HARLEY MERLIN AND THE CHALLENGE OF CHAOS

Harley Merlin 8

BELLA FORREST

Nightlight Press

ONE

Harley

"Talk to me, Harley," Imogene urged.

Fury burned in my stomach, dampened only by the tears that kept falling. I realized I hadn't said a word for a few minutes. I'd just been sitting there in my own private torment, thinking of all the ways I wanted to destroy Katherine—for Isadora, Suri, Jacob, Shinsuke, Tess, my mom, my dad, and every other person she'd killed or hurt for her own sick amusement.

The unfairness of it all made me want to tear a hole in the universe or pick up Imogene's desk and throw it against the back wall. She'd insisted I join her in her office, but I knew it was just a way to get me out of the infirmary, far from anything sharp or dangerous. One moment, I was geared up to fight, the next... I just wanted the ground to swallow me up.

"What do you want me to say?" I replied. A few hours had passed, but it didn't feel like it. Finding out about Isadora might as well have happened five seconds ago, because it still felt pretty freaking raw. "Nothing I say is going to bring my aunt and Suri back. It's not going to fix Jacob and bring him out of his coma. It's not going to bring the magical detector back."

"I know you're hurting, Harley. We all are." Imogene sighed. "We all want answers, but I don't want you to destroy yourself over this. That won't do anyone any good, least of all you."

I glared at her. "So, you're saying I should just get over the fact that my aunt was brutally murdered?"

"No, I want you to speak honestly. I want you to vent everything you're feeling, so that you can use that pain to fuel what's to come." She paused. "When someone you love dies, they take a piece of you with them. You can't get that piece back, no matter how much time may pass. Even if you were able to resurrect them, the pain of the initial loss would remain. Look at Alton—he looks at Astrid with the pain of that loss, the grief he felt when he thought he might lose her forever. The Mage Council knew what he did for her after that terrible encounter with Katherine, which is why we allowed it without any repercussions. It is only natural to want to save those you love, and it is all the more painful when that is impossible. Your pain is no different. It will linger for the rest of your days. I'm simply asking you not to keep everything to yourself, so that your emotions don't corrupt you from the inside out."

The tears started to fall again, hot and bitter down my cheeks. "I hate all of this." My hands trembled into fists. "I want to smash Katherine's stupid face into the dirt for what she's done. I want to stomp on her chest until her heart explodes so she can feel what I'm feeling right now. I want to see her pay the price for the lives she's taken, and I want to be the one to collect that debt."

"That's better. Release your anger."

"I want to march Alton right down to the Crypt and keep him there until he can bring Isadora and Suri back." I heaved out a choked sob. "I want him to tell me he can do it. I want him to keep trying until he does. I don't care if he's saying that Katherine has tampered with their bodies. I don't care about the spirit rules. I want him to drag them back into the land of the living. I don't want to hear, 'I'm sorry, there's nothing I can do.' It's not good enough. They deserve more."

Imogene nodded sympathetically, her eyes still puffy from her own crying. "I'm sorry that Alton wasn't able to restore them to life. It must hurt all the more, to know that he has done so on several occasions but couldn't for them. But his failure is Katherine's fault. She did something terrible to them, to make their spirits flee so quickly."

I held my face in my hands, the tears flowing through my fingertips. "Yeah, I know Alton did everything he could, but I can't deal with the fact that they're really gone. I keep thinking of them walking around, breathing and talking and laughing... but they're never going to do that again."

"I know, Harley. I know." Her tone was soft and sad, but that made it worse. Isadora would've shown me tough love, urging me to get on with the Grimoire for the sake of the world. I didn't need sorrow; I needed a kick in the ass. Otherwise, I'd just wallow until Katherine had won.

"And then there's Jacob," I muttered, looking up at her. "I know Louella's trying with her broken Telepathy, but Kenneth did a number on her head. It's not enough to know he's in there—I want him back, with us, where he's supposed to be. Where they're all supposed to be. It's like everyone's got these abilities, but nobody can do a damn thing to make any of this right. It makes me want to flip your freaking desk."

"I'd prefer it if you didn't." She offered a nervous smile.

I shook my head. "There's all this pressure on me, and I don't know what to do with it. And there's nothing the Rag Team can do to help me. It's not like they can find these stupid spells for me. Frankly, I'm sick of Chaos, and I'm sick of Katherine."

"Your friends are doing what they can," Imogene replied. "At this very moment, they're investigating what happened in the infirmary. Even with the CCTV ruined, they are endeavoring to find evidence of how Katherine was able to do this. They have yet to give up, and neither should you, as impossible as all of this feels right now."

"They won't find anything. She's too clever for that. They'll only find out what we already know: Katherine knew exactly when to come in and do this," I shot back. "She was waiting, all this time, for the detector to be completed. Isadora, Suri, and Jacob likely got in her way, so she killed them and put Jacob in a coma."

"They may find something more. We can't assume anything at this moment."

I glanced at Imogene, a moment of clarity emerging from the foggy mist in my head. An unsettling thought was forming, and it left a sour taste in my mouth. I wasn't even sure I could say it out loud, but I knew I had to, if only to put my sense of unease to rest. One way or another. "You were the first one on the scene, right, before anyone else?"

She frowned. "I was."

"Don't you think that's a little interesting?" I held my hands under the table, ready to pour Chaos into them if this went south. I didn't want Imogene to be in on this, but there was no denying it was a bit suspicious. Besides, I had enough grief and anger in me right now to take Imogene down, if she was in any way connected with that evil bitch. Emotion had always served me in the past, and I hoped it'd do so again, if I had to fight her.

"Interesting?" She arched an elegant eyebrow. "I hope you're not insinuating anything, Harley."

I couldn't look at her, hardly believing what I was about to say. "You were in the infirmary, and so was Katherine, before anyone else could get there. That's a little suspicious."

"I can understand your wariness, considering your current state of mind, but allow me to clarify before you come to the wrong conclusion," Imogene said. "You must remember, I arrived to find Rita Bonnello in the infirmary, not Katherine. I was confused when I saw Isadora and Suri in a pool of blood, and then I saw the detector flashing up Katherine's name as Jacob pointed it at her. I strove to fight, the moment I realized that Katherine was masquerading as Rita."

I kept my hands flexed, staring at Imogene intently, trying to detect any holes in her story.

Imogene continued. "She injured me in the attempt, using that moment in which I was stemming the blood to knock Jacob unconscious and steal the detector. I tried to help your aunt and Suri, as soon as I was able, but they were already dead, and Katherine had vanished. I did everything within my power to help Jacob, but he was on the floor, unmoving." A muscle twitched in her jaw as she blinked away a tear. "You can't know the guilt and regret I feel, that I didn't arrive sooner. If I had... there may have been something I could do to stop her. I'll replay my actions over and over in my mind for a long time to come, wondering if I might have done something differently. Had I not paused for coffee, might I have arrived in time? Had I not spent hours on the phone with the Seoul Coven, might I have saved them? It's not easy to come to terms with."

I sank back in my chair, still mulling things over. My suspicions hadn't exactly evaporated, but they were starting to ebb. She had the wounds to back up her story, but there was one thing still nagging away at the back of my mind, a hesitancy in Imogene's actions that kept me wary. "Have you got plans to deal with Rita? What if she's working for Katherine? Heck, what if she still *is* Katherine?"

"We've arranged an interrogation. I'm going to ask Astrid to execute it, using Smartie's technology. I would ask you to sit in with her, to feel out Rita's emotions, but this is much too personal for you. You would already be on the attack, the moment you stepped in the room." She paused. "Once the initial interrogation has been conducted, you can check Rita to ensure she isn't a Shapeshifter. Until then, she will be kept under close watch."

I frowned, sensing the genuine concern in Imogene's voice. "You get why I had to ask about you, right?"

"As much as it hurts to hear you accuse me, I do." She brushed away a stray tear. "Katherine must have had spies close to the tight-knit circle we've forged. At this point, we must admit that everyone is a suspect. And, if it makes you feel better, you may continue to suspect me, too. But it won't change the truth. I'd be more than happy to have you test and interrogate me, alongside Rita, if it will put your mind at ease."

"I don't think anything can put my mind at ease right now." I gave a bitter laugh. "I'd like to ask one more thing, though."

"Go on."

"Can I read your emotions?"

She smiled. "Of course. Your mind is likely running wild right now. So, here, allow me to settle your paranoia." Imogene reached for the bracelet on her wrist, the one that blocked her emotions from Empaths like me, and removed it. She set it on the desk beside her and waited. It was a gesture of open honesty, and I appreciated it.

Encouraging my Empathy to do its job, I felt tendrils of emotion flowing toward me, from her. Anguish, grief, pain, terror, frustration… it was all there, weaving a story of her struggles. They weren't the emotions of a spy, or the emotions of someone who'd played a part in murder and knocking a kid unconscious. They were the emotions of someone who was genuinely devastated and frustrated.

"How did you get that thing, anyway?" I nodded to the bracelet.

"I found this piece many moons ago after realizing I needed to acquire something to prevent Empaths from sensing me, for my own protection. I had a rather unpleasant experience with an Empath, you see, and it made me wary of appearing vulnerable. Plus, people don't like to see weakness in those in positions of power, and I wear this bracelet to stop others sensing my weaknesses—my fear, my nerves, my sorrow."

I sighed. "You would've made it easier on me if I'd felt crazy glee or something."

"As I've said, I cannot alter the truth. I arrived too late, and I'll have to think about that for years to come." She echoed my sigh.

I slumped back in my chair. "I guess, if you were involved, you wouldn't be stupid enough to hang around. You'd have ridden off into the sunset with the Queen of Evil and the magical detector." I dug my nails hard into my palms. "Katherine said she'd push me to my breaking point. She promised she'd bring me misery. It looks like she got what she wanted."

"It pains me to know that her influence has spread this far, even to the edges of our inner circle," Imogene replied. "It will make things all the more difficult, if everyone is to be suspected. They may not even realize that they're party to her manipulation."

"Well, there's one person we can cross off the list, as much as I'd like to pin the blame on him," I muttered.

Imogene frowned. "You mean Leonidas?"

I nodded. "He's still in the ICU, and still comatose."

"What about Wade?" She sounded hesitant. "He was briefly affected by the hex on your pendant. Perhaps the hex ran deeper than we first thought?"

"No, no way. I kept feeling out his emotions when he had that hex on him, and I didn't feel anything… suspicious." I knew I had to suspect everyone, but I couldn't bring myself to accuse the guy I was in love with. Was I being biased? Maybe. Was I willing to change my mind? I'd have to wait and see.

"You may be right." She smiled sadly at me. "I'll try to find a replacement pendant for you, one of these days."

"You don't need to do that. If you hadn't destroyed it, Wade would still be trying to tear my throat out."

"No, but I'd like to, nevertheless. It's the least I can do." She looked like she might cry again, and I didn't know if I could deal with that. My heart and soul were already teetering on a knife edge of self-destruction, and any sight of shared grief or kindness would make me topple over.

"There's one thing that's bugging me, though," I went on, avoiding her teary eyes. "Why did Katherine let Jacob live? Don't get me wrong, I'm glad; otherwise, I'd be a puddle of uselessness right now. But, surely, in her book, that's messy—leaving a potential witness behind."

Imogene picked up a pen and toyed with it. "Perhaps she still needs him for something."

"What, she's keeping him on ice?"

"It's possible."

"But what would she want him for?"

Imogene tapped the pen against the side of her jaw. "I suppose she no longer requires a Portal Opener, so it can't be that."

"Well, not in the way we might think." An idea jumped into my head, emerging from a memory of something Krieger had said. "Maybe she needs to add his abilities to her rare magical directory. Krieger said something about abilities having to exist to be used, and she'll want to be able to create magicals with every ability possible. With Isadora dead, Jacob is the only person left, as far as we know, who has the Portal Opening ability. If she'd killed him, too, she wouldn't be able to use that power in any of her new magicals."

Imogene nodded thoughtfully. "Ah yes, the theory that Chaos abilities cannot be created from nothing."

"If that's the case, then it makes sense that she'd keep him around, though she'd want him quiet since he's a witness. Plus, Katherine might've been worried that Jacob would try to portal Isadora and Suri out of there, in an attempt to get them to Krieger or to some kind of medical help, or even Alton. That would've created more witnesses, if they'd somehow... survived." The word stuck in my throat. "That could've been what spurred her on to knock him out when she did."

"That's a definite possibility. It makes a great deal of sense."

"But why leave him here? Why not take him?"

Imogene frowned. "I believe my interruption may have prompted her to act more rashly than she may have planned. Perhaps she didn't have time to take him without me intervening further. I was injured but I would have fought to the death to keep Jacob here if she had attempted to snatch him. That would explain why she left him in this state."

I narrowed my eyes. "Plus, she probably knew it'd crush me to see him like this."

"She's a cruel woman." Imogene stared listlessly at the desk. "However, there are other theories that conflict with the main Chaos theory. There's a theory that a Child of Chaos can create a new ability, as long as they have the core power from another magical. Take Telepaths, for example—the root of their ability stems from Empathy, but it is an advanced form. Perhaps Katherine plans to expand upon the rare abilities she's collecting, creating new magicals with powers that have never been seen before. Interdimensional travel, or Teleportation, might expand from Portal Opening... It's a frightening prospect."

"She really wants to hit me where it hurts," I murmured, half to myself. "Picking me apart, one friend at a time."

"As I've mentioned, the spy in our midst may not even know they are a spy. You mustn't be too hard on your friends, even if you suspect them."

Then maybe it's better that they're not involved at all. I knew I could trust myself. I knew I hadn't been influenced by Katherine. As for everyone else, there was no way to be sure. If they didn't know something was up in their own heads, then how could I?

The answer I'd given to the Chains of Truth, when I'd admitted that I'd sacrifice everything and everyone to kill Katherine, came rushing back. Maybe the only way to protect them would be to keep them out of it. And, maybe, that would be the only way to protect myself, too. But could I really do this on my own? Could I really take the steps to end

Katherine without any backup whatsoever? I needed to think long and hard before I made that decision. At least, this time, I didn't have the spectral trio breathing down my neck for a reply.

"All isn't lost, though, Harley." Imogene's voice knocked me out my reverie.

"Huh?"

"The Grimoire, Harley. You still have it, and that means there's still hope. With that, you may find the key to destroying Katherine." She gave me an encouraging smile, but I couldn't muster any kind of joy on my face. It would've felt wrong.

I shrugged. "Yeah, if I can figure the damn thing out."

"You haven't made any progress? I realize that, with everything that's happened, I haven't had the chance to speak with you about it." She paused. "I don't wish to add any pressure to what you're already feeling, but there's an undeniable sense of urgency surrounding your ability to utilize its power. Now more than ever before."

"I found one spell, but it was in riddles," I replied. "From what I can gather, it seems to be made up of three pieces. It kept talking about trios and threes, so that's my conclusion, anyway. It mentioned memories, and hidden fragments, too. I've been thinking about it a lot, to try and make sense of it."

"What do you think it means?"

"I might be way off, but I think the three pieces refer to three specific memories. It mentioned family ties, too, so I'm thinking these memories have to do with *my* family, since it's their Grimoire. One memory from my mom, one from my dad, and one from me. Maybe."

She nodded. "That sounds very Merlin-esque, from what I can remember of their work."

"Basically, I think I need to find the three pieces and put them together, like a puzzle. The spell talked about Euphoria, too, and I know that's based in memory and dream states, from my own experience. Euphoria is used to go deeper into the subconscious, right? So that would suggest I'm looking at hidden memories, rather than ones that are in the easy-to-reach part of my head."

"I see..." Imogene said.

A clearer idea began to form, as though the Grimoire was giving me permission to figure it out properly. "There might be something embedded in those hidden memories. And, in order to retrieve the three pieces I need, all three parties need to perform Euphoria to open up those memories and get the pieces."

"Ah." Imogene sounded disheartened, and I knew why. Hiram and Hester were dead. How could they perform Euphoria if they weren't even on this plane of existence anymore? I thought about asking for Tatyana's help, but she could only deal with spirits who were still in this world—the ones who hadn't crossed over. Beyond that, it was unexplored territory, which meant this whole thing was insane and impossible. She knew it, and I knew it.

Imogene's phone beeped, making me jump. She swiped her finger across the screen and nodded to herself. Putting the phone back in her suit pocket, she glanced at me. "Are you in good enough spirits to head to the Bestiary?"

"Now?"

"Yes, Alton has called an impromptu meeting, and it'd appear that you and I are the honored guests. Well, that's perhaps putting it a little too poetically—in a nutshell, they're waiting for us. I knew he was going to call the team together, at my request, but I wanted to gauge your state first." She waved the phone at me, before sliding it into the pocket of her sleek cream suit. "There's no pressure, if you don't feel up to it. I'm sure everyone will understand your absence."

I shook my head. "No, I'm good to go."

"I'm glad to hear it." She smiled encouragingly. "Shall we?"

A flicker of hope reignited in my heart. I couldn't give up on the Grimoire yet. And, perhaps, I had one last card left to play, in order to make this thing work. That text had granted me one last reprieve.

Alton.

TWO

Harley

Fifteen minutes later, we were standing in the familiar surroundings of the Bestiary, which had been fixed up since the fallout from Echidna's theft. All the beasties were locked inside their glass cages, and most of the debris had been cleared away. The main atrium buzzed, the bright wires thrumming with energy. Wade, Tobe, Alton, and the rest of the Rag Team were present, though Louella was still in the infirmary, looking after Jacob. Krieger was still in the infirmary, too, keeping an eye on Levi.

Everyone was staring at me like I'd grown antennae, a mixture of grief and concern flowing out of them. *Don't ask me how I am. Don't ask me how I am. Don't ask me how I am.* Most of them still had the puffy eyes of people who'd recently been crying, and the whole mood was somber. Losing Isadora, and, to a lesser extent, Suri, wasn't something we could all just snap out of. There were no words to explain this depth of pain. Even emotions couldn't quite cover it.

"Thank you for coming, during this trying time," Imogene said, breaking the tense silence. It meant nobody had the opportunity to pity me, and I was grateful for that. "If we weren't on a very strict schedule, I would have given you all more space to deal with the recent tragedies. I hope you won't think me callous, but, as you all know, we don't have a second to waste. We must discuss our options, going forward."

Wade skirted around the group and came to stand at my side. I leaned into his chest, letting him take the weight of my weary body as he put his arm around my waist. It didn't make my pain any less unbearable, but it took the edge off. I hadn't lost him, and I hadn't lost the people who were standing around me. Because of them, I had to continue. I had to keep going until we could stand together again, with the threat of Katherine eradicated.

But what about your answer to the Chains of Truth? I swallowed that memory, praying it would never come to pass, praying I wouldn't have to lose another one of my friends. More and more, I was starting to imagine my future steps toward ending Katherine without them in the picture. That was the only way to fully ensure nobody else died on my watch—by separating myself from the pack. Even Wade.

"We must find a solution to contend with Katherine. I realize you already know that, but we need to be on the same page," Imogene continued. "As far as the Grimoire is concerned, Harley was just telling me of a spell she discovered. However, we've hit something of a snag. Harley, would you care to explain?"

I snapped out of my private thoughts. "Uh... yeah, of course. The Grimoire." I cleared my raspy throat. "I managed to find the Hidden Things spell, but there's a massive problem with it."

"If it needs Echidna, so help me God, I'm going to start throwing windmills," Finch muttered, swinging his arms to show exactly what he meant.

"No, it has nothing to do with Echidna." I sighed. "It's even worse than that. It requires my mom and dad. As you all know, they're... they're dead, and they have been for a long time." That word, "dead," knocked me sick, my mind immediately jumping to Isadora's blood pooling through the door of Krieger's office.

Tatyana frowned. "In what way does it require your parents?"

"It needs their memories—hidden ones, to be more specific—but they have to be the ones to find them, deep in their minds."

"I'm guessing there's no spiritual shrink who can pry those bad boys out?" Finch replied. He was playing the joker again, and I knew it was for my benefit. A slice of normalcy, to keep me steady.

I shook my head. "I don't think so, not with them in the afterlife. Is that right, Taty?"

"Nobody knows what lies beyond. I don't know of any Kolduny who could converse with spirits once they'd crossed over. It's unknown territory, I'm afraid." Her tone was heavy with disappointment. I could feel that same emotion flowing from everyone else. This wasn't the good news they wanted; it was just another blow, after the barrage we'd already taken today.

Alton opened his mouth, as if he was about to say something, but he quickly shut it again and dropped his gaze. I eyed him, wondering what was on his mind, but I didn't call him out in front of everyone. He and I were going to have a private conversation soon enough, whether he liked it or not. I wasn't letting go of that fragile coil of hope that something could be done about it.

"With that in mind, we need to think of an alternative," Imogene said. "I will leave you to discuss it awhile. As for myself, I have an appointment with the California Mage Council, to talk about the clear evidence of Katherine's magical influence in the higher circles of the magical world. With these pills in circulation, I need to decipher whom I can trust from the wider spread of Mage Councils, not just my own, and that will require the organization of a summit. I'll be discreet about it, as their loyalty will need to be deciphered in secret."

"I was just about to suggest that," Alton replied. "We need to know, in no uncertain terms, who has and hasn't been compromised."

Imogene nodded. "I'll see to it that the preceptors are also involved, once I can be sure there's no foul play where they're concerned. Speaking of which, Rita is currently being held by the security magicals, but we must be quick in our questioning. Astrid, do you still have the means to assist with this?"

"I do," she replied. "I've still got all the polygraph material from our last set of interrogations, and they should be able to verify whether she is who she says she is. I've also arranged to bring Gregoire LaSalle in, for his Empath skills." She looked to me apologetically.

"It's okay, I know I'm too close to the situation," I replied. "It's better that you bring someone else in. I'm not exactly in an objective state of mind."

That wasn't entirely true. I did want to help in the interrogation, but I supposed they were right. There was a pretty high risk that I would lunge across the desk and try and pummel the truth out of Rita. And, though I didn't know Gregoire LaSalle personally, the name rang a bell. He was one of the former Angels who had come to the SDC to retire from the elite world of the European magical secret services. He had a more impressive resume than I did, for sure.

"Can you get Bellmore back?" Santana asked. "We could probably use her, especially with all this pill stuff going around."

"I will make some calls, but her leave was already agreed upon before I became the director. It would appear she's dealing with some health concerns, so that may not be possible, but I'll certainly try." Imogene looked tense, as if the weight of the world were on her shoulders. I knew the feeling.

"What about those kids?" Dylan chimed in. "We need a plan to get them back from Katherine."

"I'm going to speak to the Mage Council in greater detail about that and make plans for their retrieval, no matter how many private armies I have to gather to achieve it," Imogene replied. "I'll even ask for the assistance of the Angels. I'll be damned if I let that woman kill innocent children for her rituals, especially children who were supposed to be safe under my care." Her voice cracked with anger and determination, her eyes glinting with a bitter sadness.

"Would the Angels really help?" Raffe frowned. "I know you've said that LaSalle agreed to help with the interrogation, Astrid, but he's one of us—he's got a personal stake in uncovering any spies. The other Angels might not be so easy to persuade, since they're not exactly known for giving their U.S. neighbors a hand."

"I believe this is a matter of universal importance," Tobe answered solemnly. "If ever there was an opportunity for global cooperation, I imagine this would be it."

Imogene smiled. "That's my hope, Tobe. We have both of the LaSalles in the coven, after all, so I may also need to speak with them once these interrogations are over. They'll have avenues and persuasive means that I lack, in my current position, but only time will tell whether we can rely upon Europe for aid. They may still believe that this has little to do with them."

"I doubt it," Wade cut in. "They know what's at stake. Katherine's already spread across Europe."

Finch nodded. "Yeah, we heard some of her operatives talking about it when Harley and I were in the cult. If they don't help, it's nothing but blind ignorance. That, or Katherine's gotten to them, too. I'm not sure which is worse."

"Then let's hope they learn to see more clearly after I tell them of recent events, and that they aren't under Katherine's influence." Imogene gave a quick farewell before exiting the Bestiary and leaving us to come up with an impossible solution.

I watched her go, feeling unsatisfied with her plan of action. It was all ifs and maybes and vague, wishy-washy possibilities—there wasn't a solid idea in sight. It all relied on people cooperating and people not already being under Katherine's influence. As we'd learned from the security magicals and Levi, those influenced people were pretty difficult to pick out of a line-up, let alone from a bunch of calls. But at least Rita was being dealt with, although I was annoyed that Imogene wasn't overseeing the interrogation personally.

To be honest, I was starting to get the feeling that Imogene never really put her money where her mouth was. She talked a big game, sure, but the execution of it… not so much. She was trying, within the limits of her capabilities, but maybe her reach wasn't as broad as I'd thought it was. I mean, she wasn't the president. She was a small fry, in comparison, and I was only just starting to realize that.

Moreover, she'd always painted this picture of infallibility, but the holes were starting to appear. The abduction of the magical children, for example. Those kids could easily have been sent away to some remote part of the world—the Arctic, Siberia, the Sahara Desert, or something. Instead, she'd kept them in California, through some misguided sense of self-confidence. Yeah, she'd put them in a high-security facility, but

Katherine battered through those for breakfast. Imogene had dropped the ball on that one, in a big way, even though the kids being stolen wasn't officially her fault. We'd all made mistakes like that. *I* had made mistakes like that, but I'd expected more of her. And that was the problem—we'd all been expecting too much of her, thinking she had a cure-all for everything, overestimating her ability to fix our problems. That infallible image was fading, fast.

"Anyone got any ideas on how we can get to the Big Cheese, then, now that she's steamrolled everything we had?" Finch forced a bright smile onto his face. "You know, anything we haven't already tried and failed at?"

"I do," Wade replied.

Finch rolled his eyes. "Of course you do. Is it a bird, is it a plane—no, it's Wonderboy!"

"You saying you don't want to hear it?" Wade smiled wryly.

"Nope, you go ahead. I'm just glad someone has an idea. I thought there'd just be a chorus of crickets and a well-timed ball of tumbleweed."

Wade glanced down at me. "What if we could get close to Naima, close enough to manipulate her into giving us an accurate location for Katherine? It might not help us with the takedown, but there's no use figuring that out if we can't actually find Katherine."

"Naima hasn't been spotted recently, either, aside from Jacob's encounter with her, but I imagine she'll be easier to locate in the short-term," Astrid replied. "Katherine won't stop looking for rare magicals, now that she has the detector, and I'm guessing she'll keep sending her Recruiter to do just that. How do you suggest we get closer to her, if she can be found?"

"Harley," Wade said simply.

I frowned. "Me?"

"Your ability to control Purge beasts," he explained. "If we can help you hone that, you might be able to use it on Naima and get into her head. Even though she's a superior type of Purge beast, she's still a Purge beast."

Tobe's eyes glinted with excitement. "Yes, that is entirely true. We are created from the same fabric of Chaos as less self-aware Purge beasts, if you will. It may require a great deal of exertion, but I would be only too happy to assist you in your training, Harley. I am as Naima is. I would be the perfect individual to experiment upon, and I don't mind being a guinea pig on this occasion, though I am a rather large guinea pig."

"It sounds like a good plan." Alton smiled at me, though he still had that strange look in his eyes, like there was something on his mind. "Only if you're entirely up to it, though. Nobody would blame you if you needed to take a couple of hours off."

Tatyana nodded. "We weren't even expecting you to come to this meeting, considering… well, you know."

"I'm up to it." I lowered my gaze defensively. I might have been broken, but there was still fuel in the tank.

"You should probably make a start on those 'less self-aware Purge beasts,' in case you accidentally put Tobe in a fit of hysterics or something that he can't get out of." Santana's tone was warm and encouraging, making me feel calmer.

"Yeah, it was freaking weird seeing a lion-man sobbing in the infirmary." Finch chuckled, though it didn't reach his eyes. "No offense, Tobe."

Tobe shot him a warning look.

Finch looked embarrassed. "Sorry, I haven't taken my polite pills today." As if remembering, he slipped his hand into his pocket and took out a brown bottle. Tipping a yellow tablet into his hand, he tossed it into his mouth and swallowed. *Chasing your demons away...* I wished there was a pill that could chase mine away, but that was a slippery slope I didn't want to be heading down.

"It sounds like a good plan to me, too, and I'm ready to go whenever the rest of you are. But I agree on the less self-aware beastie angle. You're the same as Naima, Tobe, but I might need a more unwilling participant than you. Thing is, you want to help me, and you're a friend of mine who wants to see me succeed, which means you might not go all-in to try and defeat me. But I'm sure there are some beasts in your Bestiary who'd be the kind of aggressive participant we need, like Santana said."

Tobe smiled. "You make an excellent point. I will arrange something suitable."

"Thanks, Tobe." I steeled myself, standing tall beside Wade.

They were right, it was a good idea to go after Naima, but my mind wasn't exactly focused on that right now. Instead, I had two clear roads ahead of me: Alton and the Grimoire. I needed to move now, before I got entangled in this Purge-beast manipulation training. "But before we do, I was wondering if I could have a word with you, Alton?"

My words hung in the air for a moment, with everyone turning to look at our former director. He didn't seem too surprised by my request. It was almost like he'd been expecting it, ever since I'd mentioned that I needed my mom and dad to fulfill the Hidden Things spell. Well, this was his moment to tell me what he'd wanted to say. But not here.

He nodded. "Of course. Should we step outside?"

"You read my mind," I replied, before looking to the others. "If you all get things ready, I'll come back and start training."

Leaving the rest of the Rag Team to get on with their tasks, mainly my training prep and proceeding with Rita's interrogation, Alton and I crossed the Bestiary together and stepped out into the hallway beyond. There were a few security magicals wandering about, prompting us to continue walking until we found a private alcove far enough away from the main entrance of the Bestiary. There, Alton glanced around before turning to me.

"I know what you're going to ask," he said.

"You do?"

He paled. "I hope I'm not right, but I have a feeling you want to ask me to resurrect your mother and father so you can complete the spell to find hidden things. I saw it in your eyes, back there."

"Maybe you can read my mind, after all."

He shook his head. "If that's what you really want to ask of me, then this isn't the time or the place to discuss it. If you decide on this course of action, then we'll have to meet up later, in absolute privacy. A Necromancer can receive a lifetime sentence in Purgatory for even joking about something like this."

"Fine, then we'll talk about it later. But we're going to talk about it."

"I thought you might say that." He sighed in exasperation. "I'll just give you this one warning. Before you come to me, I want you to think long and hard about what it is you're asking. I want you to think about the consequences, and the improbability, and the effect it may have, not only on you and me, but on them, too. If you still decide you want to talk about it, then I'll be waiting."

I didn't say a word. I just kept on looking at him. I should've been feeling disheartened or worried, but I wasn't. We'd had so much doom and gloom in the last twenty-four hours that I had no room for more. Instead, the very fact that he hadn't immediately said, "No, it can't be done. There's no way," bolstered that tiny flame of hope that flickered in my chest. Instead of snuffing it out, he'd unwittingly added fuel.

And I was going to keep that damn flame burning.

THREE

Harley

Frustrated that I'd have to wait to speak to Alton about resurrecting my parents, I went back into the Bestiary to join the others. Alton had gone on his way to see if Imogene needed help with her Mage Council meeting.

"I had a thought about your training, Harley," Tobe said when I arrived. "It will take some time to prepare, but I will inform you when everything is ready. I assure you, it will be worth the wait, as I would hate for you to waste your valuable time by working upon imps and leprechauns. Please, accept my apologies for the delay." He paused. "Although, I am certain it is past time that you rested. Sleep, my friend, and return when all is prepared."

I glanced at the others, who seemed a little shifty. I could feel a tiny hint of guilt slithering away from them—nothing major, but enough to convince me that they'd colluded on this while I was out of the room with Alton. They clearly wanted me to get some rest, after everything that had happened, and had seized an opportunity to clear my schedule for a bit. I probably looked as hideous as I felt, but resting up was the last thing on my mind. I wasn't even sure I'd be able to sleep. Nightmares would be waiting; I was pretty sure of that.

I nodded. "Sounds like a good idea." I didn't mean it, but I didn't want to get into an argument with Wade and the others. They were worried about me, and their concerns came from a good place. If I had to lie and say I was going to get some rest, just to ease their own grief-stricken minds, then so be it.

"We're just going to stay here a while longer, to help Tobe," Santana said. "Wade will take you back to the living quarters, and if you need anything—anything at all—you just drop one of us a text, you hear?" She gave Wade a less-than-subtle nod, before flashing me a warm grin.

"I will," I replied, as I turned away and started to walk toward the living quarters. Wade hurried to catch up, the two of us falling in step. He didn't say anything; he just held my hand, giving it a gentle squeeze every now and again. It was enough for him just to be there. The only trouble was, if I was going to continue my journey without him, I'd have to learn how to walk alone.

"Do you want me to come in?" Wade lifted his hand to my face as we paused in the doorway of my room. "I can hold you until you fall asleep, if you want. Or we could talk for a while. I know you probably don't feel like sleeping, but it might be easier if you're not by yourself, thinking of everything."

I dropped my gaze and covered his hand with mine, bringing his fingertips to my lips. I kissed them gently, fighting back tears for the millionth time that day. "I'd prefer to be on my own, if that's okay. I need to sit with my thoughts. And if I need to scream into my pillow, I'd rather you weren't there to see it. I know you wouldn't mind, but… call it a pride thing."

"Okay." He leaned closer and put his arms around me, kissing my hair. "I love you, Harley."

I held him tightly, burying my face in his chest. "I love you, too."

"If you change your mind, or it gets to be too much, you know where to find me. Call or text me anytime, and I'll be here before you know it."

"I will," I murmured. "I will."

"I'm so sorry, Harley."

I held him tighter. "I know. Me, too."

Two hours later, unable to bear the silence of my bedroom, and knowing the others would be busy, I slipped out of the living quarters and headed through the mostly empty coven, not stopping until I reached the Crypt. With news of Isadora's death having spread rapidly through the SDC, those who had other places to go had taken the opportunity to do so, sharing in their shock and grief away from the site where she'd died. Fear had urged them away from these hallways, too, and I didn't blame them.

I made it through the thick, iron doors that led down into the belly of the coven, the security officers letting me pass after I sent a wave of reverse Empathy at them. I wasn't wasting any time on debating why they should let me pass, so I'd persuaded them with emotion instead. Now, they couldn't look at me, and mumbled awkwardly, but I didn't care. They weren't important. I just wanted to see my aunt for the very last time. I knew I wouldn't get the chance to speak with her spirit, the way I'd done with my mom, but I had to say goodbye however I could.

Heading through the rock-hewn passageway to the set of stairs that led into the main body of the Crypt, I froze. In the center of the wide, flat expanse, in front of the towering wall of mausoleums on the far side, lay two altars. Someone had put them here, presumably Alton. Two still bodies lay on the plinths, their shapes visible but vague beneath black silk cloths. I noticed gold embroidery across the silk, forming a spread of charms. *It's too late for charms now.* If Isadora and Suri's spirits had already passed on, as Alton had said, then what was the use of protective hexes? What was the use in glyphs, to guide them into the afterlife? They were already gone.

Steeling myself, I headed down the stone stairwell and made my way toward the bodies. Skirting around the smaller of the two, and feeling sick to my stomach that a teenager had died, I paused in front of Isadora's altar. I wanted to see her face, but, at the same time, I didn't know if I could handle what I might see. *You have to. You owe it to her to look at her when you say goodbye.* With my hand shaking, I drew the black silk carefully down to my aunt's shoulders.

Her face was deathly pale, her lips colorless, her eyes closed. Someone had done their best to clean her up, but I could see a few spots of dried blood across her neck and on the underside of her jaw, in the shadows there. Touching my thumb to her icy cold skin, I brushed away those rusty flecks, hating the way they marred her. I didn't want her to be buried with any hint of what Katherine had done evident on her body.

I tucked a strand of her dark hair behind her ear and glanced down at her unmoving face. Everyone always said that the newly dead looked as though they were sleeping, but that wasn't true. There was a tension around my aunt's mouth and eyes, leaving an echo of her final expression—anger and sadness and fear. Her death mask, to be worn to the grave.

"I'm sorry," I whispered, my knees buckling. I clasped her hand beneath the black silk and held it tight. "I'm so sorry, Isadora. I don't know if you can hear me, but… please don't leave me. I need you, now more than ever."

Silence boomed back.

"But you've already gone, haven't you?" Tears trickled down my cheeks, falling onto the silk. "You're gone, because I couldn't save you. I couldn't stop Katherine, and now… now you're dead, and you're never coming back." I sank down to the dusty ground, my hand still gripping Isadora's. "I've lost you and I don't know what to do. I know you weren't physically in my life for very long, but you were always there, I know you were. And, when you did come back into my life, you were the one to give me guidance and to keep me on the right path, but how do I know which way to go, without you here to tell me?"

The continued echo of silence stung like a barrage of arrows in my chest.

"You never gave up on us," I went on, desperate to fill that painful quiet. "You never gave up on me or Jacob. The moment we both met you, we knew we had family. I had a link to my past and a hope for my future. I had your stories, and your memories, and your love, and I'll never forget any of it. I'll miss you until the day I die, and I'll love you beyond that, until I see you again, one of these days. You might not have been tied to Jacob by blood, but you were so much more to him than a friend—you were a mom, a tutor, a guiding light. We both loved you so very much. I don't know how I'm going to tell him, when he wakes up… *if* he wakes up." I shook my head in despair. "I couldn't protect him, Isadora. I should've been there. I should've stopped her. I should've known that

Katherine would come down hard on us as soon as we finished that freaking detector."

A figure appeared at the top of the stone staircase. Cast in the flickering shadows of the torchlight, I couldn't quite tell who it was until they were almost at the altars, but I didn't sense any danger. I just felt an overwhelming surge of grief, added to my own.

"Louella?" I saw her, at last, as she came to stand between the two plinths. Her eyes were red and puffy, her lips cracked from the salt of her tears.

"I didn't know you'd be down here," she replied quietly. "Wade came to the infirmary. He said you were asleep."

I shook my head. "I couldn't sleep."

"I can go if you want to be on your own." She dropped her gaze. "I just wanted to come and… say goodbye." Her voice caught in her throat, and she covered her face with her hands, her shoulders shaking as the sobs came.

"No, no, you have as much right to be here as I do." I moved around to her side of the altar and put my hand on her shoulder. "I know you and Isadora were close. She thought very highly of you. We all do." Louella was yet another stray that Isadora had taken under her wing. We all had so much to thank my aunt for, and now that chance had been taken from us.

She nodded. "I just can't believe she's gone. She made me feel like she really, truly cared, when I thought I'd never have anyone to look out for me again." A sob escaped her throat. "It's like losing the Devereauxs all over again."

"I'm sorry, Louella." I put my arm around her shoulders and pulled her into a hug. She was still just a kid herself, and she'd already lost so much. Even here, where she'd thought she'd be safe, she was still losing people she cared about. And now, she was the only person who could do anything about Jacob. That was a lot of pressure, given the stakes. Jacob was her friend, and that desperation to wake him up would eat away at her if she wasn't careful. I could already see signs of it in the dark circles under her eyes and the raspy tone of her weary voice.

"No, *I'm* the one who should be sorry." She pulled away slightly and rubbed the tears from her eyes. "I shouldn't be the one crying like this. This has got to be way more painful for you. I'm so sorry. I wasn't even thinking."

"Hey, you've got nothing to be sorry for. We're all in pain right now. Nobody is hurting more or less than anyone else. Feel what you have to feel. It won't do anyone any good to bottle things up." I realized I was relaying the words that Imogene had said to me, but they were pretty useful.

"I was so harsh to Suri, too." Louella glanced down at the still-shrouded face of the dead girl. "She must've thought I hated her. I didn't, I really didn't. I just wanted to keep Jacob safe and stop him from risking his neck. But I didn't manage to do that, did I? And now she's gone, and he's... well, he's stuck inside his own skull and I can't get him out."

"I'm sure she knew you didn't hate her," I replied. "She'll have known you were only looking out for Jacob's best interests. And we all know you're trying your best with your Telepathy. It's going to take time, and... and we all need to understand the possibility that he might never snap out of it. I don't want you to snap under the pressure of fixing him."

Louella stared hopelessly at me. "I have to, Harley. I have to fix him. We have to know what happened in that room, and we have to have him back with us. I'll work and work until I've got nothing left, to bring him back."

I smiled sadly. "I know you will. I just don't want you putting yourself in a hospital bed while you're trying to help him. Promise me you'll take care of yourself?" Why did it sound like I was already saying goodbye to my friends? I shook the thought away. I hadn't made that decision yet.

"I will, as long as you promise the same."

"I'll try."

Louella sighed and straightened out her graphic tee. Today's design was the *Jurassic Park* logo, with "Dinosaur Supervisor" written underneath. I would have laughed, if I'd had the energy. "What do you think of all this?" She gestured to Suri and Isadora. "What happened in Krieger's office, I mean, not... well, not the obvious. I keep going through everything, to think of what we might've missed—like, if we should have noticed something that would have let us know an attack was coming. I can't stop thinking about how weird the timing was. Like, how would Katherine have known to strike after we'd finished the detector?"

"I've wondered that, too."

Her eyes widened. "It *is* weird, isn't it?"

"Katherine's playing some kind of game with us. I don't know if Rita is involved, but I'm guessing we'll find out soon enough."

"Astrid and LaSalle finished interrogating her about ten minutes ago, as far as I know."

I frowned. "What did they find?"

"According to Astrid, the Rita that's in the SDC right now is clean. She's not a Shapeshifter, and LaSalle couldn't sense any deception in her emotions. She was just frightened and horrified that Katherine had used her image. She's even promised to wear one of those old bodycams, to prove her innocence."

"Is it weird that I wanted it to be Rita, that I wanted her to be the culprit?"

Louella shook her head. "I think we all did, just so we'd have an answer."

Volunteering to wear a bodycam was a bold move, and it went some way toward lessening my suspicions of Rita. They hadn't gone away entirely, and probably never would, but at least she was being proactive in trying to defend herself and show she hadn't been involved.

Katherine has been watching me... She might've been in the freaking room with me, and I wouldn't have known. That was the problem with Shapeshifters—you never knew if you'd been talking to a real person or a Shapeshifter version, not unless you knew what you were supposed to be looking for. No matter how hard I racked my memory, I couldn't figure out which Rita had been in the same room as me. Had Katherine switched in and out as necessary, without the real Rita knowing? Had she been right beside me, and I hadn't sensed her?

Paranoia clawed at my chest, and my breath came in stifled gasps. I struggled for air, feeling like I was dragging oxygen through a windpipe filled with cotton. My body began to shake violently, my cheeks flushed with heat, while a cold sweat spread down my back.

"Harley?" Louella looked worried. "Harley, are you okay?"

I shook my head. "I don't think so."

"Breathe. You need to breathe."

"No… No, I need to get out of here." I blinked the black spots out of my eyes. "I'm going to go and speak to Astrid myself. I'm sorry, Louella. I'm sorry."

I hurried away from the altars, and my unrelenting pain, trying to push away the vision of Isadora's pale face. I was practically sprinting by the time I'd reached the corridor of cells and was just about to head up the stairs into the main body of the coven when I almost crashed into someone coming the opposite way. Strong hands held me by the shoulders, stopping me from falling backward.

"Harley? Hey, hey, what's up?" I stared into Wade's worried eyes.

"I… I can't breathe," I wheezed, holding onto him.

"You're okay. You're okay, beautiful. I'm here."

I collapsed into his arms, hugging him for dear life. He hugged me back twice as hard, propping me up physically and emotionally and stopping me from crumbling right there and then. He kissed my forehead over and over, breathing slowly in and out until my own breaths started to match his and the tension in my chest began to fade.

"I'm not going to let you fall, Harley. I've got you. I've always got you," he murmured against my hair. "I love you so much. I just wish I could take some of your pain away."

"I need it," I whispered back, nuzzling into his neck. "I need the pain. I just need to figure out how to channel it, instead of letting it overwhelm me."

"Don't rush it, Harley. Don't do anything you're not ready to do." He squeezed me harder. "Please, I don't want this to destroy you."

I don't want it to destroy you, either. That was why I had to separate myself from him. That was why I had to separate myself from everyone. Isadora's death had brought me to my breaking point. If I lost more people by having them fight at my side, then I wouldn't have the strength to carry on. It would crush me to the point of annihilation. And if Wade ended up hurt or, worse, killed, then it'd be game over before I even started.

I refused to have him or anyone else involved in what I was about to do. That was the only way I could keep them safe and keep myself from ever having to properly face the answer I'd given to the Chains of Truth.

"We're with you every step of the way," Wade continued. "The Rag Team is already looking into what happened in Krieger's office. Rita has agreed to wear a bodycam and everyone is planning to start up interrogations of the magicals in the SDC, to narrow the field of suspects. We're all going to do everything in our power to support you."

"That's good to know." My mind was elsewhere, thinking about my upcoming conversation with Alton. If Astrid had dealt with Rita, and the rest of the Rag Team members were looking into interrogating everyone else, then that meant I was free to look toward the next step in my mission. I had to keep it to myself, not even telling Wade, in case Katherine *was* still lurking around here somewhere, eavesdropping.

While Alton hadn't gone into the specifics earlier, he hadn't told me it was impossible to do. Normally, a Necromancer couldn't resurrect someone whose spirit had already "passed on" to the afterlife. My mom and dad's spirits had passed on a long time ago. So, there had to be more to what he *wasn't* saying. There had to be a hope, or he'd have squashed the idea the moment it had come out of my mouth.

"I can take you to Astrid now, if you'd like, to put your mind at ease. Or to the Bestiary so you can start your training with Tobe. Whichever will take your mind off things." Wade pulled away and gazed reassuringly into my eyes. "The rest of the crew are putting feelers out to find Naima, so you don't have to worry about that. She's our next target. I think O'Halloran is organizing a covert offensive operation, too, to select prime fighters to go after Katherine once we find her."

I frowned. "O'Halloran? I thought he was under the influence of those pills."

"Imogene had her man in Seoul send over an antidote. It seems to be working on him. I've tried talking to him about Echidna and Levi, and he's not holding back anymore."

"That's a relief."

Wade nodded. "Yeah, it really is. O'Halloran is still the test subject, but we're hoping we can use the antidote on everyone else who's been affected by the pills soon enough. I mean, we might not be able to summon an army, given how deep Katherine's influence has spread, but we can at least try to outnumber the cultists and be certain that our people are really on our side, thanks to that antidote."

I was too distracted to focus properly on what he was saying. "I need to get away from this for a bit. Can I meet you in the Bestiary later?"

"Uh... sure. Whatever you need. Do you want me to come with you?"

I shook my head. "No, I'll be fine. I just want to go and lie down in a dark room. I'll see you in a bit."

I couldn't wait any longer. I needed to speak with Alton. Now.

FOUR

Katherine

I swear, if I have to wear another cream suit I may tear my clothes off and go full Lady Godiva. All of these draped fabrics and expensive clothes were driving me crazy. What I wouldn't have given for one of my dresses. Yes, they were expensive too, but I was desperate for a bit of color. Pure, perfect Imogene—man, she was dull. But at least she'd gotten me out of that close call in the infirmary, so I couldn't exactly complain.

I'd never doubted that I'd get out of it untarnished, of course. I'd built my own version of Imogene up from the real one for the purpose of getting me out of close shaves, and it had paid off, but I'd had to do a little improvising. Usually, that kept life interesting, but that run-in with Isadora and Jacob now meant I had to do a bucketload of work on collateral damage. To say I wasn't happy about it was an understatement. And all the tears… *Ugh.* I hadn't cried in almost twenty years, so that had been one for the method actor in me. I'd had to dig really deep to get real ones to squeeze out of my dried-up eyeballs.

I took a moment to look around my new digs. The SDC director's office. It was pretty modern, but so painfully monochrome, mostly white and blues, to keep up with the Imogene image. I could've had the New York directorship if I'd wanted it, but that ship had sailed a *long* time ago.

Plus, why settle on something so measly, when there were bigger thrones to sit on? I liked a big throne. More ass room.

"So, I trust you all know what needs to be done, and the time constraints we're working against?" I addressed the faces staring at me through the video call. Very crass, and totally glitchy, which made for some interesting facial expressions when the screens froze, but not exactly efficient. I'd already seen Nicholas Mephiles stall as though he was mid-sneeze, which was a sight I wasn't going to forget anytime soon, his jowls in the throes of a frantic jiggle. Disgusting.

"Yes, Imogene," the California Mage Council chorused back. I had to admit, I enjoyed that. Obedience gave me a thrill like nothing else. It went right through me, in the best possible way.

"Thank you for your time." It was delicious. I was sending them on a wild goose chase to look into how far my influence had spread, and they wouldn't find a damn thing. I'd been careful. I was always careful. That's what pissed me off about Harley and her crew. They kept underestimating my skill, not realizing that they were already against the ropes. I was simply waiting for the bell to ring.

With a flurry of saccharine farewells that I couldn't be bothered with, I switched off the video conference and looked to my newfound bodyguard. He was waiting so very patiently, his body as stiff as a Beefeater. I wondered if he'd even blink, if I suddenly ran up to him and shouted, "Boo!" Probably not. O'Halloran was completely under my influence. I could've taken off these Imogene trappings and revealed myself, and he'd have just nodded like a lapdog.

I'd told the Rag Team that I was trying an antidote on O'Halloran, but I'd just replaced one mind manipulation with another, courtesy of my dear friend Kim Dong Wook of the Seoul Coven. An actual genius with medical mind manipulation—there was nothing that man couldn't conjure up, with the right threats applied. Although, I supposed that could have been true for just about anyone. The Rag Team were none the wiser, of course.

"Imogene?" There was one video call still flickering. I'd presumed it had just frozen, but apparently not. Remington was staring through the hologram screen.

"Remington?"

"Are you sure this is where we should be focusing our efforts? It hasn't turned up much so far. I didn't want to say anything in front of the others, but I was wondering if we should be directing our efforts at finding Katherine. Cut the head off the snake, and the rest dies, right?"

You won't be cutting the head off this glorious snake, thank you very much. I'd show him just how reptilian I could be. Arrogant ass. He was going to be trouble. The rest of the Mage Council were sheeple, eager to follow someone, but Remington… he was a little too independent for my liking. Always had been. And those tattoos—so tacky. Though I had one I'd like to add to him, one way or another. He'd look quite handsome with a golden apple on his body, and I'd be only too happy to apply it myself. I wasn't a fan of men, in general, but I couldn't ignore a stone-cold fox when I saw one. Remington looked like he belonged on a rock poster, rather than on a stuffy Mage Council.

"We need to discover how deep this runs," I insisted. "If we can do that, we may find Katherine through one of her hidden cultists."

Remington nodded. "That's fair." He paused, making me tap the video device to make sure it was working. "I'll get back to you as soon as I hear anything."

"Much obliged."

"Take care of yourself, Imogene."

I smiled sweetly. "And you."

As he signed off and closed his end of the call, I sat back in my chair and sighed. Remington was a growing concern, and so was Levi, despite his current zombie state. I almost wanted to somehow unleash that djinn of Raffe's on the sly, so he could finish the job on old daddio. An ex-director with a shattered skull was way easier to explain than a man with suspicions about the woman who'd taken over. Men like Levi hated women in power. I wouldn't have gone so far as to say *all* women, but he'd never been my, or rather *Imogene's,* biggest fan. He'd have jumped on the accusation train, if he was awake, and I had a sneaking suspicion he'd still jump on that irritating bandwagon when he finally did come around.

Well, I had plenty of ways of dealing with nuisances. Once they witnessed my overwhelming power and influence, they'd have no choice but to join me. If they didn't, they'd die. It really was that simple a choice. It'd be the same choice I gave everyone else, when the time came. Until then, they were still useful. Remington was a decent little investigator, and I wasn't the type to just do away with folks for the hell of it. There was always a logical purpose to my killing. If people could be used, they could be spared, until they no longer served a purpose, or until they became more of a problem than a tool. *A lot of them are still tools, even at that point.*

Suri was the perfect example. She'd served her purpose, and now she was dead. Like a battery that ran out—where else was I going to put her but in the trash? Isadora was a more unfortunate loss. She'd still had potential, but the way she'd chattered on… anyone would've put a knife in her heart, to shut her the hell up. Call it a *crime de passion*. I couldn't keep a lid on that all the time. There was still a speck of human left in me, and that came with its impulses. Sometimes, people were just so annoying that they needed to be ended.

"O'Halloran, could you go and check on things in the infirmary?" I looked to my lapdog.

"Yes, Ms. Whitehall." He dipped his head and exited. I was surprised he wasn't drooling at the mouth, after the massive dose of mind control I'd put in his water.

As soon as he'd gone, I walked over to the plush cream rug that lay in the middle of the room. All the cream, all the time. I pulled the rug aside to reveal a Strainer pentagram. On the wall opposite, I'd hung a ceiling-to-floor mirror. I stared at Imogene, hating her. She'd served her purpose, too, but we were coming to the end of that. Another one for the trash.

Sending a ripple of Shapeshifter goodness through me, I watched as delicate, ethereal, dull-as-dishwater Imogene faded away, replaced with my eminently more interesting face and shapely physique. *That's more like it.* Now, in an emerald dress, with the contrast of my copper hair against it, I finally had that flavor of color I'd been craving. I was going for Celtic goddess vibes, and I hit the mark. This was the type of woman people wanted to follow.

Taking out five bowls from the desk, complete with the trinkets and herbs that got this portal show on the road, I set them out, stood in the middle, and spoke the necessary words: *"Ex terra ligare Munera tua potestate ut educeres nos iter est."* Latin always felt good in my mouth. I couldn't believe the cheek of Echidna, when she'd said I was butchering it, back in Lethe. Well, I'd butchered her, so I guessed we were even.

I reappeared in the glass-fronted building of our latest installment of Eris Island, now situated off the coast of Oahu. A beautiful part of the world. Not that I got much time to see it. Relaxation didn't exactly fit my current MO, but there'd be time for that once I had everything in order. There was one massive benefit of being here, though—the Honolulu Coven was so laid back they were practically horizontal. I could've taken up residence right in the middle of one of the main islands, and they wouldn't have noticed.

"Eris, you have returned." Naima stood waiting. Another of my loyal lapdogs, though she'd put me through the wringer of late. I was starting to wonder if she was worth the hassle, not that I could do much about it. She and I were bound by Chaos. If I killed her, I'd kill a part of myself, too. If she continued to prove herself to be worthless, I'd have to get someone else to do it. Not ideal, after the last couple of mess-ups with delegation, but a girl had to do what a girl had to do.

"Did you think I wouldn't?" I replied.

"No, of course not, but you have been gone longer than I expected."

I smiled. "Aww, were you getting worried?"

"Always, Eris."

"As much as I'd love to hang around and chat, I've got things to do. This new world order isn't going to stop for anyone. So, first off, I'd like to see the magical children. I'm sure they're missing me, too."

Naima bowed her head. "Of course, Eris."

Without the ancient ruin of the old hexagon at Fort Jefferson to accommodate my main compound, it didn't quite have the same impact that it used to. The building was still hexagonal, but I missed the familiar ruins. That served me right for thinking I'd always end up back in Dry Tortugas

—my grandfather's favorite place. It was just another reason to hate Harley. She'd messed up my aesthetic, and that was tantamount to treason. At least we were safe here, though. One bonus to having a jumping island that could go wherever it wanted. Or, wherever *I* wanted.

A short while later, I arrived outside the laboratories, where we were keeping the rare magicals. The guards on duty bowed to me as I entered. That would never get old. I loved a bow, especially the really low, really awkward kind.

Inside, a group had gathered. They were watching the rare magicals, who sat around in a clinical room beyond, through a one-way mirror. So far, I had nine, including the tiny Necromancer, whose cat I had exploded after he'd bawled all the way from LA. *Try bringing it back to life now, Micah.* And that sullen teenager, Marjorie, who'd made the fatal mistake of wanting to come to LA with the others. *Foolish girl.* Not that she'd have escaped me if she'd stayed with Harley and her do-gooders. I already had plans for retrieving Louella. Marjorie had just made it easier on me.

The gathered group bowed to me as I paused in front of the one-way mirror, observing the magicals. Micah was still being comforted by Marjorie, snuffling disgustingly. Well, he'd be joining his puss before he knew it, and then he could finally stop his incessant whining. That day couldn't come soon enough.

Ifrit Laghari, Coral Falkland, Bakir Khan, and Delphine Basquiat stood before me—my trusty quartet, taking over from Tess after that colossal disappointment. Delphine had been the one to explode that damned cat, actually. It was good to have a Cellular around, for just that reason. If I needed someone blown up, she was my girl. However, they had one person standing with them with whom I'd only recently been acquainted—Herman Striker, a skilled Electro pilfered from Frankfurt and a massive waste of potential. I'd have preferred to let him replace that treacherous Crux bitch, but I needed him to die in the last ritual. It was a huge shame, considering how skilled he was and how malleable he might have been, to fit my needs. But hey, you win some, you lose some. And there'd be a lot more people in the lost category before my Challenge was complete.

"Herman the German, it's a pleasure to see you again." I smiled, while the young man struggled against his magical restraints. He wasn't enjoying himself, but I was. "I trust you're ready to face your destiny? You made quite the fuss last time I was here, so I hope we won't be getting any more of that, or I'll have to dump you in with the rest of them."

"You don't have to do zis, Eris," he replied. "You don't have to keep me in zese restraints. My sacrifice is willingly given."

"If I let you wander around without restraints, you'd just run off. Everyone says they'll willingly sacrifice themselves until it comes to the actual moment, and then they get all freaked out, and they start to cry, and it's irritating for everyone. It's much better if we all know where we stand. This way, you know what's coming, and so do I. Everyone's a winner. You get to be part of a great destiny, and I'm giving you that gift. Not everyone gets to say that."

Herman narrowed his eyes. "It is murder! It doesn't matter how you dress it up. It is murder!"

Bless, his bluff didn't work. They never did. Nobody really faced death willingly, not when push came to shove. Even if it was a glorious gift to me.

"I'm not trying to dress it up." I flicked my wrist casually. "I know what it is. I just thought you might like me to describe it in a different way, to make it easier to swallow."

"You are a murderer! You will pay for zis!"

I rolled my eyes. "Can someone take him away, please? Put him in with the others. His voice is starting to grate on me. I don't know if it's the German thing, or if that's just how he speaks, but he needs to go."

Delphine and Ifrit jumped to it, leading the howling Herman away and shoving him into the clinical expanse beyond the one-way mirror. As soon as he was inside, he hurled himself at the closing door, almost knocking himself out in the process. *Why don't they learn?* It was comical, really. I'd watched them all try a thousand ways to escape, but they all ended up in a heap on the floor, in the end. A fitting metaphor for ordinary life. Always trying to achieve something and always falling short. Not my life, naturally, but that was a given—my life was extraordinary, and I was going to get what I wanted, but I couldn't say the same for these sad sacks.

"Have you made any progress on the last two?" I turned back to Coral, Bakir, and Naima. My inner circle had shrunk somewhat, thanks to the Tess debacle. Even from the five of them, I only really trusted the women. Men served themselves. They could never fully be trusted.

Coral shook her head. "We're working on it, Eris. It won't be long until we track them down."

"Good, it had better not take long. We don't have time to waste," I shot back. "And I know I don't need to tell you what the consequences will be if you fail me. Although, I've brought you a little treat, to help you along."

"Oh?" Coral sounded surprised.

Opening out my palms, I delved deep into the interdimensional cache where I'd hidden the magical detector and watched as it appeared. They stared in wonder—they were so easily pleased. I had to admit, the detector was a pretty impressive piece of engineering. And it was all the more impressive, considering what it would get me… those last two magicals. *Evasive little worms.*

"What is it?" Bakir asked.

"It's a magical detector. I trust you won't have too much trouble figuring it out, Bakir?" He was supposed to be the brains of the outfit, but he'd yet to prove that formidable IQ to me. I didn't need a confirmation from MENSA. I needed evidence. Hard, cold facts and practical application. That's what got my proverbial cogs whirring.

Bakir dipped his head. "I will begin looking into it immediately, Eris."

"Ah, music to my ears." I handed it to him, and he obediently set it down on one of the laboratory benches to begin his mystical tinkering. Coral joined him, though I didn't know what use she'd be. All she could do was force blades out of her body, like some sort of spiny hedgehog. Interesting to watch, but not exactly useful unless someone pulled her in for a hug, or she ran full-pelt at an enemy.

"If I may be so bold, why have you not taken the Grimoire, Eris?" Naima's voice took me by surprise. "I had thought you might return with it."

I whirled around and eyed her darkly. "Isn't it strange how people say, 'If I may be so bold' and don't wait for a reply to confirm whether they *may* be so bold? It's like saying, 'No offense, but...' and then saying something highly offensive."

Naima looked sheepish. "I meant no offense, Eris."

"Well, now that you've pointed it out like a gigantic sore thumb, might I be so bold as to remind you that I can't touch the damn thing?" I replied acidly. "It's warded against me, the whole thing entirely Katherine-proofed, like I'm a baby trying to get into a drawer full of knives. It's a sentient being, able to pick and choose whom it allows near. Do I need to tell you, again, what happened to the people I sent after it? Don't you remember the aftermath of that?"

It still irked me, even now. All of those cultists, flooding back in failure from New York, with scorched hands and hexed bodies, some of them reduced to jabbering idiots, others missing limbs, others speaking in tongues and seeing things that weren't there. Some had recovered and were still part of the cult today, providing they hadn't died in another mission along the way. The rest had been put out to pasture. It was the kindest thing to do.

Naima shook her head. "No, Eris. I remember well."

"Really? Because it seems like your mind's a bit patchy. I can put you back in your glass box, if you're still not fully recovered from Tartarus?"

"No, no, that will not be necessary. I am recovered, I assure you."

"Glad to hear it." I sighed. "Besides, I still need Harley to get into those hidden pages. Do you think I wrecked Odette's brain for nothing?" I gave a wry chuckle, thinking of the meek little Librarian whose mind I'd torn apart to get to her secrets. "I'm not going to get stuck in some otherworld, like the other Children. I want a physical body, so I need that spell poor Odette told me about. Annoying that it had to be in the same book that those sickening specimens wrote, but there's a delicious irony to it that tantalizes the soul. That book was never intended to do anything but destroy me, but spells can be altered if you have the right mindset. And there's one in there that's vague enough to be changed to suit my needs—Odette revealed it, once she hit breaking point. One to be used by a Child of Chaos, but they clearly didn't factor in the idea that I *will* be one of those. Idiots. And since angelic wee Harley is the only one who can read out the spell that will create that divine loophole, I need to keep her around. So, don't question me again, Naima. Not unless you feel like being domesticated for a bit."

I had gone to great lengths to delve into Odette's mind, and it had paid off enormously. I'd cracked open her brain like a walnut, sifting through the chaff to find the superior wheat—the one thing that would allow me to bridge the gap between the human world and the otherworlds that I'd otherwise end up languishing in.

Not for me. No thanks.

The torture had been so intense, making me really flex my brutalizing muscles, but it had been worth the added effort. I could still hear her screams if I closed my eyes and thought about it, like a sweet lullaby to my ears, the soundtrack to my great and wonderful future as a Child of Chaos.

"I am sorry, Eris." Naima dipped her head in a bow.

"I do hate helping that Merlin bitch, though," I muttered. "Having to pretend to be all sweetness and light is turning my stomach. My fingertips literally itch whenever I'm near her, wanting to squeeze the life out of her. She's made progress, at least, on one of the spells. A spell that uncovers hidden things."

It was an undeniable risk to let Harley keep something that was created to destroy me, which was another little tidbit I'd learned from Odette, but some things were worth a calculated hazard. Having the ability to traverse all worlds was one of those worthy things. And I wasn't about to let her read out anything that could harm me. *What do you take me for?*

Naima frowned. "She has?"

"Again with the doubt. You're starting to give me a complex." I cast her a warning look. "Alton might have a solution. Harley's already approached him, so everything is moving along nicely. It's funny, really, that Alton would be willing to step into the darkest realms imaginable, all for the sake of destroying me. And he's given me all that hassle for rule-breaking. *Tut-tut*. The hypocrisy!"

"That is good news, Eris."

"Yes, it is. See, there's benefit to keeping the Grimoire around, in the hands of someone who can actually use it, as long as it's somewhere I can keep an eye on it. Imogene is paying dividends," I replied, with a chuckle. "These people don't realize that everything they're doing to stop me is actually helping me in the long run. It's poetic, it really is."

Naima bowed her head. "I am sorry to have questioned you."

"Well, maybe I should do some questioning of my own. Namely, I'd like to know where you're up to on number eleven. The time is a-ticking on finding these last rare magicals." I tapped my wrist, though I wasn't wearing a watch. Time was a human construct that I didn't much care for.

"I am endeavoring to find the eleventh, Eris," she said.

"Then endeavor away. Don't let me stop you. I have an idea of who I might like to complete my dozen, but it wouldn't hurt to pick up some extras, if you can manage that."

Naima bowed. "Of course, Eris."

The cult had access to sensitive information from all the covens, all across the globe, now. With the magical detector in our hands, too, we had no excuse for not being able to find the right people for the last part of the Challenge, before that ridiculous clock ran out. I might not have been one for the construct of time, but Chaos was a sucker for it.

FIVE

Katherine

I sat in the Eris Island Bestiary, tending to my pretties. There was something simple and comforting about gargoyles. They did what I asked and never questioned me.

Blind obedience was always a preferable quality, and that was the trouble with the more sentient kind of Purge beast, like Naima. She was loyal to me, but she had thoughts of her own. They needed to be kept in check, unlike with these beautiful creatures. Even now, I had one gargoyle doing loop-the-loops, just because I'd made it. It didn't talk back, it just did.

This ability reminded me of what I was reaching toward—the goal of turning everyone on this planet into a variation of these gargoyles. Obedient to a fault, doing whatever I asked, whenever I asked.

I was slightly concerned that Harley might delve into her version of this ability—that she could control Purge beasts. It disappointed me to think of what she might have been if I'd managed to get to her before the SDC had. I could've had a readymade sidekick. And it would have been so damn easy. I could have layered the family angle on thick and given her the mom she'd never had, even though the whole maternal thing didn't come too naturally to me. She'd have lapped from my palm like a kitty. *You screwed me over on that one, Hiram.* Another strike to add to his extensive list.

I supposed her ability to control Purge beasts was a minor inconvenience, at best, considering the power I'd amassed. It was pretty much impossible to stop me now. Harley and her little buddies had failed countless times. Even they had to know it was pointless now, though they continued to flog that poor, dead horse. I wasn't worried, though. I'd thought of everything. As soon as she'd uncovered the Grimoire's secrets, I'd make my move, binding her to my will to ensure she only read out the things I needed her to. Namely, the body spell Odette had revealed to me under the breaking point of her torture.

"I've taken all the right precautions," I said to my gargoyles. "I've made the right moves and put the right people under my influence. I'm the queen on the board, and we're edging toward checkmate. I'm so close now, my friends. So close." My insides were buzzing at the prospect of completing the Challenge, as if my cells had been replaced with hornets.

Seriously, this power inside me was addictive. I'd never been one to drink or play with recreational drugs, since that just turned people into uninhibited idiots who ended up naked or making terrible life choices, but I imagined this was what it felt like to be high. All the rush, none of the comedown. I'd never needed any social lubricant to be the life and soul of the party, and I didn't need it now. The only trouble was, despite the strength growing within me, it had its limits. At least until I ascended.

Everyone had always identified Hester as the social butterfly—the lauded sister who never did wrong—but I was the one people talked about. I was the one they stared at, whenever there were parties or dinners. I knew how to make an entrance, and I knew how to keep their attention. I was the one making people howl with laughter, and the one who could charm the bigwigs with my sharp mind. Even at eighteen, the old director of the New York coven would push me toward visiting guests, knowing I'd be able to win them around to whatever grant or loan he was trying to squeeze out of them. And, man, I could flirt my way around a crowd like nobody's business. A flutter of the eyelashes, a graze of my lip, a well-timed chuckle, and those men were putty in my hands.

Although, that had always been my last line of defense, if the rest hadn't worked.

And yet, people would just harp on about how sweet and beautiful Hester was. When she was standing beside me, it was like I suddenly became invisible. It never made sense to me, since we looked so similar. What had she had, that I hadn't? I was smarter, I was feistier, I was more vibrant. But everyone preferred her. She'd taken everything from me: my future career in the coven, my family's respect… and Hiram. It only seemed right that I should've taken everything from her, too. *Divine justice.* I'd spoken to her while she was imprisoned in that jar quite a few times, but Hester hadn't been particularly forthcoming with her replies. Stubborn as ever.

That's something they never teach you when you're young—people turn on women so quickly. One rumor, one affair, one spread of gossip, and that's it. Game over. Everything you've built gets torn down. I was called jealous and spiteful, and even my family turned against me, because they thought I was overreacting, and that I ought to "get over it" where Hiram was concerned. They didn't know I had a baby growing inside me, because of him. They didn't get that I was mad because of that —because he'd cast me and my child aside, as if I were yesterday's news, all for perfect freaking Hester. I could've told them, I could've told Hiram, but they didn't deserve the truth by that point. They'd already shown their true colors toward me, and I'd painted the walls with those colors.

Black Christmas, the papers had called it. Santa had left a little more than anyone had expected that Christmas morning, although red has always been a delightfully festive color. The shock on their faces when I killed them was the funniest part. It was like, even then, they couldn't understand it. They couldn't understand why I hated them so much. They'd turned me out of their house, and their hearts, and they still thought they were free of guilt, and that I'd just roll over and take it. Like their deaths weren't inevitable, after the way they'd treated me. My mom had even gone so far as to call me insane and suggest I be committed to a mental hospital, after I fought with Hester and Hiram in my childhood home. The fight that had resulted in me being thrown out. And yet, her eyes were the widest when I ended her life.

I'd never missed my grandfather more than in that moment, when I'd murdered them all—all but the two I'd wanted to kill the most. I'd saved them for last, so I'd have the delicious pleasure of seeing Hiram kill his dearest love. My grandpa would have backed me. He'd have understood. Hell, he'd have probably helped me kill them, if I'd asked. He'd have said, "They deserved it." He was the only one who believed I could achieve anything. The rest just wanted to hold me back and see me squashed under the success of everyone else, letting Hester run out in front while I lagged behind. Letting her take Hiram while telling me I was crazy not to just forget about him, as if I'd been nothing more than a plaything to him. Well, I was showing them.

I often thought about Hiram when I'd looked at Finch. They didn't look so similar that it hurt *every* time, but maybe that was because the memory of Hiram's face had faded with the years. Still, there were aspects of Finch's character that reminded me of Hiram, a few glimpses of his father in his features. That was the worst part—trying to love something that brought back so many uncomfortable memories.

Finch had never stood a chance of being loved. I didn't have that emotion in me. I'd thought I'd loved Hiram, but when he left me for my sister, that semblance of a feeling disappeared forever. Love just made people weak, and I wasn't weak. It had even weakened Finch, who should've been the formidable sidekick I needed. His desperation for affection had always been nauseating, but it'd been useful for a while. Now, Harley had manipulated that need in him and managed to win him over. And Hiram was still coming out of this whole thing smelling of roses. Finch didn't blame his dear old papa for his shortcomings—he blamed me, instead. I'd offered him everything on a silver platter and given him chance after chance to make amends, and he'd thrown it back in my face.

"I know I tried to have him killed, and that was wrong of me, but I never really wanted him dead. I suppose I should've gone about things differently. If I had, he might still be on our side, no persuasion necessary," I said to the gargoyles. "But now, he's becoming a problem. A big one."

At least I'd had the common sense to keep him in the dark about a few things. If there was one thing I'd learned, it was that family could turn on a person in an instant, same as anyone else. Finch had proven my point, though he could probably say the same about me. It was better that I'd kept my cards close to my chest, hiding a few aces from my son. He didn't know I was Imogene, which might have been the biggest ace I had to play. *That reminds me...* I had a loose end to tie up.

Leaving the island Bestiary, I arrived at the new location of my beach house and stepped inside. I padded down the hall and inhaled the salty air, before heading for the room at the back of the main corridor, where my grandpa slept. I say slept, but that was a little too polite—the guy was a living prune. He lingered somewhere between life and death, stuck inside his glass coffin like a mummy on display. I knew I should have properly killed him by now, but I couldn't bring myself to do it. He'd always championed me. I couldn't have sent him back to the afterlife, not for all the power in the world.

Sorry, Gramps. I brushed my fingertips to my lips, then placed them against the coffin. It left a slight smudge, matching the countless marks that already smeared the case. He really was horrific to look at, his face all shriveled up and purple, with one eye half rotted out of his head while his leathery skin strained against his skeleton. The Norman Bates flavor of this wasn't lost on me, but he'd kept me going, reminding me of why I'd set out on this path, and that was as good a reason as any to keep the raisin around.

I went to the back of the room and pushed through a door into an annex beyond.

"Good morning, sunshine." I smiled at the faint sound of chains rattling. Someone stirred in the windowless gloom. When I flicked the switch, an anemic bulb sputtered to life, casting a dim glow. Slumped against the far wall behind the bars of a cage, covered in her own filth and misery, was the real Imogene Whitehall.

I took my job very seriously, and that included keeping up appearances. Playing the role of Imogene Whitehall wasn't as easy as I made it look. Even Meryl Streep would've needed a helping hand with this one. If I didn't get an Oscar after this, then something was rigged. So, I'd kept the real Imogene around, using her for information and torturing her into submission whenever I needed something important: lists of names, valuable artifacts, that sort of thing. I'd been playing her for so many years now that I'd lost count. Four, perhaps? Maybe longer.

However, her time had come to an end. I no longer needed her. I had everything I wanted, and all my pieces were moving into the right positions. I had the magical world at my feet, right where it needed to be. It had taken years of dedication and careful orchestration, building to this exact moment, and now it was just around the corner. Soon, I'd ascend and take magic away from everyone—those who were faithful and deserving would get suitable powers; those who weren't would stay human until they died, or until I killed them for disobedience. An empire needed slaves, after all. Humans were perfect for that job.

My new magicals would gain authority over this world. They would rise up as the superior species, taking their deserved place at the top of the food chain. No more hiding from the humans. No more tiptoeing or walking on eggshells. No more shame in our abilities, instead of celebrating our power and making those weaklings fear us. The entire planet would know of Eris and her magnanimous nature. They would pray to me and worship me and beg me for a slice of power, because I'd walk in their world like no Child of Chaos before me. *Thanks to Harley.* It would be a beautiful thing.

And then, I'd use Jacob and his Sensate abilities—after I'd whipped him into shape, of course—to keep track of those I'd gifted with Chaos. The young were easier to break down and mold however I saw fit, once they'd been crushed into submission. And Jacob certainly had potential, if I allowed him to retain his Portal Opening abilities. He could zip here and there, keeping an eye on my people, making sure to nip any rebellions in the bud. After all, I wouldn't have the time or the inclination to go around doing all the hard work, after I'd ascended. That was the main point of having minions, right? To get them to do the stuff I didn't feel like doing. Naima would be at my side, as usual. Finch, Jacob—they'd all bend to me, after some re-education. Maybe Alton, Levi, and Remington would join me, in the end, and whoever else decided to be smart and work for me, instead of dying. Or, worse, becoming mere humans.

"Katherine?" Imogene blinked up at me.

I chuckled. "Who else? Did you think someone had finally come to save you?"

"Release me, Katherine. Release me, and I won't say a word."

"You never do change that record, do you?" I smirked. "Well, I'm here to say that today is your lucky day."

"What do you mean?"

"I'm going to release you."

Imogene's eyes widened. "You are?"

They really never *see it coming, do they?* "I am. The time has come."

I stepped up to the bars of the cage and reached out to Imogene. Shaking, she took my hands in hers and held them tight, a desperate woman looking to her captor for help. It was pathetic, how low she'd been brought. This Imogene Whitehall wasn't anything compared to my Imogene. My Imogene wouldn't have allowed herself to be captured in the first place. In a few minutes, my Imogene would be the only one left, until I finally dispensed with her, too. *It'll be like taking my bra off after a long day. Blissful.*

"You will soon be free, Imogene," I whispered. "You have suffered long enough."

"Thank you, Katherine. Thank you." Tears rolled down her dirty cheeks, leaving trails across her skin, like a grubby slug had gone wandering.

I tugged on Imogene's hands, sending her sprawling forward, her head hitting the bars of the cage. "*Ossa tua: ut conteram eos. Turn illa pariter. Ossa vestra iactata fatiscit, sed solum cinis donec manet.*"

As the words left my mouth, tendrils of black shot out of my palms and slithered into Imogene. I smiled down at her as the coils of Chaos threaded under her skin, turning her veins gray. She stared back at me in horror as the curse began to do its thing.

A scream escaped her throat. Her body folded in on itself like human origami, her lungs collapsing and stifling that howl with a pleasing gurgle. The crunching of her collapsing bones reminded me of car tires on gravel, from vacations I'd been on as a kid. Only, this time, my dad wasn't coming to take me out of the back seat, asleep, and carry me into the house. It's funny how you never realize something is going to happen for the last time. Take Hiram. If I'd known when he was going to hug me for the last time, I'd have used this curse on him there and then and put the dust of his remains in a fancy vase, to look at in darker days.

Imogene's skull cracked, black veins spiderwebbing across her face, rotting everything away to nothing but dark gray ash. Her mouth was still open in a terrified "O" when it disappeared completely, the dust of her drifting up with the breeze that filtered in from outside the door. Soon enough, there was nothing left but a smear of black dirt on the ground. A streak of the woman that Imogene had been.

"It was a pleasure." I chuckled to myself, before striding out of the room and locking it behind me.

Heading out of the beach house, I paused on the veranda. Across the sea, the sky had darkened to a stormy swell of clouds. My time was coming. I could feel it getting closer by the second. And, with it, I sensed the agitation within Chaos as the winds whipped up around me, clawing at my clothes and my face. *You don't have the power to stop me. Chaos rules, remember?*

"Cry all you want, little Children." Grinning, I looked up at that blackening sky. "I'm coming for you, and, once I'm done with you, there'll be no bitch badder than me. You'll be laying out the red carpet, whether you like it or not." I said it out loud so the Children of Chaos would know that the days were numbered for one of them.

Thunder growled in the distance, the sound widening my grin. *I guess they didn't like that.* Not that I gave a hoot what they thought. I was on my way, and they couldn't do anything about it, no matter how hard they stomped their feet or threw their tantrums.

I was going to ascend. I was going to be a Child of Chaos. It was no longer a matter of if, but of when.

SIX

Harley

I hadn't spent much time in Alton's new, non-director office. He'd taken up a smaller study along the main corridor of the SDC after he'd resigned from the position. It was cramped and didn't really have an Alton vibe to it, with mahogany walls and dusty furniture and a way smaller desk than he used to have. But I guessed, if he didn't have the big job anymore, he couldn't have the big office. Right now, he sat in a plastic office chair, looking worried at my sudden arrival. He'd known this moment was coming, but I supposed he'd thought he had more time. Carefully, I locked the door behind me and focused on the reason I was here.

"I'm ready to talk," I said, with a firmness that didn't leave it up for discussion.

Alton pressed his lips together before speaking quietly. "I suggest we up the security. We can't risk anyone listening in." Rising from his chair, he crossed the room to join me at the door. Together, we started to put up hexes to keep out any potential eavesdroppers.

After the memory dump that had flooded my brain back in New York, I had a bevy of new spells I'd never known before. I put them to good use, pressing my palms to the wall and whispering the unfamiliar phrases as they leapt onto my tongue, almost by instinct alone. Blue light pulsated beneath my fingertips, flowing across the walls and the door in rushing waves, reminding me of water lapping against the shore. Once I'd finished with that, and Alton seemed to be done with his own security measures, I wandered through the room with my palms up, scanning for any unseen hearing devices or hexes, just the way Finch had taught me.

"I think we're clear." I settled down into the guest chair—another plastic, half-assed affair that had probably been nicked from an old storage room.

Alton took the chair opposite and nodded wearily. "First, I'd like to ask you a question."

"Go on…"

"How are you?"

My heart sank. This wasn't what I wanted to talk about. I was doing my best to compartmentalize everything, but people asking about my state of mind wasn't helping with that. I knew they meant well, but it was easier to swallow everything until after Katherine had been dealt with. Still, when I met Alton's concerned gaze, I felt my resolve crumbling a little.

I shrugged. "As good as can be expected."

"I'm worried about you, Harley. Grief affects people in a multitude of ways. Sometimes it drives them to do things they might regret. I don't want that to happen to you."

"Isn't it better to channel my grief into something constructive?" I realized I probably sounded like an automaton, but I couldn't let my guard down. If I did, I'd melt into a pool of tears, and Alton would be left to try and put me back together again. Right now, that wouldn't do anyone any favors, with the weight of the world resting on my shoulders.

"That's not what I mean. Channeling grief can be helpful, especially in the healing process, but I just want you to know that you're not alone in this. You don't have to soldier through this by yourself. You have so many good people around you, and I would hate to see you push them away because you're in pain."

"We're wasting time, Alton." I cut him off before it got too psychiatric. "I can cry every last tear I've got when Katherine is in the ground, so let me get straight to the point. I know you can bring my mom and dad back. I saw it in your eyes when I mentioned that spell, and I heard it in your voice when you didn't immediately tell me it was impossible. So, I need you to do it."

Alton gaped at me. "That's not necessarily true."

"Don't BS me, Alton. I know you can do it. I've heard things." I hadn't, but he didn't know that.

"Heard what things?"

"That there is dark, illegal Necromancy that can bring people back from the afterlife." I remembered the prune in Katherine's beach house. That wasn't exactly the same, since Drake Shipton's body had been put on ice and his spirit had been locked to his corpse. But still—something in the look Alton had given me made me think he knew of some other spell.

"How did you know?" Alton's words came out as barely more than a whisper.

"I didn't."

His eyes widened. "What?"

"I didn't, until you just confirmed it."

"Who's to say I *did* confirm it?"

I smiled. "You wouldn't have asked to speak with me in absolute privacy if there wasn't something massively illegal and dangerous that you wanted to talk to me about. Necromancy is a sketchy, gray area as it is. I put two and two together. You'd have crushed the idea outright if it couldn't be done. Plus, I've seen the failed result of a similar kind of Necromancy, though it wasn't quite the same."

A flicker of anger crossed his eyes. "Well played."

"I had a good teacher."

"Coldness doesn't suit you, Harley. This is exactly what I was talking about."

"You'd have given up the truth if I'd just asked?"

He sighed. "I've been of two minds about it ever since we spoke. It's not something I'm comfortable discussing."

"Screw comfort. Do you think Katherine is doing what's *comfortable*? No, she's ripping up every rulebook in the game and risking everything to achieve her goal. We have to match that if we're going to stand a chance of beating her." We needed to find a way to bring my mom and dad back, so we could get the three hidden memories and discover what the heck that would lead to. If it led to ending Katherine, then it was worth risking everything.

For a moment, Alton said nothing. "You're right... of course you're right, but that doesn't make it any easier. What you're asking of me isn't just ripping up some rulebook. It's toying with the very fabric of the universe, and the cords that tie the living and the dead together. It's delving into unknown territory. And I mean it when I say it's *unknown.* All we have on this subject are theorems and possibilities—nothing has been tried and tested, for good reason. It's illegal, for a start, but it's also horrible and deeply unethical. What is dead is supposed to stay dead."

"You resurrected Astrid at least three times, and you resurrected the cultist who killed Adley and Jacintha. What's the difference between that and what I'm asking?"

He sighed. "They were recently dead, and thus not within the illegal realm of Necromancy. What you're talking about is the resurrection of individuals who have been dead for a long time and have crossed over. It's unknown territory, as I've stated. Why do you think nobody knows if there's an afterlife or not?"

"Because nobody has dared to figure it out?"

He took a sharp intake of breath. "No, it's because it's ridiculously dangerous. It could open up a void that causes the living world and the afterlife to collide, resulting in all of those passed-on spirits flooding back through to our world, potentially trapping them here, away from the heaven they've been gifted. You told me about All Hallows' Eve on Eris Island. Think of it like that, but on a global scale, with everyone who has ever died and crossed over tumbling back into this world."

"You're skirting around the simple question, Alton."

He frowned. "There's a simple question?"

"Can it be done?"

"Theoretically... yes. Yes, there is a way to briefly bring your parents back. Again, and I stress this, it is entirely theoretical, but it's probable that it can be done." He looked pale. "But, if I were to agree to this, there's another problem, aside from the colossal disruption of the physical and spiritual planes."

"What problem?"

"I can't do it by myself," he replied, after a shaky pause. "I would need a second Necromancer. A strong one. A *very* strong one. And one who doesn't mind bordering on the highly illegal."

Necromancy seemed to have illegality woven into its nature, but I could see his point. That skill was a rare one, and we were running out of time to find someone who might fit the bill. Although, I was curious to know more about why he needed a second.

"Will it take that much energy?"

"It's not just the energy, it's the entire operation," he explained, his tone strained. "Hiram and Hester have been dead for a long time, so they have no viable bodies remaining. Not only that, but, as you know, their spirits have crossed over to the afterlife. No Necromancer, as far as I know, has ever brought a spirit back from beyond that boundary. It's just not done, and it's entirely different than bringing a spirit that's still in our world back into its body. But there have been theories, over the years."

I frowned. "You're confusing me. Can it be done or can't it?"

"I'm getting to that." He flashed me a warning look. "I was thinking we might use the bodies of Isadora and Suri, but they've been tainted by Katherine, making them unusable. Plus, I'm not sure that would sit too well with me, which I know sounds insane, considering what I'm discussing."

"So, we need fresh, untainted corpses?"

He nodded. "In a nutshell, yes. However, using fresh corpses comes with its own set of difficulties. Should Hiram and Hester actually make it back, their memories might be jumbled with those of the corpses' previous inhabitants. Since the whole reason we're doing this is to find hidden memories, there's a chance those memories might be so mixed up in the other person's brain that they can't be found."

"They really didn't want to make it easy, huh?" I gave a bitter laugh.

"I imagine they thought they'd still be alive, when they wrote it," Alton replied sadly.

"Yeah… I guess they must have." That notion stabbed at my heart: the idea that they'd written this in the hopes that they'd be the ones to stop Katherine, if worst came to worst. Hiram must have realized that wouldn't be the case when he'd written that strange, unreadable spell—the one with the weird, almost Arabic lettering. He must have known, then, that the Hidden Things spell would be nearly impossible to achieve, but there wouldn't have been any time to go back and change it. Katherine had made it that much harder to end her using the Grimoire, without even knowing. She seriously had to be the luckiest witch to ever walk this earth.

"Also, there's a risk that Hiram and Hester will come back as dysfunctional zombies, with no speech or motor skills. Naturally, that presents the same problem—there'll be no way to find these memories, if that happens. Euphoria requires a conscious, focused state of mind. Zombies don't tend to have that."

My confidence was dwindling by the second. For some stupid reason, him not immediately telling me it was impossible had given me a surge of hope, but I should have known that it would come with a million provisos and risks. He wasn't painting a particularly optimistic image.

"And nobody has ever done this kind of thing before?" I asked.

He shook his head. "Nobody, aside from a few unproven rumors."

"So, it's majorly illegal, huh?"

"All of the resurrections I've done so far have been legal, as I mentioned before, but absolutely nobody in the magical community is comfortable with this ability. Ever. If it needs to be done, then it gets done. But everyone turns a blind eye. In this case, we're talking about an abominable, potentially catastrophic act, not only because of the possible collision of realms, but because your mom and dad have been dead for so long. Using borrowed corpses is unethical, for obvious reasons, and risky as hell. Illegal doesn't even begin to cover it."

I tried to grip tight to my hope. "And we need a second Necromancer who's cool with that?"

"Exactly. That may be the truly impossible part."

"You can't resurrect them both?" I figured it was best to ask, on the off-chance.

"I'm not even sure I can resurrect *one* of them, or what trying will do to me. I already go into a Purge when I resurrect someone legally. Imagine what may happen if I try this—something I've never done before that's beyond the known limits of my ability."

I sank back in the chair and gave myself a moment to think it all through. After everything he'd told me, I could see just how massive this task was, and the enormity of what I was asking. The grave-robbing would have been bad enough, but risking a collision of worlds, too?

WWKD? What would Katherine have done, in this position? I knew the answer to that, without hesitation. She'd have held two Necromancers at Chaos-point until they did what she asked, not giving two hoots for the potentially catastrophic aftermath. I had to be that ruthless if I wanted to stop her. I needed those hidden pages. They were the only thing standing between our current world and the utter calamity that would emerge under Katherine's rule. This was legitimately our last chance to stop her before she ascended.

I gave my answer to the Chains of Truth. I have to give that same answer now. I'd told them that I would be willing to sacrifice everything and everyone, in the pursuit of killing Katherine. My heart already knew the truth—I just had to force the words out of my mouth and take action.

"I need you to do it," I said, at last. "Desperate times call for insane measures, and we have to be willing to break every rule, for the sake of this world. I don't like it any more than you do, but Katherine hasn't given us a choice. Too many lives are at stake."

Maybe it would change me forever and skew my moral compass beyond repair, but it had to be done. I just hoped we could avoid the catastrophic aspect. I remembered the fear I'd felt on Eris Island when those spirits had come floating through the walls. I didn't want to see that happen again, all across the globe. But I trusted Alton. He'd be careful—he, more than anyone else, knew what might happen if he wasn't.

Alton stared at me, as though he was trying to read my expression. I was tempted to use my reverse Empathy on him, but I was already pushing the unethical envelope a little too far. Instead, I poured every scrap of hope and rage and determination and bitterness into my eyes and prayed he understood just what we stood to lose if we weren't bold enough to take this terrible step. Meanwhile, the minutes ticked on, pounding from the old clock on the dusty mantle.

"Then I suppose I'll have to do this." He looked like he wanted to run for the hills.

"But you can't tell anyone what we're planning," I urged. Our tight inner circle had loosened, after the events with Katherine in Krieger's office. I couldn't risk anyone leaking this to Katherine, but that wasn't the only reason I wanted it to be kept on the down low. There was another, more personal reason, which nagged away in the back of my head, put there by the Chains.

"We'll need help—"

I shook my head. "It has to be just you, me, and whoever we get in as the second Necromancer. I don't want Wade or Finch, or anyone else, getting involved. I won't lose them, too. If what we're going to do is as dangerous as you say it is, then I don't want them being put in harm's way. I'm not having anyone else die on my watch. I wouldn't survive it, and if I don't have the will to go on, then all of this is for nothing."

"But—"

"No buts, Alton. Please. We can do this on our own." My voice gathered in strength. "And when we have the memories and we find out what purpose they serve, I'll push forward until Katherine is gone."

Alton frowned. "While that's very noble, there's no harm in having more people help us, should anything go wrong. I know how much pain you're in and what grief like that can do to a person, but you can't push everyone away. They want to help you, Harley. And besides, you can't stop them from getting hurt in the battle to come. You can't stop them from fighting."

"I can, and I will. She's not destroying them, Alton. She's not!" My hands balled into fists, all of my grief and agony rising up at once, in one sudden burst of wild emotion. I tried to hold it all back, but it was like it didn't even belong to me anymore. Before I could stop it, a blast of Telekinesis exploded out of me, my body lighting up a blinding white. All around me, books were thrown from their shelves, and every hint of glass in the room shattered with a deafening crack, the shards raining to the ground in a glinting torrent.

Alton looked horrified. "Okay, okay, it was only a suggestion. We'll do it your way. Just you and me and this second Necromancer. Nobody else has to know." He was panicked. My anger had thrown him off guard. *Good.*

"I mean it—nobody is allowed to know," I said.

He raised his hands in surrender. "Okay, nobody will know. We'll focus all of our efforts on getting the Hidden Things spell completed, and then we'll talk about bringing the others back in. Does that sound fair?"

"For now."

"Well then, I suppose I should try to find a second Necromancer." He ran an anxious hand through his hair, which had grayed a little more in the past few months. "I'll call you when I have a lead. In the meantime, you should try and vent some of your emotions. Working on the Naima angle with the rest of the Rag Team might be the best bet. Using your abilities to control Purge beasts would be a better way to channel your feelings."

I sighed. "Let's hope so." Otherwise, they might end up tearing this whole place down.

SEVEN

Harley

Heeding Alton's suggestion, I headed for the Bestiary, after sending a quick message to Finch and Wade to meet me there. They were waiting for me, alongside Tobe, all of them standing awkwardly in front of the main atrium. I paused for a moment to look at them, tucking myself away behind one of the glass boxes.

I hadn't really allowed myself to show much emotion since I'd broken down in the infirmary, but now the tears came, and my heart swelled in an unexpected way. I loved those two guys so much it hurt. Tobe, too. He'd been the one to stop me from crumbling when my world had threatened to fall apart, and I'd never forget that. But Finch and Wade were more than friends—they were family, one by shared blood, one by shared souls. My boyfriend and my brother, standing side by side, waiting for me as if they'd always wait, as long as I asked them to.

But I can't keep asking. My love for these two, and for Tobe, and Alton, and the rest of the Rag Team, only cemented the truth of our intertwined futures: I had to push through the battles to come on my own so that they'd live. So that their hearts would keep beating, even if mine stopped. I wasn't trying to be a martyr; I was just trying to do the best thing, for their sakes.

Wiping my eyes, I emerged from behind the glass box. They smiled as

I came closer, giving me the courage I needed. Even if I died in order to kill Katherine, they'd learn to smile again, like this. And that was worth fighting solo for.

"Sleeping on the job, Sis?" Finch grinned.

"Huh?"

He chuckled. "Wade told me you'd snuck off for a snooze. Wish I could get hold of some of Krieger's famous sleeping pills. I can't remember the last time I had a good night's sleep."

"Oh... yeah, I couldn't sleep. I figured I should make myself useful instead." I remembered the lie I'd told Wade. I hated to admit it, but it was probably going to be the first in a big line of lies to come.

"And you don't need any more pills," Wade teased.

"Oof, harsh." Finch nudged him in the arm, though he seemed genuinely amused. "My nutjob pills have a list of side effects as long as my arm. One of them is insomnia. Seriously, I've watched endless repeats of *Duck Dynasty*, and even that's not enough to knock me out."

Wade laughed, and the sound made me want to throw my arms around him. "What are the other side effects? Rudeness? Foot-in-mouth syndrome? Bad jokes? A love of trash reality TV?"

"Ah, so you're familiar with them?" Finch smirked, but his expression suddenly changed. "You know I'm only joking about the sleeping, right? You deserve to get some rest."

I nodded. "I've learned to take most of what you say with a hefty pinch of salt."

"Good... just wanted to check." He ran an awkward hand through his hair. He'd gone back to blond with a little temporary Shapeshifting, but not the platinum shade from before. Now, it was more of a golden tone, verging on strawberry. A shade all his own, not tied to his past or his mother. I knew things had to be bad, if he was starting to check himself when it came to his jokes. He had no idea that his humor was one of the things I loved the most about him, because I knew it would bring a smile to my face when almost nothing else could. His humor, Wade's kisses, and Tobe's stoic presence—they were my pillars.

"All of the preparations have been made for your training, Harley."

Tobe smiled at me. "I thought we might begin with the gargoyles, as they will provide excellent practice for you."

"They act like puppies around her, seriously." Finch snapped out of his uncertainty. "Big, ugly, leathery puppies."

I mustered a small chuckle. "Let's hope they still listen to me. Murray's not in there, is he?" I remembered that particular gargoyle from our encounter months ago.

Tobe shook his head. "He is in a box all of his own. He does *not* play well with others."

No, he freaking doesn't.

We made our way through the Bestiary, passing the feathered serpent from Santana's Purge. I guessed that cute little snake was too small to practice on, given the time constraints—we needed bigger fish. Continuing on, we headed toward the gargoyle enclosure at the back of one of the branching halls. It was a vast glass box that reminded me of a weird aviary, only there were no birds flapping inside. Instead, black smoke twisted and twirled, bashing into the glass every so often, before dispersing back into the misty expanse within.

Tobe approached the glass box and retrieved his enormous set of keys from inside the ruffled feathers of his wings. He found the right key almost instantly and slid it into the lock. My heart lurched as it clicked, and he opened the door. A ripple of energy passed across the threshold, faintly revealing the forcefield that kept the gargoyles from escaping. Magicals could pass through it, but Purge Beasts couldn't, with the sole exception of Tobe.

"You may begin whenever you feel ready," Tobe urged.

I nodded. "No time like the present."

"Knock on the door and we'll get you out," Wade said, his hand on the small of my back.

"Yeah, wouldn't want our last chance of ending Katherine to be turned into gargoyle chow." That was probably Finch's form of encouragement.

"Thanks for the vote of confidence," I replied.

He smiled. "Any time, Sis."

Gathering my nerves, I stepped through the forcefield and tried not to back away as the door closed behind me, the key turning in the lock. *They're just gargoyles... nothing to be worried about.* I tried to convince myself that was true, but I'd seen what these suckers could do to people they didn't like. Memories of them escaping pounded in my skull, but that was in the past now—that had happened before I knew I could control them.

As I stared into the swirling smoke, shapes began to appear, and I set to work on mustering the right kind of juice. Delving into myself, I tried to remember what I'd done the last time, on Eris Island. As I tried to find the tendrils of my reverse Empathy so I could send them out at the gargoyles, the black mist expanded into limbs and faces and wings as the gargoyles came out in force, curious to find out who'd dared to enter their realm. Black liquid dripped from their pointed fangs, and they beat out a drumbeat with their leathery wings. But they seemed to be keeping their distance, more intrigued by me than wanting to gouge out my eyes.

Come on, how does this thing work again?

I was about to shout out a command, when one fluttered close, forcing me to stand still—my "if I don't move, it won't be able to see me" strategy. This gargoyle seemed overly familiar, as if it thought it knew me. I tried to recall whether I'd met this one before, when we'd all fought to get these creatures back into the SDC, but they all looked the same to me. *Murray?* No, Tobe had said he was in his own box. Still, it seemed almost friendly. It flapped even closer, until I could feel the wind of its flight whipping across my face. Its tongue shot out of its mouth and slathered my cheek with a streak of thick, oily mucus. I struggled not to shudder.

No sooner had its tongue made contact than it reeled back, an almighty screech tearing out of its throat. As that bloodcurdling sound shivered through the glass box, the mood changed. The gargoyles focused more intently on me. Their mouths opened in an echo of that screech, until the deafening cacophony made me cover my ears.

"Listen to me!" I shouted frantically, trying to send out a wave of reverse Empathy. Either I'd missed every single one of them or I wasn't getting it right. None of them stopped. Instead, my voice only seemed to make them angrier.

The first gargoyle swooped in, its jagged claws scratching for my face. I ducked out of the way, only to sprawl to the ground as another gargoyle divebombed me from above. All hell broke loose, with gargoyles coming at me from all angles in a frantic flurry of fangs, claws, and the stench of something rotten. I tried to defend myself, sending out another wave of reverse Empathy, but I could already feel the first stings of open wounds.

"Listen to me!" I yelled again, sending out a third pulse, but it wasn't doing anything.

Leaping to my feet, I raised my palms and sent a powerful blast of Telekinesis outward, sending them all flying back like leaves in a tornado. It only angered them more. They came flying back with a vengeance, forcing me to get creative with my Elemental magic. Fireballs flashed from my fingertips, and violent gusts of Air rushed at the oncoming creatures, holding them off for a few seconds before they rallied for the next onslaught.

"You must utilize your control over these creatures, Harley." Tobe's voice seeped in, distant and muffled, from beyond the box.

You don't say. How was I supposed to concentrate with these things flying at me non-stop? It'd been way easier with just the one, but this was a horde of gargoyles. I was starting to think I should've started smaller, but I was in this now, and I refused to knock on that door to be let out.

"Let your fear fade away," Tobe encouraged. "They have no power over you. You are the one with the power."

"Obey me!" I shouted, trying to get that echoey rasp going in my throat. It had worked before, but I didn't know the actual details of *how* it worked. "Obey me!"

I faced the gargoyles head-on and reached deep inside for the overflowing emotions that boiled in my core. I grasped for grief and heartache. I hoped they would help me get the echo I needed, as they were the strongest emotions I had right now. Pulling them out of me, I felt the physical tug as I let them flow toward the oncoming horde. To my horror and disappointment, it didn't do a damn thing. They flinched for a millisecond, before continuing their incessant attack, prompting me to send out another wave of Telekinesis, just to keep them back.

"Stop!" I shouted, but my voice came out ordinary.

Don't give up. Don't give up. If I couldn't do this, how could I hope to face Katherine one-on-one? I had to prove that I was powerful on my own. This was as much a test of my ability as a test of my determination, and I wouldn't fall at the first hurdle.

I reached for hope and a sliver of happiness, gained from the sight of my brother and my boyfriend together. Half-closing my eyes, I dug deep and let it all pour out of me, the way I'd done back in the infirmary, when I'd brought everyone to tears.

"Obey me!" Again, my voice sounded ordinary, but there was an edge of *something* to it.

My body pulsated, and my veins lit up with a subtle glow, my skull throbbing with the pressure of so much emotion. The well of emotions threatened to overwhelm me completely. A sharp pain shot between my eyes and stabbed at the backs of my retinas. It didn't feel right, but I couldn't stop now. I could deal with a little physical pain if it meant I got these beasts under control.

"Come on, OBEY ME!" A slight echo reverberated through my words.

Furrowing my brow against the pain and forcing more and more of the reverse Empathy out of me, I saw something that made time stand still. In the center of the gargoyle horde, one of the beasts suddenly dropped to the floor. It folded its wings behind its back, its eyes fixed on me, blinking slowly. Instead of a screech, it let out a small, high-pitched whine, its head dipping and rising in a weird rhythm.

I couldn't believe it. *It worked!* The gargoyle was just sitting there, watching me, while it bowed in that strange way. As I lessened the strength of my emotions, my sharp headache quickly disappeared, though it left a lingering sensation of nausea in my stomach, like I was getting over food poisoning.

I was so fixated on the obedient gargoyle that I almost forgot the rest of them. My reverse Empathy hadn't affected them at all. I had to duck as one swiped for my head, my arms rising to protect myself. Air hissed through my teeth as I felt the nick of its claws, tearing a massive hole in my leather jacket and scratching the skin beneath. The obedient gargoyle snapped out of its trance and joined the rest of its leathery friends as they swarmed in a fresh attack. This time, no amount of reverse Empathy, or

Telekinesis, or Elemental magic was going to help me, not if I wanted to get out of here alive. A true fighter knew when it was time to retreat, and I was waving my white flag.

Sprinting for the door, I banged on the glass. Tobe immediately unlocked the door to let me stagger back into the Bestiary, while the gargoyles screamed as they tried to push themselves through the force-field. Tobe moved past me and entered the box, working his Beast Master magic on them, his voice rising from the back of his throat in a curious, mystical song. It was so eerie and beautiful that it brought tears to my eyes, the whole box thrumming against the vibrations of his rich tenor, as if Chaos itself were listening. His music manifested as a calming mist that drifted across the gargoyles, turning them back into black smoke.

"Are you okay?" Wade grabbed me and made me sit down on the cold marble. "Jeez, you're covered in cuts." He had a first-aid kit in his hand. Tobe had probably anticipated something like this and had given it to Wade in the event of some minor injuries.

"I'm fine," I protested, but he was already pulling out antiseptic and cotton balls.

"You're not fine," Finch interjected, his face a picture of concern. "You just had your ass handed to you by a bunch of gargoyles, and you've got tears running down your freaking face. So sit back and let Nurse Crowley see to you. Doctor's orders."

"Does that make you the doctor?" I replied distantly.

"In this scenario, yeah."

I was still entranced by Tobe's song, my mind elsewhere. It troubled me how easily Finch could see right through me, even though I was supposed to be the Empath. Was it because we were siblings? Was there some subconscious bond between us? I had no idea. Right now, my head was pounding and my skin was on fire, and that was pretty much all I could think about.

"What's that?" Wade's voice brought me back around. My eyes widened as I saw what he was looking at. Through the gash in my leather jacket, a tiny speck of gold peeked through—the sickening, gilded threads that had leaked out from the main body of my disgusting tattoo. I scrambled to cover it, holding the edges of the leather together, while my eyes desperately sought out Finch's.

"It's nothing. I've been trying out a new bracelet, that's all. I don't think it suits me, so I'm probably going to get rid of it." My cheeks were red and hot. I knew he'd probably understand if I told him how I'd gotten this horrible tattoo, but I was too embarrassed to show it to him. He'd given me strict instructions to be careful on Eris Island, and, while I had, I hadn't been able to avoid getting this. That had been part and parcel of the subterfuge. I didn't want him to pity me for the pain I'd been through. And I definitely didn't want him to blame himself for me being permanently scarred. Even if I told him it wasn't his fault, he'd blame himself. That was just how he was.

Finch pretended to look outraged. "Hey, I bought you that!"

"It's just not to my taste." I struggled to keep the truth from tumbling off my tongue.

Wade was staring at me, half confused, half suspicious. "Finch bought you a bracelet?"

I shrugged. "Yeah, it was meant to be an apology gift. I've been trying to wear it, for his sake, but I usually keep it covered since it doesn't suit me."

"Pfft, there's gratitude for you," Finch muttered, but his eyes were sympathetic.

That is gratitude, Finch. Thank you... thank you.

"I might have to find a new jacket." I broke the silence that was starting to stretch between us.

"I'll get one for you," Wade replied, making me feel even worse.

"You don't have to."

He smiled. "I know, but I want to. You love that jacket."

"Yeah... I do." *Because you bought it for me.*

"I've got one you can borrow until Wonderboy cleans out Dolce & Gabbana for you." Finch smiled down at me. "Now, let us clean you up before these things get infected."

Tobe emerged from the glass box, closing the door behind him. It gave me the distraction I needed to press my arm to my side, keeping Wade from seeing what was really under the fabric.

"It may be wise to take a brief recess from the gargoyles, for now," he said. "They are much too infuriated, and I do not wish you to come to further injury."

"Good idea," I replied.

As Wade dabbed the cuts around my face and neck, Finch took over on my forearm, turning it gently toward him. Keeping his eyes on me in a silent promise to keep my secret, he pressed the soaked cotton ball against the cut just south of my Apple of Discord, careful not to reveal the gold of it through the gap in my sleeve.

As if you two weren't already making it hard enough to do this on my own.

EIGHT

Harley

Wearing a beat-up biker jacket that smelled strangely of a very feminine perfume, the three of us—Wade, Finch, and I—reunited with the Rag Team in the Luis Paoletti Room, missing only Louella, who was still working on Jacob. Finch had retrieved the jacket from one of his hidden caches around the SDC, and though it looked like it had belonged to him, given its larger size, I couldn't ignore that faint scent. I'd wanted to tease him about it and say it wasn't exactly the cologne I'd expected, but the way he was looking at the jacket was weird, too. As though it meant something to him. I realized, with a sinking feeling of gratitude and sadness, that he'd probably given this to Adley to wear. The perfume was her perfume. It must have pained him to give it to me, but he'd done it anyway.

Thank you, I mouthed.

He shrugged and mouthed back, *No problem.*

"Do we have any hits on Naima?" Wade had gone into business mode as he looked around the room at the others. It pulled me back into the task at hand. We needed to find Naima in order to find Katherine.

Astrid glanced nervously at O'Halloran, who'd been instructed to join us. It was hard to tell if he was fully cured, after the antidote that Imogene had given him, but he seemed to be his old self. He wasn't jabbering like an idiot whenever anyone mentioned Echidna, which was a good sign.

"Look, I know I must've given you a shock when I went all crazy, but you don't have to be wary of me anymore," he said sheepishly. "I know that's easier said than done, but the effects of those pills have worn off, I promise. I'm back in business. Same old O'Halloran, even though I feel like I'm having the worst hangover of my life. It's all coming back to me in dribs and drabs, but so far I don't think I did anything embarrassing. So, maybe not quite like the worst hangover I've ever had. There was this one time, on a bachelor party trip to Boston… uh, never mind, you don't need to know about that."

Astrid relaxed slightly. "Do you have any news?"

"Actually, I've been tasked with recruiting magicals for a solid offensive against Katherine once we find her." He smiled proudly. "So, it's important that I'm here, because I need to know where to send these soldiers once Katherine is found. Otherwise, how're we going to kick her ass?"

"Good point." Dylan nodded appreciatively. "We've got brains by the bucketload, but we're going to need brawn to end her."

No... no, you're not. I was going to get the Hidden Things spell done before it got to that point. I had to. There could only be gold at the end of this messed-up, mega-complex rainbow, and I was going to get my hands on it before any of my friends, or any of those soldiers, could so much as pick up a weapon.

"That's all well and good, but we need to focus on Naima. She's our way in to wherever Katherine is hiding out," Wade replied. "There's no point having an army if we can't find the enemy."

"Touché," Raffe said. "Couldn't have put it better myself."

Santana nodded. "Then we keep searching for her. We scour every possible outlet until we find her, and then we bring Harley in and force that cat-woman to purr."

"I've made some headway," Astrid added. "Smartie will find something soon, I'm sure he will."

Tatyana leaned over the workbench. "If you need anyone to help, just let us know. We're all on hand to do whatever needs to be done."

"I've got people in LA that I can speak to, if that'll help," Garrett chimed in. It was nice to see him back in the fold, and I knew Finch appreciated having him around, even if they had yet to fully rebuild their bridges.

"That'd definitely be useful." Astrid gave him a small smile, which made Garrett lower his gaze. I wished the two of them would get their act together and admit they still cared about each other, but that was going to be a hard thing to do with Astrid still dealing with the gap in her soul. Once all of this was over, I was determined to find a way to help her. After all, if my parents could be brought back from the afterlife, which was supposed to be an impossible thing, then fixing the hole in someone's soul would be a piece of cake.

"What do you think?"

I looked up and realized Finch was talking to me. I'd retreated into my own head, the discussion sinking into the periphery.

"Uh… yeah, sure. I'm good with whatever everyone else thinks," I answered, a little too quickly.

He arched an eyebrow. "You sure?"

"Yeah."

"You don't sound sure."

I rolled my eyes. "What is this, the Spanish Inquisition? I'm all in. I've got the cuts to prove it. Let's get Naima."

Finch kept looking at me, like he didn't quite believe what I was saying. I had no idea where this sudden suspicion was coming from, but it was written all over his face. *If he thinks something's up with me, I'm going to need to take some extra precautions.* I couldn't have him trying to help me, not after the answer that he'd given to the Chains of Truth. He'd said he'd sacrifice himself for me, if he had to, and I refused to see that come to pass. No way.

Still, my reasoning didn't stop me from feeling terrible that I was going to go it alone. Hopefully, one day, they'd realize that I'd done it for their own good, and they'd forgive me. Taking an army into Katherine's domain was suicide, and I knew it. Maybe they all knew it too, but having that one, solid idea of attack to focus on was better than succumbing to Katherine's influence and admitting defeat.

"Has Smartie picked up anything at all?" I put more enthusiasm into my voice as I turned to Astrid. I could still feel Finch's eyes on me, but the glare wasn't burning quite as much.

She nodded. "His system is set to pick up any trace of Naima or other known cult members. I already have some under surveillance, so, hopefully, that'll lead us to Naima. Sooner rather than later."

"We don't have a lot of time," Garrett replied. "What if Smartie and the surveillance can't find her in time? It might be better if we go on the offensive and capture a known cult member, instead of watching them. Then, we could force him or her into giving up Naima's whereabouts."

"You going to suggest waterboarding next?" Finch muttered.

Garrett sighed. "I know it sounds extreme, but we're out of options. We have to act fast and firm, or we'll run out of time."

"If we're pushed to it, we might have to do it your way," Astrid admitted. "But I'd rather watch for a while longer before we start crossing moral boundaries."

"That's fair." He offered her a smile.

"If it's okay with you, I'm just going to head out for a bit," I said, and felt their eyes snap toward me. "I'm not feeling too good after the gargoyle mess. Sorry to just up and leave, but my head is banging." That wasn't exactly true. My stomach still felt a bit unsettled, but my head was just fine. Truthfully, I just wanted to be on my own again so I could work through my next plan of action.

Santana frowned. "You need me to brew you up some of Mexico's finest coffee? It might perk you up."

I shook my head. "I'll be okay, but thanks." I stood and made for the door. Wade's voice called me back.

"I can come with you, if you want." He smiled earnestly. "We can take a look over the Grimoire some more. Who knows, you might find some meaning in the pages you can read. Or we can take a walk in the dragon garden to clear your head?"

"No, it's okay. I've got this. I just need some time to get rid of this headache." Before anyone else could offer me a remedy, or protest me being on my own, I walked out. Grateful for the silence of the empty hallways, I headed for the infirmary. Jacob had been on my mind, and I wanted to see him. With everything else that had been going on, I felt like I'd neglected him.

I wasn't even halfway there when I heard footsteps echoing in the corridor behind me. Turning sharply, I saw Finch skidding to a halt in front of me, stooping to catch his breath. He grinned up at me as I waited for an explanation.

"I'm coming with you."

I shook my head. "I said no to Wade. What makes you think I want you following me around? I just want to be on my own."

"Not going to happen, Sis. You're mentally unstable. I'm not letting you out of my sight."

"Thanks for that," I replied curtly. "I'm not mentally unstable. I just want to be left alone so I can deal with some things."

"Yeah, and I know what things. You can fool everyone else, but you can't fool me."

"What are you talking about? I'm not trying to fool anyone."

He smiled. "Sure, and Pamela Anderson's boobs are real."

"Seriously, all I want is some time on my own."

"So you can plan something outside of the Rag Team's mission?"

"No, so I can deal with this headache—which you're making worse, by the way."

"Man, you really need to learn how to lie. It's like watching a little kid tell me they didn't eat the last cookie in the jar, when there's chocolate smeared around their mouth."

I sighed. "I'm not lying."

"And I'm the King of Azerbaijan." He chuckled. "Don't be too hard on yourself. Not being able to lie is the sign of a fundamentally good person."

"So how come you're so good at it?"

He frowned. "Are you saying I'm a good person? I'm confused."

"Yes… no. I don't know. You've gotten *me* confused with the Azerbaijan thing." I lowered my gaze. "Finch, you've helped me out massively with so many things, but I need you to stop this time. I need you to not pursue this. Just focus on what the Rag Team is doing and let me do my thing. Please."

He shrugged. "Whatever you say."

"What?"

"Whatever you say."

"Seriously?"

He nodded. "Deadly."

"Okay, well… thanks." Puzzled, I turned and walked away, leaving him standing in the hallway, watching me. I wondered why he wasn't pursuing this further, since he was usually as stubborn as a donkey. Did he have something else up his sleeve that he was planning to do? I couldn't tell. *Not that it matters.* All hell was about to break loose, anyway, if I succeeded with the Hidden Things spell. Maybe literally, if we got it wrong.

NINE

Katherine

I kept checking my phone every two seconds, like a teenager waiting for a bite from some dude who wasn't interested. This had all the same anticipation, but if Naima didn't call, there'd be considerably bigger consequences. I'd always found it funny how she even typed in the numbers with her big old paws. She'd cracked a couple of screens already with those claws of hers. Fortunately, we had insurance. Always get insurance, for everything. That was my motto. Take Imogene—she was my insurance against Harley, the SDC, and the wider world of magical authority.

Naima was supposed to be retrieving the eleventh magical I needed for the last ritual, but I didn't have particularly high hopes. My little sidekick had started off with such promise, but she'd only become more of a disappointment as my Challenge had gone on. Don't get me wrong, I was fond of the beast. She was like a friend and a pet rolled into one, and who didn't want a pet who could speak?

But this was Naima's last chance to prove her worth. I'd put her in charge so she could show she was worthy of the responsibility, but if she outlived her usefulness… well, I'd have no problem getting someone to put the kitty down. I couldn't do it without causing myself pain, being her Purger and all, but I guessed the feeling would be different if someone else did the dirty work.

I had no room for weaklings in my future world. Naima had already had her ass handed to her more than once by Harley and the Misfits. *Good name for a band.* Perhaps I'd be generous and just lock her in my Bestiary and draw her power to sustain the island. That could work, too.

Okay, maybe there's still some use in the old girl yet.

I never let stress get to me—it was a pointless feeling—but I was getting so close to the finish line that the nerves were building. I was in the wings, waiting for the curtain to go up. The greatest performance ever created. My shining moment in the biggest spotlight this world had ever seen. I couldn't wait, but there were some little pests threatening to dull my shine.

Louella was one. Her Telepathy seemed to be coming back, and that was a major wrench in the works. I'd had Kenneth clamp down on that to avoid issues with my Imogene performance, but he obviously hadn't done a good enough job of destroying it completely. *Useless, cloying little worm.* Killing him had been a glorious moment. I'd been waiting for so long to shut him up. His very presence had always left me feeling dirty, like I needed twenty showers just to wash off the stink of his desperation.

I couldn't tamper with Louella again without someone catching on, and I needed to be careful not to out my true identity, so close to the end. I needed to keep my distance from her, if only for a short while.

A knock at the office door made me slip the phone back in the pocket of yet another cream suit. "Come in," I said.

Alton peered around. *Speaking of cloying little worms.* He was taking the job of unofficial assistant to the director way too seriously. I could barely go a couple of hours without him popping up like an incessant jack-in-the-box.

And to think I'd kissed him once at a Christmas party. *See,* that *is what happens when you allow yourself to have a drink or two.* Those bubbles had gone right to my head, and my head had made a beeline for Alton, who was all weepy after breaking up with his ex for the millionth time. Prime smooching territory, no strings attached. Still, it was an awkward encounter that he and I—or, rather, Imogene—hadn't discussed since.

But it had set tongues wagging for a while. Ironic, since it had been his tongue wagging at the time. He'd have died if he found out it was me doing the smooching. I supposed I could keep that on the back burner, if I ever needed a quick way to get rid of Alton. Remind him of that encounter, tell him it was me the whole time, and watch his mind explode.

"Alton, what an unexpected pleasure." I put on a sweet smile and sank back into the well-worn character of Imogene. It was second nature to me now, after so many years in her skin.

"Are you busy?"

Seriously? Am I busy? Understatement of the century. "I am a little, yes, but I have some time for you if it's urgent."

"I was hoping to have a word with you about Harley."

Ooh, this just got a little more interesting. "Of course. Please, sit." I sank down in the big armchair behind the desk and gestured for him to sit opposite. He did, dwarfed by the enormous seat. He looked like a little kid who'd just been allowed his first big-boy chair. I fought not to laugh.

"Has something happened?" I prompted. "Is she doing well? I realize that's unlikely, given the circumstances, but I hope she'll recover, in time."

"That's part of the problem. I suppose I expected her to be wandering around like a zombie after the news hit, but she's starting to scare me slightly."

Scare you? Stoic, hard-as-nails Alton Waterhouse? Pathetic. "How so? Is it something I should be concerned about? Do you need me to speak with her?"

He shook his head. "I wanted to talk with you first, to see what you thought. She seems to have skipped grief completely and has gone straight toward self-destruction."

"That's very troubling. In what respect has she gone toward self-destruction? Has she tried to harm herself?" There was no way I was letting Harley off herself before I'd squeezed everything I could out of her and could finally end her myself.

"No, not directly." He sighed uncertainly, like he wasn't sure whether to continue.

"You can tell me anything, Alton. No matter how concerning it might be. I'm here to help Harley, to look out for her best interests. If she's in some sort of danger, then I must know, so I may help, however I can." *Don't you clam up on me now.*

He nodded slowly. "It's this Hidden Things spell."

"Ah, she must be disappointed that it can't be done. I imagine that isn't helping her current state of mind."

"Actually, it's the opposite." That took me by surprise, and that didn't happen often.

"Oh?"

"She asked me to help her resurrect her parents so she can get the spell completed. I should've just told her it was impossible, but, when the moment came, I couldn't lie to her. She made a lot of good points about the dire straits we're in with Katherine." He looked at me reluctantly. "I don't know how much you know about Necromancy, but there are theories as to how something like that can be done. I'm worried it might end in catastrophe, but I couldn't say no to her."

"I see..."

"We've got to be bold, I know that, but her determination is frightening. It's like she's lost her moral compass. When I tried to tell her it wasn't a good idea, and that she needed to think about what she was actually asking, she exploded. Literally. Her Telekinesis went haywire, and she ended up flinging books and shattering all the glass in my office. I'm worried she's losing it, Imogene."

Well, well, well... This was tantalizing and concerning in equal measure. If what Alton was saying could really be done, then they had a way of revealing the hidden pages. The sneaky wretches had found a secret trapdoor in that dead-end street, one that might bring dear Sis and her backstabber husband back to life.

Once Harley had access to those pages, she'd become the perfect weapon against me. But I needed to use Harley. Catch-22 didn't even cover it. Harley's body had the Primus Anglicus juice that would create the ideal vessel to hold my future Eris self, allowing me to walk free between worlds. I could've used Finch, I supposed, but that was a major plan B. Getting stuck in my son's body wasn't exactly the vision I'd created in my head, even with a few Shapeshifting alterations. It would still be Finch's body, and that left a sour taste in my mouth. No, that was too close for comfort, in the familial sense. I'd given birth to the sucker—I didn't want to have to deal with being stuck inside *his* body, in any way, shape, or form.

Not that it matters. By the time Harley figured out the right spell from the Grimoire to use against me, I'd already be a Child of Chaos, practically unbeatable. And ready to use her for my needs. It was too little, too late. *So close, Merlins, and yet so far.* The only way to kill me then would be if Harley herself ploughed through those irksome rituals, and regardless of what Alton said about her lack of moral compass, I doubted she'd be willing to do what I'd done. She didn't have the ovaries for it.

"That's very worrying, Alton. Even without the extreme illegality of the matter, there are so many risks to consider," I said, playing the concerned confidant. "Such an act would have terrible consequences for the living world, wouldn't it?"

He shrugged. "It's never been done, so I don't know. But it's weighing on my mind."

"As it should." I paused. "You must be fairly confident in your ability to achieve it... Otherwise, you *would* have told Harley that it was impossible. I confess, I've never heard of such a thing being done before."

"The theories are sound. They align with the nature of Necromancy. It's just a way bigger ask than anything any Necromancer has done before. And I don't know if I can do it—both strength-wise and morality-wise." He shook his head. "I made a promise to Harley, but I feel sick to my stomach whenever I think about it. I almost didn't come to you, because I know you'd have every reason to send me to Purgatory for even mentioning it, but I had to speak to someone who understands what's at stake. I needed a fresh perspective, either to encourage me, or to tell me to nip this in the bud."

"If you're concerned about a prison sentence, then you don't need to fear that from me. I would certainly choose to turn a blind eye if you decided to proceed. If the situation weren't desperate, my reply would be different, but you're a logical man—if you didn't think this was necessary, you wouldn't have entertained the idea." I hated the flowery way I had to speak as Imogene, but that was part of her nature.

"So, you approve?"

I smiled softly. "I wouldn't say that I approve, and I cannot authorize this in an official capacity, since that would be aiding and abetting an illegal spell, but I'll look away if you wish to go ahead with it."

"Seriously?"

"Did you want me to give you a different answer? I can, if you think that's the right path."

He shook his head. "No, it's not that. I just never expected you to agree with something like this. You're known for your righteousness. And this isn't exactly righteous."

"Ordinarily, I would've protested with every ounce of oxygen in my lungs, but these are very special circumstances. It's past time for the covens to play somewhat dirty, or we'll all go down in flames." I met his gaze. "Don't misunderstand me—I don't approve of the nature of this, but if it must be done for the greater good, then who am I to stop it? It's not as though I have any less dangerous answers to our problem."

He sat back in his chair and ran a hand through his hair. "Then I guess we have to do this. If you think it's our only option, then I'm inclined to agree. I suppose I just wanted someone to dispel my doubts, and you've done that, more or less."

"You still have some?"

"I've still got doubts about my ability to actually do it, yes," he replied. Alton had always put on a big show of being heroic and brave, but I knew better. He'd buckled immediately when I'd threatened his daughter. Another reason why he'd never deserved the job here in the first place. To be a leader, there had to be no weaknesses in someone's character. It didn't make someone more human, it just made them vulnerable, and there was no place for vulnerability in a position of power.

"You are powerful, Alton." Ugh, that stuck in my throat. "You likely have more potential than you realize. There's no precedent for this, but you're a capable Necromancer. I won't stop you, as I've said, but I worry that you may be the one stopping yourself."

"I needed a pep talk." He chuckled weakly. Everything he did was weak. He didn't deserve to have the skill of a Necromancer. Once I ascended, I'd see to it that he ended up completely powerless.

"So you'll go through with it?"

He nodded slowly. "Yes... but I'll still need another Necromancer to get the job done. This isn't a one-man task."

"A second Necromancer?"

"I can cope with resurrecting one of Harley's parents, at a push, but two? I think it'd kill me."

I smiled, an idea forming. "Then you had better get started on those calls. There aren't too many of you left in existence."

"Well, there are definitely two I won't be able to get hold of. Micah is missing, and Harley told me that Katherine had murdered another Necromancer, after he botched some spell. I don't know the details of it, but she said it was pretty horrific. So, that leaves three."

My eyes threatened to narrow, but I kept them bright and open. So, Harley had found her way into my beach house, had she? She'd evidently seen my grandfather, given what Alton was saying. *Silly cow.* It was a grave disappointment that she'd been amongst my cult and I hadn't seen through her disguise. I'd actually been amused by Volla Mazinov. That was the type of person I wanted around, but I couldn't say the same about the Merlin twerp. I didn't know if I was more appalled that she'd actually had the audacity to sneak into my precious cult, or that she'd had the gall to look upon my beloved grandfather. But it was just fuel for the fire, baby.

"Then time is of the essence," I said. *When isn't it?*

Alton nodded. "Thank you for speaking to me, Imogene. You've put some worries to rest, though I'd urge you to keep an eye on Harley, whenever you can. She needs good people around her, to stop her from destroying herself."

Oh, Alton. I'm touched. He thought I was a good person. The poor dear had no idea who he was talking to. It would have been the greatest pleasure in the world to be in the front row at Harley's destruction, and I still planned to be there, with my popcorn, when it happened.

"I will," I lied.

Alton got up and left, leaving me to absorb everything I'd just heard like the beautiful, powerful sponge that I was. The idea I'd been having was starting to expand, just the way I liked. Alton had given me more than a heads-up; he'd given me a way to control Harley's fight, going forward. And he'd done it without even realizing, which made it all the sweeter.

I knew one of the three remaining Necromancers. It didn't exactly fill me with joy to have to reach out to him, but it was high time he chose his allegiance. He'd been sitting on the fence so long he had splinters in his butt cheeks. He'd helped me on a mission in London, but he'd yet to actually join the cult. I suspected he'd only refused in order to tease me, to make me want him even more. To make me want him to join, I mean. A "treat 'em mean, keep 'em keen" type of scenario. When I'd tried to convince him, he'd told me he didn't like to commit to anything.

Typical man.

Back then, I hadn't pushed it. But now, I would have to insist.

TEN

Harley

Under the cold, clinical lights of the infirmary, I sat at Jacob's bedside. Louella sat in the chair opposite, trying to keep her eyes open, one hand constantly fixed on the side of Jacob's head. She looked worn out, the poor thing, her whole face splotchy with tears—tears of grief, tears of loss, tears of frustration. She'd taken it upon herself to fix Jacob, and I got the feeling she wouldn't quit until he woke up.

"You should take a break," I said.

She shook her head. "I'm fine." I didn't push it. She and I were in similar boats, and I knew how I felt about people trying to get me to rest up and take things easier.

"Is anything coming through, or is it still jumbled up in there?"

"It's still a mess. A total mess." She sighed and rubbed her eyes with her free hand. "It doesn't make any sense. My Telepathy is getting stronger by the hour, but it's not making any difference. I can't get a single, clear thought. Just a bunch of gibberish thrown together."

"He knows you're here. He knows you're trying."

"I thought he might, but now I'm not so sure." She turned her face away from me, but I saw the tear as it dropped.

Leaving her to her private sorrow, in case it embarrassed her, I focused on Jacob. He looked peaceful, his head nestled in the pillow, his chest rising and falling in a steady rhythm. I was glad that he hadn't ended up on a slab in the Crypt like Isadora and Suri. If Jacob had been there, too, dead and cold, I didn't know if I'd have had the strength to go on. Death was always terrible and sad, no matter what the circumstances, but it always seemed worse when it came for the young. It was like nipping a flower from its stalk before it had even had the chance to bloom.

Guilt gripped my stomach as I took Jacob's hand and held it tight. I couldn't help but feel responsible for what had happened, not only to Jacob, but to Isadora. If I'd just left them in hiding, at that house in the middle of nowhere. If I'd just let them travel down their own path, just the two of them, like Isadora had asked me to... but we'd never have gotten this close to ending Katherine if I had.

Everything comes at a price. That's what Marie Laveau and Papa Legba had shoved down my throat, and they were right. Everything had a cost, and I was still trying to figure out if edging toward Katherine was worth this. Anger flickered in my chest, my thoughts bristling with hatred toward that evil woman. It only strengthened my resolve to work alone from now on, to avoid ever having to see any more of my friends in a hospital bed or on a slab. That was a price I wasn't willing to pay, no matter what I'd said to the Chains of Truth.

"Tell me you're not serious." Louella's voice broke me out of my reverie.

"What?"

"None of this is your fault, Harley. The last thing you should do is go through this alone."

I froze. "You heard that?"

"I didn't mean to. Your voice just came into my head." She looked away shyly. "You must have been pouring your thoughts out without realizing. It can happen. I wasn't prying, I swear."

I didn't reply. Instead, I thought about everything I stood to lose, and all of the people we'd already lost—Quetzi, Isadora, Jacintha Parks, Suri, Shinsuke, Tess, Echidna... The body count was racking up, and it was only going to get worse if I allowed my friends to help me. I pictured them, scattered and broken, remembering that vague image of a bright landscape with the sounds of pain and suffering all around me. I filled in the blanks, for Louella's benefit. I put my friends, including her, in that landscape, so she could see the enormity of what might lay ahead. I envisioned Astrid, dead beside the altar in the Asphodel Meadows, with blood running down her cracked head. I let the memories of Alton's desperation flow through me, and how he'd battled to bring her back to life.

Finally, I pictured Katherine, back in Tartarus, when she'd promised to bring me to my knees by destroying everyone I held dear.

Louella lowered her gaze. "Oh."

"Do you see?"

She nodded. "I see."

"Can you understand?" My voice was strained with emotion.

"When you paint it like that... yeah, I suppose I can." She looked back up. "I still don't think it's a good idea for you to do this on your own, though. Everyone knows what's at stake. We know what we might have to sacrifice, when the last fight comes."

"Nothing. That's what you'll have to sacrifice. Nothing." I smiled sadly. "That's why I have to do this alone, so that nobody else dies, and nobody else winds up like Jacob. You don't have to worry about me. I know what I'm doing, and I know why I'm doing it. So, please, understand... and, please, don't tell anyone what you've heard."

She nodded slowly. "I shouldn't have been listening. For as long as I can, I won't say anything."

"Thank you, Louella." I fed a strand of Empathy toward her to make sure there was no deception coming off her. All I felt was sadness and exasperation, but no hint that she wouldn't keep her promise. "You really should go and get some rest. You look exhausted."

"I could say the same about you," she replied, with a small smile. I had to admit, I wasn't feeling too peachy. My head had started to bang for real, and my stomach was still churning. Maybe it was just tiredness, the stress and strain and grief making me ill. Not that I was planning on taking a break anytime soon.

I chuckled bitterly. "Thing is, I couldn't sleep, even if I wanted to."

"I don't blame you."

"But you should try, if you can."

Louella smiled. "I could probably use a bite to eat, to keep my strength up. And the Banquet Hall has chocolate eclairs today, which is always a bonus. Do you want anything?"

"No, thanks."

"Okay, well… I'll be back in a bit. I'll bring you something just in case. You should eat, even if you don't feel like it. Mrs. Devereaux always used to say that whenever I was in one of my funks." A flicker of pain washed over her face. "I might see if I can take a power nap after, but I'm not counting on it."

"It might do you some good." I kept forgetting that she'd already lost two people she cared about, on top of Isadora. With foster kids, when things went wrong, we always ended up feeling like we were the jinxed ones—like anyone we got close to would somehow get snatched away. I guessed that was why she was so intent on fixing Jacob.

I watched her leave, wishing she'd had a better life than the one she'd ended up with. She reminded me a lot of myself, and I hoped with all my heart that she'd never lose her fighting spirit. The foster system made us tough, but we had our limits, same as anyone else. I didn't want the hand she'd been dealt in life to make her cold, the way I'd seen it do to others like her.

Spinning around on the hospital chair, I turned to look at Levi, who was in the next bed over. He was still deep in unconsciousness, the heartrate monitor beeping steadily. I hated those things, but at least it meant he was still alive. I didn't know if Raffe would be able to handle it if Levi didn't pull through this. They might not have been each other's biggest fans, but Raffe hadn't been the one who wanted Levi dead. That had been all Kadar. Still, Levi must have been more stable, since Krieger had stopped clucking around him like a worried mother hen. At this very moment, he was in his office with the door locked, no doubt trying to have a power nap of his own.

"You in there, Levi?" I gave him a tentative nudge. He didn't move. "Guess not."

"As a matter of fact, I am. And I don't appreciate being prodded like a science experiment." Levi's eyes flew open, almost making me topple off my chair in fright. The voice coming out of him didn't sound like the Levi I knew. It had a weird, gravelly echo to it, and the tone was deeper somehow.

But that wasn't the most unsettling part. At first, I thought my eyes were playing tricks on me, but I quickly realized they weren't. Levi's eyes were a bright, startling red, glinting like rubies, while a faint scarlet tinge had flushed across the visible parts of his skin.

What the—!

"You're... You're a djinn?" I had to choke the words out, my hands gripping the ancient vinyl of the seat. I was rooted to the spot in fear, not knowing whether to scream for help or try and restrain the beast myself. But he wasn't moving, and it didn't look like he was about to leap from the bed to attack me.

"How sharp you are," he replied sarcastically. All the djinn certainly seemed to have that tone in common. "And my name is Zalaam, not 'a djinn.' I find that highly offensive, though what else should I expect from a meager magical?"

"But... how can Levi have a djinn?" I was still reeling from the shock, but I had the common sense to speed dial Raffe without Zalaam seeing, leaving the phone on call so he could hear all of this.

"How do any djinn find themselves attached to mere mortals?" He shot me a withering look. "Leonidas and I were bound at birth, the same as all Levi men. It is their gift and our curse, unfortunately, forged many, many, many years ago by the will of a Persian warlock who took unfavorably to the comments of an unruly, impetuous member of the Levi clan. A trait that has not faded with time, from what I have witnessed. Not all djinn are fated to this, I hasten to add, and most exist autonomously. But an unfortunate few are forced into symbiosis with the men of the Levi family, as per the rules of the curse that was forged with Erebus. We do not get to choose as it is a lottery of sorts, but we must obey."

I stared into his red eyes. "But I've never seen you before. I've seen Raffe's djinn, but... well, Levi never mentioned he had one, too. Unless he only lets you out when nobody else is around?"

"'Lets me out?' *'Lets me out?'* You dare to say that I, a mighty djinn, must be permitted my freedom of speech?" Zalaam glowered at me like he might have wanted to crush *my* skull like a watermelon. "I am as much a part of this body as Leonidas. I need no permission. I was reborn into this human form, my rich djinn essence dragged into his during a warped variation of a purge. I hold sovereignty just as much as Leonidas does."

This djinn was clearly proud, but that didn't change the facts. "But how come we haven't seen you? I don't mean any offense by it; I just didn't even know you existed. And what do you mean by a 'warped variation' of a purge?"

"I existed before I was forced into this form, having been created by Erebus himself, but I was 'reborn' in this vessel. It is part of the curse. We call it a purge to keep it simple. Nevertheless, I had free rein to do as I pleased… until our true love died," he replied tersely, though his eyes twinkled blue for a fleeting moment. "Grief works upon a djinn in strange ways. It allows the vessel to suppress us. Leonidas used that, the sneaky devil, until Raffe's djinn almost succeeded in murdering him. As you can see, Leonidas has yet to awaken, but I am here, so who is the mightier one now? Hmph. And I have no desire to be suppressed again. I have been forced down for much too long."

"Your true love? You mean Raffe's mom?"

"An angel in human form. But, yes, if you must put it so crudely. She was more than Raffe's mother, and she was more than Leonidas' wife. She was the other half of my being, and she might still be alive today if she had not birthed that incompetent wretch. The manifested djinn was much too wild—the djinn wasn't ready, and our love suffered for it."

I glanced down at my phone, but Raffe had ended the call. I was grateful he hadn't heard that last part. Although, if he'd ended the call, then where was he?

I found out a few minutes later, when the infirmary door burst open and Raffe came barreling into the room. No sooner had he appeared than his entire being changed, his skin flushing red and his eyes glinting scarlet. Smoke wisped away from his body. I braced myself for a fight, in case Kadar tried to kill Levi again. Instead, he staggered back as though he was scared for his life.

"I said nothing to Raffe, I swear it to you." Kadar's voice hissed out of Raffe's throat. "I kept your secret, as I promised I would."

"You impudent fool," Zalaam shot back. "If you speak the truth, then how is it you have come here the moment I have awoken? Suspicious, is it not?"

Kadar cowered. "I... Raffe found out. He heard you through the phone."

So Kadar knew Zalaam but had never let Raffe in on the secret? I had no idea why, but one thing was for sure: Kadar was freaking terrified of Levi's djinn. Which meant Zalaam had to be one badass djinn, to instill that level of fear in someone as fearsome as Kadar. And I would've bet money on the fact that Zalaam wasn't too pleased that Kadar had tried to have his vessel murdered.

This isn't going to end well...

ELEVEN

Harley

"He heard me through the phone?" Zalaam eyed me. "Would you care to explain, Harley?"

It took a moment for me to find my voice. "You know me?"

"I might have been suppressed, but I am able to see all that Leonidas sees and hear all that he hears. Now, would you care to explain?"

I scrambled for a reply. "Uh… I must've called Raffe by accident."

"Don't play me for a fool. *Why* did you call Raffe?"

"I thought he should be here," I replied, feeling genuinely worried. One djinn was bad enough, but having two in the same room was a recipe for disaster, especially as there appeared to be some serious beef between them.

"That wasn't your decision to make!" Zalaam snapped.

"Why, because you've both been lying to Raffe all this time?" I shot a look at Kadar, who hadn't taken his eyes off Zalaam. "I didn't realize I was letting out some big secret."

"Foolish magical," Zalaam muttered, before glowering at Kadar. "As for you, did you think you could get away with attempting to kill my vessel without any retribution? As if I would allow it. If Leonidas had not suppressed me so intently, I might have fought you to the death."

He tried to sit up, but it looked like Levi's unconsciousness was having an immobilizing effect on the djinn's movements. I guessed there really was a symbiosis between magical and djinn, made all the stronger over time. If Zalaam had been with Levi since birth, then it stood to reason that the two of them were intertwined even more than Raffe and Kadar—down to a more physical, cellular level, by the looks of it.

The red flush faded from Kadar's skin as Raffe emerged. A sheen of sweat glistened on his forehead, letting me know it had taken a lot of energy to regain power over his djinn. I sensed the two of them were going to be in an ongoing fight for supremacy during this encounter with Zalaam. Both of them likely had things they wanted to say.

"Why did you ask Kadar to lie for you? Why didn't my dad tell me he had a djinn inside him?" Raffe strode up to the bed and slammed his hands down on the rail. Kadar might have been terrified of Zalaam, but Raffe wasn't backing down without some answers.

"Kadar isn't a name I would have picked. I would have said so, if Levi hadn't forced me so far down." Zalaam sounded miffed.

"Well, that's his name!" Raffe barked. "Stop changing the subject. Why did you ask Kadar to lie?"

"It was for the best," Zalaam replied, his tone softening slightly. It was a strange sight to behold. All of Zalaam's pomp and circumstance had disappeared the moment he'd heard Raffe defend the name he'd given to his djinn. He wasn't throwing "puny magical" insults around anymore, at least.

"What the heck is that supposed to mean? Best for whom?"

"For you, and for your father."

Raffe shook his head angrily. "I've never seen you. In all my life, I've never even heard a whisper that you existed. I want to know why. Is he ashamed of you? Is that it?" He gripped the bedrail, his knuckles turning white. "Do you realize how alone I've felt all these years, thinking I was the only one? It's not like I could have asked my grandpa, since he died when I was, what, two? If I'd known about you, I could've... Things would've been different. I wouldn't have felt like a massive freak, for one. My father has always acted like he's scared of me and Kadar, or like he felt ashamed of us, when he had *you* all along! He was exactly the same, and he never said a thing! And don't try and blame Kadar—I'll be having words with him soon enough about this secret-keeping, you can count on that."

"Leonidas had reason to be afraid, Raffe. We both did."

I glanced at Zalaam. "What do you mean?"

"Kadar is my son, in a manner of speaking. He became my son when he was 'reborn' in your body. The familial ties that bind you, bind us. I know what he is capable of. There is reason for fear. As for your grandpa, Raffe, you wouldn't have wanted to know his djinn. Nasty piece of work. Made Kadar and me look like benevolent fairies."

Raffe stalled, like he was buffering. His body began to spasm violently, his skin shifting between his usual olive tone and the spread of crimson that let me know Kadar was pushing through. Eventually, the crimson won out, Kadar's ruby eyes blinking as he forced his way in.

"*You* are afraid of *me*? That is ludicrous!" Kadar spluttered. "All you've done is push me into a corner ever since I was purged with Raffe. I've spent my whole life fearing *you* because of how powerful you are. How can you say that I'm the threat?"

The parallels were startling. Kadar and Zalaam seemed to be dealing with the same familial mess that Levi and Raffe were, with the father trying to suppress the son out of fear. I couldn't wrap my head around it, especially as I'd never heard of Purge beasts being related. Were djinn somehow different from ordinary Purge beasts because of that "warped variation" Zalaam had mentioned before? It certainly seemed like it. Even so, why would Levi and Zalaam be so afraid of Kadar? Sure, he was powerful and scary, but Zalaam didn't exactly give the impression of being some wilting wallflower.

"Because you are," Zalaam said simply.

"Is that why Levi kept trying to stop Raffe from naming me? Was that your doing?" Kadar didn't seem scared anymore, as he leered over the hospital bed. "You should know, better than anyone, that being named results in greater control from the vessel. If you were so afraid, you would have urged Levi to make Raffe name me. It sounds to me as though you are spouting garbage."

Zalaam sighed. "That was my fault. It had nothing to do with Leonidas."

Raffe poked through, the rapid blending of the two making my head spin. One minute, his skin was scarlet and his eyes were red, and the next, he was my friend again. Right now, however, I wasn't sure which one of them was the most alarming. Both were furious, but Raffe definitely had the edge.

"What do you mean?" Raffe demanded. "My father was the one to tell me not to name Kadar. And since I didn't even know about you, how can you say that *you* were the one responsible? Are you trying to cover for my father?"

Zalaam snorted. "Of course not. I do as I please. Indeed, that is how I sought to ensure that Leonidas would not encourage you to name your djinn. I manipulated Leonidas's mind from within, unbeknownst to him, and pushed him to force you into not naming Kadar." He paused. "I knew that, if you and your djinn found balance and managed to get along in a more amenable manner, you would easily be able to overpower me and Leonidas in combat. I did not even have the opportunity to emerge when Kadar attacked us the other day. That has always been a concern."

"So, are you saying this is all a freaking pride thing?" Raffe's jaw dropped.

"No, it was a matter of self-preservation." Zalaam stuck out his chin. "While I may have a fondness for my son, I cannot accept being the weaker amongst the Levis. I will not."

Raffe narrowed his eyes. "This *is* a pride thing!"

"No, it is self-preservation."

This is going to go around in circles. "Wait, you said you've been with Levi since birth, right?" I interjected, before the broken record could keep spinning.

Zalaam eyed me curiously, as though he'd forgotten I was there. "That is correct."

"And every Levi man ends up with a djinn because of that Persian warlock, or whatever you said it was?"

He nodded. "Were you not listening? Do you lack ears?"

"No, I'm just trying to get things clear in my head," I replied. "Does that mean that every Levi man kills his mother at birth, then?"

Zalaam shook his head. "Many do, but not all. Our true love was a capable magical, but her body could not take the birth and the Purge process at once, given Kadar's strength. Several women who have married into the Levi family have suffered similar fates."

A wave of sadness hit me, but it didn't belong to me. It was coming from Raffe and Kadar and pummeling me hard. A few tendrils of grief were drifting away from Zalaam too, though the emotions felt weird and spiky, without the human buffering of Levi to soften their edges.

"Let me speak to my father," Raffe said, shaking off his sadness. I could sense a flicker of longing in him, like he wished Santana were here for moral support. I guessed she'd been somewhere else when I'd called.

Zalaam laughed coldly. "That will not be happening. I have control of this meat suit now, and I have been suppressed far too long. I do not intend to give this body up again. As my vessel still has a great deal of healing to do, I have nobody to protest, and he will be weaker when he finally awakens. All the better to take control of. He will never force me down again. Never."

I cast a worried look at Raffe, who met my gaze with a frown. "Harley, can I speak with you outside for a minute?"

"I was just going to say the same thing."

Zalaam smirked. "Could you make it any more obvious? My ears will be burning."

"They're already looking a little red," Raffe shot back.

Skirting around the bed, in case Zalaam suddenly swiped at me, I followed Raffe out into the hallway beyond the infirmary. With Zalaam weakened by Levi's unconscious state, he wasn't a flight risk, so at least we could leave him alone in the infirmary without worrying about him escaping or tearing someone to shreds. However, we still had a lot to worry about where Zalaam was concerned.

"He needs to be locked up!" Kadar emerged, and he wasn't happy.

"You need to be locked up." Raffe shifted back for a moment. "Don't think I've forgiven you for keeping this from me."

Kadar snorted. "Pfft, you lock me up, you lock yourself up. With demented Katie on the warpath, I doubt you'll be doing that anytime soon. Face it, you need me. Yes, I may have told a little white lie, but you have no idea how terrifying Zalaam can be when he wants to be.

Have you always gone against everything *your* father has said? No, you have not. So get out of your glass house before you start hurling your stones."

"Guys!" I barked. "Hash it out later. Right now, we need to figure out what to do with Zalaam."

"Well, we can't leave him on the loose like this, that's for sure," Raffe replied.

I nodded. "I was thinking we could put him in a charmed cage, or in that cell you use. Just until we can get a better idea of what he wants, now that he's free of Levi's suppression."

"Or, we could consider him an ally?" Kadar emerged again.

I rolled my eyes. "You literally just said he should be locked up."

"What can I say, I have a flexible mind. And that's not the only thing that's flexible." He flashed me a wink.

"Kadar, pack it in! What have I told you about hitting on my friends?" Raffe shifted back.

"To do it at every given opportunity?" Kadar laughed. I really couldn't keep up with their melding in and out of control. "Look, all I'm saying is, Levi has been powerful enough to hold Zalaam at bay for this long. All we have to do is wait until Levi comes to, and then he will more than likely take over again. Even if he is forever doomed to live under Zalaam's will, we could utilize a djinn. He is powerful, and he is as wise as the day is long, gifted with the memories of all djinn who've gone before. He has probably seen and heard things that may be of use to us against the Queen of Evil."

"You should listen to my boy! He has a very wise mind!" Zalaam's voice bellowed out into the hallway. "It runs in the family!"

"So, there was no point in us coming outside, then?" I glanced at Kadar. "Thanks for the warning."

"I didn't know he could hear us," Kadar protested. All of us were embarrassed. "I would have saved myself the walk if I'd known. I've got to take good care of these sexy thighs." He patted them like they were the neck of a horse, which did nothing to help my churning stomach.

"Come on, we're wasting time out here." I led the way back into the infirmary, where we gathered around Zalaam. He smirked, an expression that he shared with Levi. Funnily enough, I felt the same urge to smack him in the face that I did whenever I was around Levi.

"I would've warned you that I would be able to hear every word you said, but I didn't want to take your 'storming out' moment." Zalaam grinned. "I have had so little time for personal pleasures, so you must forgive my small entertainments."

I cast him a withering look. "Do you want to hear what we have to say or not?"

"I thought I already did." He chuckled.

"What do you say we make a deal?" Kadar jumped in.

"Color me intrigued," Zalaam replied.

This time, Raffe was doing the talking. "We won't lock you up, if you promise to help us in the coming days. We need all the information on Katherine we can get, and with you being an older and wiser djinn, I'm sure you've got something in that head of yours that might be useful."

Evidently, he agreed with Kadar, which gave me no choice but to agree, too. *Couldn't hurt, right?* Plus, it might mean that the Rag Team had someone powerful to defend them while I continued on my mission alone.

"Or, I could just tear your head off and be done with it, Raffe." Zalaam smiled darkly. I let my Empathy edge toward him, feeling out his true emotions. Instead of anger and bitterness, or a hint of malevolence, I felt nothing but sympathy and excitement.

"Quit it with the bravado, Zalaam," I cut in. "I can sense your emotions. You're full of crap. You want to help—you don't want to rip off anyone's head. And I think there's been quite enough head-squishing to last us all a lifetime."

Zalaam laughed. "You're funny, Harley. Leonidas never gives you much credit for your amusing demeanor. I rather like it."

"Does that mean you'll help?" Raffe pressed.

He shrugged. "I suppose I have nothing better to do. However, I will need to dig through the annals of my mind first, and dip into the djinn repository, if I'm going to find anything that has to do with Katherine and her cult."

"The djinn repository?" I replied.

"All djinns are intrinsically interconnected, as we are all the fruit of Erebus. Do they teach you nothing in these places?" Zalaam muttered.

Raffe frowned. "How come Kadar can't do that?"

"He is much too young. As time passes, a thread of Chaos grows within us that connects us to the rest of the djinn—a collective memory of sorts. That may be the simplest way I can describe it, for your puny mind. Kadar's thread is not yet matured, and so he is not yet able to connect."

"He's not going to like that," Raffe mumbled.

"You're damn right I'm not!" Kadar emerged for a split second, before Raffe pushed him back down.

"You'll do that for us?" I focused my attention back on Zalaam.

He smiled. "As long as you do not lock me in a cage, I don't see why not."

After all the bad news I'd received lately, this was one slice of optimism that I could get on board with. It meant trusting a djinn, which was always a risky thing to do, but if Zalaam could really delve into this shared djinn memory and speak to other djinn across the globe, then maybe another djinn somewhere had witnessed something that might be useful to us in the fight against Katherine.

The Hidden Things spell was still my main goal, but it didn't hurt to have options.

TWELVE

Katherine

Ah, London. With my ability to portal where I pleased, at least I didn't have to contend with the outright vulgarity of the Tube, with sweaty bodies cramped side by side and commuters tussling to get closest to the perilous edge of the platform. As if that would, somehow, miraculously get them to where they wanted to go that little bit quicker. I hadn't been to London too many times before, but I'd always had the urge to shove one of those suited and booted idiots onto the tracks as the train was coming through the tunnel, just to teach them a lesson.

Deciding against that particular pleasure, I'd portaled into the middle of Grosvenor Square Gardens. It seemed fitting since, once upon a time, this area of London had been known as "Little America." A slice of home away from home. If memory served, this part of Mayfair had been the HQ for US personnel during World War II. They'd even put up a statue of good old Franklin D to commemorate our part in that global catastrophe. With me in charge, nobody would ever have to worry about war again.

I was met by the usual British welcome of gray skies and spitting rain. The park was pretty much empty, though I didn't care who saw me. I pulled the collar of my deep green trench coat closer to my chin—even fearsome operatives could always afford to be fashionable—and ignored the smack of the icy droplets on my face. Strolling to the east of the leafy park, I headed out onto North Audley Street, before taking a left into Lees Place. This was where I'd find that pesky Necromancer. *Stupid, sexy Davin Doncaster.*

His house was a sheltered, opulent building tucked away down an unassuming road, with white steps leading up to an arched doorway. It looked like something out of an Austen novel, but Davin was no Darcy. And I *definitely* was no Elizabeth Bennett, unless she'd had a secret penchant for world domination that we didn't know about. A golden knocker lay ostentatiously—or, rather, *austen*tatiously—in the center, just begging to be rapped.

I paused, collecting myself before I knocked. Davin Doncaster had been living in London as a Neutral, evading the gaze of the London Coven by keeping his head down. He was one of the five Necromancers still living, Micah and Alton included. And, if he played his cards right, he'd be one of a rather more elite group of four once I was done with the last ritual.

Naima had wanted to come with me, making some comment about Davin being an imp who couldn't be trusted, but I needed her to retrieve the eleventh magical, sooner rather than later. I had an idea of who I wanted to be twelve, but the logistics of swiping Louella were currently a little sticky. Besides, it was always good to have extras. So, here I was, on my lonesome, about to knock on the door. The nerves, as I stood on the top step, were a new sensation. There was just something about Davin that got me all worked up.

I smoothed down the front of my trench coat, fiddling with the lapels until they lay perfectly flat. Underneath, I wore olive pants and a bottle-green blouse. I pulled the knocker and let it swing back, the clang echoing inside. *A buzzer would be more efficient.* But I guessed that was the Brits for you, clinging to tradition like nobody's business.

My heart raced as I heard footsteps approach. The door opened, and there he was. Standing over six feet, with a casually tousled mane of autumnal hair. His piercing baby blues shot right into me. He looked me over with a pleased grin on his seductive lips. That face… *ugh*. My ovaries were about ready to blow. He walked the line between *Esquire*'s front page and rough-and-ready hero, with a fine graze of stubble across his jaw.

"Well, well, well, and here I was, thinking it was the milkman." He flashed me a grin, his teeth perfect. His dentist needed a raise.

"Not quite." I found my voice, determined not to show that I had a soft spot for him. "Though I suppose I am here to deliver."

He arched an eyebrow. "Is that so? Then I imagine it would be rude of me to leave you out on the doorstep. Please, do come inside." He spoke with a clipped British accent that made me think of boarding schools and Buckingham Palace. "Might you care for some tea? You must be parched if you came all this way for little old me. I believe I remember how you like it. The American way, if I'm not mistaken? I could rustle up some scones with jam and clotted cream, if you're peckish. Sometimes, I like to think of you eating those as if there was no tomorrow, when I took you to Claridge's the last time you were here. Smearing it all around that mouth of yours, with crumbs dropping… well, it wouldn't be polite of me to say where."

I fought to stop my cheeks from flushing. I'd forgotten about that. "I could eat, now that you mention it."

"Then come through to the drawing room, and I will see to it that Mrs. Mason brings in some delights to tantalize your appetite." He chuckled, the sound like a tender caress. *Snap out of it, Katie!* I was here for one reason, and one reason alone. I couldn't allow myself to be side-tracked.

"Drawing room?" I smirked. "Who has a drawing room in their house?"

"You should get one. They're all the rage, though I daresay I lack the opportunity to entertain worthy guests such as yourself. Mrs. Mason will be thrilled, for she's starting to fear that I've become a eunuch." He led me down a wide, grand hallway, complete with chandelier—*of course he has a chandelier*—and portraits of the Doncaster Dynasty on the walls. Even in oil paint, he looked stupidly handsome.

The drawing room itself was incredible. A piano sat in the corner, and the walls were lined with rows upon rows of leather-bound tomes. It was almost as impressive as my library, though on a far smaller scale. As I sat down on a velvet, emerald-green couch that probably cost as much as this whole house, he ducked out for a minute to speak to the mysterious Mrs. Mason, before stepping back inside. I knew why he'd done it—so I could get a better view of him, silhouetted in the doorway. He was dressed in a navy-blue, three-piece suit that would've put Tom Ford out of business, the fabric hugging him in *all* the right places.

"Do you play?" I nodded to the piano, aware I was gawking.

He crossed the room and sat down, beginning the first bars of Beethoven's "Moonlight Sonata." "A little," he replied, with a smile. *A little?* Who was he kidding? He played it as though he'd written the damn thing. "You know, I always imagined that Beethoven wrote this for his 'immortal beloved.' How remarkable is that, to have someone who has enraptured you so wholly that you would refer to them in terms of immortality—of a love that transcends the mortal world? Perhaps it is the Necromancer in me, or perhaps it is simply the romancer."

"Must be," I muttered. He continued to play, and my eyes were transfixed on the emotion on his face.

"You can hear the sadness and the longing in the tender notes, can't you? The heartache of a tortured musician. Nothing so crass as today's popular music," he said. "This is love, right here. This is the artistic binding of two souls. It is poetry in motion."

"Yes, well, I'm here for the Necromancer, not the romancer," I said quickly. I needed to put my foot down with Davin, otherwise I'd end up… well, somewhere I didn't have time to be.

He stopped playing. "Oh? Then you have my attention, Ms. Shipton. Although, you always do."

"I suppose you've heard about the progress I've made?"

"I confess, it's hard not to have." He smiled. "I, for one, wouldn't mind being under your intoxicating influence."

"You say that, but you've yet to choose a side." I called his bluff.

He laughed. "Is that why you're here, to force me into submission? I think I have some cuffs lying about, if that's your intention."

"I would prefer it if you came voluntarily."

His gaze held mine. "For you, always."

"Again, you keep saying that, but when I asked you to join my cult the last time, you refused, giving me some BS excuse about not being into commitment." I narrowed my eyes. "You've helped me before, and I was grateful for that, but it's time for you to join the cult or suffer the consequences. You can't be a Neutral forever, in any sense of the word."

"I love it when you talk like that." He showed no sign of being intimidated, which irked me even more. He was making a joke out of this, and it wasn't a laughing matter. *Why are the good-looking ones always so arrogant?* Usually, I'd have found that a turnoff, but this was Davin we were talking about. He could've been waving a Third Reich flag and my ovaries would still have been screaming like groupies at a rock concert.

I had to keep hold of my position of authority over him. I wasn't leaving this house until I had him on my side. He was an asset to the cult and, if he proved to be loyal and reliable, then he'd get his powers back when the time came. Those who obeyed wouldn't have to suffer, and I wanted to make Davin obey.

"I see you didn't bring the feline with you," Davin observed. "You must be feeling particularly bold, to have come here without your loyal lieutenant. Although, I have to say, I'm glad to have you alone. Naima ruins the atmosphere somewhat, with all her snapping and snarling. I lay an innocent touch upon you in conversation, and she's on me like a tigress, scratching at my hands until they look as though I had a disagreement with a coil of barbed wire."

"Well then, you'll be happy to know that she dislikes you as much as you seem to dislike her. She's otherwise engaged with important cult business, so you don't have to worry about fitting in a manicure for your precious hands," I replied. "And I don't need to be bold to come and see you. You don't intimidate me, as much as you'd like to think you do. But you're getting off the subject. Nice try."

"Can't we have some niceties before we get down to it?" His eyes glittered with mischief. "It's been much too long since you were last on that couch. And I do so enjoy our little tête-à-têtes."

I rolled my eyes. "What have you been up to since I last saw you? It doesn't look like you're strapped for cash. Weird, considering you're a Neutral. They're normally struggling to make ends meet."

"I have taken to briefly bringing back the recently deceased for the wealthiest magicals in England. Non-magicals, too, if they manage to find me. They are so very eager for one last, precious moment with their passed loved ones, so they can get some closure, and who am I to rob them of that?" He chuckled.

I frowned. "The authorities should be on to you by now, if you were up to that sort of thing." It was rule number one of the covens not to use magic for profit in the human world, but that was exactly what Davin was doing. I guessed it was a bit hypocritical to call him out on it, but it interested me nonetheless.

"Blackmail is a potent motivator, Ms. Shipton, as you well know." He looked me straight in the eyes, holding me in that intense blue gaze. *I knew he'd be trouble.* "No one would dare to report me, lest I leak the more unsavory side of their lives to the magical press. In this day and age, people fear the media more than anything else."

"Hey, it's no sweat off my brow."

"Coarsely put. I see you're as American as ever."

"It's the land of hope and glory—you should try it sometime. My point is, magicals should be allowed to profit from wherever they want, however they want." I smiled at him. "Wasn't that what brought us closer, in the first place? Our shared belief in a world where you could do what you wanted, freely, without risking a life sentence in Purgatory?"

"But how can a man be truly free, if you want to put shackles on him?" A serious note edged into Davin's pristine voice.

Because men need to be shackled? Because they're only out for themselves? Because they don't deserve true freedom? Davin was no exception to my generally bad opinion of men, but there was something about him that always sucked me in. I'd have said those things out loud if it had been anyone else, but I couldn't find the words with him looking at me like that, like he wanted to throw me onto the piano and have his wicked way. I hated that power he had over me. Nobody should have had power over me. But I couldn't resist him for much longer, not if he kept smiling like that.

"They aren't shackles. Stop being dramatic, it doesn't suit you," I replied. *Even if you do look like a movie star.* "Once I ascend, you'll be free to do what you like. Extort all of the magicals and humans you want. As long as you serve me, and don't cross me, I don't care. Speaking of which, it's time you decided—are you going to serve me or not? I'm not feeling very patient today."

Davin gave a wolfish grin that made me want him to devour me. "Need I remind you that I said I would, once you actually ascended? Don't get your knickers in a twist. I have all the faith in the world that you're the one for the job, but I like to be certain before I give my word on such matters. It wouldn't do to back a horse who falls at the last fence, now, would it? I would look rather foolish. Not that you aren't the finest filly I've ever seen."

"Why wait, if you say you have faith in me?"

"Call it hedging my bets."

"Have you been reading *Horse & Hound* or something? What's with all the racing talk?" I smirked. "I could force you if I wanted to. I could break you in, since you seem intent on talking horse."

"Would you, though?" He smirked. "I know you like me, Katie." *Katie...* It sounded so much more exotic in his mouth. "I know you appreciate what I can bring to the table, or you would have turned me into a mindless automaton by now. You *want* me to come willingly. Otherwise, where is the satisfaction? You want me to join you of my own accord because you want so much more from me, aside from my allegiance. Tell me I'm wrong... I dare you."

I watched him closely, wishing I could meet his challenge. But, the truth was, he was right. There wasn't much fun to be had in forcing someone like him to work for me. It was so much better when they did it willingly, which was precisely why the cult had grown the way it had. My subjects were loyal and eager, all of them signing up because they wanted to and because they trusted in what I had to offer as a leader. The validation in that was unmatched.

"All I want is your allegiance," I said, at last.

"Oh, Katie, we both know that's not true, though I appreciate your attempt at a lie. Wouldn't you rather have the pleasure of a worthy gentleman, who stood at your side out of choice?"

I snorted. "You need to stop reading all of these books and playing that music—it's messed with your head. This isn't a romance novel. This is the real world, and I demand loyalty, pure and simple. Those who sit on their impartial fences will receive the same treatment as those who refuse to join me."

"Easy, Katie," he purred. "I'm not saying I won't join you. My promise still stands. Once you ascend as a Child of Chaos, I will happily join the Cult of Eris. I will come to you willingly, with my arms open. Until then, I am forever at your service—if I am able to assist, that is."

"So, basically, you don't want the full commitment of the cult?" *Typical man.*

"If you have to put it so boorishly," he replied, with a small laugh. "I hope that doesn't prove to be a wedge between us. I'd hate for anything to come between us, now that I've seen you again. I'd forgotten how much I missed you."

So, all wasn't completely lost. His words implied that he wouldn't be able to say no to anything I asked of him. He was still useful, despite his refusal to comply entirely.

I sighed, unwilling to push it further. I wasn't going to get the answer I wanted right now, but that didn't mean it wouldn't come, in due time. He was so sexy and charming, and yet unpredictable—it annoyed and exhilarated me at the same time. But he'd said his piece, and nothing I added was going to change his mind.

"There's something else I need from you, since you're so eager to offer your services," I said.

"Oh yes? Name it." He licked his lips subtly. He couldn't have been more distracting if he'd tried, which was the most annoying part about him—he wasn't even trying.

Giving him the simpler version, I told him about Alton and Harley's mission to reveal the Hidden Things spell and the issues that Alton had run into, regarding needing a second Necromancer. Davin already knew about the existence of the Grimoire, as we'd discussed it during our last encounters, but he wasn't aware that it was geared toward ending me.

That revelation had come much later than our last meeting, during Odette's last moments of having a functioning brain.

He listened with interest as I revealed everything, his attention completely focused on me, the occasional sound of curiosity rumbling in the back of his throat. I liked that. He admired me—that wasn't a show for my benefit. I'd been around enough men to know when they were faking and when they weren't. It was what had made Hiram's betrayal all the more hurtful. I hadn't seen it coming. We'd shared a genuine, profound connection, and then he'd severed it without warning, pulling the rug out from under me. People say that love is blind, but my eyes had been wide open the whole time. Hiram had loved me, he'd said as much himself, until my sister had flaunted herself in front of him. *Jezebel would've been a better name for you, Sis.* Not that I was prone to blaming the woman for the weaknesses of men, but, in that particular case, I'd made an exception.

"Why would you want this Merlin girl to read those pages if they contain something that may destroy you?" he asked, as I finished my tale.

"There's a spell in there that will do anything but. It will make me truly majestic, able to bridge the gap between worlds," I replied. "Besides, it doesn't matter what other spells she finds in those hidden pages that could potentially harm me. I'm so close to completing the Challenge. By the time Harley finds any kind of spell like that, it'll be too late. It's like going into battle with too many weapons; by the time you've picked, someone's already skewered you through the heart."

"Charming visuals, as ever. You have a most poetic tongue." He paused. "Even so, that is taking a rather large risk, if you don't mind my saying."

"Have you ever known me to take the easy route?" I smiled. "And, besides, it's a necessary risk. My unbridled energy is going to need a body, and it's going to need one with the right oomph. One that can withstand all that I become, because of powerful bloodlines. Harley is my loophole."

"You can always have my body," he replied seductively. "My bloodlines are pure."

I smiled tightly. "I need something a bit more 'committed,' but thanks for the offer. And it's not purity I need, it's ancient strength. The Doncasters came in a bit too late for that."

"Touché. A hit, a palpable hit."

"I swear you actually speak with some common, local accent and put all of this posh business on as a front." I chuckled wryly.

"But what a shame that you'll have to lose your voluptuous, sensual figure for the sake of this. That is the very thing that brings men to their knees. I'll mourn the loss of it, though I hope you'll allow me to take full advantage before such a day occurs, to help heal the grief in the days to come."

My tongue tied itself in knots, just as Mrs. Mason granted me a reprieve, bustling in with a tray of scones and a teapot shaped like a thatched cottage. It looked so out of place amongst the rest of Davin's finery that I burst into laughter, my shock melting away in a pool of hysterics.

"Are you amused by my ceramics, Katie? I'd hate to think you were laughing at the prospect of my suggestion. My ego wouldn't be able to bear it. I'd wilt like a flower in autumn." He came over to sit beside me on the couch, a little too close for comfort. "You know, the French have a word for women such as yourself: *pulpeuse*."

"Should I be insulted?"

He shook his head. "Not at all. Roughly translated, it means 'luscious.'"

Oh...

Mrs. Mason hurried out again, casting a terrified glance back at me. I couldn't tell if she was a magical or not, seeing as she looked like an ordinary, slightly overweight middle-aged woman, but I imagined Davin had her under the same constraints of blackmail as everyone else. He was clever like that, but at least he had no dirt on me. I'd made sure of it. That was one reason I'd never taken him up on his countless offers to whisk me away to his "chambers," as he probably would've called them.

"Here I was, thinking you the perfect English gentleman, and then you go and put *that* on the table." I gestured to the hideous teapot, ignoring his seductive ploy. My cheeks were already hot under his gaze, like standing under spotlights.

He grinned. "I like chintz, what can I say?"

"You're distracting me again," I replied softly.

"Am I? How delicious for the pair of us." He leaned closer, brushing a strand of my hair back off my face. *Nope... not gonna happen, pal.* He might've looked like a freaking angel, but there was a devil inside him. We had that in common.

I sat back, away from his wandering hands. "Look, the bottom line is, I need Harley to perform the Hidden Things spell. It's the only way I can get to the spell that will give me the right body, and I've been waiting years for the opportunity. Chaos is a sneaky bastard, but you already know that. It's made it abundantly clear that I can't just off her, which would be my preferred route. Anyway, if Alton is going to help make it happen, he needs two capable Necromancers. I'd prefer he use someone that *I* trust—someone who's in my service, even if he's not ready to go the whole way."

"Oh, I'm ready to go the whole way, but delayed gratification makes it worth the wait." He smiled at me, with that devil-may-care look on his face.

I shook off that sultry magnetism that threatened to draw me in. "Alton is strong enough to pull off one of these resurrections, I'm sure of it. He's insecure, but he's always been powerful. But he'll need a second who's just as strong, but who has that will to please Eris inside him, if you catch my drift."

Davin pretended to snatch something out of the air. "Oh yes, I've caught it. And you'll no doubt be wanting me to take a peek when it's done, to feed you some tasty morsels?"

"I'm glad we're on the same page." I smiled. "Any information you can gather about what's in the Grimoire, you give it to me."

"With pleasure."

"I have to reiterate, this is about resurrecting people who've already crossed over. One of them almost twenty years ago. This isn't child's play. I need to know you're up to the task."

"But it's such an abhorrent thing to do." He tapped his chin in thought, before his face broke into a smile. "I would definitely like to be a part of this."

I smirked, satisfied to have a like-minded creature beside me. "Now, you won't be the first person that Alton reaches out to, but I'll make sure you'll be his last and only choice for this."

"How will you do that? Do you have him on a leash? Should I be jealous?"

"You can be jealous if you want, but it's not like that. I have my ways." I wasn't going to tell him about my role as Imogene. That was my secret, and my secret alone. *Well, mine and Jacob's...* But Jacob wasn't going to wake up anytime soon, to spill his guts. If he did, he *would* be spilling his guts.

"Secrets, secrets." He tutted.

"And you're a saint?"

He barked a laugh. "Not at all, nor do I profess to be. They lead such dull lives. One saint severed off his very own crown jewels, just to avoid the temptation of the fairer sex. You'd never find me doing something so drastic."

"Glad to hear it," I replied, allowing myself to flirt a tiny bit. After all, what was the point in dealing with Davin Doncaster if I couldn't have a smidgen of fun? "When the time comes, I want you to do the spell with Alton. After that, you have to make yourself disappear. I'll handle the rest."

He waved his hands in front of his face. "Poof, I'll be gone. Abracadabra and all that jazz."

"Good."

"Although, I hope we won't be parted for too long."

"We'll see. It all depends on how many splinters you're intent on getting in your backside."

"Will you pick them out for me, Katie?"

I chuckled. "You're insufferable."

"You love it."

"Does this mean you'll do it?"

He shrugged. "Anything for you, Katie. And I can't say I'm not intrigued to meet the Merlin heir. How sneaky, to have avoided you—and everyone else, for that matter—for so long. I bet she's a corker."

"A what?"

"A firecracker, a dervish, a sass queen—choose a more suitable term, if you will."

That made my skin itch with irritation, but I forced myself to grin. "Enjoy that meeting, since it may very well be the last time you see her alive."

THIRTEEN

Harley

The next day, I sat in the Banquet Hall with Dr. Krieger and the rest of the Rag Team, sipping coffee and going over all of the insane stuff that had happened since yesterday. Particularly, this recent development with Levi and Zalaam. *Just when we'd thought things couldn't get any weirder.*

"If he screws us over, I'm blaming you," Raffe muttered under his breath.

"How about a 'Thank you' or a 'Great idea'? It'd make a nice change." Kadar poked through for a second. The two of them had been bickering like siblings since we'd sat down to explain everything to everyone, and it didn't look like it was going to let up anytime soon.

"You might get a 'Thanks for not getting us all horribly killed,' if he pulls through for us," Raffe shot back.

"Hey, I'd be doing this myself if you'd hurry up and grow faster. It's not my fault you measly magicals take so long to mature. If you were smarter, perhaps, that thread of mine might have connected itself up to the communal hive mind, and we wouldn't have to rely on *my* father. Speaking of which, at least one of our fathers is helping. Yours has caused nothing but trouble," Kadar snarked. There wasn't enough coffee in the world to make this seem normal, and my head was already thumping.

Raffe's eyes narrowed. "You leave my father out of this, Kadar! Let's not forget who put him in that hospital bed, and who kept the secret that he even had a djinn! I still haven't forgiven you for either of those things."

"It was your anger that made me attack your dumb daddy, so you can get off your high horse. I'm driven by *your* emotion—it's not the other way around. I was following what *your* mind wanted me to do, so if you want to blame anyone, blame that useless gray matter that's stuffed inside your skull. It doesn't seem to be good for much else."

Raffe's knuckles whitened around his coffee mug. "I swear, I will lock us both in our cell if you don't pack it in!"

"No, *I* will lock you both in your cell if you don't pack it in," Santana replied coolly. "I hate to be the one to agree with Kadar, but this might actually work in our favor, and you two sniping at each other isn't helping anyone. Enough, I mean it!"

"I knew I'd win you over." Kadar chuckled.

"You haven't. It just sounds like the best idea we've had in a while, which is pretty much scraping the bottom of the barrel right now. That's right, your idea is barrel detritus, so *you* can get down off your high horse. From what you've said, Zalaam is more afraid of you two than you are of him, which puts us in a decent position for this to actually work. Unless you two tear each other apart, in which case we're back at square one." Santana flicked Kadar in the arm. "Now, bring Raffe back."

Kadar pouted. "I don't see why. I'm the one you want to be talking to. Raffe doesn't bring anything to the party except me, so why not speak to the organ grinder instead of the—"

"You heard her. That's enough from you." Raffe emerged again, sweating profusely. "And try and call me a monkey again, and I'll have you ripped out, one way or another."

"Can you keep hold of the reins?" Santana sounded worried.

He nodded wearily. "Yeah, I've got it covered. Don't worry. And, actually, it is a good idea, but I didn't want him getting his ego any more inflated. Otherwise, we wouldn't fit through the door."

We all waited for Kadar to make another flash appearance, but he seemed to have gotten the message, loud and clear. Everyone went back to drinking their coffee and picking at the remains of their breakfast.

"What are we going to do about Levi, when he wakes up?" I looked to Raffe. "Zalaam might be useful, but he also might be trouble. He's pretty stuck at the minute, since your dad is out cold, but that might change when he's conscious again. The last thing we need is a loose, unpredictable djinn—one that we don't know, I mean." I didn't want him to think I was making a dig at his circumstances.

"Kadar and I have spoken about it," Raffe replied. "We're going to wrestle back control from Zalaam, as soon as my father wakes up. If he's as frightened of Kadar's power as he says he is, we should be able to force him into submission."

"So, what was all that arguing about, then, if you'd already decided what you were going to do?" Garrett asked.

Raffe shrugged. "That's just how we do things."

"It shouldn't be too much longer until Levi can be safely brought out of his magical coma," Dr. Krieger said. "His body has stabilized considerably, so I'm hopeful that he'll awaken with no ill effects."

"Yay for good news!" Dylan raised his mug, but nobody cheered with him. "Or not..."

"Yay for your enthusiasm." Tatyana leaned into him and smiled. I'd never heard Tatyana say "yay" before, which was cause for celebration in and of itself. Their sweetness was a nice thing to see, after the endless toil of the last couple of days. It made me want to nestle into Wade and never come back out again, but that wasn't going to happen. He and I would have to go our separate ways soon enough, and I didn't know if we'd ever get to come back together again. That wasn't easy for me to swallow, but sacrifice came in lots of different forms. This would be mine, even if it shattered what was left of my broken heart.

"How are you faring with your monsters?" Astrid shifted the conversation away from the lovebirds.

"Well, I'm healing from the last round, which is good. No infections, thanks to Nurse Wade and Doctor Finch," I replied. "Tobe wants me back in the Bestiary sometime this morning, so I guess I'll know more after that."

"I'm a wizard with the old antiseptic." Finch grinned.

"You're a wizard anyway," Wade replied, smirking. "And I was the one who applied the antiseptic."

"Eh, no need to split hairs. And it's 'magical.' Let's not be archaic about it, even if wizard does sound way cooler. Warlock's better, though. That sounds majorly powerful." The two of them seemed to be getting along a lot better after my last encounter with the gargoyles, which almost made the scratches worth it.

"Actually, you'd be more likely to be a warlock or a sorcerer than a wizard," Louella said brightly. "A warlock is someone who gains magic from a higher power, a sorcerer is someone who gains magic from within, and a wizard is someone who gains magic from books and learning, which we all know you're not a fan of, Finch."

"Hey, I have dust allergies!" Finch protested. "If I get within a few inches of those ancient books, I'll be sneezing for weeks. You should be thanking your lucky stars I'm *not* a wizard. There'd be boogers everywhere, seriously."

"Do you hear that, everyone?" Wade replied. "Finch has a book allergy. *That's* why he hates learning."

"Oh, that's right, gang up on the degenerate." Finch smirked, clearly pleased by all the attention. "I'll have you know, I'm actually a very learned man. Street smarts, not book smarts, am I right, Harley? And I read plenty of books, just not dusty old ones."

"Don't bring your sister into this," Wade retorted. "That's calling for bias. And comic books aren't books."

Finch looked horrified. "Who told you about the comic books?" He glanced at me. "Sis, I'm wounded. That was our secret. Anyway, I'll have you know they are the perfect vessel for literature. You're just saying that because you probably can't read them. Here's a hint, it goes left to right, same as any other book."

"You keep telling yourself that." Wade smiled.

"I read novels, too," Finch muttered.

The rest of the Rag Team chuckled at Finch and Wade's little repartee, which made me smile properly for the first time in what felt like forever. It'd been a while since I'd sat with the whole crew like this, just drinking coffee and shooting the breeze. It felt nice to be with them, at the same table, talking like we did in the early days, long before this Katherine nightmare began to unravel. Granted, we had new folks, like Finch—of all people—and Louella, but they only added to the good vibes. Times had changed, and so had I. We all had.

This was exactly why I had to work alone—so that I could keep every single one of these people alive. Losing Isadora and, in a way, Jacob, had changed my perspective irrevocably. Now, I couldn't ask for my friends' help, no matter how alone or lost I felt, or how much I needed them. I just needed to keep reminding myself that I was doing this for their sakes.

We all looked up as Imogene entered the Banquet Hall and made a beeline for us. She looked stressed, but she was dressed as pristinely as ever, in a flowy blouse and trousers combo with a cream cardigan over the top.

"Ah, there you are," she said, as she neared. "I've been looking all over, and none of you have been answering your phones. I was so worried."

I checked my phone, which had been on silent, to find a couple of missed calls. "Sorry, Imogene."

"It doesn't matter now," she replied, with a sigh. "I've found you."

"Has something happened?" Astrid asked.

She shook her head. "Not exactly, but I thought it important to update you all on what's currently in the works." She gave a half-smile that made me feel guilty. With everything that was going on, this woman had to be under one heck of a pile of stress.

"Could I have one of these?" She pointed to the cafetière of coffee and the empty mugs beside it.

"Sure, fill your boots," Santana urged. "It's the good, Mexican stuff. I made sure."

Imogene chuckled. "Then I'm grateful for your influence, Ms. Catemaco." She poured herself a mug and took a long, satisfied sip before speaking again. "Ah, that's much better. Now I can feel somewhat human again."

"Are you sure nothing's happened? You look kind of on edge. No offense," Finch said.

"I'm sure you would be, too, in my position," she replied, not unkindly.

"Fair point."

"Now, as you know, O'Halloran is busy recruiting people for a secret army, but the cult's influence has spread much farther and wider than we had anticipated. Remington has discovered that it is far worse than we had previously imagined," she explained. "Too many magicals from the upper echelons of society are acting strangely. For that reason, we have come to the unfortunate conclusion that no one can be trusted within the realm of magical leadership, as it presently stands."

"I was worried about that," Wade murmured.

Imogene nodded. "As was I, and I hate to see that I was proven right. I'd have been all too happy to be wrong in this instance. However, I wish to assure you that I'm doing all I can, along with Remington and O'Halloran, who are two of the few people I can still trust. Yourselves included, of course."

"Even after pill-gate?" Santana replied.

"O'Halloran has shown no signs of residual effects, and my friend in the Seoul Coven was adamant that the antidote would work. He's a top alchemist in his field, so I have little reason to disbelieve him." She paused. "Speaking of 'pill-gate,' as you put it, we're still trying to catch up with those who are circulating the tablets. They may be gone from the SDC, but their influence is rife everywhere else, as far as I can tell. One of the cult members is bound to slip up soon, and when they do, we shall hopefully be there to accost them so that we may get to the root of the problem. An antidote can only fix so much, but it can do very little if those pills are still in circulation."

"I guess it's also hard to tell who's been taking the pills, if their memories are blacked out, right?" Garrett said.

"Precisely. It's like trying to grasp at water. The moment we think we have something, it trickles through our fingers." Imogene took a longer sip of her coffee. "In addition, we're also hard at work trying to get a lead on Katherine's current whereabouts, though that's also proving to be tricky. Have you made any progress on that?"

"Well, actually, Harley has been—" Astrid began, but I cut her off.

"We're doing some searches of our own, across the grid," I said. Astrid and Santana looked at me in surprise, prompting me to send out two faint tendrils of reverse Empathy, using threads of contentment I'd been feeling a moment ago to keep them quiet. They didn't seem too pleased with my unannounced decision not to tell Imogene, our coven director, about my monster training and the goal of finding Naima. Fortunately, nobody else at the table realized what I'd just done. I had my reverse Empathy down to a fine art these days, which meant it could go relatively unnoticed, even in a group.

However, one set of burning eyes made me turn slightly, my skin prickling. It appeared I'd managed to hoodwink all but one person at the table—Finch. He sat there, giving me the stink eye. *For once, Finch, couldn't you have just gone along with it?* He didn't look too impressed by what I'd done, but we'd probably hash that out later.

"That's good to hear," Imogene replied. "Speaking of leads, have you made any progress with the Grimoire?"

"I'm working on it," was all I said.

Wade glanced at me in shock, along with the rest of the Rag Team. Evidently, they all thought I'd given up on the Grimoire, too, since I hadn't mentioned it since yesterday, and the last they'd heard, it was a dead-end street.

"You are?" the Rag Team chorused.

"I've got some ideas, but they're all pretty up in the air," I replied, not going into detail. I wanted to feel out Imogene's emotions, to make sure she hadn't learned anything new from Alton, but she had that blocker bracelet on. Then again, she hadn't mentioned Necromancers, which gave me a sliver of hope that Alton had kept his promise.

"Well, I hope you keep at it, if you feel able," Imogene encouraged. "You're a very capable magical. You all are. We'll stop Katherine one way or another, even if that doesn't come from the Grimoire. Don't lose hope—we still have time to make this right." She downed the rest of her coffee and set the mug on the table like a cowboy throwing back tequila slammers in a bar. "Now, I must continue in my work. Don't hesitate to call me if you discover anything new."

"We won't," Wade replied, his eyes still on me.

Straightening her cardigan, Imogene turned on her heel and walked out of the Banquet Hall, leaving an air of confusion to settle across the table. I focused on the coffee in my mug, feeling the intense gaze of the others on me. Why had Imogene brought that up, in front of everyone? I knew she didn't mean anything by it, but it was a bit inconvenient right now, since I was planning on doing the Grimoire thing alone.

"Do you want to work with me and Finch on the Grimoire?" Wade asked, his hand on the small of my back. "We made a pretty decent team the other day, and to be honest, the kid's starting to grow on me. Like mold, or a rash."

"Eh, less of the kid," Finch retorted. "And there's no ointment for me, so don't even try. Once you learn to love me, there's no going back. I'm like magical herpes."

"Finch, that's disgusting." Santana laughed.

He shrugged. "Facts are facts, *mi amigazo*."

"Where'd you learn that?" Santana's eyes widened.

He smirked. "I may have a dust allergy, but I read. Weren't you listening? I know things. Now, Sis, what do you say to testing the limits of that allergy a little more and getting to grips with that ol' Grimoire?"

I shook my head. "I don't really feel up to it, to be honest. I'd rather go and join Tobe and do some more Purge beast training. It lets me vent a bit more than the Grimoire. I'd just lose my mind if I had to sit and stare at those pages today."

"Now that you mention your beastie training, how come you didn't want to tell the Woman in White about it?" Finch eyed me suspiciously.

I shrugged. "I've learned that, sometimes, it's better not to tell people everything you're doing, especially with all this pill stuff going around. Plus, I'm not sure if Imogene would be able to hack it. Everyone thinks the sun shines out of her ass, but it's been all talk and little action with her. I'm sure she's trying, but we're running out of time. We've got to handle this on our own."

"Harley..." Tatyana's voice held a warning.

"I know, I know, I'm probably being massively unfair, but if Katherine's influence is spreading as fast as Imogene says it is, then there's no telling when it'll reach the SDC's upper echelons, too. For all we know, it already has, and we're better off trusting each other and nobody else."

"I'm inclined to agree with Harley's logic," Dr. Krieger replied, to my surprise. "One too many people knew about the magical detector, and look where that got us. Yes, we've since learned that the real Rita is innocent of any wrongdoing, but Katherine was able to use her image to get where she needed to be, and we have yet to explain *how* she knew when to strike. For all we know, there may have been times when we were speaking with Rita when we were actually speaking with Katherine. At least, within this group, we all know that we are who we say we are. Harley's Empathy can attest to that."

I offered him a grateful smile. "So, forgive me if you think I'm feeling you out, in the coming days. I'm just making sure everyone is who they're supposed to be."

Krieger had made a valid point. At some point soon, I needed to go over who knew about the detector. If Rita was off the hook, then that left the others who'd been near it, or had known about it, somewhere along the line. There was every chance that it had simply been Katherine masquerading as Rita, and countless other coven individuals, and that everyone here was innocent. But there was also a chance that they weren't. One of them could've leaked the information to Katherine, giving her suspiciously perfect timing.

Which left one cold, hard fact: the only person I could trust right now was myself.

FOURTEEN

Harley

Being back in the Bestiary brought me an unexpected sense of calm. In the glass box, I could be alone with my abilities and my thoughts, preparing myself for more than just manipulating Naima.

Louella and Krieger had gone back to the infirmary after breakfast so that Louella could try some more of her newly returned Telepathy on Jacob, who was our last viable witness to what had happened that day in Krieger's office.

Meanwhile, the Rag Team members were busy working on more leads to get them to Naima. Astrid was scouring the globe with Smartie's help, from the comfort of her cozy little headquarters, with Garrett and Santana pulling together a dossier on possible locations, though I got the feeling Garrett just wanted to be closer to Astrid. Tatyana and Dylan were on the hunt for two known cultists who'd been seen in the California area—Ozymandias Fleming and Constance Pipistrelle. They were two of the most made-up names I'd ever heard, but, apparently, they were legit.

With no Portal Opener at our disposal, Tatyana and Dylan had been forced to take a car along the coast to Pasadena, to follow the trail of these two cultists. I'd heard them arguing as to who was going to do the driving as they left.

Raffe, as far as I knew, had retreated to his personal cell so he could speak with Kadar about how they were going to wrestle with Zalaam for control of Levi's body. I guessed there might have been the possibility of it getting a little ugly, considering the other things they had to talk about, which was why Raffe had chosen to lock them both up instead of having the conversation out in the open.

The only two who didn't seem to have anywhere else to go were Wade and Finch, who'd insisted on joining me in the Bestiary, even though I'd told them I'd probably do better without an audience. They hadn't taken the bait, and were standing together while I spoke to Tobe about what state the gargoyles were currently in.

"Shouldn't you be doing something more useful, Crowley?" Finch muttered. "Seems a waste of all that private school money, if all you're going to do is stand here gawping at Harley. What would your mother and father say? Mr. Ivy League, skimping out on his duties."

"You don't need to be here, either," Wade replied.

"I'm the one with the first-aid kit," Finch protested.

"Then hand it here and you can be on your way."

Finch shook his head. "No, I *do* have to be here. I've got to stay at Harley's side. That came from the top."

"No, you have to be watched over. Imogene never said it had to be Harley who did the watching, and she's got enough on her plate without having to babysit degenerates."

"Then does that make you the babysitter?" Finch grinned. "You should be honored. I'll let you watch the free, triple-X channels if you let me stay up past my bedtime."

Wade rolled his eyes. "You never stop, do you?"

I couldn't help but smile at them. On the outside, it looked like they hated each other, but the frost between them had thawed considerably since they'd met again, post-Purgatory. There wasn't much venom in their banter anymore.

"The gargoyles are somewhat sprightly today," Tobe warned, pulling my attention away from my brother and my boyfriend. "I thought they might settle after your last encounter, but they have continued to be... excitable. That is the most pleasant way I can phrase it."

"So, what you're saying is, they're going to claw my eyes out?"

Tobe smiled. "I would not allow that. I should not have allowed them to scratch you as they did, but I will be better prepared this time. If I sense their aggression is too much for you to handle, I will pull you out of there."

"With that singing you did last time?"

He looked slightly embarrassed. "You heard that?"

"It was beautiful. What was it?"

"Every Purge beast has a song that they respond to. When I was given life by my blessed Selma, I was also given the gift of these songs. They are innate within me, and they come to me when control becomes necessary."

"Could I use them?"

He shook his head slowly. "Sadly no, otherwise I would grant you my gift. Only those who are like me may use those songs, for only our lungs can bear the vibrations."

"It was pretty impressive," I replied.

"I thank you." He gave a small bow.

"Besides, I'm betting I'd send the Purge beasts running for the hills if I started to sing." I chuckled. "I'm not exactly a songbird, though the shower never seems to complain."

He flashed his fangs in a smile. "I fear I would shatter the glass in my own bathing facilities if I attempted such a concert." I couldn't imagine Tobe singing showtunes into his shampoo bottle, but then I couldn't imagine Tobe dousing himself in shampoo, full stop. Still, it was a good way to ease my nerves before I stepped back into the glass aviary of slashing claws and screeching beasties.

"I suppose I should get on with it." I stretched out my tense muscles.

"Are you certain?" Tobe replied.

"Yep, I'm good to go."

"Remember to focus your energies on your reverse Empathy. You cannot win this with Elemental magic or Telekinesis, not with Naima."

I nodded. "Reverse Empathy. Got it."

He approached the huge glass box and unlocked the door, the force-field shimmering as he gestured for me to enter. I stepped inside and took up my position. The swirling black smoke expanded and solidified as the gargoyles emerged from the ether into their true form. Before they'd all fully formed, I gripped my hands into fists and reached deep inside myself for the strongest emotions I could find. I focused on love and contentment, picturing myself around the Banquet Hall table with the rest of the Rag Team.

Keeping my eyes open, I held the emotion in the pit of my chest, letting it gather strength as I drew my Chaos into it. A few seconds later, my whole body was jangling with energy, every cell practically throbbing with the strain of keeping it all together. I'd felt like this once before, after I'd first broken my Suppressor and had to deal with all of that raw power pulsating through my veins. I took control of that now, forcing the vibrating energy to hold inside my chest until it felt as though I had a giant ball of power swirling inside my ribcage, threatening to burst out at any moment.

This must have been how John Hurt felt in Alien, *seconds before that thing exploded out of him.* They'd called it a "chest-burster" for a reason. Now, I had my own. Only, I didn't quite know what might happen when I let this out. *Yeah, I've really been spending too much time with Finch.*

I held it back for as long as I could, reminding myself that I was the one in control now. That was hard to get my head around, since I'd been treading a fine line between Dark and Light, control and total lack of it, and it'd been weighing me down ever since the Suppressor had broken. But I had to master this, or else we'd never get to Naima and, eventually, to Katherine. And then, all the Grimoires in the world wouldn't be able to help me.

I was just gearing up to send out a violent wave of reverse Empathy, when the gargoyles began their aerial assault. Shadows flitted in front of my eyes, and claws slashed at every available speck of skin. All of the energy I'd built up ebbed back into my body, my power losing its grip. My hands shot up to cover my face, but it stung as they cut my neck, my shoulders, my arms. Their stench was overwhelming, like rotting garbage and mothballs.

I turned to see Wade and Finch banging on the door, trying to get past Tobe. The Beast Master stood in their way, holding them both back with his mighty paws. It would've been a funny sight, if I wasn't getting dive-bombed by gargoyles. But I was grateful to Tobe for keeping them out. They couldn't keep coming in to save the day with their white-knight complex. It warmed my heart, it really did, but I needed to learn how to stand on my own two feet, with no safety net to catch me if I fell. There wouldn't be one, soon enough.

"I've got this!" I roared, flashing them a warning look through the glass. Wade and Finch stopped immediately, backing off with surprised expressions.

Fending off attacks with flurries of Telekinesis, I dug deep once again and dragged my emotions and my Chaos into the center of my chest. Only, this time, I didn't choose the good emotions. I chose the bad ones. The anger and the grief and the bitterness. That was what these creatures responded to best. If I wanted to win them over, I had to think like Katherine. They obeyed her for a reason, and now they would obey me.

The ball of broiling energy swirled again, my skin tingling with anticipation. My muscles tensed as I opened out my hands and puffed out my chest, finally releasing the wave of pent-up power. It swept out across the glass box, and the gargoyles stalled.

"Obey!" I bellowed. "Serve me! Honor me! Obey me! If you don't, I'll make you suffer!" My voice came out strange, my throat raw from the volume and depth of the sound. It was my voice, yet not. I recognized it from my past encounters with Purge beasts, but this was on a whole other level. Was this a magical's version of what Tobe could do? My lungs were definitely struggling with the intensity of the sound—they were practically on fire. But I couldn't give up now.

Some of the gargoyles dropped to the ground and folded their wings behind them.

"I said, OBEY! If you don't, I'll turn your wings into handbags!" *Whoa, a little too Katherine there.*

More and more of the gargoyles obeyed as I sent out wave after wave of reverse Empathy, filling them with all the deviousness and all the pain and all the anger that seared inside of me. Every terrible thought I'd ever had, I used against them. And they listened.

"I will roast you alive!" I roared to the gargoyles that still flapped in confusion. "I will tear out your fangs and use them as jewelry!" My lungs were threatening to explode as my eerie voice boomed out of my throat, my mouth filling with the familiar, metallic taste of blood that had risen up from my raw esophagus. But it was working, slowly but surely, all thanks to the Katherine flavor that I'd thrown into the mix. That didn't sit too well with me, but everyone had a drop of deviousness inside them, right? What mattered was what people did with it, how they used it. Right now, I was using it for good, to get these beasties under control.

After all, this paled in comparison to what I was doing to my friends —keeping secrets, telling barefaced lies, keeping important things to myself, blocking out my brother and my boyfriend and my friends because I wanted to protect them. *Man, I sound like a broken record.* Once this was over, once Katherine was dead, once I'd ensured that they were all safe, I swore I'd change the tune.

FIFTEEN

Harley

I stared at the gargoyles, my lungs burning, my heart racing, sweat dripping down my face.

They were all crouched on the ground, awaiting further instruction, and their black eyes blinked with uncertainty. It seemed to panic them, not to know what to do next. But not a single one of them made any attempt to take to the air again. They just kept watching and waiting, their wings rustling.

"Lie down!" I commanded. They did, sticking out their bony arms like hideous dogs, their oily chins lying flat to the floor. A thick ooze dripped onto the glass as their tongues lolled. "You may fly again when I leave."

They stayed put as I walked to the door of the glass box, where Tobe was standing, his paw on the lock. His golden eyes shone with pride, a wide smile revealing his fangs. He looked like a big, furry dad watching his kid from the sidelines of their first soccer game. With a turn of the key, he opened the door wide for me and stood aside as I walked past. The moment he closed the door, the gargoyles took to the air, disappearing in swirls of black smoke.

"They listened to me," I said, my voice barely a whisper.

"I knew they would," Tobe replied. "All it required was focus and strength, which you have in abundance, when you set your mind to a task."

I grinned. "They freaking listened to me!"

Finch and Wade approached, looking a little awestruck.

"Nice job, Sis." Finch put his hand on my shoulder and gave it an awkward squeeze. "You really told those leathery pests who was boss. Not sure about the whole 'I'll turn you into a handbag' vibe, though. You wouldn't exactly see a supermodel parading around with one of *them* hanging off their arm. The stench alone would make people hurl right onto the catwalk."

I smiled at him. "It worked, though."

"Yeah, I guess. You went a little Shipton in there," Finch murmured.

"I did what I had to," I replied. His tone worried me. Had I been too like Katherine?

"You did a good job, you really did." Wade muscled in, putting his arm around me. "I'm proud of you. I knew you had it in you, but that was impressive to watch."

"The way they dropped like flies, man. *Pyoo, pyoo, pyoo*!" Finch acted out what had just happened, clearly not wanting to be the one who put a downer on my success. He was right, though—I had gone a little Shipton in there. But, if it worked, what was the harm, right?

"You see, Harley, you found your own song, in the end." Tobe gave me a small, reverent bow that made me feel as if I should be in a ballroom or something.

I chuckled. "Not quite as melodic as your singing, though. That was a bit more thrash metal than operatic beauty."

"To each their own." Tobe smiled. "Now, do you feel well enough to attempt something more challenging? Gargoyles are troublesome, but they pale in comparison to the sentience of someone like Naima. They are as mice to humans, if I were to strike a contrast."

I frowned. "Do you have something in mind?"

"Some*one*, yes. A worthy adversary who is far closer to the level of Naima's consciousness."

"Why do I feel like I'm going to want to stick with gargoyles?" I said nervously.

"We do not have to proceed if you require rest. It is entirely your decision." Tobe waited patiently, while I glanced at Finch and Wade. They looked just as anxious as I did, and I could feel concern radiating from Wade. I only had limited knowledge of the creatures in this Bestiary, and I had no idea which enemy Tobe had chosen for me. But, if it was closer to Naima's level of badassery, then I had reason to be nervous.

I shook my head. "Lead the way."

"Are you sure?" Wade chimed in. "There's no harm in taking a break."

Finch nodded. "Yeah, what Wonderboy said."

"If he's Wonderboy, what does that make you? Robin?" I flashed him a grin, refusing to show just how scared I was. The gargoyles had been tough enough, and I was still sweating buckets, but I didn't have the time to play things cautiously.

Finch looked horrified. "I'm not Robin! Do you see me wandering around with my undies over a pair of stockings? No, you'd have to burn out your eyes if you saw that. You've wounded me real deep with that one." He paused, a grin spreading across his face. "Besides, Robin is the 'Boy Wonder,' so that would make me Batman."

I rolled my eyes, with a soft chuckle. "I'll send you back to your bat cave if you don't hush up. We've got things to do." I focused on Tobe again. "So, who's up next?"

"If you would care to follow me. The superheroes may follow, if they do not have the Joker to contend with, although I believe he may already be amongst these two." Tobe chuckled to himself as he turned and began to walk through the hallways of the Bestiary. Finch looked as though his eyes were about to bulge out of his head.

"Tobe knows about the Joker?" He hurried to catch up as Wade and I followed the Beast Master.

"I have not been under a rock all these years, Mr. Shipton," Tobe replied, over his shoulder. "I do have some grasp of popular culture."

Our good spirits faded as we entered a hall toward the back of the Bestiary. It lay empty, aside from a solitary box in the center. A wave of déjà vu washed over me, but I knew this couldn't be Echidna's hall. That had been off limits since the theft, and that box didn't have anyone in it anymore. This one definitely did. I could see the black swirl of smoke in the middle, surrounded by the splintered edges of frost that was in the process of thawing. Realization hit me like a roundhouse kick to the chest.

"Leviathan," I whispered.

Tobe nodded. "Very perceptive, Harley."

"I thought he was on ice, like his mother." I swallowed the note of panic in my voice.

"I took the liberty of thawing him when you left yesterday, as I was certain it would only be a matter of time before you succeeded with the gargoyles," Tobe explained, as he walked the rest of the way up to the ominous box.

"Aren't we running before we can walk, here?" Wade interjected.

"It is quite the leap, I confess, and it is rather dangerous. However, if Harley is to pursue Katherine's lieutenant, then she needs to be able to manipulate creatures who are far stronger, and more intelligent, than gargoyles." Tobe took out his keys and found the right one. "By my observations, I would say that Naima is as powerful as Leviathan, but she is not superior to him, as she is much smaller. However, her agility may be greater."

Wade shook his head. "This is way too risky, Tobe."

"Pfft, how's that for moral support?" Finch retorted. "Harley's got this in the bag. And Tobe's got the chutzpah to cut in if things go south. What's the worst that could happen?"

Tobe sighed. "While I admire your tenacity, there is a great deal that could go awry. It is not in my nature to pit someone against such a formidable foe, but these are exceptional circumstances, in which we must all strive to do more. I would not have thought to thaw Leviathan if I could not feel the power undulating from Harley."

"You can feel that?" I asked. I didn't know whether to be pleased or embarrassed. Now, I understood why people didn't like having their emotions read—it was a vulnerable position to be in. Tobe had been born from pure Chaos, so perhaps that was why he was a bit more sensitive to my energy.

He nodded. "Oh yes, it is rather potent. I would compare it to static electricity. Ever since you walked into the Bestiary, my fur has been standing on end. Have you not noticed?"

"I just thought you hadn't brushed through your mane or something," I replied. He had looked a little scruffier than usual, his mane sticking up in all directions, but I'd put it down to the same stress that everyone else was going through. None of us were looking our best at the minute, not even Wade, despite the usual sharp suit.

"Rude," Finch muttered playfully.

"It has made me certain that I am not offering you a challenge you cannot triumph over," Tobe went on. "Otherwise, I would never have dared to suggest it. I am not the sort to take uncalculated risks, but I believe this one will serve you well, should you be victorious."

Wade stepped up. "Harley, you don't have to do this."

"I don't have to do any of this, but that doesn't mean I'm not going to." I offered him a comforting smile. "Like Tobe said, we've all got to strive to do more, under these circumstances. Am I crapping my pants? Sure. But will that stop me? Nope."

"Should've worn your brown pants." Finch laughed.

"Black should cover it," I replied, trying to save face by staying jokey.

Tobe slotted the key in the lock, the scraping sound making my insides twist. "Now, a word of warning before you enter."

Oh crap... That was never a good way to start a sentence. "What do I need to know?"

"Leviathan was once known as an abomination of the seas, and he is a creature of biblical proportions. That is not an attempt at dramatics. Within this box, he has been reduced to a more humanoid semblance of his former self, but he is no less powerful for it." Tobe was starting to sound anxious, which did nothing for my growing nerves.

"Moby Dick, eat your heart out," Finch mumbled.

"He may well eat your heart out, so be cautious," Tobe replied.

Great. "Got it." I closed the gap between me and Tobe, readying myself to enter the frozen box.

"If you need help, I will be right here," Tobe said, as he turned the key and opened the door.

"Thanks."

Taking a deep breath, I stepped through the shimmering forcefield and heard the door close behind me.

SIXTEEN

Harley

I stood there in the box for a moment, gathering my emotions into my chest, the way I'd done with the gargoyles.

This time, remembering what I'd learned from Echidna, I focused on the more positive emotions inside me—love, friendship, longing for my parents—combined with the recent slew of all-consuming grief at having lost my aunt. Surely, he'd empathize with those feelings, after the death of his mother.

The air rushed out of my lungs as the black smoke unfurled, revealing a hideous creature perched atop the coil of his sea-serpent tail. His skin was a mish-mash of scales and armor plating, shifting between oceanic blues and glinting black. Some sections were completely transparent, covered in blue lights that glowed in the gloom inside the box, as if I'd delved into the murky underworld of the Mariana Trench. I could see organs shifting inside his body.

Beneath him, the mace-shaped end of his tail thrashed. Black spikes protruded from his spine, while two tentacle-like fronds flickered from the hollows of his cheeks, each one moving as if it had a life of its own. His arms were covered in armor plating, leading to hands that bore long, silver claws. He had rows upon rows of sharp teeth, his jaw jutting out like an angler fish's. A fleshy white appendage dangled over his face and held a glowing green orb that pulsated in perfect rhythm with his luminescent spots. However, his eyes were completely human. They were an impossibly pale shade of blue, almost white, and they were peering right into my soul.

"The Merlin girl, at last." The monster surged forward, the green light of its antenna flashing in my eyes. I closed them instinctively, not sure if that thing could hypnotize me, the same way angler fish did with their prey. My heart threatened to burst out of my chest. I braced for Leviathan's tail to wrap around my body and crush my bones to dust, or for his fangs to sink into my skin, but nothing happened. Nothing but bile rising up my throat as I inhaled the rotten, fishy scent of his cold breath as it crawled across my face.

I hurriedly gathered my emotions back into my chest and sent out a wave of reverse Empathy, letting it flow into Leviathan. He reeled back, swaying on top of his coiled tail, the way his mother had done.

"You have lost what I have lost," Leviathan hissed, his voice echoing as though he were shouting into a well. "Her duties are mine, now."

I fought to keep the wave of reverse Empathy going, though at least I could open my eyes now, without that thing dangling in my eyes. "What do you mean?"

"The promise." He slithered farther back into the box, making me work double-time to get the reverse Empathy to reach him. My heart sank. With Echidna gone, I'd assumed the deal to let her name my first-born was off, but apparently not.

"You know about that?" I asked.

"I inherited my mother's knowledge, as all her children do."

"I guess I should've expected that," I replied, battling with the wave of emotions. My voice was coming out normal, unaffected by the reverse Empathy. That needed to change if I was going to get Leviathan to obey, but the terror in my veins was making it harder to concentrate. I didn't want to get gobbled up by this thing. Although, if he thought I still owed him something, maybe that meant I was off the hook with the whole dying aspect.

"A favor is owed. My mother's due—the promise you swore. Katherine must suffer."

"You and me are on the same page with that, pal." I tried to make my voice echo, the way it'd done before, but it wasn't cooperating. *Maybe I should have taken that break first.*

"Your tricks do not seem to be working," he said, with a cold laugh. "They tickle, that is all."

I frowned in surprise. "What?"

"Your tricks. I do not mind them, but they may prove fruitless." He spoke in a weirdly soft tone for something so terrifying. I'd expected instant savagery from him, the moment I stepped into his box. A soft-spoken monster was somehow infinitely more frightening than one who came roaring forward with all the bells and whistles of evil. It made him unpredictable, and I didn't like that.

"Is that so?" I sent out another wave, more to prove a point than anything else.

"Katherine is the enemy, not I. She must burn. She must rot. She must die for what she has done." Leviathan's white eyes narrowed with fury, his luminescent spots turning red. This guy was definitely more ancient than Katherine, and though he wasn't a creature of many words, his disdain for her was obvious.

"She killed your mother." I stated the obvious. "Just like she killed mine."

"As I said, you have lost what I have lost."

"And you want her punished?"

He flashed his fangs in a sour smile. "I want her destroyed."

"Then we're definitely on the same page." I hadn't expected to be having a reasonable conversation with this beast, but weirder things had happened. He was clearly in pain, his emotions throbbing through those lit-up specks.

"The Challenge should never have been possible," he said bitterly, still swaying as though he was trying to dodge my reverse Empathy. *Crafty creature.*

"Chaos is unpredictable as heck. You think it's going to do one thing and then—*bam!*—it goes and does something else, leaving everyone chin-deep in crap."

Leviathan laughed darkly. "Indeed. It makes errors, then spends millennia trying to fix them in secret."

"It's like you're in my head," I replied. "Chaos just blurts out these major hiccups, tries to resolve them without 'direct intervention,' since that's against the rules—you know, it drops a spell here, a thought there, channels a few ideas through a couple of people, scrambling to make the best of the gigantic mess it made."

"The Merlin Grimoire, for example." He surged forward, his eyes fixed on mine so I couldn't look away. He let the words hang in the air, while I struggled to keep the reverse Empathy flowing and not give too much away. It was a juggling act, and I was failing miserably. My reverse Empathy didn't seem to be having any effect on Leviathan whatsoever.

"You've heard about that?"

He smirked. "That's the trouble with you magicals. You hear only what you want to."

"Do you know much about it? You must be pretty old. No offense."

"There is no offense to be found in age, Merlin. With age comes wisdom. Youth is not all it is claimed to be." I pushed down the nausea that threatened to spill out of my mouth, as Leviathan's stench filled every sense. "As for the Grimoire, I know a great deal."

My heart lurched. "You do?"

"What would you care to know?" He flicked his wrist casually, as though he was asking what my order was at the drive-thru.

"What's in it? Is there something in there that can kill Katherine?"

He chuckled. "Perhaps there is hope for you. You ask the right questions." He reeled back, the angler fish lamp glowing white instead of green. "There is magic within those pages that can kill her. I listen and I hear all. Even frozen, my ears and eyes are open to Chaos and its whisperings."

"What magic?" I pressed, forgetting about the reverse Empathy completely for a minute.

"There is a spell that will destroy her. It is intended for that specific purpose. It is Chaos's final resort. And it is there, within."

"Can you tell me anything else about it? I need details, Leviathan. I hate to sound rude, but I really need everything I can get right now." I paused. "And I'm guessing, since you haven't killed me yet, you need me to do this so that you can have your revenge, too."

He rose up on his coils, his tentacles snapping. "There is always time for me to change my mind."

"Well, if you kill me, then Katherine will get away with it. She'll get away with killing your mother, and my mother, and everyone else who's died because of her. And there'll be more to come, if she ascends. If you think you'll escape with your life, you're wrong—she'll use you for her Bestiary, pumping the life and Chaos out of you until there's nothing left but a shell."

The words poured out of me like gunfire. He might have been acting reasonable, but he was still a monster—he didn't have to let me out of this box alive if he didn't want to, but I was determined to fight my corner. Especially now that he'd given me that slice of pure, genuine, vibrant hope. There was an actual spell in the Grimoire that could destroy Katherine. An actual freaking spell, crafted for that sole purpose. This wasn't a wild goose chase anymore, full of uncertainty and a bunch of ifs and maybes. Leviathan's words had cemented the fact that I was on the right path, headed straight for the weapon that would stop Katherine in her tracks, once and for all. And that was worth everything.

"But who's to say you will be victorious?" Leviathan's eyes narrowed, his lamp glowing red now. Did that mean I'd pissed him off, or had I just hit a nerve?

"Nobody, but I'm your only shot at getting revenge for your mother."

He chuckled. "It is always fun betting on the underdog. That is you, in case you needed clarification."

"I'm aware of that."

"Why have you finished with your tricks?" He swayed from side to side in a hypnotic rhythm. "Have you given up so quickly? That hardly inspires confidence."

"I just thought I'd lure you into a false sense of security." I smiled, gathering a powerful ball of raw emotion in the center of my chest, dragging every sensation into its core to boost it up. All my anger, my hope, my sadness, my faith, my love—all of the strongest emotions available to mankind. If he thought magicals were puny, he was about to get a taste of what we could really do.

"I will not make it easy," he purred. "My mind will not break quickly."

"I wouldn't want you to. My real enemy isn't going to, so why should you?" I held my ground and felt the swell of that ball of energy inside me. My cells and veins were jangling, the way they had back in the gargoyle box, sweat dripping into my eyes as I battled for control.

Leviathan swept forward, moving at blinding speed. I staggered back into the glass to avoid him and slammed my head against it, but I kept hold of the ball of energy even though pain hammered at my skull.

He lunged again, slashing his silver claws at my face. I feinted out of the way, gripping even tighter to that precious ball. I couldn't drop it now —I couldn't let it ebb away, or I'd be back at the starting line, and I didn't know if I had the stamina to keep going.

I was about to leap back up to my feet, when the lash of his tail caught me in the back of the legs, swiping me off balance and sending me tumbling to the ground. The air escaped my lungs as I hit the deck hard. I scrambled back up, but Leviathan had disappeared into a mist. Shadows danced behind the haze, making it hard to figure out what was real and what wasn't.

Leviathan exploded out of the fog, thundering right at me. I ran at him, skidding to my knees and sliding right past him. Blue and purple lights pulsated through the mist. I kept my eyes fixed on them, clawing breath into my burning lungs. I ducked rapidly as sparking orbs shot through the haze. Like homing missiles, they followed me wherever I ran, and the box wasn't exactly big. One smashed into the glass as I darted out of the way, bursting into a flurry of blue sparks that transformed into icicles, splintering as they hit the floor. I let another of the orbs get that little bit too close, then leapt out of the way. It slammed into the glass, and purple sparks erupted, transforming into oily blobs that slithered as if they were alive.

I kept my eyes peeled for Leviathan himself. He was lurking in the mist, waiting for his moment to strike. I almost missed his tail sneaking around my feet, but I jumped away before it could do damage. My heart was pounding now, blood rushing in my ears.

I can't do this for much longer. I was at the opposite end of the box now, as far from the door as it was possible to be, which meant I couldn't call for Tobe.

Holding on to the ball of energy in my chest was getting harder by the second. I needed to unleash it or lose it. But I couldn't even see Leviathan, so how could I direct my energy at him?

Pressing myself up against the glass, I tried to edge toward the door. The sparking orbs kept coming at me—blue, purple, red, green, white—each one containing a different horrifying entity. There were icicles, those oily blobs, vortexes of fire, clawing fronds of barbed seaweed, and flashes of bright light. My legs were already torn up from the barbed seaweed that had clamped around my ankles and thighs and had sunk their thorns into my skin.

I tried to duck away from a white orb, a fine sprinkling of dust falling into my eyes. The pain was instant, spreading across my face like a rash, itchy and sore and stinging. My head ached, my limbs felt like stone, and this ball of energy in my chest was about ready to disintegrate me from the inside out.

I screamed in pain as another round of barbed seaweed clamped around my stomach, piercing right through the thick leather of Finch's jacket. Another orb exploded. Something thick and wet and sticky landed on the bare skin of my neck. I felt something slide across my throat, cold and creeping, and a strange pressure pushed down hard on my windpipe. *Not this again.* I lifted my hands to try and scrape the oily creatures away, but the blobs covered my fingers, their unexpected strength working like glue to sandwich my fingertips together.

This is it... I'm dying here...

Something smacked me in the back of the legs, bringing me to my knees, right where Leviathan wanted me. I couldn't see, and the pain was only getting worse. However, I sensed Leviathan approaching from the right-hand side, my other senses working overtime to compensate.

"Do you submit?" His voice echoed nearby. "I confess, I thought you'd be a more worthy adversary."

"Never!" The word came out raw and ragged, booming out of my throat until I tasted blood. "I'll never submit! I'll never give up, as long as my heart's still beating!" The glass around me vibrated with the sheer volume of my voice.

"How…?" Leviathan trailed off.

"I. Will. Never. Give. Up!" I screamed, the box trembling, the aftershocks shivering through my legs. "Do you hear me, Katherine? I'm never backing down!"

Leviathan had gone completely silent. *Did I do it?* Still blinded by the dust of the white orb, I had no way of knowing.

SEVENTEEN

Katherine

Showtime.

I turned back the sleeves of yet another cream ensemble, sick of them dragging in everything I encountered. Coffee, ink, mysterious dirt —everything. All these shades of white were just begging for stains. It really had to be the most impractical color, especially for someone who, through no fault of her own, seemed to be a magnet for blood and assorted viscera. Granted, Isadora and Suri had definitely been my bad.

Satisfied with my reflection in the mirror—well, as satisfied as I could be when I had to stare at Imogene's boring face—I left my office and headed for the infirmary. I'd really gotten into the swing of the SDC and my directorship. As it turned out, it didn't matter where you were, places like this were always the same. They wanted a leader, they followed a leader, and they did what they were told, begging for instructions like griping schoolkids. What could I say, they loved me. After Levi and his total incompetence, who could blame them? I'd come along like the savior that I was and brought them all back from the brink of complete embarrassment. It really would've been a mess without me.

Then again, the world was. But that'd soon be changing.

I pulled a sour face as I stepped into the infirmary, bombarded by the clinical glow. Hospital lights were the most unflattering in the world, no question.

Scanning the empty main ward, my eyes fixed on Levi and Jacob. *Morning, my darlings. I hope you've been behaving yourselves.* I chuckled to myself as I crossed the room toward them, but I paused just short of Levi's bed. Something was up. I could sense it, like smelling burning toast right before a stroke. My gaze shot to Levi, who was wriggling beneath the covers like a worm on a hook. He definitely seemed more conscious than he had yesterday. *Well, that's a problem.*

"Leonidas?" I said, peering closer.

"Im… Imogene?" he rasped back. *Yeah, not good.* The sucker was conscious, when he was supposed to still be out cold. I hated unexpected events, and this was way up on my list of inconveniences. I was glad I'd managed to get to him before anyone else could. There was no sign of the German, and the blinds were down in his office. *Sleeping on the job, Krieger? Tut, tut.* I was actually pretty impressed that he'd been able to go back in there, after the bloodbath I'd made of his workspace. That was German efficiency, right there. I wasn't about to smother Levi with his own pillow, though it did cross my mind. But I had to be careful now, after the close call with Isadora and Suri. Another death with me nearby would be way too suspicious. *Pity.*

"Leonidas, can you hear me?" I sat down beside his bed with a concerned expression, playing Imogene to perfection. Oh, the tenderness. *Just call me Mother Theresa.*

He blinked his eyes open. "Imogene?"

Yes, we've been over that. I was Imogene, he was him, and I wasn't about to go in pointless circles. "How are you feeling?"

"Strange." He writhed as if he were in pain. I glanced at his intravenous drip, wondering if I should up his meds. Not that I had any idea how to do that. Magical supremacy was one thing, medical stuff was another. I'd be as likely to kill him as take his pain away. Although, maybe, if that just *happened* to be the case, and that jumping green line just *happened* to flatline, I'd get away with it. I could pin it on Krieger and his exhaustion after losing Isadora. Doctors made mistakes all the time, and even Krieger could slip up.

"Strange how?" I decided against it. It was too much hassle, fiddling with knobs and whatnot.

He shook his head. "It's nothing. I'm okay. I'll be okay."

"That's good news," I replied, putting on that clipped voice that I despised. It was sexy as heck coming from Davin, with that delicious British accent, but he made it sound natural. Imogene was upper-crust American, and for me, it was a chore.

"How long have I been out?" He struggled to sit up, and I let him. His hands looked particularly clammy, and I didn't want to get within ten feet of those sweaty palms. I'd evaded him at enough drunken Christmas parties to know it'd take a tank of Purell to get rid of his cold touch.

"Several days." I did my best to look worried. "Are you sure you're feeling better? You look very pale. Can I get you some water?"

He gaped at me like a beached fish. "Several days?"

"Yes, you took quite a hit."

"From… From Raffe?" He furrowed his brow, and I could almost see the cogs whirring as he tried to piece everything together.

"The djinn," I corrected. "Raffe is very distressed by the entire incident."

His face contorted, his hands balling into fists. "Everything's a bit hazy."

"I'm sure it is. Are you sure I can't fetch you something? You seem to be in a great deal of pain."

"No, I've got it under control," he snapped back.

"I was only asking." I feigned hurt, though I didn't give a hoot what he said to me. He'd get all the appropriate punishments when I ascended. And it took a lot more than a snappy tone to wound me.

He sighed. "I'm sorry, Imogene. I'm not… quite myself."

"That is only to be expected after what you've been through. You had us all extremely worried."

"What happened, exactly?"

I sat back in the chair. "Where do I begin? It would seem that the djinn took over control of Raffe and tried to harm you. Jacob and Louella managed to save you and bring you here before any severe damage could be done. Dr. Krieger has worked tirelessly to ensure you were healed.

From what I have heard, the djinn attempted to crush your skull with his bare hands, which is absolutely horrifying."

"I thought I dreamt that," he said sadly.

"Then, I'm sorry to be the bearer of bad news."

"Not to worry, someone had to tell me," he replied. "Has anything else happened since I've been out?"

I bit my lip, putting on a good show of apprehension, even though I was absolutely gagging to tell him everything. This was going to be deeply satisfying, to make him see just how incompetent he really was. The jester of the coven world. A total laughingstock. I hadn't even had to use any of my pills on him—he'd made all of those mess-ups by himself. Oh, I was going to enjoy this, and, frankly, I needed a bit of fun. My meeting with Davin had stolen my mojo a bit, and I needed a decent ego boost to get things back on track. This would do the trick, and then some.

"I'm afraid it has," I said, squeezing the brim of a tear into my eyes for good measure. "Isadora is no longer with us, alongside a poor human who was caught in the crossfire. Shortly after the incident with Raffe's djinn, Katherine managed to infiltrate the SDC and murdered Isadora and the poor human girl in cold blood. She was masquerading as Ms. Bonnello, which allowed her to perpetrate this awful tragedy. To make matters worse, she took the detector, and knocked dear Jacob unconscious as she escaped. I attempted to stop her, but she was much too strong for me. My own wounds are still healing, though I imagine the ones inside will take far longer to heal." I brushed a fingertip across my cheek, more to make sure the cut was actually still there than anything else. *Imagine if I'd accidentally healed it!* Fortunately, I could still feel the ridge of it, slicing across my cheek. Perfect.

"What?" Levi gasped, just the way I'd wanted him to.

I nodded. "It is terribly sad. We were forced to tell the girl's parents that she died during a fatal mugging, though we can't release her body to them as of yet. They are devastated, as are we. I believe Jacob had some feelings for the poor thing, so perhaps it's best that he doesn't know what happened to her." I paused. "What's more, Katherine's influence continues to grow, now that we are reaching the end of her rituals. With only one left, it's all rushing toward us at a rather alarming pace, and we're struggling to keep up, in order to stop her. I'm getting increasingly worried, so I'm grateful that you've finally regained consciousness. We can use all the help we can get."

A cold bark of a laugh rasped from Levi's throat. "Is that right?"

"Yes, we're quickly running out of time."

"And I bet you're just loving watching that clock run down, aren't you?" A faint blush of red had covered Levi's skin, his eyes turning a dark, unsettling shade of crimson.

I leaned closer, intrigued. "Levi has a djinn?"

"Didn't you know? He's gone back to sleep, if that's what you're worried about. I know how much you hate witnesses, Katherine. It is lucky for you that Raffe's djinn isn't able to detect you, given his juvenile state. If he were connected to the wider hive mind of Erebus, he would have seen what I have seen."

I smiled. "Well, this *is* an interesting twist. I'd like to say I never suspected it, but I always wondered if you ran in the family, so to speak. I know how you creatures of Erebus like your routines, and what's better than a family of willing hosts?"

"I wouldn't call them willing. A curse is a curse, even if some of us happen to get along better than others."

"And I'm guessing that's not the case for you and Levi?" I chuckled, delighted to see someone more my speed. Monsters were infinitely preferable to magicals, and anything was preferable to Levi.

"We have our differences."

"Ooh, do tell."

He smirked. "I wouldn't want to give you all my trade secrets, Katherine."

"Eris, if you don't mind," I replied. It wasn't a request.

"Nice choice."

I smiled. "Thanks. I love a rich history, don't you? What can I say, hers struck a chord. Or, rather, a discord."

"You're funny, too? I didn't expect that."

"There's no fun in being predictable." I eyed him curiously. "Speaking of which, I don't always expect fear and terror from the people I meet, but it helps. And you don't seem to be scared of me at all. I'm not sure whether to be impressed or insulted."

He laughed coldly. "Why would I be scared of you?"

I shrugged. "Most people find some reason to be."

"I'm not a person, I'm a djinn."

"Potato, potahto."

"You dare call me a potato?"

I chuckled. "What else should I call you?"

"Zalaam."

"You missed a trick there. I'd have gone for Alakazam."

He narrowed his ruby eyes. "It means 'darkness.'"

"Is that supposed to intimidate me? Katherine means 'pure,' and you can see how that turned out."

"Names mean more to a djinn, evidently."

"Yeah, evidently." I laughed. "You'd have to blame my parents for that one. They were clearly hoping for something different, but what kind of bar were they setting? I'd never have been able to live up to that. Now, Hester, on the other hand—"

"It means 'star.' It is Persian in origin; I am more than familiar with it," Zalaam interjected.

"Well done. Ten points to you." I shot him a warning look. I didn't like being interrupted while I was getting into monologue mode. "She was definitely a star, until she wasn't. She got the better end of the deal, if you ask me. Even now, people talk about her like she was a celebrity. I just thought she was a ball of hot air, all glow and no substance. I guess both fit the bill."

"You like to talk, don't you?"

I fought the urge to push up the button on his meds. "I enjoy the art of conversation, if that's what you mean. Although, good conversation requires two minds of equal intellect, so I can forgive you if you're struggling."

"What game are you playing, Katherine? Why are you playing this role of Imogene?" Zalaam looked me over. "I can tell you despise it. Others might not be able to sense that, but I can."

"Good for you," I replied. "A bit disappointing if that's all your djinn powers can do, though."

"They can do so much more, as you well know."

I grinned. "Again, are you trying to intimidate me? It takes more than a few empty threats to pique my interest."

"You should be scared of me."

I allowed myself a quick glare. "No, Alakazam, *you* should be scared of *me*. You should be very scared of me, because I've got the power to end your entire lineage, right here, right now. And once I ascend, I'll have the power to wipe out all the djinn from existence. I'll tweak Chaos itself, if I have to. It could use a tune-up. Far too much trash has been allowed to slip through, these past decades."

"My name is Zalaam," he muttered, though the bravado had slipped from his voice.

"And it's Eris to you," I shot back. "You'd do well to remember that, if you want to live. I reward those who join me, and I punish those who don't. Choose your side carefully. *Very* carefully."

"You don't scare—"

"Yes, you've said. But I've got the feeling that might change," I said sharply. "Oh, and if you're thinking of threatening me by swearing to tell Levi you know who I am, just know that I'm already onto you. I made a deal with Erebus back in Tartarus, but I'm guessing you already knew that? That hive mind of yours is a wonderful thing. But the crux of that deal is, your lips are sealed, whether you like it or not. You can't say a word about me. You're bound by Erebus's rules, and he's got a vested interest in me. He doesn't want me picking him for the final Challenge, now, does he? So, if you say a word, he'll snuff you out before you even open your smoky little mouth."

Zalaam sat in stunned silence. "How can you know that?"

"I've got a hive mind of my own. You wouldn't believe what I've got locked away in here." I tapped the side of my head, glad I could nip any betrayal in the bud before he started throwing warnings about.

At the time, that deal with Erebus, to stop him from killing me in Tartarus, had been a thorn in my side. Harley had almost caught me out with that particular move. But, now, it was paying dividends. Erebus wasn't an idiot—he realized what he had in his grasp, when I'd been put in that position, and he'd sworn to stay out of proceedings as long as I didn't choose him for the last Challenge. I was a woman of my word, as long as he kept his pesky djinn in line. There was no way Zalaam would dare to cross his maker, not unless he had an instant death wish. All djinn were born of Erebus, and it was his power that connected them all. If Zalaam tried anything, Erebus would come down on him so hard it'd make his ruby eyes pop out. I could see all of that running through the djinn's head as I watched and waited.

"You are a learned woman," he said, at last. "I underestimated you."

"Don't be too hard on yourself. Most people do, and they come to regret it."

"Although, you should know, I haven't spoken of you previously to Leonidas, though I sensed who you were a while ago. Not as long ago as I might've liked, but I certainly had an inkling. You see, at first, it was harder to detect, but as your strength has grown, so has the telltale power signature that you are not who you appear to be."

"You said nothing because you weren't able to." I gave a wry chuckle. "Levi had you squashed right down, unable to influence him or speak to him in any way. That's my guess, anyway, judging by the fact that he almost got his head caved in by Raffe's djinn and you didn't miraculously pop out of nowhere, all red and fiery. And he'd have used you if he could, rather than have his brain turned to mush, which would suggest you were buried *way* way down. So don't try and pretend your silence about me was anything other than Levi putting a big djinn gag on you."

He dipped his head in a jaunty bow. "I can see it would be foolish of me to pretend otherwise. But I must ask, what do you want from me now that you know of my existence?"

"Who says I want anything from you?"

"If you know so much about what I am, then you know I can be useful to your cause. You wouldn't have mentioned Erebus, otherwise. You want something. What is it?"

I smiled, cracking my knuckles in satisfaction. "Oof, now you're talking my language…"

EIGHTEEN

Harley

The searing pain faded away from my eyes, and the milky mist retreated so I could actually see what was going on inside the box. Leviathan stood right beside me, swaying like a drunk after last orders. I could see that he was fighting my reverse Empathy tooth and nail. Dragging myself to my feet and kicking away the barbed seaweed, I stared at him. Tentatively, I approached.

"Can you hear me?" I asked, but he didn't respond. "Hello? Anyone home?"

Silence. Well, silence and a lot of weird swaying.

Holy crap!

I turned around to look at Wade and Finch, whose faces were plastered to the glass. Tobe still stood by the door, waiting for me to come out. A smile spread across my face as I looked at my brother and my boyfriend, who were grinning through the box.

"I did it!" I shouted.

"What?" I couldn't hear Finch, but I could read his lips.

"I said, I did it!"

"You hit him?" Another bad lip-reading from my brother, though I seemed to be quite good at it.

I rolled my eyes. "No! I. Did. It!"

"Oh!" Finch mouthed. I guessed he was shouting, but I couldn't hear him. "Yeah, you did!" No sooner had the words left his mouth than his grin suddenly faded. Wade's did, too.

Wade banged his fist against the glass, jabbing at something behind me.

I whirled around, but Leviathan was nowhere to be seen. He'd disappeared back into the mist.

I should've known it wouldn't be that easy. Although, that was the trouble, it *hadn't* been easy. I'd been brought to my knees, thinking I was about to die, and even that hadn't been enough, apparently. I peered through the thick mist, which was getting thicker by the second. It'd gotten so dense that I couldn't see those pulsing dots anymore.

A blur whizzed past my head, and I ducked just in time, as a tentacle shrank back into the gloom. Crouching low to the floor, I tried to see if I could spot Leviathan where the mist was thinnest, but that slimy beast was impossible to see. For a creature so big, he was pretty good at hiding himself.

I reeled back as another tentacle shot out of the haze, collapsing in a heap on the floor as it knocked me off balance. Apparently, those things sticking out of his face could extend at will. I tried to jump back up, only to feel something slimy and muscular wrap around my waist, squeezing until I thought my ribs might crack like an egg.

Clawing for breath, I placed my palms against the tentacle and pounded round after round of Fire into it. The slithering appendage snaked away, smoking slightly, and filled the whole box with the stench of cooking fish. *As if I wasn't already feeling sick.*

Staggering a little and feeling majorly lightheaded after almost having the life squeezed out of me, I backed into the corner of the box, figuring it lessened the number of angles he could strike from. Another tentacle shot out, but I dodged it, narrowly avoiding braining myself on the glass. I started to gather my emotions back into the center of my chest. If I'd done it once, I could do it again. I just had to make it stronger this time, though I had no clue how I was supposed to do that. My last bout of reverse Empathy had been the strongest yet, and that had still fallen short. This was starting to feel less like a test, and more like a fight for my life. After all, Leviathan stood between me and the door.

I leapt out of the way as Leviathan charged out of the mist, barreling straight for me with breathtaking speed. He hit the glass with a thud that made the whole box shudder. If I hadn't gotten out of the way, I'd have been mulch right about now.

Finch twisted his hands over and over, playing out some kind of charade. He covered his face with his palms, like he was sobbing, before moving them away and laughing weirdly. *What is he saying?* Was he trying to tell me to use reverse Empathy? That seemed like the most obvious conclusion. Unless he'd just lost his mind.

"Control him!" Wade mouthed slowly. I resisted the urge to glare at the pair of them, considering I had a massive Purge beast to deal with. What did they think I was doing? Twiddling my thumbs and hoping for a miracle? The last part was sort of right, but I was already doing everything else.

Sprinting for the other side of the box, I skidded to a halt as Leviathan tore out in front of me, blocking my path. How was he moving so freaking fast? All of that armor plating on him should've been slowing him down, but apparently it didn't weigh a damn thing. How was I supposed to get control over him, when he was moving so fast? A massive wave of reverse Empathy might've done it, one that surged through the whole box, but I'd already tried that.

"You thought you had me there, didn't you?" Leviathan chuckled.

"I did, for a second. Admit it."

He flashed his fangs. "I fooled you. If you are so easily tricked, you don't stand a chance."

Great, now the big fish-snake thing is calling me weak. I moved backward until my shoulders hit the glass, keeping my eyes on Leviathan. I'd already lost my grip on the ball of emotion, but my goose wasn't quite cooked yet. Gathering it again, I focused on the swirling vortex in the middle of my chest, trying to hold it steady enough to send out one massive wave.

Before I could even get a tendril out, Leviathan's tail whipped out like Indiana Jones on adrenaline, snapping around my ankles and dragging me to the ground. I screamed as it lifted me up into the air, the sound fading to a groan as he slammed me against the glass, right in front of where Finch and Wade were standing. They stumbled backward, as if I was going to come right through the freaking thing. To be honest, I wasn't entirely sure that I wasn't.

I'd just about shaken the dizziness out of my head when he lifted me up again, leaving me dangling off the end of his tail like a wriggling fish on a hook. I fought back, trying to reach up to untangle my feet, reminding me of those insane magicians who willingly had themselves shoved in a straitjacket and suspended from a crane or something. Bringing me closer to his face, he laughed, before smacking me against the other side of the box. This time, I felt his tail snake away, leaving me to sit there, in a daze, wondering what else he had up his fishy sleeve.

"Can you not do that?" I yelled into the mist. "I've got a phobia of being upside down."

Leviathan chuckled, the fact that I couldn't see him making it all the creepier. "You should never tell the enemy your weakness, Merlin."

His tail shot out, but I was ready for it. I leapt over the slithering thing and bolted for the opposite corner. "Missed!"

"You should also never let the enemy know where you are." His tail hissed out again, grasping me in a place that was a little too intimate for my liking.

"If you want to keep that promise to your mother, you'd better let go of me, right now!"

He instantly retracted his tail. "My apologies. It is hard to see in all this fog."

"You don't say," I shot back, making him laugh again. I was going to wipe that smirk off his face if it was the last thing I did.

Trying to be clever, I crouched to the ground and pressed myself flat against the glass floor. On my belly, I dragged myself forward, getting right under the swirling mist until I found what I was looking for. I knew I looked ridiculous, but I didn't care. I was going to get this sucker. Right ahead of me, I saw the coiled scales of Leviathan's tail, the spiky end tapping the glass lightly. *Is that how he's sensing me?* Was he feeling out my vibrations, and using that to strike? Hoping that was the case, I held my breath and continued to crawl forward at a snail's pace, making as little noise and vibration as possible.

With my eyes bulging at the strain of not breathing, I pulled myself right past the nasty creature, until I was staring at the back of him. I eyed the jagged spikes that ran down his spine, wondering how much they'd hurt if I accidentally impaled myself on one. Still, I didn't have too many options right now, and Leviathan didn't seem to know where I was.

"You can't hide from me, Merlin," he said.

Oh, can't I? Carefully lifting myself up into a squatting position, I leapt at him, wrapping my arms tight around his neck. He jolted in surprise, tossing me this way and that like I was a rag doll. It only made me cling tighter. I locked my hands together in a vise as I struggled to stay on the wildest bucking bronco I'd ever experienced. Squeezing my eyes shut and hoping that I wouldn't hurl right onto the back of Leviathan's head, I set about gathering the ball of emotions back into my chest. I had to give this everything, or I'd never stand a chance against Naima. Then again, she didn't have a tail and friggin' tentacles to deal with.

I focused on the strongest emotions that churned inside me, dragging up the most powerful memories I had and siphoning the energy from them in volatile tendrils of raw feeling. I thought of avenging my parents and Isadora, bringing my mind back to the way I'd felt when I saw the blood pooling under Krieger's office door. I thought of Suri underneath the black cloth, and Isadora's vacant eyes, her face left with that pained expression of grief and pain. I thought of Jacob, motionless in his hospital bed, with no idea if he'd ever wake up again. I thought about stopping Katherine, once and for all, and saving every creature on this spinning rock we called home. Including the people I loved, more than anything: Wade, Finch, Santana, Tatyana, Astrid, Raffe, Dylan, Garrett, Jacob, Louella, all of them. The ability to keep them safe was in my hands, but how could I hope to do that if I couldn't even control Leviathan? I had to do this. I just had to.

"You will obey me!" I howled, like I'd done in the gargoyle box, sending out a powerful pulse of reverse Empathy, channeling everything I had into it. But, no matter how deep I dug, and how many emotions I dragged into my chest, kicking and screaming, it wasn't enough. Leviathan kept trying to throw me off, unfazed by my words.

"No, I don't think I will, but nice try. That tickled more than before," he replied.

What am I doing wrong? I had about two minutes before I couldn't hold on anymore, so I had to come up with something quickly. To be honest, I didn't think I had it in me to go another billion rounds with this dude. If he threw me off, that'd be it—game over. Either I'd have to tap out and run for the door, or he'd end up breaking me, one way or another.

"Sometimes, the Darkness needs to be fed." The voice came out of nowhere, soft and gentle, slipping into my mind as if someone had whispered it into my ear. I knew that voice. I'd heard it before, back on Eris Island.

Mom?

I waited for her to speak again, willing her to, but that was all I was getting. Maybe she hadn't spoken at all, and it was just my mind urging me in the right direction. Still, it was enough to jog my memory. My mom had given me some sage advice when I'd let her out of that sickening jar. She'd told me that, sometimes, I needed to feed the Darkness inside of me.

Okay, then. I guess it's dinnertime.

Holding on to that thought, I closed my eyes and reached for the Darkness, seeking out the shadowy side of myself that I kept suppressed. Weirdly, it wasn't too hard to find. It was like the place where two oceans met, the two sides distinct. All I had to do was dip my toe into the Dark side, and the rest would come flooding out. At least, that was my theory. Finding the heavier pull of the Dark Chaos, I gripped it tight in my mind and let it flow through me, giving it free rein over my body.

Without warning, I exploded backward, my hands wrenched apart as I was flung from Leviathan's back, hitting the back of the box with a thud. This time, there was no dizziness, only a violent buzz in my veins that excited and terrified me in equal measure. I jumped up, and immediately crumpled to my knees, the Darkness throbbing inside me. It was too strong, and I was pretty sure it was about to implode all of my cells, and me with them. My body didn't even feel like it belonged to me anymore, everything crackling and sparking, my veins turning black underneath my skin. This thing was going to tear me apart, and there was nothing I could do to stop it.

And then, as suddenly as that rush of destruction had coursed through me, it ebbed, forming a thread of control that spread up and down the length of me, reaching right to the edges of my fingertips and down to my toes. I stood up, feeling as if I could flip a mountain or something. Ahead of me, Leviathan had turned, his eyes narrowed in confusion.

This was going to be fun.

Lifting my palms, I let the Darkness twist around my fingers, sparking and glinting. Trying Fire first, I sent out a blast, almost careening back into the glass as it pummeled out of my hands in a single, violent torrent that hit Leviathan square in the chest. He went flying, disappearing into the mist. *Cool.* I took a step forward, feeling that thread strengthen, the violence settling into a more bearable sensation as I shot another torrent into the haze. Judging by the wheezing groan I heard, I'd hit my mark.

Buoyed by the new energy within me, I walked into the mist. I'd taken a few steps, when Leviathan swept out of his hiding spot, striking at me with his clawed hands. The sharp edge scraped against my arm as I sidestepped the attack. The pain spurred me on to launch a retaliation of powerful Fire. This time, he was too quick, twisting away from danger. *Crap...* The Darkness had been fed, and it was proving useful, but it wasn't all-powerful. I still needed to do the work.

The fight raged on in an aggressive back-and-forth. He slashed at my face and my body, while I retaliated with Fire and Telekinesis, using them to push him farther back into the box. Soon enough, I'd begun to learn his moves without even realizing. It was almost as though there was a time lag on him, my mind knowing what he was going to do before he did it. The thread of Darkness had given me a peculiar clarity, letting my mind process his actions rapidly. Using this new sense, I hurled Fire at him, time and time again, each blast striking him precisely where I wanted it to. With every blow I landed, he started to look more and more frustrated, his eyes narrowing as he tried to twist and turn away from my attacks.

This is insane! If I could do this with Leviathan, then I already had a head start with Naima. I'd seen her fight before, and I could use that to my advantage, avoiding all of the preamble I'd had to go through with Leviathan. I mean, providing I actually survived this encounter. Tobe had assured me that he wouldn't let Leviathan kill me, but even Tobe seemed alarmed by how quick this bastard was. I'd seen him go for the door a couple of times, only to step back, a worried expression on his furry face. Even I was starting to worry, even though I knew Leviathan had a deal to keep with his mother, which should have kept me safe. But he was so into the fight that I started to worry that he'd forgotten he was supposed to keep me alive, to fulfill that promise.

Now, I just needed to find a way to make Leviathan stay still. No matter how many blows I landed on his armor plating, it wasn't doing much to slow him down, and until that happened, my reverse Empathy was fairly useless. He could take the beatings I was sending his way, and I was pretty sure his stamina would outlast mine, if it came to that.

After singeing him with yet another beam of Fire, I took a quick moment to look over his body, picking out the transparent pockets that were only half covered by the armor plating. Most of them were cloudy, as if the gelatinous layer was quite thick, but there was one tiny pocket that was entirely see-through. It rested just beneath his chest, wedged in the gap between two of the lobster-like plates. That was my target—a possible weakness that I could exploit.

Lifting my palms, I sent out an intense blast of Telekinesis, focusing it on that one sweet spot. He went thundering backward, smacking into the glass with a slam so loud that I could've sworn the box actually cracked. At the very least, he'd made it rock on its plinth. Wade and Finch jumped back in shock.

This is it—now or never. Grappling for a fresh ball of churning emotion, I felt it swirl within me, crackling and powerful. I let it surge out of me, hitting the weakened Leviathan almost as hard as he'd hit the glass.

"Obey me!" I bellowed, the sound howling out of my throat with a painful tear, my lungs burning as they struggled to contain the volume.

"You will obey me!" It hurt so badly, but I couldn't give up. Getting slammed into the box, or squeezed to death by tentacles, hurt a lot more.

Leviathan's oddly human eyes took on a faraway look. He sank down onto the coils of his tail and bent his head.

"I will obey," he said quietly. *Is this another game?* There was only one way to find out.

"Kneel for me," I commanded.

He did it, even without legs, rising up proudly before flattening himself on the floor at my feet.

"Show me your weak spot." He lifted the armored plate to reveal the jelly-like patch where I'd struck him. "Now bow to me."

His head dipped to his chest.

Against all odds, I really had done it. Even if I couldn't do this to Katherine, with all her ritual-infused power, manipulating Naima would bring us one step closer to ending her. I now had the skill to get Naima to spill her guts, which would hopefully give us the clear location we needed.

With a smile on my face, despite feeling like I was about to collapse with fatigue, I left Leviathan where he was and walked to the door of the box. Hurriedly, Tobe let me out, and I emerged triumphant but exhausted. My clothes were tattered, and I was covered in bruises and cuts, but my determination had only grown stronger.

I'd barely caught my breath when Wade sprinted over, enveloping me in his arms. I sank into his warm hug, nuzzling his shoulder.

"You're in one piece," he murmured. "Thank God, you're in one piece."

"Well, as far as we know," I replied, chuckling.

"Don't you EVER do that to us again!" Finch put his arms around both me and Wade and squeezed us tight.

"Isn't that the point, that I do it at least one more time?" I smiled into Wade's shoulder.

"Well… yeah, but don't get slammed around like that," Finch said. "You've got precious human bones, remember? They're not made of Adamantium. You aren't Wolverine. Things won't just grow back and heal like magic."

I pulled away from Wade and looked at Finch with a grin. "Precious human bones?"

"Yes, very precious," he replied. "They're Merlin bones. They're… family bones. My family bones."

"Are we skeletons now?" I chuckled, but he looked deadly serious.

"I mean it. You're literally the one piece of family I've got left—that I actually want to associate with, anyway. You're the only person in my family that I can be proud of. And if you'd been killed by that hulking sea worm, I'd have slathered him in melted butter and eaten the bastard." He smiled awkwardly, a hint of the usual Finch mischief glinting in his eyes. "So thanks for not embarrassing me. Can you imagine the humiliation?"

I smirked. "You were so close, Finch."

"Have to keep you on your toes, Sis."

My phone pinged in my pocket. How that thing was still working after being slammed around was beyond me. I retrieved it, to find that there wasn't even a crack in the screen. The message icon flashed, and I swiped it open to see a message from Alton. I stepped back from Finch and Wade so they couldn't read the sender's name, covering the screen discreetly with one hand as I read it. He had news for me. Big news.

"Sorry to duck out on you, but I think I need to hurl." The excuse popped into my head. It wasn't my strongest, but it'd have to do for now.

"What? But you just—" Wade tried to protest.

"Seriously, I'm feeling really green right now," I replied, already speed-walking toward the door. "The stench in there, it'd be enough to make anyone sick."

"Should I prepare further training?" Tobe called after me.

I glanced back. "No, I think I've got it, and I'd like to still be in one piece when we face Naima."

"But… skeletons!" Finch blurted out, making me smile sadly as I focused on what lay ahead. I didn't quite know what he was trying to say, but I appreciated the sentiment.

However, right now, me and my precious human bones had something else to attend to. And while I might have felt like crap for acting like this with them, it was all for their own good, in the end.

NINETEEN

Harley

I headed for Alton's puny study, jogging through the hallways.

The SDC had been weirdly quiet since the news of Isadora's death, with lots of the usual inhabitants choosing to keep away, but it looked like they were flocking back, slowly but surely. Groups wandered through the halls, walking infuriatingly slowly, but I tried to keep my head down and not shove my way through. I felt their eyes on me and heard the soft hiss of their whispering as I passed by. They were scared of me, not only because of my power, but because it was *my* aunt who'd died.

I wasn't assuming they blamed me for it, but a nasty pattern was emerging: wherever I went, tragedy hit. First with the president of the United Covens, and now closer to home. I was a walking, talking, breathing jinx. They didn't even need to whisper; I could feel their suspicion and anxiety bombarding me as I tried to get past them. Some of them even wrenched their arms away, in case I accidentally brushed up against them. *What, do you think you'll be next or something if you get too close?* I may as well have had some plague, from the way they were looking at me. Then again, it could've had something to do with the fact that I looked like I'd been dragged through a hedge backward, my clothes all torn up and my body covered in who knows what.

Ignoring it as best I could, my mind turned to Alton and the news he had for me. I was keeping all my extremities crossed that it was going to be the good kind. I was already on a high from controlling Leviathan, and I really didn't want anyone killing that buzz. It'd been a long while since I'd felt this positive about my mission to end Katherine. If he threw a wrench in the works, I'd deflate like a kid's balloon.

Reaching the turn-off that led toward Alton's office, I paused and shot a look over my shoulder. Someone was watching me. I scoured the passersby, trying to sense them out with Empathy, but I couldn't feel anything weird, aside from the blatant terror they felt for me. And yet, the hairs were prickling on the back of my neck, my skin tingling as though there were eyes on me. My instincts were sky-high, everything on alert. I didn't know if that was because of my Darkness's little feast in the Bestiary, or if it was just because I needed to be on my guard these days. Either way, my senses were sharp as a knife, my cells jangling in warning.

Is Katherine here? I peered back into the throngs of people, but I wouldn't have been able to spot her even if she was. There were a number of Shapeshifters in the coven, and just because I sensed a lack of emotion, that didn't mean it would be her. She'd duped us all with the Rita Bonnello disguise, and none of us had seen it coming. All her actions were carefully planned, to the tiniest detail. I'd learned that the hard way.

Puzzled, I pressed on through the corridor toward Alton's office, keeping those instincts on their highest level. I kept on walking, reaching the next turn through the endless hallways. As I turned the corner, a familiar figure pushed through the hall to catch up to me.

Finch... for Pete's sake. I'd have to be clever if I planned to lose him.

Darting into the corridor before he could reach it, I sprinted toward a smaller corridor to the left and headed down it. This was an annoying detour to have to take, but I couldn't have Finch eavesdropping on anything Alton had to say to me. I kept running and lunged into the next hallway, pressing myself up against the wall and peeking around the edge. Finch crossed the entrance to the smaller corridor, heading in the wrong direction, walking quickly. I smiled to myself. *This is all for your sake, Finch. You'll understand soon enough.*

Satisfied that I'd lost him, I continued with my detour, racking my brain to find a way to circle back. There were a few connecting corridors that led to Alton's office, and though it would take me a bit longer than expected, I was pretty sure I could get there without being spotted.

A few minutes later, heading down yet another corridor, with only one more to get through before I reached Alton, I skidded to a halt. The hairs on the back of my neck were standing up again. I glanced back, to see if I could see anyone in the hallway behind me, but it was empty. The corridor in front, on the other hand, was swarming with people.

I peered out from my hiding spot, keeping to the shadows, determined to pick Finch out of the crowd. Only, I couldn't see him at all. Being a Shapeshifter, he could have been literally any one of these people —a sly fish in the sea of magicals who were currently passing through this part of the coven.

It was close to lunchtime, and I wasn't too far from the Banquet Hall, so I figured they were on a mass exodus to get the plumpest of the chef's specialty burritos. My mouth watered at the thought of food. Kicking Leviathan's ass had taken it out of me, and my stomach was growling. But lunch would have to wait for now.

Using the crowd to shield me, I reached the opposite side of the hallway and ducked behind a dragon statue. They never ceased to amaze me, towering over the coven like gigantic bronze sentinels. If they were supposed to be the guardians of this place, they'd been slacking lately.

Slinking back into the shadow of the dragon, I took out the piece of charmed chalk that Remington had given me and scraped it against the wall, hurriedly drawing a doorway. It was wobbly and alarmingly narrow, but it would have to do for now. I really hated all this sneaking around, but I couldn't let Finch in on what I was planning. I wasn't trying to be a hero; I was just trying to save their lives.

"*Aperi Si Ostium*," I whispered, focusing on where I wanted to go. A bright light shot through the chalk markings, sparking like a lit fuse, and turning my awkward 2-D drawing into a real-life door.

Slipping the chalk back into my pocket, I turned the handle and opened the door out onto Alton's office. When I slammed it behind me, Alton jumped out of his seat.

"What the—!" Alton almost knocked his chair over as he stumbled back against the wall. "How did you get in here?"

I smiled. "You're not the only one with secret ways around the coven."

"No, seriously. How did you get in here?" His breathing slowly returned to normal.

"A spell," I replied.

"Well, I guessed you hadn't learned how to walk through walls." He offered a nervous grin. "But the fact remains—you shouldn't know how to do that spell, Harley."

I shrugged. "I've been picking things up along the way. Turns out, I can be a pretty good student when I want to be."

"You're here now, and I suppose that's all that matters." He paused. "I imagine you used that spell to get here without detection?"

I nodded. "That's about the crux of it, yeah."

"Were you followed?"

"No."

"Are you sure?"

"I wouldn't have used that spell otherwise," I replied. "Nobody knows I'm here talking to you. I'd like to keep it that way, and I'm guessing you would, too."

His brow furrowed. "Yes… Yes, I would."

"Are you *sure*?" He didn't sound like it.

"I understand your reasoning behind keeping things quiet, and I've agreed to do so," he said, after a moment. "Now, if you'll take a seat, we can discuss how things are progressing."

I crossed the room and took the chair opposite, leaning eagerly up on the desk. "So, does that mean things *are* progressing, then? I was terrified you were going to tell me you'd changed your mind, or you couldn't find anyone to help you out."

"On the contrary, I've actually reached out to all of the remaining Necromancers who I thought might be able to assist us."

My eyes widened. "Have any of them said yes?"

"I'm getting to that," he replied sharply. "Unfortunately, one of them was recently killed in a raid on the Wellington Coven's repository in New Zealand, presumably by Katherine's cultists. I didn't know her well, but it pained me to hear that she'd been murdered so cruelly. Anyway, that left me with two options."

A stab of fear hit me in the chest. If the cultists had killed another Necromancer, then that meant she was the second one to die because of Katherine, after the one who'd botched Grandpa Shipton's resurrection. Why was she going around murdering Necromancers? Surely, she needed them for her messed-up new world? Then again, I guessed she only really needed one, in order to make more.

"What about the other two?" I pressed.

"One of them vehemently refused to get involved. The mere mention of what I was asking sent her into hysterics, and she slammed the phone down on me, after screaming, 'No!' I can still hear it ringing in my ears. She didn't want to know what it was for, so I didn't exactly get to explain what was at stake. The moment I said 'Katherine' she was already out of the running."

"And the other one?" My hopes were starting to fade.

Alton sighed. "Well... he did say yes."

"What?" I gasped. "Are you serious?"

"As luck would have it, I'm very serious. However, given the highly illegal and insanely risky nature of what we're asking of him, he's insisted that we be discreet about it and tell no one. He's a very well-respected magical, and I get the feeling he doesn't want his name dragged through the dirt if anyone were to find out about what we're going to do. Or go to Purgatory, for that matter."

"That was our plan anyway," I muttered.

He nodded. "I just wanted to let you know what his terms were, so don't go shooting the messenger."

I raised my hands in mock surrender. "No guns here, Alton."

"Good."

"Who is this dude?"

"His name is Davin Doncaster," he replied. "And he's an exceptionally gifted and powerful Necromancer, so we're very lucky to have him on board. If anyone can pull off something of this magnitude, it's him."

I smiled. "Hey, you've got talent. I'm sure he's nothing compared to you."

Alton chuckled. "While I'd love to believe that, Davin is infinitely better at Necromancy than I am. He's had a lot more practice."

"Oh?" I didn't know if that was a good thing or a bad thing, given everyone's thoughts on that particular ability.

"I said he was a very well-respected magical, but there's a tricky side to him, too. Davin is a Neutral, with roguish tendencies. The elite adore him, but that's only because he offers something that they want. In some parts of the world, they revere what he can do, and that has made him arrogant over the years. Plus, it has made him extremely difficult to work with, especially since he believes the hype about himself and his abilities. But, as he's the only one willing to help, we don't really have any other options. I'd prefer not to work with him at all, but desperate times... Just be prepared for a lot of egotism and a devil-may-care manner to go with it."

I gave a nervous laugh. "You're not exactly painting the best picture here, Alton."

"I want to paint an honest picture," he replied. "Davin is unlike any other Necromancer I've ever met. He flaunts his abilities, and he doesn't care what people think of it. He thinks he's superior, and, while he has the talent to back it up, it doesn't make him a pleasant person to be around."

"You sound like you're intimidated by him." I put it out there, bluntly.

Alton sighed. "Perhaps. He's just an... extreme individual, that's all. I want you to be ready, if you decide to go ahead with this, because both of us will be the ones putting up with him. And, like I said, I'd prefer to be as far away from that man as possible, not because he's inherently dangerous, but because he can be reckless."

"I hate to say it, but reckless is what we need," I said. "We have to go ahead with this, even if he's a tool."

Alton laughed weakly. "I know we do, but it doesn't hurt to be cautious." His expression darkened. "I don't trust Davin, but you're right. We need to take risks, going forward. If we want to do the Hidden Things spell, then he's our only chance. But don't say I haven't warned you, when he starts smarming about."

"Noted." I flashed him an encouraging grin.

"All right, then." Alton braced himself. "I've given Davin the location where we're going to meet up and do this, but I'll tell you more about it when we rendezvous tonight."

"Tonight?" I almost fell off my chair.

"Too soon?" He looked genuinely worried.

I shook my head. "No, no, not at all. I just wasn't expecting you to hit me with that."

"I thought we should move quickly."

"For sure. Sorry, you just caught me off guard there."

"I'm sorry," he replied, with a smile. "So, with such a short timeframe, I suggest you spend the rest of the day collecting all of the ingredients you need for the spell. Is that doable?"

"I don't know. You tell me." I took a piece of paper out of my pocket, before sliding it over the desk. I'd written down all the ingredients the Hidden Things spell required. They'd been tiny footnotes to that mind-boggling poem, and the list was as long as my elbow.

He looked over it, nodding to himself. "Some of these are fairly rare, but the majority can be found in the coven or at Waterfront Park. I'll put you in touch with some magical smug—uh, traders, that I know, in case you have trouble getting what you need."

"You were going to say 'smugglers,' weren't you?"

He smiled. "I wasn't a director for all those years without pulling a string here and there. Just let me write the numbers down, and you should be good to go."

As he took out his phone and jotted numbers and names down, I watched him closely, grateful to have him on my side. This spell was going to be difficult, and it was going to be scary as hell. I hadn't forgotten his warning about the possibility of the land of the living clashing with the realm of the afterlife, letting billions of the dead back into our world. He'd also warned me about everything that could go awry with my mom and dad—zombies, mixed memories, all that worrying stuff. There was every chance that it could go horribly wrong, and I needed to be ready for any and all outcomes. But that wasn't going to stop me from being a little bit hopeful that we might just pull this thing off. It didn't have to be all doom and gloom just yet.

"There you go." He slid the note back across the desk, like we were finishing up a dirty deal.

"What are you going to do while I'm foraging for all of this?" I slipped the note in my pocket.

"I'll make sure we have two bodies ready by midnight," he replied, his tone strange and unsettled. "As you know, I can't use Isadora and Suri, not that I'd want to. But I have some ideas."

"It's probably best I don't know about that, right?"

He chuckled, but it didn't reach his eyes. "Yes, it's probably best."

Alton the Graverobber was a prospect I couldn't quite deal with right now, but I trusted him to get the job done. Just as he trusted me to do my part. The secrets of the Grimoire were in my grasp, so close I could almost feel them.

TWENTY

Katherine

Suitably smug about my little chat with Alakazoosh, or whatever he called himself, I had to put my perfect nose back to the proverbial grindstone.

Well, Imogene's nose.

I might've loathed her, but playing this role came with its perks. There was something so titillating about wandering amongst these people, without them having a single clue that their greatest enemy was literally staring them in the face. I got a kick out of it every damn time.

My bracelet had come in exceptionally handy. I'd been gifted it by a mystical shaman in the middle of the Arabian desert, when I was four days into a journey of enlightenment, and close to death, with no food, no water, and no hope. He'd appeared out of nowhere, leading a camel, and guided me to safety, to a Bedouin camp where the children gathered around me and welcomed me like a hero.

Only kidding—I stole it from a vault of ancient artifacts in Vilnius, Lithuania, early on in my journey to become a Child of Chaos, around the time I'd decided I needed to infiltrate a Mage Council or two. I'd lied to Harley about it being an emotion blocker; that stupid girl couldn't sense my emotions, since I was a Shapeshifter and all. She didn't know about this particular party trick. It was one of the reasons I'd gone after the pretty piece in the first place. I'd known, years ago, that if I really wanted to make the Imogene scheme work—*I love a rhyme*—I'd have to find something that would keep out pesky Empaths. Or, rather, find something that could cover the reason they couldn't sense me, and stop them from realizing I was a Shapeshifter.

What this bracelet actually did was fake emotions. It had itty-bitty canisters of pilfered emotions inside it, stolen from some poor saps and trapped within. All I had to do was pick one and push the right teeny-weeny button, and bingo—I could trick anyone into thinking I was warm and fuzzy, my insides marshmallow soft. The emotions emanated from the bracelet, not me. All I had to do was put in the amateur dramatics of taking it off, as though I were baring my soul, and the bracelet did the rest. Screw all those Tiffany monstrosities covered in garish diamonds; I'd take one of these babies, any day of the week.

Good thing I never told anyone about it. I smirked, thinking of Finch. That little worm thought he had all my secrets, but he couldn't have been more wrong. Mama had kept a few choice morsels to herself, and they just happened to be the finest cuts.

Giving the infirmary a wide berth for now, since the bookworm and the German had decided to get back to business, I headed for Geek HQ, also known as Astrid's Control Room. I knew the djinn was bound by Erebus not to say a word about me, but I didn't feel like chancing it with an audience. One fleeting hint of rebellion by Alakazam and my entire charade would be toast, and I'd worked too hard to let that happen.

I was halfway down the corridor, when I happened upon two of Harley's Merry Men. The Jock and the Russian. I never liked to think about many people by their real names. Creating amusing nicknames was part of the fun. Although, I confess, I was getting sloppy with so many other things on my mind. The Jock and the Russian were hardly inventive. *Beefcake and the Koldun-What-Now?* That was better.

"Tatyana, Dylan, is something the matter?" They looked like crap and didn't seem to be speaking to each other. *Ah, young love.* The squabbles and the making up, the squabbles and the making up, in an endless freaking cycle of hormones and weakness.

Tatyana shot a look at Dylan that could've felled a smaller man. "No, Imogene, everything's fine. We reached a dead end, that's all."

"In your pursuit of the cultists?" Oh yes, I knew everything these insipid critters were up to. I even got hourly reports, which was just perfection. Who needed the hassle of trackers when they literally texted me where they were and what they were doing?

Dylan nodded. "Yeah, we managed to find Constance and Ozzy, and we tried to go after them, but we lost them after a while. Taty said we should go one way and I said we should go another. Turns out, if we'd gone my way, we might've found them again." He sighed. "Anyway, it was a dead end. They vanished, and there haven't been any more alerts on them, so who knows where they are now?"

Back at Eris Island, where they ought to be. I'd had Naima portal them back, after a suitable period of time had passed, once I'd heard these two had planned to go after them.

"You don't know that," Tatyana shot back. This was about to get juicy. I loved a PDA—public display of animosity.

"Know what?" he replied.

"That we'd have found them if we'd gone your way."

He shrugged. "I'm just saying, I've got a better sense of direction than you. You almost sent us down the wrong turn-off on the way there *and* back."

"I was listening to the GPS!" Tatyana protested. As if you could trust those useless things.

"Arguing is not the way to resolve problems," I cut in, though I was desperate to see things turn nasty. Imogene wouldn't have allowed it to get that far, so I couldn't, either. "It's unfortunate that those cultists managed to escape, but there will be other opportunities. I was just on my way to see Astrid and the others, to see how they were coming along. Perhaps you could join me so that you can see if there are other cultists you can go after?"

Tatyana offered me a grateful smile that made my insides giddy. *No clue.* "Yes, I think that'd be a good idea. This one's phone died on the way back and mine is barely hanging on, or we would've called ahead to let everyone know what had happened."

"What, and that's my fault, too?" Dylan muttered. "I don't control phone battery."

"I wasn't saying that," Tatyana shot back. "I just meant we didn't have a way to call anyone."

"It would seem as though the stress of destroying Katherine is getting to everyone, which is only to be expected," I said. "Come with me to see Astrid and try to hug it out along the way. This is nobody's fault."

Dylan lowered his gaze. "Sorry, Taty."

She smiled. "I'm sorry, too. Being in that car—I think I've got cabin fever."

And so the cycle begins again. Turning away as they smooshed into one another, I carried on down the hall, leaving them to it. They'd catch up once they realized I'd already gone. *That* kind of PDA wasn't something I wanted to have to see, not after I'd just had my lunch.

Sure enough, they came to a halt beside me as I reached the beating heart of the SDC's technological prowess—otherwise known as a human and her silly tablet. I had to hold in a snort every time she referred to that thing as "he." I mean, the girl was pretty weird to begin with, always staring around with big, vacant eyes. She hadn't always been like that, not when I'd encountered her before, and I had a feeling that was my fault, which only made it funnier. I remembered her cracking her head open on the altar in the Asphodel Meadows, and all her little chums crying and screaming, with that big brute, Garrett, whisking her away like an action hero. It had been laughable then, and it was even more laughable now.

Clearly, Alton had resurrected her, and things hadn't quite gone according to plan. That girl had definitely been rapping on death's door when she'd hit the altar. Poor Papa Waterhouse, left with a fleshy void for a daughter.

Flanked by the Action Hero and Miss Mexico, said fleshy void turned as I made my grand entrance into her base of operations—it was nothing more than her private study, transformed into a haphazard control room. "Imogene? Has something happened?"

"No, no, nothing to worry yourselves over. I just thought I'd come to see how things were going," I replied. Yeah, it was definitely a "lights on but no one's home" type of vibe with her, now. Tom and Jerry followed sheepishly behind me, evidently devastated that they were going to have to admit defeat. *Geez, why are they all so dramatic?* They were starting to put me to shame.

"What's up with you two?" Santana nodded to the two twerps shuffling beside me. "I thought you were supposed to be in Pasadena."

Dylan shook his head. "They disappeared."

"Are you friggin' kidding me?" Santana sat back in her chair. *Easy, tiger.*

"They must have gotten wind that we were after them and made a run for it," Tatyana replied. Well, at least they were working together now. So sweet. Not.

"How's it going here?" Dylan approached the bleeping computers that surrounded Astrid. It was no CIA, that was for sure. My intelligence team was in far better shape than these punks, but then, I had the common sense to put the time and effort into my people, unlike some folks I could mention. *Levi...*

Speaking of the CIA, they'd be wetting their pants if they could see my operation. The fact that I was getting away with everything, right under the noses of the humans, was even more satisfying than pulling the wool over the magicals' eyes. At least they knew what they were up against. With the humans, they had no idea, and they wouldn't until they were on their knees, bowing to their new and beauteous overlord.

"Not great," the Void replied.

Garrett nodded. "We've been scouring every outlet, and we haven't seen hide or hair of Naima or Katherine... or anyone, really. It's like they've all dropped off the face of the earth."

Ha, Naima would rip your throat out if she heard you saying she had a hide.

As for the curious absence of any and all cultists, that was my doing. I'd warned them all to keep a low profile, though I wasn't about to cease my operations altogether. I had a world to conquer, after all. I couldn't just go into lockdown because a couple of jumped-up kiddos were trying to take me down. That would've made me a laughingstock. Besides, they didn't stand a chance. All of this was for nothing. They could scour and pursue and search all they liked. By the time they actually got into a bit of action, it'd be too little, too late.

And I'm right beside you. I felt like giving my hands a little wave or doing a little jig to say, "Ta-da! Here I am!" but I managed to swallow the urge. I'd get my satisfaction later.

"Is Raffe not with you?" I couldn't see him anywhere, but maybe they were keeping him under the desk, like a good little dog.

Santana shook her head. "He locked himself up hours ago so he could have a word with Kadar. At least I know they can't do any damage to each other. That's one benefit of having a boyfriend who's got two people in one body. No matter how heated things get, they can't come to blows."

I can think of a few other benefits. I stifled a smirk, nodding sympathetically. "It must be hard for him. I couldn't imagine it, having to deal with two personalities, never knowing which one will take control. He must be exhausted."

"Yeah, he's having a rough time, but hopefully they'll have come to some arrangement by the time he gets out of his cell," she replied.

"I'm sure they'll come to realize there are bigger conflicts to contend with," I assured her. "And it shouldn't be long before Leonidas is fully healed, which will likely ease the rift between them. I know how troubled Raffe was by what his djinn did. Perhaps Leonidas awakening will prove to be their olive branch."

"I hope so." Santana sighed.

The worst thing about being surrounded by these ingrates was seeing the colossal waste of potential. Even just in this room, we had the daughter of the famed Catemaco family, who would've been set to take over the legacy of that coven, if I didn't plan to ascend and eradicate all of those dynasties. They were too dangerous to allow to remain as they were. The same went for Tatyana and her Kolduny clans.

I wasn't going to kill everyone, don't get me wrong, but I couldn't have powerful families sticking together. That was a recipe for rebellion. They'd be separated, naturally, with those who were obedient being allowed to live, and those who weren't… well, I'd said it enough times. Death, death, and more death, executed in a thousand creative ways.

"Sorry we don't have better news," Tatyana said, so wonderfully shamefaced. It was pure poetry. "I wish we could've had something good to tell you."

There she was, a fearsome Kolduny, with the clout of that ancestry behind her. She'd have made a welcome addition to my cult, but there was a stubbornness in her that made me pretty certain she would have to be put down. *Such a shame.* I appreciated beauty, and she was beautiful not only in her looks but in her power, too. It was going to be like slicing a big rake across a rare painting, but I didn't mind destroying a pretty thing or two, if necessity called for it. Her death would certainly make the rest of the Kolduny listen up.

"Hey, it's not as if we're doing any better," Garrett replied.

I often sidelined him in my mind, but Garrett had come from a good magical family, too. He'd certainly proven useful in LA, scurrying around after me like my own personal Igor, doing my bidding and asking, "How high?" whenever I said, "Jump." Perhaps there was hope for him. I couldn't say the same for the others.

"Can't you soup up Smartie?" Dylan asked. "Isn't there some app or something you can download to let us see more?"

Oh yeah, because it's that easy. I struggled not to roll my eyes.

"He's already working overtime," Astrid replied sadly. "He's covering the globe right now."

There you go again with the "he."

I shuddered discreetly, turning my attention back to Dylan. He showed some promise, despite being more brawn than brain. I could certainly understand what Tatyana saw in him, especially in the eye-poppingly tight T-shirt he had on, but her parents must've been so disappointed. She could have had her pick of the rich, formidable oligarchs, and she'd chosen the Jock. Even Louella was a force to be reckoned with, her mind bright and her spirit strong, but she was definitely not going to see my brave new world. I needed her for a greater purpose.

"Perhaps you could visit places where Katherine has previously been," I suggested, flexing my power to send them on yet another wild goose chase. I never used the same place twice, and I never left evidence behind.

"That's not a bad idea," Santana replied. "We haven't been back to the docklands or anything. We might find something there that we've missed. I can go and get Raffe, see if he's done fighting with Kadar, and head there now?"

Ah, Raffe...

He'd have made an exceptional minion, but I'd have to see how things turned out before I made a decision about him. His lineage was mighty, with all that ancient Persian goodness flowing in his veins, and I'd definitely be forcing the djinn to toe the line. So, who knew, maybe he'd survive to see what I had planned for this world.

As for the others, the jury was still out. Some might make it, some might not. Although, I did have that promise to keep to Harley. I told her I'd make her watch as all her friends died. I told her I'd crush her under the weight of her own grief. I told her I'd destroy her by destroying them. I may have been paraphrasing, but the gist remained. And I couldn't go back on a promise, now, could I?

"I think that sounds like an excellent plan." I forced enthusiasm into my voice, hiding a secret smile. There was nothing in the docklands for them to find. My cleanup team was way better than anything the SDC had to offer.

"I'll come with you," Tatyana insisted.

"Me, too." Dylan nodded.

Of course they were going together, the romantic little quartet. It was going to be deeply enjoyable to tear them away from one another someday soon. They'd weep and wail and put on a heartbreaking show, and I couldn't wait. Who needed TV when you could have this kind of drama, with me pulling the strings? *Dance, my little puppets, dance.*

They could all have been much greater, but they were just so limited and vain. I wanted to sigh, but that wouldn't have been very Imogene. If they hadn't been so caught up in family dramas and soapy romances, they might even have seen the wolf amongst them, eyeing up the tasty sheep for the end of days. Fortunately for me, they continued to allow their paltry problems to get in the way. That was the key to success—feel nothing, aim high, and never get bogged down by the silly, unimportant stuff. It'd served me well so far.

"Should we call Harley, let her know the plan?" Astrid asked, ever the voice of logic.

That robot was never getting her soul back, but maybe that wasn't such a bad thing. The whole soulless vibe meant I wouldn't have to deal with *another* nauseating couple, pawing at each other. I could tell that was what Garrett wanted from her. *Tough luck, bucko.* With no soul, how could she love? With Davin back on the scene, I almost wished I could remove my soul for a little bit, although I was probably going to lose that at some point, anyway. Children of Chaos didn't need souls, and they didn't need pesky, sexy-as-hell, delicious men like Davin Doncaster, either.

Santana shook her head. "I think she's still busy with Finch and Wade."

"Oh? Perhaps I ought to pay them a visit, see how things are going. I could pass the message on, if you like," I said, my interest piqued. They were the only folks whose mission I wasn't clear on. I presumed they'd gone to pore over that stupid book, but maybe I was wrong.

"It's okay, I'll just give them a quick call," Tatyana cut in, a little too quickly for my tastes. *Hmmm...*

"Are they studying the Grimoire?" I wasn't about to let them hoodwink me. If they were preparing for the Hidden Things spell, I wanted to know how far along they were. I supposed I'd know soon enough, once I spoke with Davin.

"I think so," Garrett replied. "Harley's been acting weird, so who knows where she is." His words settled my creeping concerns. While the others had answered quickly, he took his time, his expression genuine. He didn't seem to be trying to lie.

"Can you blame her?" I replied, attempting sadness. "If it were me, I would have locked myself in my room and stayed there. To have lost so much... It breaks your heart to think of all she's been through. And still, she continues to persevere. She's remarkable."

Santana smiled. "Yeah, she is."

Finch could've been remarkable, but he'd only ended up disappointing me. He'd had all the opportunity in the world, handed to him on a silver platter, and yet he'd still become nothing but a giant failure. Yes, that silver platter had been riddled with obstacles, but that was character-building. How else was he supposed to have learned?

It was becoming clearer that I was going to have to kill him if I had the opportunity, if only to tie off that loose end. Even if I forced him to join me, it would never be the same. There was too much water under the bridge, and I planned to drown him in it. Plus, that would really kick Harley where it hurt. She'd finally gotten the brother she'd always dreamed about, most likely, and I was going to take that away from her.

But I couldn't do it myself. He was my flesh and blood. I'd given birth to him. I'd watched him take his first breath, though he'd naturally started screaming almost immediately. I should've known then that he would only fail me. To be honest, I hated myself for that one weakness. My son. The only way to rid myself of that was to kill Finch, but I needed someone else to do it for me—someone who could actually get it right, unlike wormy Kenneth.

If you want something done right, you do it yourself. The mantra circled inside my head, but it didn't make a difference. I just couldn't do that with Finch. I needed another way of ending him... or, maybe, I'd just strip him of all his magic when I ascended and be done with it. Exile him somewhere, where I'd never have to see his face again. Antarctica, maybe. That way, if he wanted his magic back, he'd have to surrender himself to me, forever. Otherwise, he'd just be a benign and worthless human. Or an icicle, depending on where I sent him.

You could have been remarkable, too. It saddened me and troubled me, in equal measure. Unbeknownst to my little ray of sunshine, I'd implanted a version of the Dempsey Suppressor in him when he was a baby. There was more Chaos in him than he thought. Maybe not as much as his darling Sis, since it would've cracked by now if that'd been the case, but it was enough to worry me, if it was ever released. I'd always planned to help him remove it, when the time came, but he'd shown he didn't deserve that power. It really was a shame.

There were maybe a few days left before I ascended, depending on how fast I could get the last two rare magicals I needed. Even if Finch did find out, that didn't leave enough time for him to do anything about it. It had taken Princess Harley long enough to break hers, and she had more Chaos in her than anyone deserved... aside from me, of course. I deserved it all, and I was going to get it, soon enough.

"If you're all heading out to see what you can find, I ought to make myself useful," I said. "I'll go to the infirmary and see how Louella is faring." I wasn't going to do that, of course, but I had to make it look like I was going to do something suitably mushy and Imogene-like. Dealing with waifs and strays was her hobby, and sobbing over them was her sickening MO.

"Give her our love," Santana replied.

I nodded. "Of course." *Yeah, right.* I was more likely to knock her out than pass on that lame message, given her determination to get Jacob out of his unconsciousness. She was a major thorn in my side, and I was readying the tweezers to rip her out. I wasn't going to allow her to wake him up, not before I decided to let him. I had big plans for Jakey. When my new dawn rose, he was going to be my favorite pet, zipping here and there at my beck and call. Oh yes, he'd be one of the lucky ones.

When I ascended, people would envy his position at my side. They might not like bowing and scraping, to begin with, but they'd soon see that I'd created something beyond their comprehension, something so beautiful that it would take their breath away. Their minds wouldn't be able to envision it right now, but mine could. Mine had. In my world, there would be no war, no suffering, no hiding in the shadows. Everyone would be free to be the very thing they were born to be. The magicals who obeyed would have their Chaos returned, and they would be at liberty to do whatever they pleased, as long as they didn't cross me. They could live in harmony and luxury, commandeering the humans who'd trodden on us for so long.

If someone was sick, no problem—I'd have medical magicals who could heal anyone and anything. If someone wanted to travel to some far-flung, exotic land, no problem—I'd have Portal Openers on hand to take anyone anywhere, whenever they wanted. If there was a conflict, I'd nip it in the bud. If there was famine, I'd fix it. If there was a drought, I'd bring the rain. If someone wanted more power, they could have it, as long as they proved themselves.

Once I became a Child of Chaos, all my dreams would come to fruition. I would create a world where I had all the control, where I could do anything and make anything. And they would laud me for it, cheering my name until they forgot about the way the world had once been. Once I took over, there would be no looking back.

TWENTY-ONE

Harley

With the list in my pocket, I jumped around the SDC, using the *Aperi Si Ostium* spell to collect what the coven already had: quicksilver, wolfsbane root, sweet clover, blue sage, ashwagandha, gotu kola, mountain juniper, Malabar nut, winter melon, Indian pennywort, pyrethrum, colocynth, cordyceps, and the seed powder from the black oil plant, whatever that was.

I'd also managed to nick an alchemical catalyst and a Sherlock's Eye. I'd had to call Alton to figure out what the heck I was looking for with those, but he'd told me I could get them from the alchemy lab, since there wouldn't be anyone in there. Turns out, one was a tube of dark purple liquid, and the other was a perfect orb of smooth, solid glass, which weighed a lot more than it looked like it should've, given its smallish size.

The list was huge compared to other spells I'd performed, but then, this was bigger than anything I'd done before. With only one more item on my list, I was well on my way to getting this done before I had to meet with Alton this evening. However, I would definitely need help getting this last one. I'd sent a text to the first number on the list when I'd first left Alton's office, almost two hours ago, knowing I wouldn't find that item anywhere in the SDC. The smuggler had just been under the heading, "Tiny." No real name, no nothing. The other names on the list were the same, all of them nicknames to protect their true identities.

I looked back over the message I'd sent: *Alton said you could help me find some ingredients. Meet me by the manhole covers in Waterfront Park as soon as you can, with the last ingredient on the list, if you can get it.* I'd taken a snapshot of the last item and attached it to the text before sending it into the ether.

I read over their reply: *I'll look into it.* I had no idea who was on the other end, but if Alton trusted them, then I had no reason not to. After all, this was black market business. Real names were dangerous commodities. Still, I was running out of time.

I sent another text: *Any news?*

A moment later, my phone pinged: *Be there in fifteen. Stay put. I'll bring a rose.* A tongue-out emoji sat at the end of the message, standing out weirdly. What kind of smuggler sent an emoji? I guessed I'd find out soon enough, once I got to Waterfront Park.

Opening another doorway in the wall of the repository, I ended up in the creepy maintenance room in the underbelly of Waterfront Park, complete with the clanging coolant pipes and six manhole covers in the grimy floor. The last time I'd come here, Wade and I were visiting Dennehy's World of Wonders—the spiraling, upside-down shop that lay beneath one of those manhole covers. We'd needed the ingredients for a tracer spell to use on Jacob's bracelet in order to find him. The memory made me pause, suddenly breathless. If I hadn't done that spell, Jacob and Isadora would still have been safe. *I've been over this. I had to do it, just like I have to do this.* But that didn't stop the sadness from edging through my veins.

It was dark and damp, and my mind was racing with all the memories of this place. I remembered encountering Bellmore in Dennehy's. I wondered where she was now, after her sudden departure from the SDC, due to personal problems. I wished her well, hoping for a swift resolution of whatever she was suffering through. With the whole Rita Bonnello issue, and Jacintha Parks's death, I didn't like having gaps in the preceptorship. The SDC was incomplete without a full deck of trustworthy people.

Speaking of Rita, she'd stuck to her promise and was wearing the bodycam. I hadn't seen any of the footage, but I was pretty sure that Astrid would contact me if anything fishy happened. It didn't mean I suddenly trusted Rita, but at least she was accounted for.

Astrid, meanwhile, had already sent me a text to say that a group of them were heading out to investigate some of the old sites where we'd encountered Katherine before, which eased my mind slightly. That meant some of the pressure was off my shoulders, at least when it came to keeping my friends out of the way. Finch and Wade were still a problem, in the nicest way possible, but I could avoid them as long as I kept using the *Aperi Si Ostium* spell.

I sat down on the floor in the driest patch I could find and went over the list of ingredients, making sure I had everything. Yep, there was only one more item, and I just hoped that "Tiny" came up with the goods, whoever they were.

I was busy turning the Sherlock's Eye over in my hand, trying to figure out what it actually did, when a shuffling sound on the opposite side of the room made my head snap up. A figure emerged from the gloom, head dipped, half shrouded by a black hoodie. She was definitely female. My eyes were drawn to her exposed midriff, due to the simple fact that I didn't expect smugglers to go around wearing cropped hoodies. Above the waistline of her jeans, I noticed a tattoo that I'd seen before —a pawprint, etched into her skin.

"Kenzie?" I gaped at her. I'd have recognized the Morph anywhere, even without seeing the glint of her bazillion piercings.

She tugged back her hood to reveal her hazel eyes, impish face, and wry smirk. "Surprise!"

"What are you doing here? Are you... Are you here to meet *me*?"

"You asked, I brought. Looks like you found out about my side hustle." She crossed the room, her heavy boots clomping on the floor. The last time we'd met, her mocha-brown hair had been shoved up in a bun, with an undercut over her ear. This time, she'd shaved most of it off, leaving a curly mohawk down the center that flopped over her left eye, adding to her Mad Max vibes.

"You smuggle?"

She chuckled. "I had boxes and boxes of phones and SIM cards, and this is the thing that shocks you? It's all goods to me. Doesn't matter if it's cellphones or ghoul bones, I get the stuff, you give me the cash, everyone goes home happy."

I couldn't believe it. "But this is mega illegal, Kenzie."

"Pot, kettle, black?" She grinned. "You think what you asked me for is sugar and spice, and all things nice? If you're worried about me, don't be. I keep a low profile. Nobody's going to catch me. I get the goods myself, then I use my animal pals to deliver and get the money. I've seen grown-ass men crap their pants at the sight of a six-foot grizzly at their door. Best debt collectors ever."

I frowned. "Then how come you're here now, and not one of your animals?"

"I recognized your number. Couldn't resist." She shrugged.

"Do you have what I asked for?" I wanted to chat for a bit longer, but I didn't have the time.

"Would I be here if I didn't?" She chuckled, and delved into her bag, bringing out a sleek black box. "What do you want them for, anyway?"

"Do smugglers always ask questions?" I replied, smiling. She didn't need to know why I needed the rare bones of a Bai Gu Jing, which literally translated to the White Bone Spirit. I'd done some research before I'd asked "Tiny" to acquire the ingredients for me, although I hadn't gone into nearly as much detail as Astrid would've. From what I could find, the Bai Gu Jing was literally a pile of bones from ancient female Purge beasts of Chinese origin who'd been as sentient in life as Naima or Tobe and hadn't turned back to black smoke when they'd been killed. They could still transform back into their living form on certain nights of the year, and were said to be these beautiful, nymph-like beings. These bones still held the spirit of one.

"Fair point." She handed the box over but stopped short as I reached for it. "Do you have the cash?"

I smirked. "Would I be here if I didn't?"

"Ha, I guess I deserved that."

I rummaged around in my Mary Poppins bag for the money and handed over a heart-wrenching wad. That was pretty much everything

I'd earned during my time in the Fleet Science Center archives, but Alton had promised to give me the money back once all of this was over. *You'd better, Alton, or I'll be the one sending a grizzly to your door.*

"How did you get a hold of this?" I took the box from her as I made the exchange.

"You got lucky. I know a guy in Chinatown, and he had a box of these lying around. Weird thing to just have in your house, but I don't judge."

"Seriously, though, why did you come instead of sending a cat or something?" After the way we'd left things, I'd never imagined I'd see her again. She'd been adamant about staying out of the whole Katherine thing, and yet here she was. She was a clever, streetwise kid—she had to know this had something to do with stopping the end of the world.

She shrugged. "I wanted to. I do the anonymous schtick for most magicals, but I can't trust those folks as far as I can throw them. With you, it's a bit different, y'know? What can I say, you made a mark last time. I thought it'd be cool to see you again, especially with you asking for those weird-ass thingies. You're an odd one, Harley, and odd is cool. I can get down with odd."

She nodded to the box that I was in the middle of stowing away in my bag. Out of anyone else's mouth, her words would've sounded like some cliché hood-talk, but she made it sound almost musical. Like a rapper or a beat poet, every word punchy and precise.

"Does Finch know you're here?" The thought jumped into my head. These two were kind of friends, after all.

Kenzie sighed and glanced over her shoulder. "Ah, busted."

Finch emerged from the shadows behind her, leaving me speechless. Kenzie spun a good yarn about wanting to see me again, but she hadn't come here alone. I should've known, the moment I saw her, that Finch wouldn't be far away. I supposed that was what I got for thinking I could outsmart my brother with charmed chalk and *Aperi Si Ostium* doorways.

"Sorry to gatecrash," he said, with a wry grin.

"Why?" was all I could say, staring at Kenzie.

She met my gaze, a little apologetic. "I didn't know what you were getting yourself into. I spoke to my dude in Chinatown, and he was crazy agitated about giving the bones to me. I had to go back out and Morph with a fox, and pretend to be a fox spirit, to get him to give in. The Chinese are mega scared of those creatures, if you ever need a way out of an argument with one of them. Anyway, when I Morphed back into my own body, and after he'd stopped cursing me, he kept chattering about the bones being mad dangerous." She paused, lowering her gaze. "Call it friendly concern for a cool compadre."

"She did the right thing," Finch added. "We were both worried about what you were up to. I mean, who needs ancient Asian ghoul bones? It's not as if you wanted them to cook up a stock or something. Ugh, can you imagine the taste?"

Irritation bristled through me. For all Kenzie's hipper-than-thou, don't-give-a-crap attitude, she'd gone running to the one person I wanted nowhere near this. I wanted to *Aperi Si Ostium* the heck out of there, but I realized Finch would only follow me. *Give up, please... you have to give up.*

"You shouldn't have done that," I said coldly.

"What, and just let you fiddle with your ghoul bones by yourself?" Finch replied. "No way, Sis. I want to know what you're going to do with them, and I'm not leaving until you spill the beans. I let it slide last time, but you've been acting like a nutcase."

I narrowed my eyes. "I don't have to explain myself to you, Finch." Jumping up, I made for the door of the maintenance room. If I had to be cruel to be kind, then so be it. Finch wasn't getting involved, end of story. I wouldn't lose my brother as well as my aunt.

"Actually, I've got a ghoul bone to pick with you, Kenzie." He shifted gear, knowing I wouldn't be able to resist my curiosity. "How come you went ahead with the sale, when I asked you not to?"

She looked nervous. "Business is business. You think I can say no to that kind of money?"

"You're too much like me, do you know that?" he replied, genuinely frustrated. "Look, just tell me the truth, Harley. Whatever it is, we'll figure it out."

"I'm already figuring it out. I don't need you." I hated saying that to him, but what choice did I have?

"You know what happens to martyrs, don't you?" His voice sounded strained and thick with emotion. "Heroes end up on plaques and gravestones and monuments. They don't get to live, and they get forgotten about soon enough, so if you're doing this to prove some kind of point, or to wind up in some dusty old history book—don't."

"I don't need to listen to this." I turned and strode to the door, turning the handle. I was about to swing it open when I felt something hit me in the back, knocking me hard into the door itself, my forehead banging off the metal.

"You're going to listen, Harley!" Finch shouted.

I whirled around to face him, though my head was ringing. Lifting my palms, I sent out a violent wave of Telekinesis, my powers still souped-up from feeding my Darkness. It smacked into him way harder than I'd intended, sending him flying across the room. He crashed into the far wall and slumped to the floor, looking up at me in surprise. Tears stung my eyes as I looked back at him, hating what I'd done. Torn between rushing to his side and getting the heck out of there, I knew what I had to do, and it freaking killed me inside.

Turning around, I drew a chalk doorway and whispered the spell, focusing on where I wanted to go. Finch didn't say a word. I pulled down on the handle and paused on the threshold, blocking his view of the other side. A sharp pain splintered through my temples, my brain feeling like it had swollen to twice its size. I knew I was pushing myself too hard, but I couldn't stop now.

"Keep quiet about this," I said, not turning back. "It's for your own good—yours, and Wade's, and the rest of the Rag Team's. You'll understand. I know what I'm doing, and I just need you to trust me on this."

With that, I stepped through and closed the door behind me before I could change my mind.

TWENTY-TWO

Harley

With all the ingredients secured, and my body about to pack it in from exhaustion, I was ready to crash into my pillows and catch some well-earned Zs before night fell. Finch wouldn't follow me here. Even if he banged on the door until his knuckles were raw, I wouldn't let him in. I needed rest.

It should've felt good to be back in my bedroom in the living quarters, but it took a split second to realize I wasn't alone. Wade sat on the bed. He looked up in fright as the doorway slammed, while my heart jolted in complete shock.

"What are you doing here?" I gasped, the doorway disappearing at my back.

"What are you doing, coming through one of those doorways?" His words tumbled out; he was evidently still getting over the surprise of me appearing out of nowhere. *I really need to put some extra charms on my bedroom door.* That was the only way to keep people out, even if I was secretly glad to see them. The trouble was, I knew more questions were coming, and it wasn't going to be easy to lie to the man I loved. He knew me too well.

"I was tired, and it's the quickest way to get here without running into anyone. I know they mean well, but I can't handle being asked how I am for the millionth time," I replied, putting on a weary display as I padded over and sat down next to him, leaning my head on his shoulder.

"So, I shouldn't ask how you're doing, then?" He lay his head down on mine.

"Not right now. Not unless you want a weeping mess to deal with," I said softly. "I just want to sit here for a bit, with you, and forget everything that's happening outside that door. Is that okay?"

At this point, I wasn't even trying to manipulate him away from his potential questioning. I really did just want to sit there, beside him, and forget about the rest of the world for a moment. We hadn't had a chance to be alone for a long time, and I missed just being with him, in this room. Up until recently, this had been my happy place, tucked up in bed with him, watching some dumb movie or another. He'd laugh while I asked a billion questions, and I usually fell asleep before it was over, but that was our routine. And I missed it so much.

"Of course it is," he murmured against my hair, kissing it gently.

I turned my face up toward him, taking in every contour of his face. My fingertips reached out impulsively, grazing the stubble across his jaw. I wanted to remember him exactly like this, in case I never saw him again. I glanced up to meet the intense gaze of his deep green eyes, which looked like sea glass washed up on a stormy shore, so full of emotion and love. Love for me. I could feel it flowing out of him and into the center of my being, lighting up every nerve in a way that neither Darkness nor Light ever could. This was beyond Chaos. Love—real, true love—was stronger than anything magic could conjure up.

My breath caught in my throat as I sank into those beautiful eyes, letting them erase everything else. His hand cupped my cheek. A small smile edged across his sexy lips, heightening the electric shiver before the thunderstorm of our kiss. Anyone who's ever loved someone would know that feeling. It can't be put into words. It's a tension, and a fear, and a release, all at once, knowing that everything will change the moment you kiss them, even if you've done it a thousand times before. Only, this time, it was tinged with a flicker of the bittersweet, because I didn't know if I'd get to do it ever again. I wanted thousands more, but I didn't know if I'd get that chance.

"I love you," I whispered thickly, looping my arms around his neck and clinging to him for dear life.

"I love you, too," he murmured, as he dipped his head and caught my mouth in his.

I kissed him with the desperation of someone with a ticking clock over their head. Every touch, every embrace, every movement of his lips was precious, more precious than it had ever been before. If he thought something was strange, he didn't say anything. Instead, he matched my desperation, kissing me back with a deep, burning desire.

I'm sorry. That was all I wanted to say to him, over and over. I wanted to pull away and explain everything so that I could have him at my side when I performed the spell tonight, but I couldn't do that. Even if I never got to kiss him again, I didn't want to take happiness away from him. Maybe, one day, if I didn't make it, he'd find love again, and I'd smile down on him from wherever I was, knowing that he was safe and happy because of me, even if I couldn't touch him or kiss him again. Naturally, I'd be sick with jealousy, unless there was no such thing in the afterlife.

All those thoughts brought tears to my eyes as I kissed him deeper, reaching for the buttons of his expensive shirt. I made quick work of them, pressing my body flush against the bare muscles of his torso. There was so much strength in him, and I wanted to draw that into me, so I'd have the courage to carry on, even when things got dark in the days to come. His breath had turned to short gasps as he held me, his strong arms gripping me tight as he lay me down beside him on the bed. I reached up to kiss him again, but he moved his head back slightly, his fingertips caressing my cheek as he stared down, a sad smile on his face.

"What's wrong?" I asked.

"Nothing. I just wanted to look at you."

I smiled. "I look tired, right?"

He shook his head. "No, you look beautiful. You always do. I just hate seeing you so sad. I wish I could take all that pain away."

"I don't think that's possible," I said quietly.

"Maybe one day, when all of this Katherine stuff is over."

I nodded, my stomach gripped with guilt. "Maybe."

Wade's phone went off, the buzz of it splitting the tension between us.

I wanted to take it and throw it against the wall, because I knew we'd never get this moment back. It was a harsh reminder that I couldn't just forget about the outside world. And, with so much going on, there was no way he couldn't answer it. I had to watch as he sat back up and took the phone out of his pocket, swiping the answer button and pressing it to his ear.

"Raffe?" he said. I couldn't hear what was being said, but there were a couple of "ums" and "ahs" as the conversation went on. "I'll be there as soon as I can." He put down the phone and turned to me, buttoning his shirt back up. *So, the moment's really passed, huh?*

"What's up?" I asked, sitting up and fixing my clothes.

"That was Raffe."

I nodded. "I guessed as much."

"Zalaam is asking for you."

I frowned. "What?"

"Apparently, he wants to speak to you about something."

"Why didn't he call me himself?" I asked.

"He says your phone's off."

"Oh... right." I'd switched it to airplane mode when I'd gone to Waterfront Park, to avoid being disturbed or potentially being tracked. Ironic. I wished I could've put a big "Do Not Disturb" bubble around us, just for a little bit longer. But that bubble had burst. "Did Raffe say what he wanted to talk to me about?"

Wade shook his head. "No, apparently Zalaam is being very tight-lipped. He'll only speak to you."

I didn't know whether to be intrigued or terrified. Zalaam hadn't seemed too impressed by me the last time we'd encountered one another, so what on earth would the djinn have to tell me?

TWENTY-THREE

Harley

As I entered the infirmary, Zalaam's ruby eyes flashed right at me, a look of impatience on his face. Well, Levi's face.

Raffe, Santana, and Tatyana were standing awkwardly around the hospital bed, and nobody seemed to be speaking. Even if Zalaam hadn't been looking annoyed, it wouldn't have chased away the dark cloud across everyone present.

I guessed Astrid and Garrett were still working through all of the video feeds from across the globe, pushing Smartie as hard as possible, but I wasn't sure where Dylan was. Or Alton, for that matter. Wade was standing at my side, accounted for, and Finch was probably on his way back from Waterfront Park, or having a stern word with Kenzie.

Meanwhile, Louella was in her steadfast position at Jacob's bedside, one hand fixed on his temple. I couldn't see Krieger anywhere, but a moving shadow behind the blinds of his office let me know he was keeping busy.

"Where's Dylan?" I asked, so used to seeing him at Tatyana's side.

"He went to tell Astrid and Garrett about our latest failure," Santana replied.

I sighed. "No luck with the old sites?"

"Zilch." Santana shook her head. "The place was empty. Not a scrap of evidence anywhere."

"Sorry," I murmured.

"Why are you sorry?" She smiled. "It's not like you've got your feet up, chillaxing while we bust our asses. Not like others I could mention." She shot a look at Zalaam, who smirked. "It's just massively disappointing. It sounded like such a good idea, but nope—just us slamming our heads into another dead end."

"Isadora used to say a dead end was just a good place to turn around," I said, lowering my gaze.

"And she never let us down," Tatyana replied, with a sad chuckle. "She's right. We're just wallowing right now, but we'll be back to our usual, determined selves in no time."

"Are you all quite finished?" Zalaam muttered. "Your droning on is giving me a headache. I'm almost tempted to retreat back inside Levi, if you're going to carry on. I feel like one of you is about to lead us in a communal prayer."

"That wouldn't be such a bad thing," Raffe snapped. "You could certainly do with a bit of soul-searching."

"What do you think I've been doing?" Zalaam shot back. "Why soul-search when you can search more practically? Ah, I suppose you wouldn't know anything about that, since *your* djinn isn't mature enough. Funny, I was mature enough by the time Levi was your age. I guess you were stunted somewhere along the line."

"Getting forced into a cage every time you turn a tiny bit red will do that to you." Raffe balled his hands into fists and stormed off to the far side of the infirmary. Santana followed, putting her hand on his shoulder, talking to him in a low voice I couldn't quite make out.

"Have you found something?" I turned my attention back to Zalaam. After all, that's why I was here. If he was toying with me, I'd be majorly pissed. I didn't have time for this, not unless he had something useful to say.

Zalaam smiled. "Glad to see someone understands urgency. As a matter of fact, yes, I have found something. From the moment Raffe told me to inquire about Naima, that's what I've been doing, using the hive mind to reach out to other djinn across the globe. Though, apparently, these ingrates thought I was sleeping on the job." He glowered at Tatyana.

"Get to the point, Zalaam." My tone was snappier than I'd intended.

"Rude."

"Sorry, I'm just a little tense at the moment. You know, with Katherine about to ascend and everything, I'm not exactly high on patience," I replied.

He folded his arms in a huff. "Well, if you must know, someone spotted Naima in Montana and followed her to a private lake house by Flathead Lake."

"That's a real place?" It sounded made-up. But if Naima really was there, then I guessed she'd used the Strainer to get to Montana from Eris Island. She'd chosen well—Montana was pretty rural, with nobody around to disturb whatever she was up to.

"Something to do with the Native Americans who used to reside there —the Salish. I imagine it's supposed to be a cruel joke, but that's by the by." His mood softened slightly. "Nobody else lives at that location, from what the djinn in question told me. So, you have your location. And, according to that same djinn, she wasn't alone."

"Katherine's there?" I blurted out.

He chuckled darkly. "No, the djinn smelled magic on a young magical, along with something akin to pure dread. The poor girl was terrified."

"A girl?"

"Did I stutter?"

I rolled my eyes. "I was talking to myself."

"You shouldn't do that. It's the first sign of madness."

"Then does that make you insane? You speak to yourself all the time," I shot back.

"You're a sharp one, Harley. I enjoy you." Zalaam grinned.

I ignored him. "If she's got a young magical with her, then it must be one of the rare ones for Katherine's last ritual." I turned to Wade. "I just wish we knew how many she already had. That way, I'd be able to get a better gauge of how long we've got until she makes her move."

He nodded. "But, on the upside, at least this is a valuable lead."

"It's the best one we've had in a while," I agreed.

"I believe a 'Thank you, mighty Zalaam' is in order." The djinn waited smugly.

"Thank you," I replied. "It's nice to see a djinn who doesn't follow the stereotype."

He scowled. "And what stereotype might that be?"

"That you're all untrustworthy demons who are out for death and mayhem and destruction." I glanced at Raffe. "Even the ones who seem calmer than most."

"Such impudence. If I weren't trapped in this useless body, I'd show you just what a djinn can do."

I smiled. "Ah, but then you'd only be reinforcing said stereotype."

He sat back. "You really are an interesting being, Harley. Very interesting indeed. Truly, you remind me of someone… though I can't quite put my finger on who."

I let him bask in his smugness for a bit longer as I retreated into my own thoughts. I had the Hidden Things spell to deal with tonight, but I couldn't just ignore the importance of what Naima was doing in Montana. But it was almost four o'clock now, which meant I had eight hours until I needed to be back here to do the spell. *Yeah, I can swing that. Right?* I had the *Aperi Si Ostium* spell at my disposal; I could step right into that lake house without Naima sensing a thing.

"We've got to go after her, and we've got to do it now, before she has the chance to slip away again," I stated.

Raffe and Santana came back over. "Do what?"

"We're going after Naima," I replied.

"But we should keep the intervention team small, or Naima will smell us a mile away," Wade added. "Two at most."

"How do you feel about a quick trip to Montana, then?" I smiled at him anxiously.

"Whoa, hold your horses there, *mi hermosa.*" Santana held her hands up. "You're under enough strain as it is. Two of us can go instead."

I shook my head. "You're forgetting one small thing."

"What?" She frowned.

"This is the sole reason I've been training to control the Purge beasts —so I can use what I've learned on Naima."

"Oh... yeah, I forgot about that." She smiled, but I could sense her hesitancy.

"Plus, it'll take my mind off other things." I smiled. "I've got the chalk-door spell. And I'm the one who can get what we need out of Naima."

Zalaam snorted. "Good luck with that."

"What do you mean?" I shot him a no-nonsense look.

"The lake house will almost definitely be warded against such spells. According to the djinn who surveyed it, that cabin is brimming with hexes and wards and charms," he replied. "What, did you think you'd just be able to waltz in?"

One of these days, we're going to get an easy task. It made sense that Naima would protect herself and whatever she was doing with that magical girl. Word of me stealing the Grimoire must've reached Katherine and Naima by now. Heck, mini-me had said as much when I'd last seen her in my weird, "could've been" nursery. Naturally, thanks to the freaking irritating mantra of "Chaos rules," she hadn't been able to tell me more, but she'd suggested Katherine knew that I had the book.

A shudder of fear ran through me. I hadn't thought about mini-me's warning much, but now it further opened a can of worms in my head—someone from my inner circle must've told Katherine that I had the Grimoire and about the magical detector. They had to have; otherwise, how would she know so much? *But who?*

Back in the day, my first suspect would've been Finch, but he'd proven himself already. He'd had the chance to do Katherine's bidding and get Adley back, and he'd refused outright. Plus, he'd have handed my ass over to her on Eris Island, where I'd have had no chance of escaping. Since I was standing here instead, that let him off the hook, as far as I was concerned.

Then, who else? I looked to Wade. No, it couldn't be him. Not him. Anyone but him. Then again, there might have been some residual effects on him from the pendant's hex. *But the pendant was destroyed.* Surely, if that was gone, then any effects would be, too. No, it wasn't Wade. And if it wasn't him, then that left the rest of the Rag Team—my trusted, dearest friends. The very friends I loved and was giving everything to try and protect.

One of the people standing in this room might've been the snitch without even knowing it. They might be under Katherine's influence and have no clue. The only other people it could be were Krieger, Alton, Levi, and Imogene, but they seemed less likely. Krieger would have jumped ship to work with Katherine way earlier if he had wanted to give her the detector. Levi had been out cold for days and hadn't known about the magical detector being finished. Alton wouldn't be helping me with the Hidden Things spell if he was in on it, since it was intended to finish Katherine off. And Imogene had tried to take Katherine on and gotten a nasty gash to the face in the process. Plus, she'd been with me when I'd looked through the Grimoire, and she hadn't tried to take it or destroy it. If she was working for Katherine, she'd have done both those things when she'd had the chance.

It might be one of you. I looked to my friends. This was precisely why I had to continue alone. I loved them all so much, but they were a threat to the success of my mission right now, likely without realizing it. If I let them in on what I was doing, there was the distinct probability of it getting back to Katherine, and then she'd soundly wreck all my plans in one fell swoop. And that'd crush them as much as it would crush me.

"So, we can't use *Aperi Si Ostium*?" Wade asked.

Zalaam snorted again. "Not unless you want to end up as cat food."

"Then how do we get in? Naima won't hang around, and we need to nab her before she runs off back to Eris Island again to bring her mouse home to her owner." We had to do this before midnight tonight, so we needed a quick option. But, without any Portal Openers, I couldn't think of anything. *Oh Isadora... I miss you.* Not just because of what she could do, but because her death had torn me open inside, leaving a gap that I didn't think I'd ever be able to fill.

"This time, I might get a 'Thank you, mighty Zalaam' out of you," the djinn said, smiling.

"Go on," I urged.

"I have something you might use—a portaling spell that only the djinn may use, a spell we've never shared with magicals. It is unlikely Naima will have warded against such a spell, given its rarity," he explained, pleased as punch. "You can use it to get as close to the lake house as possible."

"Okay, so what's the spell?" I pressed.

"It involves an Arabic chant that you wouldn't be able to manage, with your coarse American tongue," he replied. "And a rare emerald. One for each journey. In this case, you'll need two, unless you plan to stay in Montana."

I held back my irritation. "Tell me these emeralds are easy to get, or I might blow a fuse."

"They are known as Sahar Gems and are imbued with slivers of djinn Chaos. They are hidden in the most unexpected places, so the djinn can have them nearby whenever they are needed, for whatever reason. One must always have an escape plan, after all." His expression darkened. "In days gone by, it was not uncommon for us to have our power drained by evil warlocks, who then chose to lock us away in lamps and sell us to people for laughable amounts of money. You would be horrified by the number of djinn who've ended up on the shelves of tourists, destined to be nothing but ornaments for drab mantelpieces."

"Like a genie in a bottle?" Santana arched an eyebrow.

He scowled. "How disgusting."

"That's the myth, though, right?" Raffe backed her up.

"I suppose that is where the myth originates. A genie is a limited version of a djinn—a djinn with only a fraction of its power, enslaved by an evil warlock for profit," Zalaam replied. "Sometimes, genies evade those warlocks through various tricks. One of which is to use these Sahar Gems to replenish their powers, or to simply portal away, as far from the warlocks as possible. But it all depends on whether or not they can find an emerald."

"And where do *we* find one?" I asked.

He shrugged. "Museums are riddled with them."

"Specifics, *please*!" My temper and my volume were flaring.

"I know of two precise places where you'll find one, and you'd certainly have no trouble using your chalk-door spell to get to them," he replied. "There is one in the Tower of London, set at the front of the Imperial Crown of India."

I gaped at him. "You're kidding, right? You want us to break into the Tower of London and steal an emerald from the Crown Jewels? I don't think so, pal. What's the other option?"

"There is the cluster of emeralds fitted on the pommel of the sword belonging to Tairrdelbach Ua Conchobair, who was the high king of Ireland in the early 1100s, if memory serves, which is currently on display in the Dublin Coven's museum wing. He was also the magical king of Ireland, during those times."

"I didn't understand half of what you just said," Santana replied.

"I thought you said these gems were nearby," I added.

He shrugged. "They've dwindled in recent years, and you wanted to know specifics. I've given them to you. You can search other places if you like, but Naima may be gone by then."

"Can we put the emeralds back?" I really hoped so.

He shook his head. "They will be destroyed once they're used."

"Looks like we're going to Ireland first, then," I muttered. I didn't like the idea of ruining a perfectly good relic, but we could worry about the personal and financial complications later. At least it was in a coven, so we wouldn't be inciting the wrath of any humans. Anyway, right now, that kind of fallout was literally the least of our problems.

Wade nodded. "Back to the homeland."

"Right… I always forget you've got Irish in you. Or maybe I've just gotten used to that little twang to your accent. I don't hear it so much anymore."

"It usually only comes out stronger when I'm pissed off." He smirked.

"Same here. I get super Mexican when I'm hangry." Santana chuckled, but I could feel her nerves. She was just trying to lighten the mood, the way Finch would've done if he were here. Speaking of which, I was going to have to think of a way to lose Wade, Finch, and the rest of the crew once we got Katherine's location from Naima. As soon as I got it, I needed to distance myself from the coven to pursue her on my own, hopefully with the Hidden Things spell in tow.

This is going to be a challenge. But when had that ever stopped me?

TWENTY-FOUR

Harley

Using the *Aperi Si Ostium* spell, Wade and I stepped through to the Dublin Coven, appearing in a long, cavernous room with a curved roof.

It felt as though we'd stepped back in time, entering some grand, almost medieval world. Balconies lined the upper floor, giving an open view onto the varnished floor below, where stone busts stood sentinel. Inside the many mahogany recesses, ancient bookshelves lined the walls, the whole place a librarian's dream. Only, there weren't just books. Glass boxes featured artifacts from all over the world.

We just had to find the one belonging to… I wasn't even going to try and say his name. I'd just call him the high king of Ireland.

Everything was lit up in the soft glow of lamplight, with a faint sliver of moonlight coming in through the windows. I wasn't really a pro with time zones, but I could tell we'd hit Dublin in the dead of night. Which explained why there was nobody around.

"Do you see it?" I whispered, feeling like I ought to, even though the place was empty. It seemed a shame, given how beautiful it was.

"Why are you whispering?" he teased.

I laughed quietly. "I don't know. I can't stop."

"You're a funny one, Harley Merlin."

"But that's what you love about me, right?"

"Oh yes. More than anything." He leaned down and planted a kiss on my forehead. Anything more seemed wrong in a setting like this, as though somebody would pop out and scold us for such despicable behavior.

"You're distracting me, Mr. Crowley." I smiled up at him.

"Yeah, we should probably find this sword, huh?" He put his hand on the small of my back, ushering me down the cavernous hall. "We should check the upper floor first, if only to get our bearings. We'll get a good view from up there."

I nodded and followed him up a distant, slightly more modern staircase, until we found the corridors that led to the arched recesses. The windows looked out on the gray-stone streets of Dublin, illuminated by old-timey street lamps, giving the city a mystical, magical air that seemed impossibly romantic. Meanwhile, the faint shimmer of an interdimensional bubble rippled across the glass. I watched a few stray people walking past for a moment, some staggering, some laughing as they made their way home, and envied their obliviousness. They were just going about their business, with no idea that they were going to be enslaved by Katherine Shipton, if I couldn't stop her first.

"You lived in Ireland for a little while, right?" I asked, as we walked along. This would've been so romantic, if it hadn't been for the mission hanging over our heads.

"For a few years, when I was a kid. My mom sent me off to boarding school in Cork, actually." He paused. "But the less said about that, the better."

"You hated it?"

He grinned. "I hated it. The school was beautiful, and I love the country, but the teachers were insanely strict. I thought I'd be scarred from all the whippings."

"When did you go to school, the 1800s?" I snorted, though it reminded me of my own scars. They marked my back in faint, silvery lines. Sometimes, I'd turn in the mirror after a shower and see them. They startled me every time. People had always teased me for wearing jackets constantly, but they didn't realize I was terrified of them seeing those scars.

"Might as well have," he replied.

"Were you a cheeky kid? I thought you'd be the rule-follower."

He shook his head. "I think they just did it to make an example of me."

"That's horrible. How old were you?"

"I was there from ages seven to ten."

"I'm so sorry." I held on to his hand, entwining my fingers with his.

He shrugged. "No need to be. Everything turned back around when I came back to America, so it's not all bad, and a school like that looks good on the résumé, even if I was only there for three years. I'm not trying to pull out the violins or anything. It was tough here, but it was character-building, and it taught me discipline, which has served me well."

Wade stopped suddenly. We were about four archways down, and I didn't instantly see what had caught his eye. I peered around his shoulder. There, in the center of the recess, stood a plinth with a glass box on top. Inside it, elegantly hung from a black iron rod, was a huge sword. The pommel glinted in the moonlight that glanced through the windows, though the emeralds were too old to sparkle. They'd been dulled by the years, turning an almost milky shade of green. Then again, these weren't the shiny gems of the modern day; these were ancient jewels, rough cut, more or less the way they'd been dragged out of the ground. I guessed there'd been some alchemy at play when these emeralds had been made, because I could feel the subtle bristle of Chaos energy as I approached.

"So you've got the spell to break into this without setting off alarms?" I asked. We'd discussed what we were going to do before we got here, but it seemed a bit more unnerving now that we were standing in front of this ancient artifact.

"I have a spell prepared, yes."

I grinned at him nervously. "Just checking. If all else fails, we can break the damn thing and get out of here as fast as possible."

He chuckled. "Sounds good to me." He was about to step up to the box when I reached out and pulled him back. "What's wrong? Is something the matter?"

I shook my head. "Something's coming to me. A different spell. I think… I think it's from the memory dump I got in New York."

"To break the box?"

"Yeah… Do you mind if I give it a try?"

He shrugged. "Go ahead. You've got all sorts of spells hopping about in that brain of yours. I'm sure you've got something better than what I had planned."

Taking a breath, I stepped up to the box and put my palms flat against the glass. My mouth opened, and the words came flooding out, my Esprit glowing: *"Quod omnis turbare. Turn eam pariter in manibus. Ut nihil veniat."* It seemed to be along the lines of, *"Shatter what is whole. Turn it to dust in my hands. Let it fall to nothing,"* but my Latin wasn't exactly great.

Wade stepped back as the box did just that, erupting into a fine, glittery dust that settled around our feet like snow, leaving the sword exposed. His jaw dropped, his eyes shining.

"Wow…"

I grinned. "I've got to admit, that was pretty cool."

He reached over my shoulder, his body close to mine, and took the sword down, leaning it up against the plinth. His ten rings lit up with Fire, and he pressed them carefully to the gold fittings that held the gems in place. He melted the fittings away, loosening the emeralds until they dropped to the floor like pebbles. Snatching them up, he turned them over in his hands.

"Can you feel any power in them?" he asked, holding them out to me.

I touched a few of them, but nothing came back. They were clearly duds. However, when I touched the biggest two, which had been right in the center of the pommel, I felt that subtle pulse of Chaos shivering back into my hand. "These two."

"You're sure?"

"I guess we'll find out when we try to do the spell," I replied, smiling.

"Right then, we'd best put these babies to the test." He put the dud emeralds back and replaced the sword on its holder, though there wasn't much we could do about the box. Someone would find this in due time and wonder what had happened, but we couldn't worry about that right now.

"After you, Mr. Linguist." I nudged him in the arm.

"I haven't spoken Arabic in years."

"You can do it; I know you can." I looked up into his eyes, pleased to have more time with him before tonight. Every moment was precious now, and I had to savor every single one. I wished we could've been back in my bedroom, picking up where we'd left off.

"Keep close when we reach the lake house," he said. "If anything happens to you—"

I cut him off softly. "It won't. I've got you, remember?"

He smiled. "I love you."

"I love you more." I clung to his arm as he pocketed one emerald and put the other in the center of his palm. "You've got this. Plus, you're in your homeland. That should give you a boost."

"I'm not sure it works that way, but let's hope the luck of the Irish is with us." He laughed and turned his attention back to the emerald. Clearing his throat and closing his eyes tightly, he recited the spell in Arabic. I guessed the one we'd pocketed wouldn't be affected—Zalaam had explained the emerald had to be in your hands to be used. And, as long as I had hold of Wade in some way, it'd portal me, too.

The world around us spun, my body disintegrating before my very eyes. Wade turned into a wisp of grayish smoke. I braced for the pain, but it didn't come. This wasn't like the Strainer. This was something more refined, and infinitely more ancient.

Leaving Dublin behind, we zipped out of the coven, moving at supersonic speed through landscapes that took my breath away, even though my lungs were currently smoke and I had no idea where my eyes were. But, somehow, I could see everything. We soared like rockets over oceans and countries, passing verdant countryside and arid desert, snow-capped mountains and golden vistas, moving so fast I understood why we couldn't be in our physical forms. This would have torn the skin off our bones.

A few minutes later, we landed outside the lake house in Montana. The sky was gloomy, with clouds rolling in across the nearby mountains and the metallic tang of rain in the air. The sun would set soon, with it being just after five o'clock here, casting an eerie light across the landscape below. Wind rustled through the trees and skimmed across the rushing water of the nearby lake. I spotted the cabin just up ahead, barely a hundred yards away, as my physical body reconstructed around me.

"That was weird," Wade murmured.

The used-up emerald had vanished completely. I guessed that Irish King's sword wasn't getting it back. *Oops.*

I nodded. "Very weird."

"I can cross that off the bucket list. Been a wisp of smoke? Sure have."

I chuckled, despite my growing nerves. "Makes you wonder what else the djinn can do, doesn't it?"

"Definitely."

"Don't do anything heroic, okay?" I said suddenly, grasping his hand. "We're here to get the location out of Naima, that's all. There might be a fight, but don't get yourself killed. Please… please don't get yourself killed."

The enormity of what we were about to do had just hit me, punching me right in the heart. The last time there'd been a fight, Isadora hadn't made it out alive. *I should've done this on my own.* It was too late to send him back now, with only the one emerald, but I couldn't stop the thoughts coming into my head. Naima wasn't Katherine, but she wouldn't go down easy.

Wade glanced at me strangely. "I'm not going anywhere, Harley. I won't let that happen."

"Just promise me you'll be careful. Don't be a hero. You might be mine, but that doesn't mean you have to do anything crazy to prove it. I already know." Finch's words were hovering in my head. Heroes didn't get to live. I needed to know Wade would be okay. He was the true reason I was going on my solo mission. If anything happened to him before then, I might as well have stayed a wisp of smoke for all the good I'd be.

"I promise, if you promise." He brushed his thumb across my cheek.

"I promise." *For now, at least.*

"Come on then, let's get this beastie before she goes running back to Katherine." He gave my hand a squeeze, but he didn't let go. I was glad of that.

Together, we snuck toward the cabin and crept around the outside of the building, keeping to the shadows of the surrounding forest. There were only a handful of windows we could peep through, and most of them just showed the empty rooms of the cabin. The sight of Naima's long cloak, thrown across one of the chairs in the kitchen, gave me hope that she hadn't disappeared quite yet.

Continuing our silent investigation, Wade put up his palms and checked the cabin with heat-reading magic, trying to sense out anybody inside. I, on the other hand, used my Chaos to check for the immediate threat of any hidden hexes. After what Zalaam had said, we couldn't take any chances. I found a couple and began to unpick them, the way Finch had taught me. I was careful not to trigger anything as I dismantled the hexes, letting them fall away on one or two of the windows. After all, we'd need a way in—a way that Naima wouldn't sense.

Reaching the very back of the cabin, where a veranda jutted out into the woods, I dismantled the hexes that surrounded it and crept up onto the platform with Wade at my side. There, we edged toward the two larger windows that faced out and peeked into the room beyond. It was a rudimentary lounge with a fire burning in the hearth. Naima stood at the far side, while a girl sat on a furry bear rug in the middle, her arms bound behind her back with Atomic Cuffs. She couldn't have been older than ten, with ebony skin and a tight bun on either side of her head. Tears streamed down her face, and she was shaking violently. *It's okay, we're here.*

My optimism dwindled as I saw the pentagram of the Strainer drawn on the floor around her. With a sudden jolt, I realized what was going on —Naima was reciting the spell that would take this girl to Eris Island.

"We have to move, now!" I hissed, just as the edges of the pentagram lit up, the ingredients in the five bowls exploding.

"What?"

"NOW!" I roared, jumping up and knocking down the back door of the cabin with a powerful blast of Air.

I sprinted in, but the little girl had already begun to twist through the middle of the pentagram, getting sucked down into the unknown. If I kicked one of the pots or tried to stop the pentagram, I had no idea what state the girl would come back in, or if she'd even come back at all. With a sickening snap, she disappeared altogether, her cries echoing out. A shiver crept down my spine. Where she was going, we couldn't save her.

Naima, however, was still here, flashing me a killer look that only spelled danger.

TWENTY-FIVE

Katherine

I licked my lips in anticipation of the new arrival.

Naima had sent word a short while ago that I could expect delivery of a South-African girl by the name of Lesedi Kumalo. A suitably exotic little bird to add to my menagerie.

According to my loyal lieutenant, she had the rare ability to Morph, as well as being a full Elemental. And capturing her was all thanks to my shiny new magical detector.

As it turned out, Bakir Khan really did have the IQ he liked to harp on about. He'd gotten the thing working in no time, and now I was reaping the rewards.

I couldn't resist welcoming the rare magical myself, even if it meant taking some time out of my packed Imogene schedule. My office door at the SDC was locked. If anyone needed me, they could just keep banging until I came back. This was much too important. After this kid, I only needed one more, and I knew precisely who that was going to be.

"Lesedi, welcome to Eris Island." I grinned at the girl, aware that I sounded like a ringmaster welcoming customers into the circus tent. But this was a momentous occasion, and that called for a little enthusiasm.

She screamed.

Of course she's a screamer—they all are. That part was getting a bit tired, to be honest. Why couldn't they just come to me with open arms and understanding? They would be revered throughout history for being the ones who'd given me my status as a Child of Chaos. What greater honor could they hope for? I was giving them fame, and all they did was wail. *Ungrateful cretins.*

"Is that any way to greet your host?" I asked, giving her one last chance.

She screamed louder, snot trickling out of her nose and tears running down her face. *Repulsive.* This was why I never could've made a good mother. All that snot and crap and piss and tears and screaming. Nope, that wasn't my cup of tea at all. Plus, I was fairly fond of my beauty sleep, and children did nothing but ruin that. Did I have bags under my eyes? Not a chance. Did I have premature wrinkles? No, thank you. And that was all because I'd had the common sense to ship Finch off to Mrs. Anker as early as possible so she could deal with all of that. The Shapeshifting took care of any pesky lines, but most of this was me in my raw and delightful form.

"Lesedi, I suggest you shut your trap before it gets you in trouble." *Very last warning, kiddo.* If she didn't hush up soon, I was going to start counting.

"I want to go home!" she wailed.

"You are home," I replied.

"Take me home! Please! My parents will pay, just let me go home!"

Ugh.

"*Infelicem animam pauperis praevalebunt. reddat ei quietam. et erunt vocem eius. suscipiesque universa de manibus eius.*" I swiped my hand across her throat, severing her vocal cords. I'd given her ample opportunity to calm the hell down. What did she expect?

Her mouth opened as if another scream was about to come out, but there was nothing but blissful silence. Music to my ears. She gaped like a fish out of water, flapping her lips, her eyes wide in confusion.

"Don't say I didn't warn you. If you'd behaved, you could've kept your voice. This is what happens to disobedient little girls."

She looked like she was trying to scream hysterically, but I couldn't hear a thing. *I should've done this with all of them.* Every time I walked into that laboratory, it was nothing but shouts and cries and wailing children. It was really killing my last ritual buzz.

"Eris, what would you like us to do with her?" Coral Falkland stepped forward. *Ah, my spiny minx.*

"What do you think?"

"Throw her in with the others?"

I chuckled. "Bingo."

"Right away, Eris." Coral beckoned for two of my minions to help her, the three of them dragging her out of what I liked to call the Viewpoint. From here, I could see the beauty of my island, all handcrafted by my own fair digits.

Everything was coming up Katherine, and I couldn't have been happier with the way things were proceeding.

I did wonder why Naima hadn't come back with Lesedi, but I didn't have the time, or the inclination, to go chasing after everyone. Like a good puss, she'd come back when she was hungry. Besides, she was a big girl; she could take care of herself. I mean, she'd probably stayed to try and scout out another magical for me, trying to preempt my next request after her past failures, but she didn't have to do that. I already had the perfect one in mind. Then again, I could always use extras, in case one of them *actually* decided to die from fear. I'd heard it could happen, though I'd never seen it. And I'd definitely tried it out on a couple of prisoners, to no avail. Maybe, with this divine face, I just wasn't frightening enough.

And, if Naima wasn't here to see the grand show, then that was her tough luck. Latecomers wouldn't be admitted. I wasn't about to be diverted from my mission for anyone. Not now, not when I was so close to completing it.

TWENTY-SIX

Harley

My training with Leviathan had been geared toward this fight. At least, this time, I had Wade to help.

Naima lunged first, moving at blinding speed. Her claws flashed, but I ducked. Wade lifted his palms and slammed a ball of Fire into her face. She twisted out of the way at the last second, the fireball scorching the cabin wall. A few sparks began to catch. I drew a tornado of water from the faucet of the kitchen sink and doused the flames before they could start an inferno.

"Careful with that," I warned.

He nodded. "Thanks for putting it out."

"No problem." I skidded under another one of Naima's pounces, pounding my palms into the floorboards and sending up a net of vines. She slashed through them with her claws, cutting them to ribbons.

"You won't defeat me, if that is your plan," Naima purred.

"We'll see about that," I shot back, fortifying my words with a blast of Air that sent the kitty flying at the wall. She somersaulted backward before she hit it, landing with surprising softness on the floor.

Man, she's quick. Leviathan had been pretty freaking fast, but this was another level. Tobe had been right—she was more agile than Leviathan, who'd been held back by his bulk and all that armor plating. Naima had none of that, and it showed.

Her claws clicked on the ground as she sprinted toward us on all fours, her fangs bared. She lunged through the air, aiming straight for Wade. He tried to send out a fireball, but she was way too quick. She hit him full force, knocking him to the ground, the two of them wrestling as she tried to expose his throat for a bite. I shot a beam of spiraling Telekinesis at her, flinging her off him before she could get to his jugular. Even then, she was quick enough to graze a cut along his throat with her right fang, drawing first blood.

He'd barely gotten up when she was back on him, snapping her jaws like a devil. Desperate to get her away from him, I powered another charge of Telekinesis at her. I gripped a lasso around her waist and tossed her toward the fireplace. The flames caught the edge of her fur, singeing it slightly. She rolled along the floor for a second or two, putting any potential fire out, before sprinting right back. This beastie had energy in spades, and I hoped we could keep up. There was no trickery here, like with Leviathan, just pure, unadulterated strength and speed.

"You will tire before I do." She grinned as she arced through the air, twisting right over my head and landing behind me. I whirled around, and she jabbed her paw into my stomach, making me double over as the air rushed out of my lungs.

Naima jumped on me with her full weight. She was heavier than she looked, crushing me as she extended a savage claw. I felt it, cold and sharp, against my neck. I pressed my hands against any part of her I could reach. Forcing Fire through my veins, I let a wave of it spread out across her, the scent of burning fur filling the air as she howled, reeling back. Patting herself down with her paws, she quickly extinguished the sparks that crackled across her chest.

"You were saying?" I jumped up and stood beside Wade, the two of us facing off against her, side by side, like the good old days.

Together, we lifted our hands and sent out a blockade of raging Fire. It was a risky move in a wooden cabin, but we needed to be bold. The only trouble was, I couldn't see Naima through the wall of flames. I tried to peer through the rippling screen of bright orange and searing white heat, but it was proving impossible.

"Behind you," she whispered in my ear. I twisted around, only to go careening backward when she kicked me hard in the chest. Wade followed as she landed a roundhouse kick to his face, knocking him to the ground. Wheezing, I struggled to get up, only to find that Wade wasn't moving. He lay still on the ground, blood trickling from his nose. I crawled over to him and shook him by the shoulders.

"Wade?"

He groaned, his eyes blinking open. "I'm okay. I'm okay."

"Think again." Naima loomed over me. I tried to get my Chaos together, but she gripped me by the throat and lifted me up, leaving me dangling and fighting for air. It was hard to conjure magic when someone was crushing your windpipe. But if I didn't, she'd kill me.

Gripping her wrists to steady myself, I urged Earth through her body, the emerald on my Esprit glowing fiercely as I called on good old Mama Nature to do her best work. The ground shook, and tree roots shot up through the floorboards. They twisted around Naima's legs and worked their way up to her torso. I pulled my hands into fists, the roots following suit, gripping tighter and squeezing hard until Naima had no choice but to let me go.

I hit the deck, dragging air into my lungs and grasping at my neck to make sure she hadn't pierced the skin. A short distance away, Wade was back on his feet, his ten rings glowing. I made a beeline for him, leaving Naima to slash away at the roots that held her fast. They wouldn't keep her distracted for long, but at least we could catch our breath for a second. My heart was already pumping hard, my arms tingling from using so many types of ability in one go.

"She's tough," I muttered, using the opportunity to gather a ball of emotion into my chest. This might be the best chance I had to put my reverse Empathy to the test, and I wasn't going to waste it. I built it up as best I could, but I was having the same problem I'd had with Leviathan. It wasn't enough. I needed to get my Darkness involved, or this was never going to work.

He nodded. "You can say that again."

I closed my eyes to try and release my Darkness. I'd just reached that weird edge, where Light met Dark, when something knocked me straight off my feet. Pain shot up my legs, forcing my eyes open. Naima had Wade in a headlock, her claws out and ready to strike. Startled, I looked down to see what was causing me so much pain, and found blood pouring down the backs of my legs, my jeans torn. She'd tried to sever the tendons in the backs of my knees, by the looks of it, but she hadn't quite cut deep enough. Still, that didn't mean it wasn't stinging like a bitch.

Still lying on the floor, I unleashed a lasso of Telekinesis at Naima, wrapping the tendrils around her paws and ripping them away from Wade. He ducked out the moment her grip loosened, and whirled on her, shooting out blast after blast of Fire. She feinted out of the way, pulling against my Telekinesis and dragging me with it. I had to sever the tie, jumping back up to my feet to try something else. *I need one gap—just one chink in her armor.* But, so far, she wasn't showing any signs of weakness.

She darted this way and that, zigzagging so that none of our attacks landed. Before I knew it, she was on me again, bending me around into a headlock. I could feel her muscles rippling underneath her thick fur as she squeezed tighter, making my eyes bulge out of my head. I tried to retaliate with Fire and Air, but it didn't make a difference. It was almost like she didn't even feel it. Even as her forearm went up in flames, she just held it closer to my face, until I was forced to snuff it out with a bunch of Water. She shook herself off, still gripping me tight.

"Come any closer, and I will twist her head off," Naima warned, as Wade edged nearer.

"I don't think your boss would be too happy about that." He was calling her bluff.

As she tried to muster a comeback, he launched a precise beam of Fire at her head, and she let me go. But not before she caught hold of the back of my jacket. I slithered my arms from the sleeves and stumbled forward to join Wade. I knew he'd catch sight of my tattoo with my arms bare, but that didn't matter now. He'd understand what it meant, and he wasn't about to stop a fight to ask me questions.

"Does it still ache, Harley?" Naima chuckled, staring at the Apple of

Discord. "Or does it just kill you to know you are stuck with that for the rest of your life?"

"It only spurs me on," I replied. "A reminder of what I need to do and why."

"At least you did not scream too loudly when I poured the gold into your flesh. Most do."

I narrowed my eyes at her. "Then I guess I'm tougher than I look."

I bombarded Naima with Fire. Before I could stop him, Wade barreled through the beam of Fire, hurling himself at her, and tackled her to the ground. She fell with a thud. With his ten rings glowing more brightly than ever, he pummeled her with Chaos, urging wave after wave of Fire into her, until her fur had turned black, all of it practically melted away from her skin, to reveal the scorched, raw flesh beneath. An exposed patch opened beneath her heart, though it was hard to home in on it with the two of them wrangling like bare-knuckle brawlers on the ground.

You can do this, Harley. I had to, or we'd never get out of this cabin alive.

I grasped for a tendril of powerful Telekinesis and slammed it into her chest. She stilled, the air pushed out of her lungs. Hurriedly gathering up a ball of emotion, I delved deep into my mind and reached that stark edge between my affinities. Letting the Darkness loose, I felt it take over, my veins pulsating, my whole body jangling with the after-effects of feeding the proverbial beast.

"Submit!" I bellowed, my voice echoing strangely again. It hurt like mad, my throat on fire, but I'd gotten used to this particular brand of pain. It was almost getting easier, each time I did this. "Submit to me!" I stepped closer, until I was right over her. Wade stepped away from Naima, letting me work my magic.

"Never!" She tried to move, but I was holding the reins.

"I said, *submit*!" The words came out of my mouth as a howling scream, as though there was a banshee at the cabin door. It echoed around the room, the hairs on the back of my neck sticking up. Below, Naima grunted and snarled, but there was nothing she could do to fight this. I had control now, and I wasn't about to relinquish it. "Do you submit?" I roared, the sound deafening, to the point where even Wade had to cover his ears.

Naima gnashed her jaws. "I… I sub… I submit."

"Good, now tell me the exact coordinates of Eris Island's current location."

"21°05'31.0"N… 159°00'12.5"W." She strained against me every second, but I held fast.

"When does Katherine plan to move it again?"

She snarled furiously. "Not for at least… four days."

"Thank you," I said coldly.

"What are we going to do with her now?" Wade asked. "Should I manipulate her memory to make her forget?"

I shook my head, my mind already made up. We couldn't risk letting her loose to warn the evil bitch. I didn't even look at Wade as I crouched low and pressed my palms to the ground, the emerald of my Esprit glowing. Tree roots splintered up through the floorboards around Naima. As I twisted my hands, the roots followed my movements, wrapping around Naima's throat and squeezing tight. I wished there could've been a quicker way.

"Harley?" Wade sounded worried.

"She has to die, Wade. You know that, and I know that." I pulled the roots tighter, until her eyes turned red. "Death is a better end for her. Loyalty to Katherine only corrupts and decays the soul. Her soul, if she has one. That's far worse than death."

"You can stop now," he said, putting his hand on my shoulder. "She's dead."

"I need to check." I leaned down and put my hand in front of her nostrils, but she wasn't breathing anymore. He was right. She was dead. Black cracks were already starting to appear in her skin, small sections of her body peeling away in flakes that reminded me of ash, letting me know it wouldn't be long until she dissipated completely.

Now for the really hard part. I needed to ditch Wade, somehow.

Taking a moment to collect my thoughts, I pulled more Water from the kitchen sink and spilled the liquid over the Strainer pentagram. I washed the symbol clean off so nobody could come here unexpectedly. I might have needed to ditch Wade, but I wanted him to be safe.

Next, I searched the pockets of Naima's cloak. Wade followed me, watching me closely. What I was doing looked innocent enough—just someone checking the enemy's clothes for anything valuable. To be honest, I wasn't entirely sure what I was looking for, but at least I was buying some time to get a plan together. A moment later, my hands closed around a cluster of smooth shapes. *Perfect....*

"Find anything?" he asked.

I shook my head. "No, but I should probably bring this cloak, in case anyone comes looking for Naima. We can at least make it look like she's gone somewhere else. Her body will probably start evaporating soon, so that gets rid of the main evidence."

"Makes sense." He smiled, and it broke my heart. "Should we get going?"

"Lead the way." I forced myself to smile back.

The moment his back was turned, I scattered the entrapment stones at his feet. He glanced down at them in surprise as the gleaming ropes shot out and crisscrossed over him, dragging him to the ground. They wouldn't hold him forever, but they'd stop him from trying to stop me. And, hopefully, he'd forgive me, once he understood. As he writhed and thrashed, I hurried toward him and knelt at his side. Reaching through the shining red ropes, I rummaged in his pockets and took out the spare emerald and his phone, with him helpless to stop me.

"I'm sorry, Wade." I slipped the emerald into my own pocket and carried the phone back through to the kitchen, putting it out of his reach. Once he was out of the ropes, he'd be able to phone for help, but I had to buy some time first. Taking a second to gather my nerve, I turned back and stepped over him, hating every second of this.

"What are you doing, Harley?" he barked, his eyes angry. "Let me out of here. Stop messing around."

"I'm not messing around. I'm sorry, but you have to stay here for a while. I'll explain everything, hopefully, one day, but I can't now."

"Harley!" he yelled. "Let me go, now!"

"I love you, Wade, and if I survive what happens next, I'll spend the rest of my life making it up to you." I took a breath. "It needs to happen like this. I'm sorry… I'm so, so sorry."

I turned my back on him and headed for the door. Walking out of the cabin was the hardest thing I'd ever had to do, that fight with Naima included. Speaking of which, half of Naima was already gone, the rest of her vanishing in a flurry of ashy flakes as the seconds passed. All I wanted to do was take those ropes away and let him come with me, but his life was more important than my selfish need to have him beside me.

"Harley!" he hollered after me, but I'd already closed the door, the sound disappearing.

Once I was a short distance from the cabin, I took out the emerald and held it in my hand. Trying to remember the words that Zalaam had taught Wade, I closed my eyes and let the words come. I'd never spoken Arabic before, but I hoped Chaos would get the gist of what I was trying to say.

My body disappeared, transforming me into a wisp of smoke as I focused on where I wanted to go. It wasn't easy, considering all the thoughts racing through my head and the emotions pounding through my skull, but I held on to the location.

Zipping away from the cabin at lightning speed, the world rushing by beneath me, I tried to ignore the stark reality of what I'd just done. I'd left Wade stranded in Montana, and I had no assurances that I'd ever see him again after I faced Katherine. *I should've said more.* I should've stayed there and poured out my heart to him, in case it was the last time. I should've hugged him and kissed him and told him over and over how much I loved him. But it was too late now. I was already flying away from him, with so many things left unsaid.

Those entrapment stones would hold him for at least a few hours, if not more. Ordinarily, they held monsters, not skilled, powerful magicals, but these had come from Katherine, so maybe I had a little more time. A few hours was all I needed for the next part of my mission.

TWENTY-SEVEN

Harley

The djinn portal led me back to my bedroom in the SDC, my body reappearing from the wispy smoke.

I couldn't look at the bed without thinking of Wade and the sweet, stolen moment we'd shared before we'd gone to Montana. Tears still stung my eyes, but I had to force them back; there was no time for sentiment, not right now. I could cry and beg forgiveness later, providing I made it through. But, for the time being, I had to be strong.

Stronger than I'd ever been before.

I changed quickly out of my torn clothes, and I threw Finch's jacket over the top, even though it still had rips in it. Running over to the spot where I'd hidden the Grimoire bag, I checked to be sure I had everything on my list. It was all there, weighing the bag down.

I strapped the bag across my body and checked the clasps before opening a doorway to Alton's office. We'd have to push our plan forward, and I hoped Alton had the means to do it, considering I had no idea how long the entrapment stones would hold Wade for.

Stepping into Alton's office, I closed the door quietly behind me. Alton was standing on the far side of the room, scanning through some documents with his back turned to me. He didn't know I'd arrived.

"Boo!" I didn't know why I'd said it, but it felt right. Anything to take the edge off what I'd just done to the man I loved.

Alton jumped, almost scattering the documents across the office. "You've *got* to stop doing that!" He whirled around. "Secret tunnels are one thing, but this is plain unfair. You're going to give me a heart attack one of these days."

I chuckled. "Sorry, I couldn't help it."

"You're a little early, aren't you?"

"About that—we need to go now. I know we were supposed to meet at midnight, but something's come up. We need to do the spell as soon as possible." I lowered my gaze, trying not to give the game away. "Can you call Davin, get him to come sooner?"

Alton frowned. "Why the rush?"

"It's Katherine," I said. "She appeared on Smartie's surveillance, in San Diego." I didn't enjoy lying, but given the circumstances, I figured this was justified.

"She did?" His jaw dropped.

"I'm guessing she knows about the Grimoire, which means we have to move. Pronto."

He nodded rapidly. "Give me a moment, and I'll see what Davin can do." Taking out his phone, he dialed a number and pressed it to his ear. "Davin? Yeah, there's been a slight change of plan. How soon can you get to the location?" He paused. "Oh? You're already there? Ah, I see. You wanted to get a feel for the place. I suppose that makes sense. Well, we won't be too long, so don't go anywhere. Yes, yes, I have everything." He rolled his eyes. "Of course I'm going to do my best. I suggest you do the same. Very good, see you soon." He hung up.

"All good?"

He sighed. "Yes. He might be something of an asshat, but he's diligent —I have to give him props for that. He's already there, hexing the site with protective spells."

"He can't be all that bad, then."

"No... though I imagine it's to save his own skin and keep out prying eyes."

I shrugged. "As long as it works for us, too, I'm not complaining. Now, do you have everything ready? I've got all the ingredients for the spell, but I know you thought you had more time."

"I have what we need." He waved his hands across an open space in front of the bookshelves to the back of the room, a forcefield disintegrating to reveal two caskets pushed against the wall.

I tried not to shudder. "Do I want to ask how you got them?"

"When you're wearing a white coat and a stethoscope, people will believe just about anything," he replied solemnly. "I went to the nearby hospital and removed two corpses from the mortuary, claiming they'd been compromised with a deadly infection that could spread if the bodies weren't quarantined. I confess, I feel nasty for doing it, but… hey, it's done now. The greater good, right?"

"Right." I glanced at the caskets, wondering who was inside. And where Alton had managed to get caskets at such short notice. I didn't know if there was a hotline that Necromancers could phone to get their hands on death-related items, but clearly Alton had pulled some strings. Likely at his own expense, out of respect for the dead. He felt bad enough without leaving the poor souls exposed.

Faced with actual death, it was only natural to think about who these people had been when they were living. What had they enjoyed? Who had they loved? Who loved them? Did they live good lives? It made me think about my own life. There was a good chance that Wade would never forgive me for this, but I couldn't dwell too much on that. I had to remind myself that I was doing this for his sake, and for the sake of everyone I held dear. Did that make me a good person, despite these shady actions? I really hoped so. At the end of it all, I wanted to have lived a good life, with a story worth telling. Wasn't that what everyone wanted?

"I suppose we don't have anything more to discuss," Alton said, looking to me. "Are you ready?"

I took a shaky breath. "Ready as I'll ever be, for something like this."

"Then we should go."

"After you."

He smiled. "You're the one with the charmed chalk. If I may?"

I crossed the room and handed him the innocuous stick. "It's all yours."

Taking the proffered chalk, he lifted it to the wall and drew a large doorway, before whispering the *Aperi Si Ostium* spell and closing his eyes, no doubt focusing on the place he wanted to go. The edges of the chalk lines sparked, sinking into the wall and forging a three-dimensional doorway. Alton opened his eyes and turned the handle, pushing the door open.

Beyond, I could see the cavernous ceiling of an ancient, Gothic-style church, which had long been reclaimed by nature. An iron fence stood at the far end, the gates open to reveal a plinth with an ornate altar on top of it. The stone floor had seen better days, splintered with cracks that provided space for eager weeds to grow through, thirsty for sunlight, and covered in fallen debris.

Moonlight shone through tall windows on both sides, though some had been shattered completely, leaving the church open to the elements, and the bitter cold that swept in from outside. I stepped through first, in awe of the place. The darkness threw me off for a moment, as I had no idea where we were. I guessed there must have been a bit of a time difference, as this place was already steeped in night. An icy draft blew through the abandoned building, whistling between the eaves as if it held a secret. All around the arching church, ghostly statues were hidden amongst the architecture, their stained hands clutching musical instruments.

"Harley?" Alton's voice snapped me out of my trance.

"Yeah?"

"I'll need some help with these." He still stood on the threshold of the doorway, nodding to the two caskets.

"Of course. Sorry."

I stepped back through and grasped the brass handle on the front of the first one, using my Chaos to help me drag the heavy thing through the open doorway and onto the church's broken, weed-strewn floor. The brass studs scraped along the stone, the sound echoing around the building, as I lugged it down the main aisle of the church, the wooden base getting tangled in the undergrowth.

Finally, I reached the surprisingly well-preserved altar at the front of the space. There was no sound quite like hauling a coffin along bare stone, and it made me shudder like nails on a chalkboard. Even after I'd set my casket down, I had to listen to Alton do the same, watching him strain against the weight of it.

Turning back, I looked at the other end of the church. An exploding star of still-intact glasswork glowed above a sandstone balcony, a wooden door tucked beneath it, with a heavy, rusty chain stopping anyone from entering. Anyone without an *Aperi Si Ostium* spell, anyway.

This place was breathtaking and haunting in equal measure, as though I could close my eyes and hear the ghosts of an ancient choir singing at the tops of their lungs and listen to the sermons that had been spoken across gathered congregations. I wondered how many baptisms, marriages, and funerals had been done here—the three stages of life. Birth, love, death.

"Where are we?" I asked, as Alton approached.

"The Church of Saint-Étienne-le-Vieux, in Caen."

"That's France, right?"

He smiled. "Yes, France. Northern France, to be exact."

"What time is it here?"

"Two o'clock in the morning, thereabouts."

"Well, that explains the darkness."

He nodded. "It's better that we have the cover of night."

"Where's this Doncaster dude? I thought you said he was already here."

A figure popped up from the balcony, patting dust from what looked to be a *very* expensive, dark green suit—the kind that would have made Wade just as green with envy. It pained me to think of him, stranded in Montana, wondering what he'd done wrong. Pushing away those thoughts, I focused on the shadowy man on top of the balcony.

Light as a feather, he leapt over the edge and landed on the ground, the impact softened by a cushion of Air that he pillowed out underneath him as he soared. Standing to his full height, which had to be over six feet, he approached. In the moonlight, I could see him better as he came closer. He was insanely good-looking, that much was obvious, with a mane of oh-so-casual reddish-brown curls and the most intense blue eyes I'd ever seen. Designer stubble grazed his jawline, his posture like that of a ballet dancer, making his suit look all the more impressive.

Wow... where have they been hiding you? He looked like he'd stepped out of the pages of *Esquire,* or *GQ,* and I found myself quickly losing grasp of my voice as he came to a halt in front of me. This kind of man didn't exist in real life, as far as I knew, but here he was, a hint of mischief turning up the corners of his mouth.

"You must be the fabled Ms. Merlin, if I'm not mistaken. It is the greatest of pleasures to make your acquaintance." He actually bowed, one hand on his abdomen, the other elegantly placed behind his back. His voice was soft and masculine, with a distinct British accent that made me even more tongue-tied.

"You must be Davin," I managed to blurt out.

He chuckled as he stood. "I hope you haven't heard too many terrible things. I'm not half the rogue people love to gossip that I am, though I don't mind the air of mystery so much. One must always keep an air of intrigue about oneself, if only to keep life interesting."

He took my hand, placing a gentle kiss on it. I stared at him like an idiot, completely taken aback. This wasn't what I'd been expecting.

"Uh... yeah."

He smiled. "I confess, I've come to find you exceedingly interesting, even though we've never met. Such bravado, such gravitas, in one so young—it is enthralling, it truly is. When I received the call from Alton, I thought it to be some sort of jest, until he explained your intentions in further detail. Although, he didn't mention how rare a beauty you were." He glanced at Alton. "Shame on you."

"Uh... thanks?" I mumbled. I had to remember Alton's warning about this guy's trustworthiness, but I almost couldn't believe that someone so beautiful and well-spoken could be any of the things Alton had said he was.

"When you're done with your charm offensive, we've got things to do." Alton shot Davin a warning glance.

Davin raised his hands in mock surrender. "Are you envious, Alton?

Would it make you feel more comfortable if I were to comment upon your good looks?"

Alton shook his head. "No, it wouldn't."

"You are too coy. You always have been." Davin gave me a hundred-kilowatt smile. "When you called to ask for my assistance, how could I resist? To work alongside the great Alton Waterhouse—such opportunities don't often present themselves, nor does the opportunity to delve into the great unknown of what awaits us upon our demise. You certainly know how to tickle my fancy, Alton."

"Have you done this kind of thing before?" I asked. He gave off this intense aura of power, but, from what Alton had told me, this sort of spell was unchartered territory for any and all Necromancers, Davin Doncaster included. I did a quick Empathy check on him, remembering that this was a total stranger, but all I could feel was confidence and self-assurance, with a hint of passion that made my insides feel weird.

He shook his head. "Nobody has, which is why my interest has been thoroughly piqued. I've performed resurrections of all kinds, but this… this is beyond anything any Necromancer has done before. I have always hoped my name might echo through history, rather than simply from the lips of exquisite women, and if this proves a success, perhaps I will finally have my name in one of those tomes." He flashed me a wink that made my cheeks flush.

"Do you think you can pull it off?" I pressed, trying to look anywhere but at him.

"Usually, the more powerful the magical, the greater the chance of a not-so-disastrous resurrection. Fortunately, you have two such powerful magicals at your disposal, so let's hope we can achieve a mutually satisfactory conclusion."

I didn't know if it was my mind or his accent, but I was having some trouble concentrating right now, with those blue eyes fixed on me. There had to be some Chaos going on here that made him so magnetic. No man could naturally have that sort of energy.

"You should've been thrown in Purgatory a long time ago for all the Necromancing you've done. Illegally, I might add," Alton said. "You can't go around resurrecting people at will."

Davin laughed. "Whyever not? Why be gifted with such talents if you aren't going to use them? It is one's duty to use *everything* one has been given, especially if it brings pleasure to others. Would you deny people that?"

"You rip people off," Alton shot back.

"I grant them closure," Davin replied, cool as a cucumber. "You should try it sometime. You never know, you may like it."

"Like I said, you should have been put in Purgatory a long time ago for the things you've done for money."

Davin smiled. "A man must live, and he must live well if he can. Have I helped some old dears tell their recently passed husbands that they have loved them, without fail, for decades? Yes, I have. Have I helped to heal the wounds of a family torn apart by the death of a child? Yes, I have. Have I helped star-crossed lovers have one last moment to declare their undying love? Of course. Life is so very fragile, and we are here to bridge the gap between the living and the dead. Should I receive punishment for being the gatekeeper to those precious moments?"

"You're a charlatan," Alton replied.

"Oof, a palpable hit." Davin smirked. "However, since we're discussing illegalities, perhaps you shouldn't be so quick to point the finger. I'm not the one who brought two stolen corpses here, after all."

Alton narrowed his eyes. "I did it for the sake of keeping this world safe."

"There are always excuses," Davin replied. "I have mine, you have yours. Perhaps we should leave it at that, before it turns to fisticuffs? I should hate to have to put on such a vulgar display in front of Ms. Merlin."

"Yeah, I think that'd be best," I said dryly, a little amused by their banter, although it had proven Alton's point that Davin was into some shady stuff. "We've got a lot to do tonight, and I don't want to have to deal with any bloody noses."

"Just the living dead?" Davin's words hovered eerily in the air.

I took a breath. "Yep, that's pretty much it. And I need you two to work together, instead of sniping at each other, if we're going to revive my parents. I'll take the rest from there."

"A remarkable woman indeed," Davin murmured, smiling at me.

As soon as my mom and dad were revived, I'd tell them what this was all about—that was, if they didn't come back as mindless zombies or with mixed-up minds, in which case, we'd be royally screwed.

If all went well, I'd follow the spell and finally unveil the Grimoire's secrets.

TWENTY-EIGHT

Harley

"Help me move these," Alton said, nodding to the caskets. "We need to get them as close to the altar as possible."

"Why?" I replied, out of curiosity.

"Altars of any kind are usually positioned in spots where the fabric between the land of the living and the realm of the dead is thinnest. It's why Necromancers try to perform resurrections as close to an altar as possible, though I've got no idea if it'll make a difference for this one. I'm talking about spirits that haven't crossed over yet," he replied. "But we've got to do what we can, with what we know works."

Davin tutted. "You would ask Ms. Merlin to heave a casket? Where are your manners?" He stepped past me and took up one of the casket handles, pulling it closer to the ancient altar.

"She managed just fine before," Alton muttered, pulling the second one flush against the first so that they pointed out from the altar like two black piano keys.

"You should step behind that fence." Davin looked up at me as he unlocked the clasp that held the two parts of the casket lid together. "Not only because of what you may see within these caskets, but because of what may happen. You shouldn't be near in case the Necromancy affects you by accident."

"It can do that?" My eyes widened.

"It can, Ms. Merlin," he replied. "You may come forward once the resurrection is complete, to begin your own spell. Until then, it would be best if you didn't come too close, especially if they arise as zombies. I loathe the word, personally, but it's a very real affliction, and if we must behead... Well, it would not do to have a lady risk a bite."

My stomach churned with nerves. "Would I turn into one?"

He laughed. "Those are fairytales—the stuff of Hollywood and awful video games. You won't 'turn,' per se, but you may acquire a nasty infection of the necrotizing variety."

"Okay, stay back until they're resurrected. Got it." I retreated behind the iron fence.

I couldn't tear my gaze away as they simultaneously lifted the lids of the caskets, revealing the pale corpses inside. Unlike Isadora, these ones looked peaceful, like they could well have been sleeping. In fact, I expected them to jump out of the coffins at any moment and declare that there'd been a terrible mistake, and they weren't dead at all.

One was a young woman of around thirty, while the other one was an older man, maybe in his mid-forties. I wished they looked more like my mom and dad, but that would never have been possible, not even if we'd had all the time in the world.

"You should get started on preparations for your spell while we deal with this," Alton said, his tone worried.

"I have extra vessels, should you need any. I always carry spares. One can never be too prepared," Davin added, pointing to a small wooden chest that was spilling over with bowls and dishes and urns of all kinds. I slipped around the iron fence, trying not to look too hard at the corpses, and took three of the deep ceramic bowls, before retreating to my safe spot.

As I watched, Alton and Davin took a bowl each and set them on the chest of each corpse. Next, they put two smaller dishes on the eyes of the dead. They went back and forth between the altar and Davin's chest of wonders, taking out pouches of herbs and weird-looking trinkets: two smoothed rubies, two rabbit paws, two shriveled things that reminded me of shrunken heads, and two silver chains with charms embedded in the silver. They worked seamlessly, despite their previous snarking, putting the necklaces around the bodies' necks.

"What herbs are you using?" I asked.

"Frankincense, dried oriental lilies, periwinkle, Nepalese poppies, green yarrow, and ayahuasca," Alton replied.

"And plenty of garlic, of course," Davin chimed in.

"Garlic? Why do you need garlic?" *Please don't tell me they're going to wake up as vampires.* Zombies were one thing; vampires were something I couldn't wrap my head around right now.

"Purification," he explained. "Nothing to worry about. Dracula isn't going to come and give you a nasty bite either, though you certainly have the sort of neck any vampire worth his salt would long to sink his teeth into."

I gaped at Davin. "I'd rather nobody took a bite out of me tonight, if it's all the same to you."

He laughed. "A shame. I'll have to suppress my own vampiric tendencies." With a grin fixed on his face, he licked his right canine in a way that made me want the ground to swallow me up.

Ignoring him and turning back to my own task, I sat down on the ground and took out the Grimoire, flipping it open to the right page. After reading the instructions, I removed the herbs from my satchel. I used the three bowls I'd taken and split the ingredients equally into three parts, before adding three drops of quicksilver. The dark purple liquid from the alchemical catalyst tube would come later, once the resurrection was complete. As for the Sherlock's Eye, I was supposed to hold that while I recited the words of the spell.

With my preparations more or less finished, I turned back to Alton and Davin. They'd stopped ferrying things from the wooden box and were now adding the finer details, crumbling up the petals of the oriental lilies and letting them fall across the bodies in the caskets. It was oddly beautiful to watch.

"You need to spread the petals so that they lie closer together," Davin remarked.

"You stick to your corpse, and I'll stick to mine," Alton shot back.

He shrugged. "It will be your funeral."

"I know what I'm doing." I could sense Alton's nerves, his mood dark.

"Do you? I thought all of this was purely theoretical. I doubt either of us knows what we are doing." Davin smirked. His emotions were all confidence with a hint of intrigue and amusement.

"Do you ever take anything seriously?" I asked, drawing Davin's attention to me.

"Very few things," he replied. "Love, beauty, elegant tailoring… yes, I would say that is about it."

"Not death?" That surprised me.

He shook his head. "Never death. As a Necromancer, one learns that it's nothing to be taken seriously. It can always be reversed, even if not for very long. And we have the gift of knowing that there is *something* beyond." He grinned. "You must be looking forward to seeing them again."

I sighed. "I don't know how I feel about it."

"Really? I would have thought you'd be chomping at the bit to see them in the proverbial flesh, even if they're coming through different bodies."

I shook my head. "I haven't really thought about it. To be honest, I didn't know if we'd get this far, so anything beyond this is… unknown territory for me, too."

"Intriguing," he murmured. "Very intriguing."

"I don't see why. Neither of you knows if this will actually work, so there's no use getting my hopes up until it's done."

He smiled. "Beauty and intellect. A heady mix."

"Yeah, well, get your head back into what you're doing so you don't mess this up."

He laughed. "Amusing, too. Ah, if only you were a few years older."

"Pack it in, Davin," Alton growled. "If we fail because your eyes are wandering, I'll see to it that you end up in one of these coffins. Harley is not your plaything, and I'd prefer it if you kept your words and your mind out of the gutter. If you make another comment like that, I'll be forced to intervene. I don't want things to get nasty, so don't push your luck, do you understand?"

"I have no idea what you're talking about. My eyes and my mind are entirely focused, Alton. Honestly, the pair of *you* ought to get your minds out of the gutter before they start collecting mulch." He chuckled, clearly not bothered by Alton's threats, though I was grateful for the backup. I could handle myself, but it felt nice to have someone help to defend me. Returning to his task, Davin set two of the rubies into the eye dishes that covered the sockets of the dead, creating a weird image that reminded me of the djinn. Opposite, Alton did the same. I had no idea if they were reaching the end of their preparations, but a strange tension lingered in the air that hadn't been there before, as though something big were about to happen.

"Do you have the ghoul bones?" Alton asked.

I frowned. "I thought they were for the Hidden Things spell."

He nodded. "They are, but we need them for this, too. It'll strengthen the power of our spell. Think of those bones like a guide, to help your mother and father back from wherever they are."

"What kind did you acquire?" Davin turned to me.

"They're the bones of the Bai Gu Jing." I took the sleek black box out of my satchel and opened the lid. Set against an interior of red velvet, they didn't look like much—just a pile of white bones. They definitely didn't look human, though I wasn't sure if that made it better or worse.

"Exceptional." Davin smiled, approaching me to take the whole box.

"Will I get them back?"

He nodded. "They will remain intact. There's very little in this world that can destroy the bones of a Bai Gu Jing, not even Necromancy of this magnitude. You'll have them returned, worry not."

"Is that right?" I glanced at Alton for reassurance.

"Yes, he's telling the truth. You'll get the bones back, to use for the Hidden Things spell."

"You think I'm lying?" Davin eyed me curiously.

I shrugged. "The jury's still out." My hand accidentally grazed his as I reluctantly handed the box over, his eyes widening as we made contact.

"My goodness," he gasped.

"What?"

"You... I knew you were remarkable, but this? This is something else entirely."

I frowned. "I don't know what you're talking about."

"The power in you, Ms. Merlin. It is… intoxicating. One brush of your fair skin, and I can feel it all. Chaos is positively brimming out of you, in the best possible way. I'm surprised you aren't glowing, given the intensity of it."

"I'm not radioactive. You aren't going to grow three heads." I quickly pulled my hands away, feeling weirdly embarrassed by what he'd felt.

"No, my dear, you are so much more."

Taking the box, he returned to the caskets and set the ghoul bones on the altar in front of them. He opened the lid and placed his hands over the bones, closing his eyes. A moment later, he began to speak, only it didn't sound like his voice at all. It was deeper and darker, as though it was coming from somewhere else entirely. The tone of it sounded Chinese.

A few seconds later, the bones rattled, rising out of the box of their own accord. Instinctively, I grabbed the Grimoire and clasped it to my chest, in case this was some unexpected attack. Davin might have been charming as heck, but Alton didn't trust him, which meant I couldn't, either.

The bones floated out past Davin's hand and twisted in a spiral, hovering over the top of the two caskets. I couldn't tell if it was the moonlight glancing in through the windows, or my eyes playing tricks on me, but the bones seemed to be growing and connecting.

The limbs lengthened, and the bones disappeared as a beautiful young woman with long, flowing black hair, enshrouded in a billowing white dress, emerged. She was possibly the most stunning woman I'd ever seen, her features Chinese and striking, making her all the more ethereal. Only, she wasn't entirely solid. She was standing right between the caskets, her body passing through them as if they weren't even there. If I looked hard enough, I could even see the altar and back wall through her skin. Davin bowed to her, and she bowed back.

"Bai Gu Jing, it is a pleasure," he said.

"Why have you called me?" she replied, her voice a raspy whisper.

"There are two souls we need you to guide back to the land of the living, with the aid of a spell we're about to perform," Davin explained.

"You are Necromancers. Why call for me?"

"These souls are beyond the spirit world. They reside in the afterlife."

The apparition frowned. "The afterlife? That is beyond your reach."

"Which is why we need you," Davin replied.

"You know I do not obey the will of men. It was men who put me where I am. It was men who turned me to bone." Her voice bristled with anger.

"Then do it for me," I said, rising from my hiding place.

"And who are you?" The woman turned, sweeping through the church until she was mere inches from my face.

"I'm Harley Merlin. It's my mom and dad we need to bring back," I replied, my voice shaking. The building had turned icy cold, the hairs on my arms standing on end as my teeth chattered.

Her expression softened. "Your mother and father?"

"Yes."

"Merlin… I know that name," she purred. *Join the club.*

"My family have been magicals since the Primus Anglicus."

She nodded. "Then you have ancient blood in your veins, as I do."

"Does that mean you'll help?"

She smiled sadly. "I cannot deny the pleas of a young maiden."

"Thank you, Miss… uh Bai Gu Jing. You have no idea what this means to me." I gave an awkward bow, and she returned it.

"I understand loss, maiden." Her ghostly hand caressed my face, sending an icy shiver right down my spine. "It is deep in my very bones."

"In that case, we should get started," Alton said, staring at the ghost. "Davin, are you ready?"

He nodded. "I thought you'd never ask."

"There are no assurances that I will be able to guide their souls back," the spirit woman said, her voice echoing through the church, making it colder by the second.

"We've got no assurances that this is going to work, so we're all in the same boat," Alton replied.

"So grab an oar and join us." Davin grinned mischievously. I was in awe of the dude—he was genuinely unfazed by this.

The spirit bowed her head. "Very well. I will listen and act as I see fit."

"Davin?" Alton eyed him.

He smiled. "Ready when you are."

Alton took two sticks of sage and lit the ends, passing one to Davin. Together, they formed smoky patterns across the bodies in the caskets, both of them humming as they worked. It wasn't a tune I recognized, but the moonlight seemed to dim as they hummed, the church so cold I was turning blue, all my extremities going numb. *I should've snagged a bigger coat on my way out.* Slowly, they placed the sage into the bowls that sat on the corpses' chests, the fire igniting the herbs.

Alton and Davin raised their hands. Tendrils of purple and black light slithered around their fingers as they pressed their palms onto the shoulders of the dead. The purple light crept out of their hands and snaked over the dead bodies, sinking deep beneath the skin. Every collapsed vein lit up purple, creating a spiderweb beneath their pale flesh.

I held my breath as they began to chant, in perfect harmony. "Otherworld *animum, cuius extra scimus nostras voces ut relicto mundo ad imitandum nos. Caelum et deditionem venire ad nos. Qui nosti omnia relinquere et ad quam quondam audire solebas. Haec in corporibus sunt fructus, et adhuc vivere. Vasorum parati tenent. Pervenit ad nos intendere verbis per velamen separat mortis. Transire ab ignotis limine portae margariticae, et reditus. Opus es. Vos voluit. Convertere, quaeso.*"

They repeated it twice more. After they'd completed the third chant, the bone spirit disappeared with a snap of bitterly cold smoke, no doubt chasing after the spirits of my mom and dad, wherever they were. Meanwhile, Alton and Davin continued, while I sat there and watched. After every phrase, the church grew darker, until a frosted sheen splintered out across the ancient sandstone, the windows fogging over with ice. The purple light that surged from their palms grew brighter, pulsating under the skin of the dead bodies, until I could barely look at it without burning my retinas.

Davin seemed to be taking it all in stride, his voice booming and powerful as he repeated the mantra over and over.

Alton, on the other hand, seemed to be struggling. His voice strained as he urged the words out, and sweat poured off his forehead as he fought to keep his hands on the shoulders of his corpse. Black sparks crackled and fizzed from his palms, his veins glowing purple from the edge of his shirt collar and up his neck. It reached his face, the purple light turning black as it followed the lines of his circulation, until his features were a mess of his normal skin and this sickening darkness. His lips had turned jet black, and when I looked up to his eyes, I saw that there was no white or green left. His eyeballs had turned entirely black, with two bright purple pinpricks in the center.

"Alton, you can do this," I shouted. The church floor had begun to rumble, the walls shuddering, and I had to yell to make myself heard. "Don't let it defeat you! We need this to work. I need this to work. I need you to fight, like you've never fought before!"

I didn't know if he'd heard me, but his mouth turned into a grimace, the muscles in his neck popping as though he was trying his best to urge more power into the dead young woman in front of him. *Yes, come on, Alton!*

They continued to chant, Alton's voice getting stronger, matching Davin's volume. My gaze flitted between the two men, panic rising through my chest. Whatever they were doing looked like it was killing them, decaying them from the inside out. Even Davin looked like he was starting to struggle, the black veins now creeping across his face, too. Their hands were shaking on the corpses, sweat dripping down onto the broken stone and the overgrown weeds, both of them trembling under the strain.

One of the windows behind me shattered, making me jump. But, if Davin or Alton had heard it, they weren't showing it. Davin's eyes darkened to that same encompassing black, with the two pinpricks of purple light taking the place of his pupils. I'd been so preoccupied with worrying about the state my parents might come back in that I hadn't considered what state Davin and Alton would end up in. Right now, it didn't look good.

As the chant built to a roaring crescendo, I dropped the Grimoire and covered my ears. The Bai Gu Jing suddenly reappeared between the caskets. There seemed to be two other figures with her, wispy and spirit-like. With a scream that shattered the rest of the windows, the White Bone Spirit slammed her hazy palms into the chests of the dead woman and the dead man and disappeared in an explosion of vivid purple light. Her bones hovered for a moment over the two caskets, before they toppled back into the box on the altar.

Alton and Davin staggered backward, releasing their corpses. The black veins receded and left the two men stooped and panting on the altar plinth. I sprinted toward the caskets, just in time to see both bodies blink their eyes awake. A strange, shimmering haze rippled across them both, as if something were being projected onto their bodies. It was like watching a time lag, where one frame of an image was trying to keep up with the next one. I realized, with a jolt of nervous excitement, that my mom and dad's faces were showing through those of the dead bodies, phasing in and out.

"Did it work?" Alton rasped, wiping his face with the back of his sleeve.

"I hope it did. Otherwise, that was a useless palaver." Davin gave a weary laugh as he removed a silk handkerchief from his top pocket and dabbed it across his face.

I rested my hands on the closed halves of the casket lids and waited. *What if they're mindless zombies?* That was my first worry. What if they didn't remember anything? What if their thoughts were mixed up with the bodies they'd taken over? The young woman blinked, my mom's face appearing for a moment, blending with the features of the deceased.

"Harley?" I'd have known that voice anywhere.

"Mom?"

"Harley, is that really you?" Tears sprang into her possessed eyes.

"It's me, Mom. It's really me." Tears threatened to spill out of my eyes as I looked down at her, the spiritual shift phasing back in to reveal my mom's face.

"Sweetheart… oh, my precious little girl," she wept, sitting up slowly as she got used to her new body.

In the other casket, the middle-aged man was starting to stir. As with my mom, there was a strange overlap, with my dad's spirit phasing across the body he'd landed in. He sat up sharply, like something from an awful Frankenstein movie, only to relax as he got a feel for his new limbs. His eyes turned toward me, but they weren't the eyes of the dead man—they were my dad's eyes. I recalled them from the dreams I'd had, trapped inside the dreamcatcher that had let me remember him when I'd first arrived at the SDC.

"Dad?" I said nervously.

"Harley?" he replied. "How can it be you? How can this be possible?"

TWENTY-NINE

Harley

All my life, I'd waited for this moment, and now that it was here, I could barely move, let alone speak.

"You're so grown up." My dad's voice caught in his throat as he emerged from the casket. "How did you get so grown up?"

I stood there frozen as he walked toward me in a hospital gown, his bare feet shuffling over the stone. Tears tumbled down my cheeks when he reached out and touched my face.

"Sweetheart," my mom whispered, as she followed him.

Their spirits phased across the bodies they were using, giving me one final, heartbreaking chance to see them the way they'd been when they were alive. My mom was even more beautiful in the flesh, red hair flowing down her back. My red hair. The red hair she'd given me. And my dad… I couldn't get over it. He was here, he was right here, standing in front of me, touching my face so gently that I wanted to crumple to the ground and hold onto his legs to stop him from ever leaving me again. He was exactly the way I'd remembered him in my dreams, with his curly, dark hair and sky-blue eyes. My eyes.

"You're here," I gasped through wrenching sobs. "You're actually here."

"My little peanut." My dad grabbed my face in his hands and stared at me, like he couldn't believe it either. "I've missed so much, haven't I?" He sounded so sad that it was about to splinter what was left of my heart into tiny pieces.

I nodded slowly. "So much. I've missed you every day. I've missed you both, every single day."

"I'm sorry I had to leave you. I'm sorry. I'm so, so sorry." He pulled me into a tight hug that I never wanted to escape from. His body felt oddly warm, as though he really was alive, dispelling any creepiness I might've felt. "Can you ever forgive me? I tried so hard to keep you with me, but I couldn't let her get you. I couldn't be selfish, but I never, for a second, wanted to be away from you. I wanted to watch you grow up. I wanted to see every moment. And here you are, a young woman, and I wasn't here to see it happen."

I gripped him tighter. "I forgave you a long time ago. I just wish things could've been different, so you could've both been with me." I snuffled into his shoulder. "I saw the life we were supposed to have. I saw it, and I wanted it, and I couldn't have it. And now you're here, and I'm going to have to say goodbye again, and I don't know if I have it in me."

I felt a hand on my back and turned to look at my mom. "You're stronger than either of us, Harley. And it's never going to be goodbye for us. As long as you're still breathing, and you're still living, and you're still looking up at the night sky and thinking of us, we'll always be by your side." She smiled sadly. "We always have been."

I put my arm out to bring her into this bittersweet hug, clinging to both my parents as if I were a child again, a little girl who'd grazed her knee and thought the world was going to end. Only a kind word and a kiss on the forehead from my mom and dad could have fixed my pain then, and that hadn't changed. In that moment, I would've given everything to have kept them here. But I could already sense our time coming to an end, and that made me cling ever tighter, savoring every moment of having them in my arms.

"I love you so much," I murmured, pulling their heads against mine. "I've missed you so much. I don't want to have to go on without you."

"I love you, sweetheart." My mom pressed her forehead to mine.

"I loved you from the moment I heard you were coming into our lives. My peanut. Our peanut." My dad pulled away slightly and brushed a strand of hair behind my ear. "But your mom is right, Harley. We're not going anywhere. We might not be able to stay in this world, but we're always here, with you. Our blood runs in your veins. Whenever you feel like it's too hard, or you can't go on, just know that we're watching, and we're proud, and we know you can do anything you set your mind to. We carry you with us, wherever we go." He pressed his hand to his chest, covering his heart.

"Where have you been?" I asked, wishing Alton and Davin would just disappear. I could sense their anxiety to continue, but I wasn't ready yet. I needed longer.

My dad frowned. "I can't remember. There was peace and calm, and everything felt good. No aches, no pains, no heartbreak. But… I don't know where or what that place was."

"It's the same for me," my mom replied. "I remember feeling at ease, and I remember your dad being with me, but I don't know where that place was. I don't remember anything after you released me from Eris Island."

A pained sob clenched my chest, my lungs burning as I fought to keep hold of my emotions. It was a relief to know that, wherever they'd been, they'd been together.

"Hate to be the one to disturb such a touching display, but we've really got to get a move on if we're going to complete your spell, Harley." Davin's voice echoed through the church, making my heart sink. He was right, but couldn't he just wait?

"There's no way of knowing how long these bodies will hold your spirits, Hiram, Hester," Alton wheezed. The cracked, raspy tone of his voice made me turn over my shoulder. He was sitting on the ground beside the casket, his eyelids blinking slowly, his face pale and sweaty.

"We also have no way of knowing how long we may have until Mr. Waterhouse begins to Purge," Davin added. "The last thing we need is a rampant Purge beast running amok whilst you try to complete your spell. It will be difficult enough, from what Alton has told me, without such an inconvenience."

"Spell?" My dad frowned.

I nodded. "That's why I brought you back. I need your help with one of the spells you wrote in the Grimoire. It needs all three of us. For it to work, we all need to sink into Euphoria and find a sliver of memory that's been buried deep. At least, that's what I think we need to do. Although, it's your spell, so maybe you can help me out?"

My mom shook her head. "I… I can't remember what we wrote in that Grimoire. Can you, Hiram?"

"No, I don't think I can," he replied. "It's all a bit hazy, but it always was. Chaos channeled into us and wrote through us, but it was hard, even then, to grasp what we were actually putting into the book."

That wasn't good. I'd been so sure that they would be able to guide me through the spells they'd written down, but apparently they were as stumped as I was.

"We always had a sense of what we were writing, but the words never really connected in our heads," my mom explained, her brow furrowed.

"I do remember one thing, though." My dad stared at my mom, as though the memory of what he'd done was coming back in full force. Fresh tears brimmed in his eyes, his mouth half open, like he wanted to cry out. "I do remember writing one last spell, on my own. Your mom wasn't there. I was alone."

I struggled with my words. "I know the one you're talking about. It's the last entry."

"Chaos made me write it, but there was more urgency than there'd been before," he replied, speaking in a stilted manner, as if he were saying things the moment they emerged in his mind. "It's the single most dangerous spell that's ever been written. I remember that. I remember thinking it, as I wrote it. I was crying, though… Why was I crying? I remember anger and grief, and an internal battle… but why? I can't remember why." I could hear the frustration in his voice as he stared at Hester.

"Because you were about to kill me," my mom said quietly. "You were under the Sal Vínna curse when you wrote that last spell. You couldn't fight it. Even when you were standing in front of me, you couldn't fight it. It was too strong."

My dad's mouth fell open. "Hester…"

"I forgave you the moment I saw you and knew what was going to happen." She smiled up at him with so much love that it took my breath away. "Katherine killed me, not you. You were merely her weapon. You couldn't have resisted. I could see you battling until the very last moment, but you were too far gone."

"My love… how could I have done that to you?" Tears fell down his cheeks as he moved to touch her face, brushing back the phantom hair and gazing deep into her eyes.

"Because you had no choice." She looped her arms around his neck, as though there were nobody else in the room. I didn't know whether to look away or keep watching. This moment felt too private for anyone to see.

"Why couldn't I remember?" He brushed his thumb across her cheek.

"It was the afterlife's gift to you, to get rid of all the bad memories and leave only the good ones," she replied. "You were never supposed to remember, and I was never going to tell you. But, just know, I don't blame you. I never did. My sister took me away from you, and she took me away from our daughter, and I could never forgive her for that, even if I had a thousand more years stuffed in a jar."

"I'm so sorry." My dad pulled her into his arms and buried his face in her neck. "I'm so sorry I did that to you. I'm so sorry I didn't remember. You must have been carrying that burden for so long."

"Hey, none of that matters now," she whispered. "I love you, and I will always love you, and nothing Katherine did, or could do, will ever change that."

"I love you, Hester. I love you so much."

Davin cleared his throat, making me want to punch him right in his Adam's apple. "I really must insist that we start on your spell, Harley. Otherwise we will lose our window of opportunity."

"The last spell?" My dad looked at me in alarm.

I shook my head. "Not just yet. I need to find out how to read the Grimoire first. That's why you're here. That's the spell I need your help for. Here." I darted to the spot behind the iron fence and took up the book, bringing it back over and opening it up. I thought about flipping straight to the Hidden Things spell, but curiosity urged me to flick to the back, where that last, terrible spell was written. "Do you know what this says?"

My dad took a shaky breath as he looked at the strange writing. "No… I can't read it. Is that the last spell I wrote?"

"Yeah."

"I don't even know what language that is." He traced his fingertips across it, but nothing happened. "Hester, can you read this?"

She eyed the script and shook her head. "No, I have no idea. Is it a form of Arabic?"

"Maybe, but the symbols aren't quite the same."

"Wait." My dad froze.

"What is it?" My heart lurched.

"I can't remember the actual spell, but I know what it was intended for. It's supposed to destroy Katherine," he replied. "But, if you're going to do this, you'll need to be fast with it. There's no guarantee it'll work once she ascends as a Child of Chaos. All of these spells were intended to be used to stop her before that point, so I don't know if they'll still work afterward."

"How do you know that?" my mom said.

He frowned. "It's like remembering a dream. Bits and pieces come back to you, but not the whole thing. I think Chaos had me write this once Katherine had put the Sal Vínna curse on me." He paused. "I think I knew what I was about to do, and I knew I couldn't give in without fighting back another way. Letting Chaos take over for those few minutes must have been the best I could do. I'm sorry… I'm so sorry, Hester. And to you, Harley—I took your mom away, and I—"

"I don't blame you, Dad," I interjected. "Like Mom, I forgave you a long time ago. I was the one who found out you were under the curse. I went to New York and I looked at the pictures, and I knew you weren't the one responsible. What you did was Katherine's doing, not yours. It was all her. One day, I'll clear your name… if I make it through this fight with Katherine."

"Oh Harley…" He reached out and took my hand.

"Speaking of Katherine." I took a deep breath. "She murdered Isadora."

My dad's face fell. "What?"

"She killed her, and Alton couldn't resurrect her. He tried, but there was nothing he could do. This is why I'm here, calling on you both, so we can end that bitch for good and stop her from killing anyone else." My voice cracked.

"About time," I heard Davin mutter. I glared at him. Beside him, on the ground, Alton really didn't look good. He'd gone a waxy shade of blue, his lips colorless, his hair drenched in sweat and plastered to his forehead. It spurred me on, knowing we had to get this spell done before any Purge beasts could spring out and surprise us, wrecking this whole thing before it had even gotten off the ground.

"Usually I would tell you to mind your language, but in this case, I think it's entirely called for," my mom replied, her voice bitter with anger and sadness.

"Then we should get started on this spell, so we can make that happen," my dad agreed, his eyes swimming with grief. "Nobody else is going to die because of her. Not if we can help it. So, what do you need us to do?"

I turned the page to the Hidden Things spell and let them read through the instructions. "I just need to add the alchemical catalyst, and then we can start with the Euphoria."

"I'm sorry it's come to this, Harley," my dad said, squeezing my hand.

"Me, too. But if it stops Katherine, then it won't seem so bad." I let go of his hand and moved toward the three bowls of ingredients that I'd mixed. Taking the tube of purple liquid, I applied three drops to each one and carried them back over to my mom and dad. I handed one to each of them, while leaving the third for myself.

"We should sit," my mom said. "And put the bowl in your lap."

"Do you remember how to do this?" I asked, surprised.

She smiled uncertainly. "It's coming back to me. Do you have the Sherlock's Eye?"

I nodded and took it out of my pocket. "What do I do with it?"

"Put the Grimoire in the very center of the triangle we're about to make, and put the Sherlock's Eye on top of the Hidden Things spell," she replied. *Man, am I glad you're here.* "And the ghoul bones? You'll need those."

"Ghoul bones. Right." I hurried over to the altar and took the box of ghoul bones, which had all returned to their resting place inside. Closing the lid, I carried them back to my mom and dad.

Together, we sat down in a scrappy triangle. As instructed, I put the bowl in my lap and placed the Sherlock's Eye in the center, while my mom took the ghoul bones and scattered them in a vague circle around us. Then she took my hand while reaching for my dad's, too. Following suit, I took my dad's hand, and the triangle was complete. I waited until they'd closed their eyes before I did the same, trying to remember everything I'd been taught about getting into a state of Euphoria. Breathing deeply, I let my thoughts fade away, working through each thought in my head until there was nothing left, like clearing out a warehouse. I needed to find the hidden boxes at the back of that warehouse, and I couldn't do that with everything else getting in the way.

Moving through my memories as quickly as I could, I finally felt myself teeter over the edge of reality and into Euphoria, like I'd done with Nomura in his study.

Blackness swallowed me whole.

THIRTY

Harley

The darkness receded, but I wasn't somewhere in the depths of my mind anymore.

Instead, I was standing in the nursery that should've been mine, with mini-me Harley sitting in the lap of a gigantic bunny, wafting its fluffy paws in a wave.

This isn't right.

Euphoria wasn't like this the last time. There'd been no nursery, no mini-me, and definitely no six-foot stuffed rabbit. I should've been in the darkest recesses of my mind by now, sifting through all my memories until I found the ones I'd buried deep—ones I didn't even remember, because I'd chosen not to.

"What's going on? Why am I here?" I stared at the little version of me, who just giggled. Creepy as ever.

"Did you think you'd have to wade through all that stuff in your head?" she replied. "Ha, Wade. Get it? Speaking of that poor boy, he's still trying to wrestle free of those entrapment stones. He's not going to be very happy with you when you see him again."

I frowned. "Does that mean I *am* going to see him again?" That worried me. There were only two reasons I'd be seeing Wade again. One, if I managed to survive this and stop Katherine in her tracks. Two, if he tried to come to my aid, even after I'd tried to escape him. The first filled me with excitement, but the latter… that wasn't going to happen, not on my watch.

She shrugged. "How should I know?" Ah yes, mini-me, the all-knowing, never-telling pain in my ass. I'd forgotten just how charming she could be.

"So, why aren't I in Euphoria right now? That's what I'm supposed to be doing, and this sure as heck isn't Euphoria."

She giggled, the sound making the hairs on the back of my neck stand to attention. "You are different now, Harley. You will never come to experience Euphoria like an ordinary magical ever again. This state you are currently in… it transcends it all. Euphoria is child's play compared to what you can do with that mind of yours. Our mind."

"Can you just tell me where I am? No riddles."

"Chaos rules, Harley. Chaos rules."

I pulled a sour face. "I swear, if one more person says, 'Chaos rules,' I'm going to spontaneously combust."

She chuckled. "Chaos rules."

"Is this Chaos then?"

Mini-me pouted, like I'd spoiled her game. "In a way, yes. You are connected to the Grimoire and the Chaos within you on a much deeper level than before. You've opened a gateway, and that cannot be closed until you choose to close it… or it is closed for you." She flapped the bunny's paw, as if she was telling me off. "You should be grateful. This is much better than struggling through Euphoria, isn't it? At least, here, there's no risk of getting trapped in astral planes by desperate preceptors."

"Can I find this memory sliver here?" I looked around the room, but nothing jumped out at me. I half expected there to be a box or something, with a great big X on top, marking the spot. But this place was just an echo of something that could've been; it wasn't anything I wasn't willing to remember. I wouldn't have minded forgetting creepy little mini-me for a while, but that was beside the point. This was part of something created by my mom and dad. This wasn't my memory, so that sliver, or whatever it was, couldn't be here. Could it?

"As if it would be that simple." Mini-me laughed. "Did you think I was going to hand over your piece of the key, like a gatekeeper? Perhaps I should have raided the dress-up box for something more appropriate. A robe or something."

"Then where is it? I don't have time for your games."

"Your piece of the key is hidden in your most painful memory." Mini-me's voice suddenly turned serious, the bunny arms falling to the toy's sides. "It can be found in the one memory you have forced away, time and time again, hidden deep in your subconscious mind. And, my goodness, there have been some cowboys in there."

"Hey, that's *our* subconscious you're talking about," I muttered. "But what's the memory? If it's something awful, surely I'd be able to remember it."

"You need to dig deep, deeper than you have ever gone before, so that you can pluck up the memory and embrace it. Make peace, and you'll... well, you'll find the piece. Pretty clever, right?"

"Pretty stressful, actually."

Mini-me grinned. "You must embrace your pain, down to the last drop. Leave nothing unturned. Leave no emotions behind. Only then will you have access to what you need."

"I've got some questions first."

She shrugged. "It's your ticking time bomb. If you wish to waste valuable seconds on questions, then who am I to stop you?"

She was right, but there was something I had to know. "Why are there three pieces of this key? How and why did Chaos do that? If it was written by my mom and dad, it should only have been two pieces, so they could easily access it in the future, right? I mean, I don't think they even knew that I—I mean, we—existed when this spell was written. It doesn't make any sense."

"Chaos knew. Chaos knows all," mini-me replied.

"Chaos knew about me?"

She nodded. "You were already a seed, starting to unfurl. It sensed you. It knew you existed before your mother and father did."

"Okay, say that's true. Why complicate it that much further? Why not keep it to two easy pieces?"

"Your mother and father didn't know you were given a piece of the puzzle when the spell was written, as you've stated," she explained. "Hester was pregnant and had yet to find out, but Chaos foresaw a few choice things, as it likes to do. Katherine things, to be more specific."

Understanding dawned. "My mom and dad's deaths, you mean?"

"Exactly." She took up a bunny paw and tapped it against her chin. "Unable to intervene directly, or stop the deaths of your parents, Chaos had little choice but to leave small loopholes for the most capable of magicals to prove they had what it takes to complete these quests and get a peek inside the Grimoire."

"You mean me?"

"It would appear your head has swollen since we last met," she replied. "But yes, I mean you. Of course I mean you. Who else would I mean? There's nobody else who can get close to the Grimoire. At least not right now…"

I struggled not to lose my temper. "I just wanted to check. And what do you mean, 'not right now'? Are you talking about Katherine? Will she be able to read it when she ascends?" Panic hit me.

"Chaos rules, Harley. Chaos rules."

I swear to all that is good, I'd strangle her if she weren't me. "Helpful."

"I try." She grinned. "You see, this was never really about Hester or Hiram. They were vessels—avenues through which Chaos could set fail-safes in place. It was always about the endgame, and the one who can bring the spells to life." She smiled eerily. "Chaos prepared all of this for you. Isn't that nice?"

"Not the word I would've used."

She snickered. "I'm glad we're funny. You'll need that humor in the dark days to come, especially when it comes to actually defeating Katherine… or failing miserably. That's all on your rather masculine shoulders now. The pieces of the game have been on the board for a long time. They have just been waiting for the players to take their positions. And you have taken your sweet time."

"Well, if Chaos had just told me all of this, we'd be well ahead of this so-called game, so don't start pointing fingers at me," I shot back. Chaos was really starting to get on my nerves. If it had wanted me to know all of this, why hadn't it just said so earlier, when we weren't down to the wire? *Chaos rules.* I could've punched myself for thinking it.

"There were markers that had to be hit before this could happen," mini-me replied. "It just so happened that Katherine worked much quicker than anticipated."

"So this *is* Chaos's fault. And now I'm the one trying to scrabble everything together at the last minute because it underestimated her."

Mini-me shrugged. "If that makes it easier to swallow, then sure. Now, how about we go for a little walk?"

"Where?"

"Questions, questions. You will see." Mini-me jumped up and headed for the nursery door, grabbing a rag doll from one of the shelves and trailing it along the ground beside her. *That's right, just add to the creep factor.* Up until that moment, I'd had no idea I could leave this place and go somewhere else in this weird otherworld, but it looked like I was about to find out how far this place stretched. She turned the handle and gestured for me to follow her.

Stepping out, I entered a narrow, gloomy hallway. Anemic bulbs swung from the ceiling, casting a sickly glow on the ground below. Mini-me walked on ahead, flashing in and out of focus as she passed through the pools of dim light. I'd seen horror movies that started this way, and I sensed I was walking into some kind of nightmare. Steeling myself, I hurried after her, my boots echoing in the narrow corridor, reverberating back as though someone was following me. I kept glancing over my shoulder, just to be sure, but behind me, there was nothing but black, the bulbs sputtering out as we passed under each one.

"Would you prefer to be called Harley the Snail?" mini-me asked, turning to look at me.

"You're surprisingly fast for a little kid," I replied, defensively. "Where the hell are you taking me?"

"Language." She tutted. "Actually, this is the first stop." No sooner had she said it than a door appeared in the side of the corridor, a silver handle glinting in the gloom.

"What is it?"

Mini-me rolled her eyes. "Do I have to do everything for you? Open it, and you'll find out. I can't hold your hand through all of this, or Raggedy will get jealous." She lifted the doll, letting it dangle limply from her hand, like someone hanging from the end of a noose. *Yeesh...*

I turned the handle, opening the door wide. Beyond, I saw the red brickwork of my old elementary school. Memories came flooding back as I stepped through, the door staying open behind me. I'd barely walked two steps when I heard a ruckus nearby. Turning, I saw the back of a little girl. She was staring at a little boy, who was taunting her. *I know this.* The boy was tugging at her bag—my bag. A moment later, the strap broke, sending the contents spilling out onto the sidewalk. I remembered it all, like someone was playing the movie of my life, right in front of my eyes.

I was in first grade when I unleashed my first bout of Telekinesis, and all because Billy Brucker wouldn't stop picking on me. From the first day I'd walked into class, he'd targeted me. Some days, it had been stolen pencils, or "accidentally" dropping paint on one of my drawings. Other days, it had been pinches in the arm, and him trying to corner me in the hallway. But this day... well, after this, he'd never bothered me again. I sensed the moment before it came, watching the little version of me as she threw up her hands and sent Billy Bruckner flying across the road in front of the school. He landed on the opposite curb, blinking in confusion.

You deserved that, you little bastard.

"Anything interesting?" Mini-me appeared in the doorway.

I shook my head. "I know this. I didn't forget this. This can't be it."

"Then what are you dithering for? Time's a-wasting."

Mini-me was already pressing on ahead, leaving me to play catch-up. I headed back into the corridor of doom. A few moments later, we stopped beside another door. This one had a bronze handle, though I wasn't sure if that meant anything.

Before mini-me could hit me with another round of snark, I opened the door and entered. This time, I found myself in the bathroom of the Bradleys—they'd been my second or third foster home, though I'd been to so many that it was hard to keep count. There wasn't much room, but I was pretty sure none of the people in my memory knew I was here.

Pressing myself back against the jade-green tiles, which I remembered as if it were yesterday, I waited, even though I already knew what was about to happen. This was a memory that had haunted me for years, but I'd never shied away from it.

My eight-year-old self was sitting in the bath, playing happily with a toy boat, surrounded by bubbles. Her head whipped around as someone breezed past, through a door I couldn't see. Mr. Bradley stormed in and wrenched at her arm, trying to drag her out of the tub. The little girl fought back, terrified of him. I'd always been scared of Mr. Bradley.

"You think you're at a hotel, huh?" he snarled.

"N-no, Mr. Bradley."

"You think you can just play around in here while others are waiting?"

"N-no, Mr. Bradley." She tugged her arm away from the man's vise-like grip, crashing back into the water with a loud splash, sending water spilling out onto the bathroom floor. Mr. Bradley's cheeks turned beet-red as he launched a tirade of expletives at the poor girl. *Me.*

Frightened out of her mind, eight-year-old me tried to hide under the bubbles, the water freezing over as a whirlwind of icy Air swept around her. He'd lost his mind after that, blaming the plumbing, and I'd been carted off back to the orphanage until they could find another foster family for me.

"How about this one?" mini-me chirped.

"No, I remember this day clearly," I replied.

"Tick-tock, Harley." *As if I wasn't already aware.*

Leaving that awful memory behind, we carried on down the corridor. Through a few more doors, I saw my childhood self causing havoc without even realizing what she was doing. I hadn't known then what I knew now. I saw myself at twelve, setting fire to the Corbin family's curtains at Christmas with a stray tendril of Fire after their son had tried to touch me where I didn't want to be touched. I saw myself accidentally tearing the Gingers' backyard in two with a blast of Earth, just shy of my fourteenth birthday, because I'd said I didn't want a party and Mrs. Ginger had wanted to show me off to her friends. She'd called me ungrateful and wouldn't listen when I tried to tell her that I didn't like to be surrounded by big groups of people. So, I'd taken my teenage revenge on her garden. I saw myself in my bedroom at the Taylors' house, aged fifteen, trying to keep their oldest son, Eli, from attacking me. I'd sent a spiral of Water at him, dunking him completely, while the family pit bull, Barker, had stood guard over me, barking his head off and snapping his teeth at Eli.

But none of this was new to me. None of this was hidden.

Through the next door, I entered the parking lot of the casino. Deep down, I guessed I'd been hoping for this memory, ever since mini-me had mentioned Wade. My heart lurched as I saw him trying to find the escaped gargoyle, just as I'd seen him that night, when I'd come out to get in Daisy and drive off. Man, I'd hated him back then. He'd been so smug and arrogant, nothing at all like the Wade I'd come to love. I guessed we'd both been putting up fronts. I'd been lost, with no idea what I was going to do with my life beyond spotting cheaters at the tables and trying to pretend like all I needed was my independence to survive. My entire life had changed in that one, serendipitous encounter, and even though we'd snarked at each other like nobody's business, I wouldn't have changed it for the world. *I miss you*. I knew this Wade couldn't hear me, but I wanted him to know, all the same.

"How about this one?" Mini-me popped up at my side.

"No, this is a good one," I replied sadly. There were way too many Harleys in this image. I backed away, wanting to get out of there as quickly as possible. It was too overwhelming to see that now, no matter how much I wished I could've stayed a bit longer.

After a few more doors that didn't show anything remarkable, I reached one with a blue ceramic handle. Feeling a bit disheartened after pushing through my endless memories, with nothing to show for it, I turned the handle and entered the next room. I frowned as I looked around at the bedroom, which was steeped in a cold, blue light. Flowers snaked up the walls, and a lamp shaped like a rocket cast a pale glow on the bed, where a small version of me sat, knees tucked up to her chin. I remembered the room. I was back at the Bradleys' house again. I would've recognized that hideous wallpaper anywhere. But I couldn't quite remember this moment. Then again, I'd had a thousand moments like this while I'd been living at the Bradleys'.

A kid waltzed in. Eleven years old, with a mohawk and a pair of sunglasses resting on his head, even though it was dark out. *Seamus Bradley.* He was the Bradleys' only son and had been more of a nemesis to me than Billy Bruckner. He'd hated me from the moment I arrived at that house and hadn't made any attempt to hide the fact. Even so, I couldn't remember this incident. He'd always gone around with those stupid sunglasses on his head, but my bedroom had been off limits to him, by Mr. Bradley's terrifying decree. *So, what is he doing here?* I tried to rack my brain, but I couldn't recall it at all.

"Ugh, what's that smell?" Seamus made a show of pinching his nose, a nasty grin on his face. "Oh, that's right, it's you, isn't it? That must be what foster kids smell like."

"Leave me alone," eight-year-old me replied.

"Why should I? This is my house; I can go where I want. It's not your house. You don't get to tell me what I can do."

"Go away, or I'll shout for Mr. Bradley."

Seamus laughed coldly. "Dad's not going to do anything to me. I'm his son, remember? You're just some *thing* he picked up off the street. You want to know why?" He waited, but I didn't reply. "It's because he felt sorry for you. He doesn't care about you. He thinks you're trash. Hey, maybe that's why he picked you up. You shouldn't leave trash lying around. It's bad for the environment."

"Please… just go away."

"No, I don't feel like it, so I won't." He flicked a casual wrist. "How come you've got no mom and dad, anyway?"

Little me buried her face in the sheets. "Go away."

"They junkies or something? They out on the street, right now, with their begging bowls and sleeping bags?" He sneered. "I bet they are, aren't they? Either that, or they took one look at you and decided they'd be better off without you. You ever seen *The Hunchback of Notre Dame*? You're the ugly little thing they leave on the steps at that church. Yeah, that's what you are. And, hey, guess what I'm going to call you—Quasi. How about that?"

"Just leave me alone," I begged from under the covers.

"I mean, who would want you?" he went on. I could hear the stifled sobs of my eight-year-old self, her little body shaking violently beneath the fabric. "Oh, you're going to cry now? Why? You don't like the truth?"

"I haven't done anything to you. Just leave me alone."

"Your mom and dad probably thought they'd be better off dead than have to hang around with you. They probably dumped you and shot themselves, just to get away from you." He laughed cruelly. "That's why you're an orphan, Harley—because nobody wants you. You're not supposed to be wanted. Nobody could love a nasty, stinky little thing like you. Your mom and dad didn't want you. My dad doesn't want you. My mom doesn't want you. And I don't want you. You're disgusting. You make me want to puke, just looking at you. Gross."

My nineteen-year-old eyes widened as the memory began to creep back into my head. This was the moment when it had all gotten to be too much. I'd done my fair share of sitting by the window, hoping my mom and dad would somehow come back for me, never losing hope that I belonged somewhere. But then this had happened. I'd already gone through the incident with the bath—that was the reason I'd been sitting in my room in the first place, if I remembered right, petrified that I was going to be sent back to the orphanage. I might not have liked Mr. Bradley, but being with an actual family had been better than getting shipped back to the orphanage, embarrassed and ashamed that the foster family had given up on me. This was the first time I'd truly felt alone in this world, with nobody to turn to. It was the first time I'd understood that nobody was coming for me. Seamus's words had stung because I'd believed them. I'd believed that I wasn't wanted, even before he'd said those horrible things.

It was the only time in my life that the feeling of loneliness had become so unbearable that the Chaos inside me had reacted. It had reacted to other emotions in my life, sure, but this was the only time loneliness had driven it to snap within me. Which it did, at that moment, lighting little me up like a beacon. My body was glowing, my eyes turning a crackling shade of bronze, tendrils of Chaos wrapping around my fingertips and threatening to explode.

Seamus reeled back in horror, sprinting for the door and calling for his dad. It was the straw that had broken the camel's back with the

Bradley family. I'd been sent back to the orphanage the very next day. Seamus had told them I'd picked up the lamp and thrown it at him and tried to set him on fire with it, and they'd believed him, especially when they'd seen the lamp that had been shattered by my Chaos. I supposed it was the only way his human mind could explain why I'd been glowing.

As I glanced at the glowing figure on the bed, her emotions swept toward me, hitting me like a punch in the chest. I felt that pain all over again, that loneliness and misery, and the permeating feeling of rejection that had sunk deeper into my bones from that moment on, making me realize that I couldn't rely on anyone. The Smiths had built me back up to some degree, reminding me that there were good people in the world, but that wouldn't come for this little girl for another eight years, and she had so much more to endure before she learned that not everything was bleak and cruel. She had no idea that she'd find friends in a coven, not far from where she sat right now. She had no idea that she'd find love and open her heart again, in a way she'd never have thought possible. Eight-year-old me was lost and in pain, and nothing but time could fix that, even if I wished I could fix it for her.

On impulse, I walked to the bed and sat down, my cheeks damp with tears. This night had been the worst of my life, and I hadn't remembered any of it. I'd pushed it so far into the depths of my mind that I'd forgotten it altogether, because the thought of reliving this type of agony was too terrible to comprehend. I'd already lived through it once, so why have it on repeat? Why force myself to remember how alone and unwanted I'd felt, when I'd had to go through eight more years of that feeling? I'd been told, every day in those ensuing eight years, how unwanted I was, but this moment had been the epicenter. The seed from which I'd hardened myself and learned not to care, shutting myself off completely from anything and everyone who could hurt me.

"Hey," I said, reaching out to the little girl. "Harley?"

The girl blinked. "Who are you?"

"A friend," I replied. "And I just want to tell you that everything's going to be okay. You're going to be okay. You're going to be happy, one day, and you're going to forget all of this. You're going to find out that you're wanted, more than you could possibly imagine. You're going to be loved, and you're going to love, so you can't harden yourself so much that nothing can get through. Don't make that shell too thick, okay?"

The girl's lip trembled. "Are you lying to me? They all lie."

"No, I'm not lying," I assured her. "And you're not alone. You never have been. I know it must feel like it, and I know it hurts, but you're loved, Harley. Your mom and dad are looking down on you, and they love you so much... *so* much. All you have to do is keep them in your heart and never forget them, and they'll always be with you, walking at your side. Whenever you feel sad or alone, just think of them, and know that they're listening and they're wishing they could be with you, to take your pain away. You're not unwanted. You're so very loved, more than you could imagine."

"My mom and dad are with me?"

I nodded. "Every single day. They never left."

"Are you an angel?"

I smiled. "No, I'm not. I'm just here to tell you that you don't have to listen to the people who don't matter, because you're going to be extraordinary. You're going to have a real family again, soon enough. Just hold on. Please, hold on and don't close yourself off. Don't ever lose the ability to love, because all the happiness in the world is coming."

"Are you a fairy godmother?" A warm smile broke out on eight-year-old me's face. "You must be."

I chuckled. "Maybe, but just promise me you'll never let that spark go out."

She nodded slowly. "I promise."

"Come here." I wrapped my arms around her and pulled her into a hug, feeling her little hands grip me tight. "It's all going to be okay, Harley. I promise you."

"This is for you," she said, pulling away. From under the covers, she pulled out a strange piece of matte black glass. "It's the secret I've been holding on to for far too long." Her voice changed, coming out as a weird, deep echo.

"What is it?" I took the gift and held it, the shard ice cold against my palm.

"The key you've been looking for." I looked back at eight-year-old me, and almost screamed. Her body was starting to melt away, like a wax doll that had been put too close to the fire.

"She finally cracked it. Slow claps for us."

I turned to find mini-me standing in the doorway and clamped my hand over my mouth. She was starting to melt away, too, her face dripping onto the floor, her hand letting go of Raggedy. The doll turned to ash the moment it hit the ground, the floorboards turning to liquid underneath it.

Around me, the walls were melting, and the bed was melting, and the broken rocket-ship lamp was melting. Everything was melting. And I had no idea how to get out of this state before I started to melt, too.

THIRTY-ONE

Harley

My eyes jolted open, and a choked gasp escaped my throat.

Davin stood over me. His hands gripped my shoulders, shaking me so hard my teeth were chattering. I almost reached out to touch his face, to make sure he wasn't melting, but I managed to resist. He looked fine. No dripping skin, no screeching ghouls, just a worried expression.

"Harley? Harley, can you hear me?" he asked.

I nodded, totally disoriented. "Yes… You can… stop shaking me now."

He took his hands away sharply. "My apologies, but necessity called for a stroke of brute force. Your Telekinesis was causing havoc, as you can see."

I glanced past his broad shoulders to see that the iron fence had been mangled, half of it sticking up like a futuristic piece of modern art. A few of the instrument-wielding cherubs had lost heads, wings, and limbs, while the remainder of the windows had been completely shattered. The ceremonial bowls had all been tossed against the walls, leaving little piles of herbal debris in their wake, and the caskets had been thrown halfway across the church.

I became aware of something hard and smooth in my clenched fist. I unfurled my fingers to reveal a matte-black lens in the shape of a semicircle, with a flat edge down one side.

I have the key!

"Did you manage to acquire what was needed?" Davin looked down at the strange object.

I grinned. "Yeah, I think I did." I turned to my mom and dad, who were sitting to either side of me with their eyes closed, no longer holding my hands. I didn't know when we'd let go, but it didn't seem to have had any effect on the spell. Tears were falling down both their cheeks, their eyeballs flickering under their eyelids, like they were in REM sleep. I wanted to shake them awake, the way Davin had done to me, but I guessed they needed more time. I wasn't going to interrupt them while they were in the middle of Euphoria.

"How's Alton?" I looked toward the altar. He was rocking back and forth. By the looks of it, he could barely keep his eyes open, and black veins were spreading across his skin again. That wasn't a good sign.

"Very green about the gills. It will not be long until he Purges," Davin replied. "He's resisting as best he can, but none of us can restrain a Purge for very long. Although, with your power, I'm certain you already know that. I can last a little longer than most, but that's always been my forte."

I shook my head. "I've never done it."

"You continue to surprise me, Ms. Merlin." He shook his head in disbelief. "I was sure you would have created a veritable army of snapping little monsters by now."

"Nope, not even one."

"I have read of a magical such as yourself," he said. "A powerful woman of epic proportions—as good as she was mighty. She Purged only once in her lifetime, though she had enough strength and performed enough remarkable spells to have Purged a thousand times. Nobody knew how she managed it. But when she finally did Purge, she created something wondrous. I believe the beast still lives, taking care of the Bestiary."

My eyes widened. "You mean Tobe?"

"Ah yes, that was the name. It had quite slipped my mind. The magical went by the name of Selma."

I nodded. "I've heard of her."

"You remind me very much of her, though I didn't know her personally. I am a voracious reader, amongst other things. Nevertheless, she always held a special place in my heart. Strong women often do." He smiled, his hand still on my shoulder. I shuffled out of his grasp, feeling slightly uncomfortable at his attention.

Fortunately, at that moment, my mom woke up, blinking slowly as she came out of her Euphoria. My dad was still deep in his trance, his eyelids flickering. Focusing on my mom, I saw that she had something gripped in her right hand, and I could see the hint of black peeking through her fingers. Relief washed over me. She'd done it. And now, we just needed the third piece to the key that would open up the secrets of the Grimoire.

"Is it done?" Alton wheezed, his head lolling.

My mom turned to him. "It's done." *Why does she sound so sad?*

I found out, a second later. With a gut-wrenching scream, Alton arched back in a way that didn't look natural, his spine almost cracking in two. The black veins engulfed him, spiderwebbing out across every available expanse of flesh. His mouth opened in a howling "O" as darkness poured out of him. Purple sparks crackled all around him. His arms shot out, and he crashed into the stone where he lay, thrashing and spasming as the Purge took hold.

"Mom, NO!" I cried out, crawling across the ground to reach her. Alton couldn't hold her anymore. I threw myself at her, wrapping my arms around her and gripping her as tight as I could, in the hopes that it might somehow keep her spirit in this body. Her spirit was phasing in and out like crazy, mixing my mom's face with that of the young woman whose body she'd possessed.

"I'll always be here," she murmured. "My love for you will always keep me close."

Her arms dropped to her sides, limp and lifeless, and I knew she was gone. No amount of begging could keep her here. I tried to keep hold of her, but her skin had gone cold and the strong scent of embalming fluid and disinfectant drifted away from the corpse that had been my mom, if only for a short while.

Heartbroken, I lay her down on the ground as carefully as I could. Only, she wasn't my mom anymore. I'd never see her again, not until the day I died. *Will they let me go where you've gone, Mom?* I hoped so, with all my heart.

I was about to reach for her hand, her stiff fingers closed over the shard of black glass she'd brought back, when Davin's voice distracted me.

"We have something of an issue here," he said, his tone anxious.

"Don't you dare let my dad go," I shot back. "Not yet. He's not finished."

"I will do what I can, Ms. Merlin, but that isn't the problem. Very soon, we will have a Purge beast to contend with, and if I'm to hold your father here a while longer, I won't be able to help you."

I stared at Alton as more black smoke poured out of him, his mouth and eyes filled with it, until I could hardly see Alton beneath it all. The realm of the dead might not have collided with the land of the living, but that didn't mean there weren't going to be consequences for what Alton and Davin had done. They'd pushed the boundaries of Necromancy, and that came with a price. A terrible one, by the looks of it.

"A Mason jar. Do you have one?" I looked back at Davin.

"In my box of wonders," he replied.

Jumping up, I sprinted for the chest and snatched out a jar, tucking it under my arm as I walked toward the gathering mass of black smoke that had enveloped Alton entirely. This was giving me major Erebus flashbacks, and I would've given anything to have Santana here to help me.

I waited for the black smoke to take shape, but instead, the cloud swirled upward from Alton's body, the black veins and purple sparks dissipating. *I can't let this thing escape.* Two red lights shone through the darkness, like eyes, watching me. Holding my ground, I thought about unleashing my Darkness so that I could control this thing with my reverse Empathy. But, since it didn't actually have a physical form, I wasn't sure how successful I'd be.

The creature flew toward me, tendrils of black smoke slithering out like fingertips. Lifting my palms, I sent out a wave of Air, hoping it would push the thing back. My gust breezed straight through, hitting the back wall. I sent out a blast of Fire, but the same thing happened.

Crap, crap, crap... This thing was like nothing I'd ever faced before. I'd rather have battled Naima again than fight something I didn't understand.

I sent out a blockade of Telekinesis, the edges of my lasso spiraling around the creature, trying to find a foothold. With every second that passed, and every failed attempt, the creature swept closer, its eyes glowing brighter.

The church door exploded open and someone darted inside, sprinting full-pelt down the main aisle. They scattered a handful of entrapment stones on the ground underneath the terrifying smoke beast. The stones glowed green, and ropes shot out, the smoke solidifying, like dry ice in reverse, as they ensnared the beast, dragging it to the floor.

"Finch?" I gasped, as the figure threw back his hood.

"I know I'm a stunner, but are you going to keep gawking, or are you going to help me trap this beastie?" He flashed a grin.

I couldn't move, my whole body shaking. I was already on the edge of exhaustion after that whole debacle with mini-me and the melting faces, the fight with Naima, and pretty much everything else that had happened in the last few days. This was just another shock to the system that I couldn't quite take right now.

Finch grabbed the jar from under my arm. Racing toward the trapped beast, he unscrewed the lid of the jar and set it in front of the smoky creature. The tendrils of its weird body snaked through the gaps in the green ropes, pouring into the charmed jar until there was nothing left. Only then did Finch pounce on it, screwing the lid back on as tight as possible.

What are you doing here? I tried to say it out loud, but the words wouldn't come. I was absolutely speechless.

Finch turned to me, brandishing the jar. "Here he comes to save the day!"

THIRTY-TWO

Katherine

I whistled the tune to "The Final Countdown" as I strolled through the hallways of the coven, taking my sweet, sweet time, and really hitting those drumbeats.

There weren't any people around to witness my little pre-victory, one-woman pep rally, which was probably a good thing. Seeing Imogene Whitehall air-drumming through the corridors would have set some tongues wagging, though that wouldn't matter soon. I'd be shedding this skin before I knew it, and it was going to be the most glorious feeling in the world. I might have killed Imogene—the real one—but I couldn't wait to kill this character, too.

Good riddance, Whitehall!

I was going to make a damn bonfire and burn every single shade of cream I could get my hands on. In my new world, there'd be nothing but color—the brighter, the better.

With a satisfied smile, I took out my phone and re-read the most titillating text I'd ever set eyes on. I mean, most texts from Davin Doncaster were titillating, but this one… it topped them all: *My darling Katie, I hope this message finds you in good spirits. If not, I'm certain that what I am about to say will cheer your delectable heart beyond measure. They're reaching the end of the spell. It's almost done. Did I not tell you that I would triumph in your name?*

I hope that I may look upon you soon, so that I may seek my reward. Yours Eternally, Davin.

There was something so effortlessly charming about him, even in texts. But what did he mean about seeking his reward? It was his loyalty I wanted. But that was supposed to be his gift to me. I hadn't offered anything beyond being at the side of Earth's new ruler and getting his powers back once I saw fit to redistribute them.

So, what else was he after? I had a few ideas, with it being Davin, and they only served to widen my smile as I headed for the infirmary. Everything was slotting nicely into place, just the way I liked.

And now it was time to really get the proverbial gears in motion, so I'd be ready for the greatest performance of my life—the moment that all of this had been building toward.

I eased off on the power ballads as I entered the infirmary, checking to make sure Krieger was otherwise engaged. Not that I was going to say anything he couldn't hear. I wasn't going to blow my cover now, at the eleventh hour. I just didn't want to deal with the irritating small talk with the inhabitants of the SDC, and who could blame me? Their inane, relentless conversations about "ending me" made me want to pluck out my vocal cords and use them as shoelaces. Fortunately, Krieger was nowhere to be seen.

With the infirmary to myself, I approached Levi first. His eyes were closed, and he was snoring softly. *Aww, like a big, fat baby.*

I jabbed him in the arm with my forefinger, just to make sure he was asleep. He didn't move. *Good, stay down, doggy.* I wasn't in the mood to deal with Levi, and I definitely wasn't in the mood to deal with Alakazam or whatever his name was. Djinn had a way of leaving a sour taste in my mouth, and I didn't want anyone ruining my pre-show buzz. Although, he'd been useful, in his own way.

Moving to the next bed over, I sat down in the chair beside little Jakey and took his hand, squeezing it. Anyone coming in would see wounded-heart Imogene tending to the poor soul who'd been clonked on the head by that mean old Katherine. *I'm already here, bitches!* I'd been wanting to scream that from the rooftops, but there was a time and a place for that, and I needed to make sure nothing was going to screw up my plans before I started celebrating. Not counting the chickens before they'd hatched, and so on. Right now, my chickens were incubating nicely.

"How are you, Jacob?" I said, smirking. "I hope everything's not too messed up in that skull of yours. You must be going out of your mind… literally." I chuckled at my own joke. What could I say? I was hilarious. "Sorry it's been so long since I've been to visit you. I've been exceptionally busy, as I'm sure you can imagine. I'm very much looking forward to seeing you again. I really am. It's going to be emotional. So, you just need to hang in there for a little while longer, while I take care of the final details. You have no idea how much grunt work it takes to get an operation like this off the ground, let alone getting everything into its last stages. I'm exhausted, to tell you the truth, but adrenaline is giving me a nice little kick."

I looked up at his closed eyes, wondering what he was thinking. He'd be raging, knowing I was right here but not being able to tell a soul. *Delicious.*

"Now, I know you'd never say so, but you've got to admit I've played my game so very, very well, haven't I? I deserve a trophy, or a medal, at the very least. A big, shiny one. Sure, there have been a couple of glitches and minor inconveniences, courtesy of Miss Prim, but I haven't let it get to me. That's very important, Jakey. You must never let anything stand in the way of what you want, even if Chaos itself is against you. Aren't I a shining example of that? Despite everything you and your little band of merry men have thrown at me, I've still managed to pull through. And now, I can see that glorious finish line. Can't you, Jakey? Can't you taste it?"

He didn't say a word. The perfect audience to my favorite pastime—the soliloquy. Hamlet had nothing on me. I rattled out way more than seven before I'd even eaten breakfast. And you certainly wouldn't have found me crying about someone killing my dad and usurping my throne. I'd always admired Claudius for having the guts to take what he wanted. Plus, I'd been the one doing the patricide, when that opportunity had arisen—been there, done that, got the bloodied T-shirt. Soliloquized thoroughly afterward. As for the usurping… well, if anyone even tried it, they'd find themselves getting obliterated before they'd even poured a damn thing in my ear. Nobody was stealing my throne, not when I'd yet to set my peachy backside down on it. *But soon... so very soon.*

"Sorry, I got distracted there, didn't I?" I grinned. "You see, what people don't seem to realize is that I'm not the villain of this piece. They think I am, but I'm not. Don't misunderstand, villains are always way more interesting than sappy protagonists, but I'm going to be the hero you've all been waiting for. I'm going to change everything for the better, and then you'll all be down on your knees, thanking me for the efforts I've gone to."

I paused, letting the words come.

"They're right to fear me, of course. I am fearsome, as all good leaders should be. And this brain of mine—ooh, you've got no idea, Jakey. It's exceptional, beyond anything your weak imagination could conjure. You'll see—pretty soon, actually—and you'll wonder how you never saw it coming. All of you will, especially the spawn of Merlin. She thinks she's the brains of the outfit, but even she won't expect what I've got in store. If you thought my being Imogene was good, you're going to wet your pants when you find out what's next. Isn't that beautiful? A twist to end all twists. And, my sweet boy, it's just around the corner."

THIRTY-THREE

Harley

I stared at Finch as he lifted the jar up to the moonlight, watching the smoky creature twist and turn inside.

"Tap on the glass as much as you like, buddy, you aren't getting out. Not even if you say please." He chuckled, turning around to face me. The laughter died on his lips.

"What are you doing here, Finch?"

"Is that your way of saying, 'Hey, Bro, thanks for saving me from the big smoke beast who wanted to eat me'?"

"No, it's my way of asking what you're doing here. You're not supposed to be here." My voice trembled, partly from exhaustion, partly from the terror of seeing him in this place. I was glad he'd saved my ass from the Purge beast, but he was putting himself in too much danger, and he didn't even know it.

"When do I ever do what I'm told?"

"Finch…"

"Harley…" He held my gaze defiantly.

"Please, you have to go."

He shook his head. "Nope, no way, José." His mouth suddenly fell open, his eyes settling on my dad—our dad. Davin was still holding him in this world and didn't seem to be showing any signs of strain. Alton, on the other hand... well, he was passed out on the floor, breathing slowly. Fortunately, Davin seemed to have the strength to contend with looking after Alton at the same time as keeping my dad fixed in the land of the living.

That guy really is as powerful as Alton said he was. He was just taking all this boundary-pushing in stride, not even breaking a sweat, though maybe he was just good at covering it.

"Is that...?" Finch trailed off in disbelief.

"Yeah, it's him," I said, my voice softening.

Just then, our dad's eyes opened, a black sliver glinting in his right hand. He'd found the missing piece to complete the key. *We did it!*

So why didn't I feel happier?

He frowned and looked down at the body beside him, an expression of heartbreak passing over his face as he realized what had happened.

"She had to leave," I murmured. I knew Alton hadn't had any choice in letting my mom go, but I'd wanted longer. It had been hard enough saying goodbye to her on Eris Island, but to have to do it twice was just plain cruel.

"I was worried about that." Our dad pressed his fingers to his lips, kissing them, before placing them on the lips of the corpse. It was weird to watch, but I understood why he had to do it. It was his way of saying goodbye, until they met again. He unfurled the corpse's hand and took out the sliver of matte-black glass, putting it with his own piece. He glanced curiously at Finch as he got up and approached tentatively.

"Dad?" Finch murmured.

Hiram frowned. "You must have me confused with someone else...?"

"Actually, he's right," I said. "This is Finch Shipton. He's Katherine's son—yours and Katherine's son. But don't worry, he's on our side, not hers."

My dad looked shocked. "*My* son?"

"Surprise!" Finch said weakly, waggling his hands. Even though I couldn't read him with my Empathy, I could see the turmoil of emotions washing over his face. Sadness, anger, regret, and a flicker of something like relief. "I guess you never knew about me, huh?"

"No... Katherine never said a word." My dad came closer, putting his hand against Finch's cheek, as though he needed to touch him to believe it. "You look like me, aside from the hair."

He really does. Having only had vague dreams of my dad, I'd never realized just how much Finch resembled him, until now. Standing face-to-face, there was no denying where Finch had come from. There were hints of Katherine here and there, but the majority was Hiram, even in the wry turning up of his mouth.

"Blond isn't my natural color. It's red, like Katherine's." Finch mustered a laugh. "But all the good I've got came from you, not my mother. Not like Harley. She got the best of both worlds, in more ways than one. Do you know how crazy powerful she is?" I couldn't tell if he was serious or not, given that he was playing up his usual Finchy behavior.

"I've seen what Harley can do, yes," my dad replied, with a proud smile. "But that doesn't mean you aren't powerful. Everyone has different qualities, but that doesn't make any of them superior. I suppose I can't comment, since I don't know you, but if you have those bloodlines, then there's no way you can be ordinary."

Finch looked wounded for a moment. "No, you're right, you don't know me."

"I'm sorry for that. I promise you, I had no idea you existed. I might not even believe it now, if you didn't look so much like me." He took his hand away. "She didn't tell me, Finch. If she'd told me, I would've looked out for you. I would've done whatever I could to get you away from her. I don't believe any child should be taken away from their parents, but with Katherine it's a different story."

Finch shrugged. "It doesn't matter now. She never wanted me as anything more than a lapdog. She probably only kept me alive so she could control me in a way she couldn't do with you. Not without whacking a great big curse on you, anyway. You know, showing the mighty Hiram Merlin who was getting the last laugh."

"I'm so sorry." My dad's voice broke. "I should have known. She said she had a surprise for me. I was supposed to go and see her, but I didn't. Hester told me not to go, so I stayed away. I wonder... if I'd gone, what might've happened?"

"It wouldn't have changed anything," Finch replied. "She'd have still gone batty, and she'd still be trying to ascend, and she'd still have put that curse on you and killed everyone in her family. She'd probably have told you about me, then pushed you off a cliff or something. Something suitably Katherine. And she'd have been majorly pissed that she didn't get to see the look on your face when she told you, and that she didn't get to shove one last monologue in before she forced you under her control."

"I'm still sorry. I wish I'd known about you."

"What can I say, the latest batch of Merlins seem to be doomed in one way or another. It's why I keep telling Harley that we need to stick together." He shot me a weighted look. "She's got other ideas, apparently. Keeps running off."

My dad looked at me. "Is that true?"

"I've got my reasons." I felt like I was getting an "I'm not mad, I'm just disappointed" bit of telling off. Davin was watching with interest, an amused smile on his face. *I bet you're loving this, aren't you?* Well, at least he was useful. Without him here, we wouldn't even be having this conversation.

"What reasons?" Finch shot back.

I sighed. "I've got some, and they're good ones, and that's all you need to know. Now, you need to get out of here."

"I told you, I'm not going anywhere," he replied. "Do you know how much of a ball-ache it was to get here in the first place?"

"No, I don't. Why don't you enlighten me?" I held my ground. I wasn't going to let him make me feel guilty for saving his life, in the long run. And I wasn't going to let him or our dad persuade me to let him in on this, though he was likely putting a few of the pieces together.

"I followed you," he replied. "I've had Kenzie tracking you as a ladybug since you ditched me in Waterfront Park. Clever, I know. No need to applaud me. And before you get on your high horse, I was worried. That's all there is to it. Oh, and you're not the only one who can rustle up a bit of magic chalk when needed. So you can *Aperi Si Ostium* my ass."

My jaw dropped. "So, does that mean—"

"I know what you're up to? Yes indeedy. But don't crap your pants, I haven't told anyone yet. Mainly because I actually understand why you don't want anyone knowing. I would've understood if you'd just told me, but you forced me to use my wily ways by running off every two seconds. To be honest, I was 99 percent sure you were knocked up."

A horrified gasp escaped my dad's mouth, and my cheeks started to burn like nobody's business. The last thing I wanted was my dad, to whom I was going to have to say goodbye, knowing about my damn love life. This wasn't the lasting impression I wanted, for me or him.

"Finch!" I barked.

He raised his hands in apology. "My bad. But hey, good news—you definitely aren't, so we don't have that to deal with, on top of everything else. Although, that would probably have been easier to swallow than you feeding me a bunch of lies, even if you do have a good reason. I get why you're trying to protect Wade and the others, but it stings, Sis, that you couldn't trust me with this. I mean, I'm disposable, right? I'm ready for whatever wacko crap you're about to get yourself into. Bring it ooooon, man!"

Out of nowhere, my eyes welled with tears. "What do you mean you're disposable? You aren't disposable." I struggled to hold back a sob. "You don't get it, do you? I knew you wouldn't. That's why I didn't want to tell you what I was doing."

"That doesn't—" Finch started, but I talked over him.

"You made your promise to the Chains of Truth, Finch. Did you think I'd forget about that? I know what's at stake. I know they aren't premonitions, but if there's even a hint of anything happening to you, I'm going to do whatever I have to, to make sure it never happens!" Emotions were pouring out of me, and I had to grapple with them so I didn't end up reverse-Empathizing the crap out of everyone in the church.

Finch looked startled. "But… I've never been important. Lapdog, remember?"

"You're not my lapdog, Finch. You're not my sidekick. You're my brother, and you're my friend. And you're not freaking disposable, so don't you dare say that again!"

"She's right, son." Our dad glanced at him. "I don't know what Katherine did to you to make you feel that way, but if you've helped Harley get this far, then you're worthy of everything she's said. To have gone through what you must've suffered and come out the other side as a good man—that's remarkable in and of itself. And you said you weren't special." He gave a small, sad smile. "If I were to guess, I'd say that's your power, that's your gift. Throughout history, every hero has needed someone equally heroic at their side. That's you, Finch. I may not know you, but I can tell that much."

"That's just a nicer way of saying 'sidekick.'" Finch lowered his gaze, but I could see that he was pleased.

"You wouldn't be here if you were just a sidekick. You would've obeyed when Harley asked you to stay away. The fact that you disobeyed shows how much you care, and it shows that you're supposed to be with her, as brother and sister, facing whatever comes next." He paused. "And I'm glad that I got to see you both before I have to go again. If I'd never had this chance to meet you, I fully believe there'd have been a piece of me missing for the rest of my afterlife."

Finch looked like he was fighting back tears. "I'm sorry she killed you, and I'm so sorry she killed Hester. I hate her for stealing you away, not just from me, but from Harley, too. I used to be so mad at you for choosing Hester over her, but now I understand. I regret everything I've done for her..."

"I would have done everything to get you away from her, I promise you that," Hiram said. "But, just remember, her sins aren't yours. Even if she made you do awful things, it's not your fault. I know, better than anyone, how tight her grip of control can be. She's a manipulator of the highest order. I was fooled for a while, and I'll always regret that, but I came to my senses. And I'm so very, very glad that you did, too."

"Can I ask you one thing?" Finch said, taking a deep breath.

"Of course."

"Did you love her? Katherine?"

My stomach plummeted. *Wow...*

Our dad smiled sadly. "I thought I did. I don't know if that's the answer you want, but it's the honest one. But I didn't know what true love was until Hester came into my life. When it's real, it hits you like a punch in the face. People are right when they say, 'When you know, you know.' And I knew with Hester." He lowered his gaze. "But I certainly would have loved you if I'd known about you. That starts from today, I swear it. I might not get to see you again, but you're my son, and you're a part of me. And I love you, because of that."

I turned to Finch, expecting his customary snark, but he didn't say a word. He just stood there, letting our dad's words sink in. His face gave nothing away, but his eyes were brimming with tears. *Was that the answer you wanted?* I couldn't tell.

"And I love you, Harley. So very much." My dad reached out to take my hand, folding the last two slivers of the matte-black lens into my palm. "I wish I could stay longer. I wish I could help. I wish a lot of things, but I'm fading. Your friend over there is struggling, though he doesn't want to show it. He's losing his grip on me."

My eyes darted to Davin, who was standing motionless, like a soldier at attention. He still had a smile on his face, but it was strained. A sheen of sweat glistened across his skin, his arms shaking ever so slightly. He could've fooled anyone into thinking he had control.

"Yes, sorry about that, old chap," Davin said, his voice raspy. "I really am doing my best, but your spirit is slipping through my fingers. I believe it may tear me apart if I don't release you soon, so be a good sport and wrap it up as quickly as you can."

Panic rose up my throat, but my dad gripped my hand before I could say a word. "It's all going to be okay, Harley. You have Finch, you have Alton, you have *The Great Gatsby*." He gave a small chuckle. Apparently, he and Finch had a lot in common. "And your mom and I will always be with you, just like we promised. If you ever feel like you can't carry on, just think of us and know we're there, cheering for you, every step of the way."

"But I miss you," I whispered through my tears.

"We miss you, too. And if there was a way that I could stay, and your mom could stay, we'd move heaven and earth to find it. But our time came to an end a long time ago. You still have a life to live, and I want you to live it—really live it. Destroy Katherine and find happiness again. Find happiness in the world that you're going to save. And know we're smiling down on you."

I reached forward and collapsed in his arms, hugging him tight. "I love you, Dad."

"I love you, Harley." He held me close. "One last thing—remember to be careful with the Grimoire. Chaos used us to write it, but I have no idea what challenges await you amongst the hidden pages. So just go with your gut instinct and take your time. It's designed for you. It wants you to succeed. But that doesn't mean there won't be pitfalls. Use your head, and you'll be fine."

"That's one thing you didn't try," Finch cut in. "You should've head-butted the pages until your eyes were swimming so much that it all started to make sense. It's so simple, now that I think about it."

Hiram chuckled. "I like your sense of humor. Don't ever lose it."

"I won't," Finch replied.

"Come here." He opened out his arm and pulled Finch into a hug, both of us saying our last goodbye to the man who was one half of the people we'd become. "I love you both. Be good, look after each other, and don't let that evil witch win. You're so much stronger together than you ever could be apart. And, Finch, I'm sorry I didn't know about you sooner, when I was still alive. I would've done everything to get you away from Katherine's poison. And I'm sorry that you're still dealing with the aftermath of everything she's done to you. To both of you."

"It's not your fault," Finch murmured. I knew it was the closest thing to "I love you" that he could muster, but the sentiment was exactly the same. It was just his way of saying what he couldn't.

"I have to go now." Our dad gave us one last squeeze, and then he was gone. His body went limp, his skin cold, that same stinging scent of disinfectant and embalming fluid filling my nostrils. I stepped back, trying to keep the body from collapsing to the ground.

"Here, let me do that. Wouldn't want you reeking of death. Embalming fluid is a killer to get out of your clothes." Finch put his arms underneath the corpse's armpits and dragged him over to the young woman on the floor. I had no idea how he knew what embalming fluid did to clothes, and I didn't want to. I guessed he was trying to make me laugh, but I was too sad for that.

"Did I… Did I miss something?" Alton rasped, coming around. He looked green and shaky, but at least he was alive. No black veins in sight.

"You look like you're about to pop your clogs," Davin replied.

Alton frowned. "What?"

"You look rather peaky." He rolled his eyes at Alton's blank face. "You look exceedingly unwell, Alton."

He nodded. "I don't feel too good, to be honest."

"I'm so sorry, Alton," I said. "This can't have been easy for you. I'm so sorry to have put you in this state. If there's anything I can do, just say the word."

He smiled. "It was my decision. I'll recover. I just need some time."

"Where's my thanks?" Davin prompted.

"I couldn't have done this without either of you," I replied. "I'm very grateful. I just want to make sure that Alton is okay."

"He'll recover. He's Purged now, which will lead into the healing process." Davin gave Alton a knowing nod.

"But how come *you* haven't gone into a Purge yet?" I eyed Davin curiously. "You can't be able to last *that* much longer."

He grinned. "I can last plenty long. Practice makes perfect. And I have had much more practice than our dear friend Mr. Waterhouse, over here. It's what gives me that added stamina."

"I guess we should be grateful we don't have to deal with two Purge beasts," I muttered, trying not to look too awestruck. He had to be crazy strong not to go straight into a Purge after what he'd done. *Hats off to you.* I wasn't going to say that out loud, in case it made his ego swell even bigger, but I had to give credit where it was due.

I looked down at the slivers of the matte-black lens in my hands. But there weren't three slivers anymore. Somehow, without me realizing, the edges had fused together, creating one perfect circle. I couldn't even see where the joins were.

"Cool doohickey you've got there. What does it do?" Finch was doing his best to stay positive, but I could tell our dad was still weighing on his mind. I felt the same way.

I turned the lens over to see if there were any charms or markings etched into the smooth surface, but it was blank. "I'm not sure."

"It looks like a spyglass to me," Finch noted.

Curious, I walked to the Grimoire, which was still lying on the ground where I'd left it. I sat in front of it and flipped to a random empty page. As I peered through the lens, words and illustrations jumped back at me. It didn't make sense, since the lens was thick and matte, and totally opaque. But the words and pictures were definitely there, and I could actually read them.

Grinning like an idiot, I flipped through page after page, finding spells that would've been useful a few months back, when we'd first found out about Katherine's rituals. Evidently, the timelines hadn't quite been aligned. There was a spell to subdue Chaos in the Asphodel Meadows. A spell to cast light in Tartarus. A spell to make weapons disobey their wielder in the land of Gaia. A spell to summon the minions of Lux in the land of Lethe, straight out of the light pools. *Now you freaking tell me.* Evidently, Chaos had cut its losses and thrown in spells for just about every step of Katherine's plan, though they were no use to us now. Those ships had sailed.

"I can read it!" I gasped, continuing to flip through the Grimoire, right to the point where the filled pages stopped.

Finch smiled. "Seriously?"

"Seriously." All of the Grimoire's secrets were open, every last one. Now, I just had to find the one that would destroy Katherine.

If Davin hadn't been here, I'd have devoured the unreadable spell—the last one my dad had put in here. That had to be the one, it just had to be. It was too dark and powerful not to be, not to mention the fact that it had been written in a language I couldn't understand. That had Chaos written all over it. But I had to wait. I hated to, but Davin was still an outsider. Sure, he'd helped us, but this was a secret I couldn't risk getting out, no matter how helpful he'd been.

A little more patience. Just a little bit more.

I'd waited this long. I didn't want to ruin it now.

THIRTY-FOUR

Harley

I was so excited about finally cracking this big old nut open that I'd almost forgotten that Finch really wasn't supposed to be here. My dad might have said all those heroic things about us staying together, but, at the end of the day, I wasn't willing to lose another family member. He was the last one I had, since I'd have ripped out my own tongue before I called Katherine family.

The conundrum dulled the edge of my excitement. There was no way Finch would let me out of his sight now.

I felt something move in the pocket of my leather jacket. When I glanced down, a mouse poked its head out. I yelped as it ran right down my front, its little claws gripping at my jeans while it scuttled away, hurrying toward the floor at Finch's feet. He stooped to pick the creature up, stroking its furry little head as he brought it to eye level.

"Thanks for the stellar espionage, Kenzie. Couldn't have done it without you."

I glared at him. "Yeah, real sneaky."

He grinned. "You can hang back for now, and... uh... do whatever it is you do when you're not spying for me."

The mouse gave a sharp squeak before scurrying all the way across his arm and down his front, defying gravity as it ran the length of his leg and hurtled across the floor of the church. It disappeared out of the door that Finch had kicked open, racing away into the night. I guessed Kenzie just had to sever the tie between herself and the little creature in order to get back into her own mind. No lengthy travels necessary.

"Where did you get the charmed chalk?" I looked up at Finch. "I didn't ask before."

"I have my ways."

"Did Remington give it to you?"

He shook his head. "He wouldn't trust me as far as he could throw me. But, you know, I always think it's better to do things and ask for forgiveness later."

"You *stole* it from him?"

"I've got some pretty light fingers." He winked. "He came to talk to Garrett, and I took my shot. I knew that stuff was sentimental for him, so I figured he'd be carrying some sticks of it on him."

I shook my head. "You really won't give up, will you?"

"What do you think?"

Then how am I supposed to keep you safe? I clasped the lens in my hand and tried to come up with a plan. Right now, Finch being around was the least of my worries. Alton was still a complete mess, propping his back against the altar to stop himself from collapsing under his own weight, and Davin was eyeing me closely.

"I take it you found what you were looking for?" Davin asked, clearly realizing he'd been caught staring. "I must ask, what could be so utterly mysterious and important that it needed to be concealed with such complex and dangerous magic?"

Instinctively, I closed the Grimoire and slipped it back into its bag, pulling the strap tight across me. "Equally complex magic."

"Might I have a gander?" He smiled, his eyes fixed on the bag.

"No."

"Yeah, it's FHEO," Finch replied. I could tell he didn't like this dude, right from the get-go. I didn't mind Davin all that much, but he didn't need to know what was in the Grimoire. That was for me to know, and me alone.

Davin frowned. "FHEO? Is this some hipster word I don't know?"

"It means For Harley's Eyes Only. You couldn't figure that out?" Finch smirked.

"Ah, the Shipton snark is strong in this one. It is a fabled thing, known amongst all who have heard the tales of your mother. I see you haven't evaded that particularly droll quality."

"Do you always speak like that? You got a thesaurus stuck in your throat or something?" Finch shot back.

"It's called education, dear boy. You should try it sometime."

"They teach you to fight at Cambridge, or whichever snob school you wound up at?" Finch narrowed his eyes.

I stifled a snort. "While I'd love to stay and listen to you snipe at each other, someone needs to get Alton back to the SDC before he blacks out. He's already dead on his feet."

"We're both going back." Finch turned to me. "You, me, Alton—we're all going back to the coven. Captain Fancy Pants can do what he likes."

"Envy is an ugly emotion." Davin chuckled. "And, if you must know, my undergarments cost more than you could earn in your lifetime."

Finch shot me a look. "Undergarments? Is this guy for real? Did you spirit him out of *Pride and friggin' Prejudice* or something?"

"Nope, he really speaks like that. And no, I'm not coming back with you." I lowered my gaze, keeping one hand on the Grimoire satchel. "I've got Katherine's location now, and I've unlocked the Grimoire. I can't go back to the SDC, not until this is done."

"Well, you can't stay here," Finch muttered.

"I'm not planning to. I just need to go somewhere safe for a couple of hours so I can read through this thing without any distractions or worries. Somewhere out of the way."

"Did you leave half of your brain behind when you did that Hidden Things spell?" Finch reached down and tapped me on the head. "Hello? Ground Control to Major Harley? Anyone home?"

I gently pushed his hand away. "We're really running out of time here, and I need to make sure that the rest of the Rag Team don't get involved, for their own sakes. So, you need to take Alton back, and I need to do this. Like Dad said, we need to work together, which means you covering for me while I get this done. They'll believe you, no matter what you say.

I mean, don't say I've been abducted by aliens or anything—keep it simple."

Davin raised his hand, like the polite gentleman he was. "Forgive me for interrupting your familial squabble, but there's an important point that I need to get off my chest."

"What is it?" I glanced at him warily.

"I do not know much of Finch's mother, only what I have heard others say, but even from that fleeting acquaintance with her character, I'm certain you may need more than a few hours to decipher a means of using the Grimoire against someone like her. I have heard many alarming things. Things that would make weaker men quake in their brogues. She is a dangerous woman. Ordinarily, I would find that ever so enticing, but she is the kind of lady I wouldn't touch with a ten-foot barge pole."

"Do you have a point?" Finch snarked. "You think we'd be in some crusty old church in France if we didn't know she was a total loon? Use that educated noggin of yours, since you're so proud of it."

"Actually, I do have a point, if you would permit me to finish," he replied curtly.

"You weren't done? Sorry, I lost track of what you were saying about three words in."

"Yes, 'I do not' can be particularly taxing for less well-rounded minds." Davin smirked. "Harley, please allow me to offer you the use of my cabin in Chamonix. It's isolated, far from civilization, so nobody will disturb you. I have a man there year-round. I can make the call at a moment's notice, and he will ensure you're kept safe, with all the privacy you require."

Finch snorted. "Of course he has a cabin in friggin' Chamonix. I bet you've got houses all over the world, huh? People like you always do."

"Is that a rather large chip on your shoulder, Finch?" he replied, cool as a cucumber.

"There's no way in hell that Harley is going to some cabin. Who the heck are you, anyway?"

"Davin Doncaster, pleased to make your acquaintance." He didn't miss a beat. It was funny to hear their slinging match, but I needed to get a move on.

"Finch—" I started to speak, but he cut me off.

"No, you're not going with him. You don't even know him, Harley. Didn't anyone ever teach you about stranger danger?" He grasped my wrist and dragged me toward the side of the church. Davin immediately moved forward, a worried look on his face.

"I would never cause Ms. Merlin any harm. I merely wish to offer her safe refuge so she can continue in her endeavors," he urged.

Finch whipped out a stick of chalk and began to draw, glancing back over his shoulder. "Yeah, and I wish the Chargers would win the Super Bowl, so I guess we're both going to be disappointed."

Davin rolled his eyes. "Must everything always come down to your little games of hand-egg?"

"What?" Finch snapped.

"Well, it isn't a football, is it? There is no ball, and there are no feet involved. American football should be called hand-egg, and I refuse to believe otherwise."

"Call it what you want, Harley isn't going to Chamonix."

I sighed. "Finch, I can fight my own battles."

"Not with this smarmy punk you can't. He'll hypnotize you with his baby blues, and I'm not about to see Wade sobbing in a big ugly pile on the floor because Mr. Cambridge Education has smarmed all over you, wooing you with fancy cabins and hot chocolate on tap." Finch whispered the *Aperi Si Ostium* spell, the edges of the doorway sparking as it turned into a three-dimensional opening.

Before I could argue, Finch yanked me through the doorway, with the Grimoire and the lens in tow, and slammed the door shut behind us.

Davin made no attempt to follow us, though he looked disappointed. Through the narrowing gap, I saw Alton staring helplessly at the bodies on the floor. If we jumped ship now, we were leaving him to deal with all of that. Guilt twisted in my stomach.

This wasn't supposed to be the way things went down. Finch wasn't meant to be in control.

"I'm sorry!" I yelled, seconds before the door closed and disappeared.

"Don't worry about it!" Alton shouted back. "Just do what you have to do!"

Staring at Finch, I realized I was stuck with him now. If I wanted to make this work, I had no choice but to carry on with him at my side. But, try as I might, I couldn't forget what the Chains of Truth had said.

Don't make me say goodbye to you, Finch, or I swear I'll drag you back from the spirit world and kill you myself.

THIRTY-FIVE

Harley

It took me a moment to realize where Finch had brought me, my mind racing with a million other things: Alton, the corpses, Davin, my mom, our dad, the Rag Team, and that stupid promise that Finch had made.

My stomach dropped like a stone.

I was standing in my bedroom in the SDC, surrounded by the clothes I'd thrown around in my hurry to get ready for the Hidden Things spell. My bed was still ruffled from where Wade and I had shared that sweet moment, right before Raffe had interrupted with his call about Zalaam. Only, it didn't quite feel like my room anymore. It felt like it belonged to some other girl, and I'd stepped into her domestic world, intruding on her ordinary life.

"You're the one who's lost your freaking mind!" I snapped, irritated beyond belief that he'd brought me here, of all places. "What part of 'safe and out of the way' didn't you understand? The SDC? Seriously? Weren't you listening to a word I said?"

"Just take a damn moment before you start pegging me to the wall, Sis!" he shot back. "You don't need to be out of the way. Hiding in plain sight is just as good. Wade isn't back yet—he's still stuck in Montana, and he's not going to be back for ages, thanks to you fixing him up like a

Thanksgiving turkey. Oh yeah, Kenzie gave me all the goods on that, so there's no point looking sheepish. Anyway, The Rag Team is busy preparing their mission to go after Katherine. They're pushed to their limits. They're not going to come looking here."

I frowned, trying to calm my rapid breathing. "Once Wade gets out of the ropes, he can call for help. I left him his phone—I just put it out of his reach. The cat will be out of the bag as soon as he makes that call. So, yeah, this was still a crappy place to pick."

"Sis, you are stone cold."

I ignored him and walked over to the desk, sitting down. Taking out the Grimoire and spreading it on the table, I flipped the page back to my dad's last spell—the one he'd written just before he'd gone to kill my mother.

The moment had come. There was no Davin to worry about, and Finch had given me enough assurance that I wouldn't have to worry about the Rag Team bursting in either. I could sense anguish coming out of the pages, shivering through me as I trailed my fingertips across the weird writing. I still couldn't read it, and no words wanted to come pouring out of me.

Grabbing the black lens, I moved it over the strange scrawl, but nothing happened. *More secrets? Are you kidding me?* How many more flaming hoops did Chaos want me to jump through? Hadn't I proven I was worthy by doing the Hidden Things spell? I remembered what my dad had said about pitfalls and wondered if this was one of them.

However, as I moved the lens around the page, desperate to find *something,* I paused. There, in the very center of the weird writing, hidden unless I looked through the lens, was the same Veve of Erzulie that I'd seen on other pages. Curious, I pressed my fingertips to the symbol and focused on my dad's emotions that were brimming out of the page. *Show me... show me what I'm supposed to see,* I begged inwardly.

A moment later, the Grimoire's strange voice began to echo inside my head, repeating the heartbreaking words that my dad had spoken when he'd written this thing. *Show your forgiveness,* it boomed inside my skull.

"What?" Finch said.

I glanced at him. "I didn't say anything."

"You didn't just say, 'Show your forgiveness' to me?"

I shook my head. "That was the Grimoire."

"Weird."

Closing my eyes, I focused on my dad again. With my fingertips on the Veve of Erzulie, I delved deep into my emotions and found the tendrils I was looking for. The love and forgiveness and heartache I'd felt when I'd been forced to say goodbye. I reached for the memory of finding his mortuary photo in the New York Coven as well, remembering the relief I'd felt when I'd seen those marks on his neck that had proven, once and for all, that he'd been under the Sal Vínna curse when he'd done all those terrible things.

Gathering that into a ball in my chest, I sent the emotions out as a tight stream, forcing it directly into the Veve of Erzulie—the voodoo symbol of love, the perfect "X" to mark the spot of what I needed.

"Uh, Harley." Finch tapped me on the shoulder.

"What is it now?"

He gulped and pointed at the page of the Grimoire. "The words are moving."

I looked down and saw that he was right. The strange words that I couldn't understand were twisting and turning, each one morphing into a letter I recognized. It wasn't English, and it wasn't Latin, but it was written in the Roman alphabet.

"Do you know what language this is?" I asked. Finch knew more about dark and dangerous spells than I did.

He nodded. "It's Ancient Greek. Well, the words are, but not the alphabet. It's Romanized it for you." He paused. "But I can't focus on it. Every time I hold onto a word, the next one disappears. It's like it doesn't want me to read it. Can you read it?"

"Yeah… I think I can." My eyes devoured the words on the page, though I didn't start saying anything, the way I'd done when I'd almost summoned Erebus. Instead, the Grimoire's voice echoed in my head again, translating the words as my eyes passed over them. It was bizarre and thrilling, all at once:

Though Darkness may come in many forms, not all who seek shadows bathe in evil.

A balance beyond time and space, required to keep the world's order.

Look to the Darkness and find what you need, and offer what you must in return.

Call it to you and feel the power of the obedient, brought low to your heeding cry.

Ask what you will and find yourself answered, though be prepared to give of yourself.

Let it come to you and seek not to covet its power, for in envy lies failure.

Bring the Chaos into being, in the form destined by Origin itself.

All Mothers seek to protect their own, as all Children must break free of past bonds.

Call the Darkness to you and feel the wealth of knowledge, granted you by its tentative hand.

Ask what you will and bring questions of value, though all questions come with a price.

Let it come to you and do not ask too much, for in greed lies destruction.

Bring the Chaos into being, in the form destined by the Mother herself.

All beings must bend, otherwise...

Otherwise what? The spell seemed to cut off just as it was getting to the good part, leaving me on one heck of a question mark.

The Grimoire's voice fell silent, giving me nothing else to go on, as my head continued to swim with the words. Somehow, they felt familiar, as if I'd heard them before. Not quite the same, perhaps, but with the same sentiment I'd experienced on a different occasion. My mind instantly went back to the spell I'd read out in the New York Special Collections—the spell that had summoned Erebus, which I'd been thinking about a moment ago. There was something about that spell and this one that set an alarm bell ringing in the back of my brain. It was like that first spell had been the starter pack to this one.

But why had it cut off like that? Was I missing something? Or was this the whole spell and I was reading too much into it, expecting more somehow? I mean, it was short for a big, scary spell. Other powerful spells I'd performed had been way larger than this one. *You're just being paranoid.*

Now, I was starting to understand why Katherine was so terrified of this book. I could literally flip to any page and look through the lens and

I'd find spell after spell designed to stop her. As I'd discovered earlier, most of them were useless now, intended to be used before she'd reached this point in the rituals.

But there was still this big one. I didn't need to read it out to know that it was a powerful curse, meant to summon *something*. My money was on a Child of Chaos. A Dark one. *Erebus, maybe?* It certainly fit with the feeling I was getting, but I wasn't completely sure. There also seemed to be a hint of some kind of trade in the spell, but I had no clue what I was supposed to give in order to get. Only one thing was certain—Chaos had clearly prepared for the eventuality of Katherine reaching the last ritual.

I gripped the edge of the desk, my heart thundering. I had everything I needed right here, but there was one problem: How was I supposed to prepare for these spells and aim them at Katherine? And how was I supposed to know which one to choose? A big, shiny spear to throw at her, and plunge into her heart? There was always a chance I could miss. Maybe a massive sword that could cut her in two? But, then, I'd have to be sure I could get close enough. There was one spell that showed a way to break down powerful forcefields, but if I had to use that one *and* one to forge a weapon, as well as the one that would stop Katherine from absorbing the magic to finish the final ritual, I wasn't sure my mind would be able to cope.

I need a plan... I definitely need a plan.

Finch's phone beeped, snapping me out of my borderline breakdown. "Can you put that on silent? I'm trying to concentrate." I knew I was being snappy, and he was bearing the brunt, but this Grimoire was much bigger than I'd ever expected. All of it was much bigger than I'd ever expected. And I was starting to feel the weight of that crushing down on me.

He ignored me and checked his phone, his expression darkening. "Leave that for now."

"Are you insane?"

"I mean it. You need to come with me to the infirmary, now." He looked at me, obviously worried.

"What is it? What's happened?" *If anything's happened to Jacob, I won't be able to go on.* Worst-case scenarios exploded into my mind.

"Louella finally tapped into Jacob's noggin."

I shot up. "Then what are we waiting for?"

I shoved the lens and the Grimoire into the satchel and slung it across my body, sprinting for the door. Being a lone wolf could take a back seat for a minute. Right now, the pack was more important. I could go back to pushing Finch and the Rag Team away once I knew Jacob was okay. If nothing else, it would give me the courage I needed to get on with this thing. Plus, if we had a lead into Jacob's mind, we'd finally find out what had happened in Krieger's office, and that was worth putting everything to the side, if only for a short time.

I darted out of my bedroom, with Finch in hot pursuit, tearing through the SDC. I didn't stop for a moment, eager to reach the infirmary as quickly as possible. Finch caught up a few moments later, running at my side.

"You're going to have a lot to answer for," he warned.

I flashed him a look. "I can manage."

A small smile turned up the corners of his lips. "Wade's going to be so pissed when he finally gets back from Montana. I mean, you left him in *Montana*."

"Hey, it's beautiful there."

"It's in the ass end of nowhere!"

"He'll understand."

Finch snorted. "You better hope he does."

"Look, just don't tell anyone what I've been doing, okay? Please, Finch. It's important to me. You said you understood why I was doing this, and I need you to prove it. Keep my secret… please. I'm clearly not going to be able to get rid of you, and I can't waste any more time pushing you away. But, if you want to help me out, I need you to do this. I need you to keep quiet."

He flashed me a grin and pulled his fingertips across his lips. "Not even the KGB could get it out of me. But, if you try and give me the slip, I'll tell the Rag Team everything."

"Are you blackmailing me?"

"I guess I didn't forget *everything* my mother taught me."

I shuddered. "Fine. You stay silent, and you can keep helping me."

"I'd call that a deal, Sis. The Merlin siblings at large again, taking down Katherine Shipton side by side. Eris Island, mark two, locked and reloaded."

I chuckled wryly. "Don't make me regret this."

Despite my laughter, I already did. He might've convinced himself that he was disposable. But, to me, he was anything but.

THIRTY-SIX

Harley

We reached the infirmary ten minutes later, barreling into the room to find Imogene and Louella standing at Jacob's bedside.

Levi was fast asleep in his hospital bed, snoring softly, oblivious to the momentous occasion that was happening around him. *At least that means Zalaam is down for the night, too.*

It was only seven o'clock in the evening here, but my concept of time was all over the place. I'd just come from France, where it had been the wee hours of the morning, and now I was back to San Diego time. It was disorienting, to say the least.

I slowed to a walk and approached Jacob's bed. I'd been waiting for so long for some sign that he was still sane inside that precious head of his, and I was impatient to find out what Louella had tapped into.

"How is he?" I jumped right in, sitting down and taking Jacob's hand in mine.

"I managed to capture a few streams of his consciousness," Louella replied. "It wasn't very clear, but it felt like he was trying to tell me something. He mentioned your name, Harley, and he mentioned Imogene, too. That's why I called you both here. I couldn't reach you on your phone, Harley, so I tried Wade, then Finch." She smiled. "I knew you'd be with one of them."

I nodded. "Yeah, my phone's been on the blink for a while. I think it was all the portaling back and forth, before Jacob got hurt. It's wrecked my SIM card."

"Well, at least you're here now," she replied. "That's all that matters."

Imogene looked at me with worried eyes. "Is Wade not with you?"

I swallowed my rising anxiety. "No, he had to go and look into something at Waterfront Park. I think there was a rare herb he wanted to get."

"Tibetan cordyceps, I think he said," Finch chimed in.

"Wow, he'll be lucky getting those at Waterfront Park. He'll be lucky getting them anywhere," Louella said. I'd forgotten she had the knowledge of someone twice her age, but she wasn't giving me any suspicious vibes. She was too focused on Jacob.

"He should have come to me," Imogene replied. "I would've been happy to try and source some for him."

"Well, if he doesn't find any at Waterfront Park, I'll get him to go to you." I smiled at her gratefully. I envied Imogene for her ability to stay calm through just about anything, her face a picture of serenity, with only a hint of worry on her smooth brow. *I need some of what she's having.* Finch and I were a complete mess, both of us panting like we'd run a marathon, sweat dripping down our faces. And I didn't even want to know what I looked like in the mirror. Bedraggled wouldn't have covered it.

"Can you get hold of those streams again?" I asked.

Louella nodded. "I was just waiting for you."

Taking a deep breath, she placed her palms on Jacob's temples and closed her eyes. "He's talking about what happened in Krieger's office… He walked in with Isadora and the detector, after they'd tested it out in the Banquet Hall… He saw Imogene and Suri… Imogene was mad at him for bringing a human into the SDC… The detector started to whirr into life, and it showed… wait, no, that can't be right…" Her brow furrowed, her mouth opening in a startled "O" of terror.

"What did it show?" I urged. I wanted to know what was scaring her so much.

"It showed… It showed the detector identifying Imogene as… as Katherine." Tears began to roll down Louella's cheeks as those words sank in.

My eyes widened, and my heart damn near stopped as my blood ran cold. Time seemed to slow down completely, as if I'd wandered right into my worst nightmare. Beside me, Finch stiffened, his eyes snapping toward Imogene, his hand reaching for my shoulder like he was about to drag me out of there. Clearly, he hadn't known any of this.

"Suri stabbed Isadora," Louella went on, her voice trembling. "She was working for Katherine… She wanted to be a magical… Katherine revealed herself and killed Suri… and then she killed Isadora." Her words got clearer, as though the streams of consciousness were coming at her faster, tumbling out of her. "She plunged a scalpel into Isadora's heart and cut herself so she could fool us all. She knocked Jacob out and put him in a strange stasis so he wouldn't be able to breathe a word. Imogene is Katherine. For years, she's been Katherine."

I couldn't take my eyes off Imogene as she stood calmly at the foot of Jacob's bed, a smile spreading across her face. A smile that Imogene would never have worn. It was a smile I recognized. Katherine's victorious grin.

My limbs felt like they were frozen. This wasn't possible. It just wasn't possible. Jacob had gotten it wrong—he had to have. And yet, that smile spoke volumes. *No, no, no, no, no, no, no…* I'd trusted Imogene. She'd been there for me in my darkest days, and now Louella was telling me that she'd been Katherine all along? *No, that can't be.* She was a shining light, while Katherine was pure, dark evil. She'd given me that pendant, as a reminder of my family. She'd had it made so I'd have something to remember my lineage by.

Realization slammed into me like a wrecking ball. I felt sick to my stomach, bile rising up my throat. *That pendant made Wade try to kill me…*

Sliding my hand into the satchel, I took out the black lens. It was as though my hand didn't even belong to me, like something else was driving me to do this. The Grimoire? I didn't know, but I couldn't stop it. My fingertips were shaking, barely able to hold the lens in my clammy palm. This lens was supposed to reveal hidden things. Did that mean people, too? Enemies who'd been hiding in plain sight this whole time? I had to know.

Raising the lens, I peered through it, my throat completely dry. There she was… long red hair, wild green eyes, wearing one of her elaborate gowns beneath that expensive suit.

The devil herself.

THIRTY-SEVEN

Katherine

I felt like taking a bow and basking in the abject horror that was positively thrumming from each and every one of these idiots. I would've preferred applause for all my time and effort, but I'd take what I could get, and shock and terror had their own brand of thrill. The cat was out of the bag, and, frankly, I couldn't have been happier. It was like an enormous weight had been lifted from my shoulders.

It was almost as though I was meeting them all for the first time, as Katherine and Imogene, all wrapped up in one glorious package. It was a strange sensation, and I probably should've been looking for an exit, but I wasn't going to walk away from this. It was all too beautiful. I loved it. And besides, if you weren't living life on a knife's edge, you were taking up too much room, and right now I was dancing along that sharp blade, about to jab it right into their hearts. Their beloved Imogene was a figment of my imagination. I'd been pulling the wool over their eyes. And, by now, they were all running through every encounter they'd ever had with Imogene, realizing just how stupid they'd been. I'd been right in front of them, this whole time. Dramatic irony at its most satisfying. And *what* a payoff! I couldn't have planned it better myself.

And why look for an exit, when I already knew I was getting out of here alive? I *always* had backups for my backups. This was no exception.

I'd been thinking about this for a while, ever since that incident in the German's office. And now, I had the control. Just the way I liked it. Ultimate domination, sunny-side up. I knew it would reach this point. With Louella's lovely little power returning, it had only been a matter of time before Jacob's memories started causing trouble, revealing the oh so shocking truth. I could've stood here all day, drinking in their shocked faces, as they tried to wrap their feeble minds around it all.

"Isn't it hilarious?" I grinned. "I've played you all for so long, and you didn't even know. Off you all went, looking in all the wrong places, while I was standing right in front of you. You poured your hearts out to me. You looked to me for guidance. You even accepted gifts from me, without realizing that I had the power to hex them whenever I pleased. All this time, you were one step shy of worshiping Eris—she just had a different name. Imogene Whitehall. Oh, I've had so many wonderful nights, just laughing myself silly that not a single one of you noticed. You should see your faces! I wish I had a camera so I could savor this moment."

Harley lunged out of her seat, just as I'd known she would. Little Miss Wounded Heart. All of this revenge stuff was getting painfully tired, and she was so hilariously predictable. I could have counted, to the second, the moment she launched into attack mode. Opening my palms, I sent up a forcefield, the thin veil rising as smooth as butter. She could slam her Chaos against it until her heart gave out, and she wouldn't be able to get in.

Finch grabbed Harley around the waist and threw her backward, pushing a wave of Telekinesis into her to keep her away. Again, I could've done a countdown to him getting involved. It was all so boring. Did they really think they could just pummel me into submission?

"Get the hell out of here, NOW!" he roared.

"No way. I'm not—" she tried to reply, but he cut her off.

"Leave, NOW!"

Ooh, when did you grow a pair, son of mine? It was almost sweet, but I didn't go in for all that saccharine stuff.

Safe behind my forcefield, I sent out a veritable thunderstorm of Electro, nicely gathered from that Crux bitch. It hit Finch full in the chest, his body going into an immediate spasm that made me want to howl with laughter. He looked ridiculous, flopping to the ground and thrashing around like a fish who'd made a bid for freedom. Harley stared at him, clearly not knowing what to do with herself. *First rule of Chaos Club... never hesitate.*

Right on time, a Strainer portal tore open a hole in time and space, a rush of wind crashing through the infirmary. Davin Doncaster stepped out, looking like James Bond in the flesh, flanked by a small group of my loyal cultists. He was wearing a dark green suit, which would have been an unusual choice, but I knew there was a deeper meaning behind his fashion selection. He never did anything without putting a great deal of thought into it. *Aww, he wore my color, just for me.* And man, did he look good.

They blocked Harley's exit, and I could actually see the moment she started to panic, her eyes wide and frantic. It was yet another sumptuous blow to her fragile ego, and my heart was singing opera. I might not have been the fat lady, but this wasn't over until I started singing, and I was close to breaking into a damned aria. It was all so perfect.

"Davin?" Harley's voice came out as a choked gasp. *Ah, you didn't see that coming, either?*

"My apologies. I realize this may come as a shock, but my loyalty has never been to you or your cause." He smiled roguishly, making my heart pound. I had no idea how he did it, but seeing him taunt her made him even sexier.

"I should've listened to Finch. You snake!" she snarled. "What did you do to Alton? Where is he?"

"Temper, temper," he purred. "Alton gave me the slip, but he is on his last legs. We had quite the fight, and he did not make it out of the conflict unscathed. No, I imagine he is already dead. He wouldn't have managed to get far before his heart gave out. Not after everything he put himself through, for you."

"I did warn you I was everywhere," I added, just to really rub that salt in deep. "Davin, could you round these nice folks up?"

"Of course, my darling. Get the girl," Davin commanded, pointing to Louella. *I love it when he takes charge.* Half of the cultists sprinted forward, leaping over the hospital bed. She tried to run, naturally—they always tried—but the cultists grappled her to the floor, pinning her there with her arms behind her back and clapping Atomic Cuffs on her wrists before she had the chance to drop an arm and make a run for it. That left one horse in the race. The prize mare, who'd lost sight of the finish line.

Harley backed up, keeping an equal distance between herself, me, and Davin. Raising her palms, she launched a barrage of powerful attacks as she stepped into the gap between Jacob's and Levi's beds. I could see her fumbling for something in her jacket pocket.

I laughed. "You think magic chalk is going to save you?"

Her eyes flashed at me, spilling pure rage. "You won't win, Katherine!"

"Oh, my sweet, stupid girl, I already have."

As Davin and the remaining half of the cultists closed in on her, she stood her ground, sending wave after wave of Fire, and Water, and Air, and Earth, and Telekinesis at them. Every time they went hurtling backward, they just got up again, knowing I'd be the one to kill them if they didn't capture Harley. I was far scarier than a little girl who was in way over her head. Although, I had to admit, it was pretty impressive to watch Orphan of the Year fight back in such close quarters.

She knew there was no way she was getting through my forcefield, so she hadn't even tried. That was slightly disappointing, but hey, I could deal with it. Poor thing had a lot on her plate.

"I'll kill you all! And I'm going to start with you, Katherine!" Harley howled, her face a picture of useless determination as she continued her barrage of attacks, until she'd backed herself against the wall. One hand was still fumbling for the piece of chalk. She was clueless. She'd barely get a single line drawn before one of my people stopped her, and then she'd have to live with the embarrassment of knowing she'd wasted time on drawing a silly line that was never going to get finished. She had tenacity, but I was getting impatient for this to be over. I had things to do. Clearly, she had no respect for *my* mission. *So selfish.*

"Give up, Harley. You're not going to win this," I said, taunting her just a little. I had to get my kicks somewhere.

"That's where you're wrong," she replied, with an unnerving calm. *Bluffing, are we?*

I snorted. "Well, you know that's not true. Either you submit, or we make you. I know which one is more dignified. Look at the state of you. Anyone would think you ought to be locked up. You're acting like a crazy person."

"You don't have the upper hand this time."

"Must we always fight? Wouldn't it be so much easier if you just gave in and joined me? You might like it. I offer some serious perks."

"Go to hell!" she snapped.

"We were there together, remember? Or did you forget? Have you forgotten about poor Shinsuke already? Shame on you." I grinned.

She closed her eyes and began to mumble something under her breath. Bright green smoke emerged from her skin, spiraling around her in a powerful vortex. It wasn't like anything I'd ever seen before, and I'd seen most things. A moment later, it shot out in an explosion of tendrils, forcing me to duck as one strand made a beeline for my head. I heard the whoosh of it as it whizzed by, bouncing off the side of my forcefield.

I didn't appreciate being made to duck, especially not when I'd gone to the trouble of putting up a shield. Unfortunately, one of my cultists wasn't so lucky. The tendril hit him full in the chest. He screamed as his skin melted away, leaving a puddle of milky goop on the floor where he'd once stood.

"Not exactly sporting of you, Harley," I snarled. I didn't like surprises, either, and this little trick had definitely surprised me.

Her mouth opened, as if she was about to come back at me with some ever so stinging retort, when Levi's eyes snapped open, flashing red. Zalaam had the reins, as any good djinn ought to. He sat up and lurched toward Harley before she even saw him, tapping her on the back of the head.

"Alnuwn alan, waedam alshueur bi'ayi 'alm. Tagmid eaynayk wadae alnasyan yati astayqz eind alaitisal bik. Walakun lays gabl dhalik. Alnuwm alan, walsamah laha yakhudhuk," he whispered, the Arabic rolling off his tongue like music to my ears. In essence, he was putting her to sleep. It was all over, in less than a minute. Jacob was out. Harley was out. Finch was out. Louella was writhing in Davin's arms, making me slightly jealous. But at least she wasn't dropping limbs left, right, and center. The Atomic Cuffs had seen to that.

"Lucky number twelve," I purred, more to myself than to anyone else.

On the other side of the infirmary, the door opened and Herr Doktor walked in. His face was a picture. He looked at Davin and the cultists, his eyes moving around the room, settling on Finch, Harley, Louella, and Jacob, all of them down for the count, aside from the pretty little Telepath. Before he could open his mouth, I brought down the forcefield around me and transformed into my real self, letting myself breathe without all those flimsy fabrics wafting around me. He stared at me, totally baffled.

"Pleasant evening, isn't it? You really should have gone somewhere else." I raised my hands and sent a shockwave of powerful, raw Chaos through the infirmary. It wasn't a specific ability. Oh no, it was more than that. So much more. A new skill I'd picked up that I'd been so very eager to use.

The crackling torrent hit the infirmary walls, sending sparks across the interdimensional bubble that held this entire show together. As the tendrils spread out like veins, they sapped the bubble of its energy, tearing holes in the ceiling, the walls, everything. Soon, there would be nothing left. All of this would come tumbling down, just like the rest of the world, once I was in my seat of power.

Davin sent out a blast of Air that swept Krieger right off his feet, slamming him into the back wall so hard that he didn't get back up again. He crumpled to the floor, his head lolling to the side. Beyond the infirmary door, I heard the rumble of boots approaching. The security magicals were on their way, but it was too late. I'd already done my damage.

"Thank you, Davin." I walked toward him, as the infirmary crumbled around us. *This* was romance. Standing together while a coven fell to pieces. Part of me hoped he'd be standing at my side when the rest of the world followed, so we could rise from the ashes together. *Maybe I'm a romantic after all.*

"Do you need anything else, Katie?" He gave a smooth bow that looked effortless.

I shook my head. "No, you've done everything I could have asked for. You'll be rewarded, I promise you that."

He smiled. "I look forward to worshiping you, in every possible way."

"So, you still won't join me until I've ascended?"

"You have given me plenty to think about. Perhaps my mind is already changing."

I gazed into his intense eyes. "Then I look forward to the day you finally submit to me."

"Oh, that day has already been and gone, my darling. I am yours, body and soul. Soon enough, once you have become the goddess that I have always known you to be, I will worship you, as I have promised."

"Patience isn't one of my virtues," I warned.

"It will be worth the wait, I assure you. Delayed gratification at its finest."

"Don't disappoint me."

He took my hand and kissed it gently. "Never."

"Then I suggest you follow me."

"I would follow you to the ends of the Earth. My divine goddess. My Eris." He'd never called me that before, and it threw me for a moment. Somehow, it sounded even more wonderful coming from his lips.

"Then we should go." I sent out three strong strands of Telekinesis, wrapping one each around Louella, Harley, and Jacob. Holding them steady, I swept my palm across the air in front of me, my hands sparking with vibrant light. A burst of energy shot out of my fingertips and tore open a hole in the universe. I waited until the edges stopped crackling before I stepped through, trailing my three captives behind me, my cultists waiting to follow.

Finch could die in the crumbling infirmary for all I cared. That way, I would finally get what I'd been wanting without having to hang around to watch the life leave him.

I paused at the portal threshold and turned back. "Thank you for your help, Zalaam. You should probably get out of here if you want to survive. Not that I'm particularly bothered if you stay."

He glared at me, his eyes flashing. "I didn't want to help you. I was just upholding my end of the bargain."

"I know—that's what's so wonderful about it." I chuckled. "At least you know that Raffe and Kadar will be safe. Aren't you glad? They get to live because of you. You should give yourself a pat on the back. Not everyone will be so lucky."

Zalaam had bartered for Raffe and Kadar's lives, and I'd been only too happy to grant him that, for the right price. I knew a bargain when I saw one. Having a djinn on your side was always useful. And he'd come through in the best possible way. Harley had walked right into the trap without even realizing it had been set. Everything had been planned down to the minute, the moment I'd known Louella could blow my cover. And now, I had her to finish my ritual. And I had Jacob to use in my new world.

And I had Harley, the clock stopping for her at the eleventh hour. There wouldn't be a reprieve. She wasn't going to stop me—she was going to help me. After all, thanks to her, the Grimoire had revealed its secrets. With it, I would take what I'd stolen from Odette's head and give myself the body that I needed in order to be a true goddess. No raw, flailing energy for me. I would be whole—a solid person to be worshipped by all on Earth. I'd seen the spell I needed in Odette's mind, and I knew what I was looking for within the Grimoire's pages. A spell that could be modified to meet my needs, once I had completed the final ritual. A spell that could be used by any Child of Chaos. I guessed Chaos never expected me to reach the finish line. *Fools.* Well, I was going to show them just how dedicated I was.

Every step that Harley had taken, this whole time, had been for me, without her even knowing it… and that was going to sting like an absolute bitch.

THIRTY-EIGHT

Harley

My eyes shot open, like I was lurching out of the worst nightmare of my life. My clothes were drenched in sweat, my breathing rapid. I looked around wildly, somehow expecting to still see the infirmary, but we weren't in Kansas anymore.

No, we were as far from the SDC as it was possible to be.

I felt something rough and solid behind my back and tried to bring my arms forward. They wouldn't budge, bound together with Atomic Cuffs.

As I blinked through the pounding headache that threatened to explode my skull wide open, my vision cleared. Greenery surrounded me on all sides, crumbling ruins poking up through the vines that had reclaimed their territory. Creatures howled in the branches of the endless rainforest canopy, rustling leaves in their panic to get away from the intruder who'd burst into their world. I sat at the edge of an open glade, a ferocious waterfall crashing down on the far side, disappearing into a gaping crevasse below. Wildflowers grew on narrow outcrops of rock.

We're in the Land of Gaia... Only, this wasn't the same spot where I'd tried to fight Katherine before. There was no altar and no reminder of President Price. Instead, we seemed to be in the decimated corpse of an old temple, though most of it had given way to the rainforest. A few blocks of stone showed where the floor might've been, and lichen-covered spires stood abandoned.

In the center of the open expanse, there was a giant slab of stone, circular and marked with eroded figures. I could make out the face of a monkey, and maybe a dragon, but the rest had been worn away by time, splintered with weed-strewn cracks.

When I turned my head to the side, my heart jolted. Standing on the eastern edge of the ruins was a shaking, quivering, weeping line of children, some so small it made me want to cry. Twelve of them, all bound in Atomic Cuffs, tears streaming down their faces. Micah was there, his head buried in Marjorie's stomach as she tried to hold him with her bound wrists. The only one who wasn't crying, who stood proudly with her head held high, was Louella. She was trying to be brave, her eyes fixed on me.

I'm going to get you out, I mouthed, but she didn't move. She didn't even acknowledge that she'd seen what I'd said. I would've shouted it across the ruins, but the sight of Katherine kept me silent. It'd only put Louella in the firing line, urging Katherine to kill her first. I knew why these twelve magicals were here—this was the final ritual.

Scanning the rest of the ruins, I saw Jacob a short way off, still unconscious. As for Finch and the rest of the Rag Team, they were nowhere to be seen. *They aren't here... she left Finch in that place.* I remembered hearing the rumble of the whole place collapsing in on itself, which meant Finch had been stuck there, knocked out, with no way of escaping.

Davin stood beside her, looking smug as he paraded around like a peacock. I wanted to punch him almost as much as I wanted to swipe Katherine's head off. I could've kicked myself for not sensing trouble with him. Finch had a stellar bastard detector, and I hadn't tuned in to it.

"Ah, start up the band, Harley finally has the decency to join us. I hope you've packed your tap shoes, because it's time to dance, niece of mine." Katherine turned to me, dressed in a long emerald gown, a silver crown atop her red hair. The same hair I had. She looked so freaking pleased with herself. She'd played us for so long, and this was her payoff.

"I won't be dancing to your tune, Katherine," I spat back.

"Oh, but you will. You still don't understand, do you? It's over, Harley.

You tried and you failed, as I knew you would, and now you get to see everything I've been working toward, all these years. I've earned it, wouldn't you say?"

"Where's the real Imogene? I felt her emotions. She showed them to me. There's no way you could've been her, all this time, without me realizing." I wanted that to be true, I really did, but Katherine had always warned me that she had everything planned, down to the last detail. I hadn't believed her, and I'd paid for it.

She chuckled. "You and Jakey are so alike. He didn't believe it either. I must have been *that* good. I mean, of course I was. I never half-ass a theatrical role." She lifted her wrist and showed Imogene's bracelet, unclipping it and dangling it from her fingertip. "A simple trick. Sideshow stuff. I press a few buttons, and boom, I can give the illusion of having a heart."

My stomach dropped. "It was you… it was always you."

Katherine slow-clapped, the sound sending shudders up my spine. "Now she gets it. I've put my entire life into this endgame, Harley. I told you time and time again that I had it all perfectly orchestrated, and you still thought you had the upper hand? I bet you almost popped a vein when you found out about the Grimoire. I bet you thought it would be your panacea—your cure-all, to get rid of me. Well, I've got news for you. Chaos is particularly stupid. Spells can be changed. And spells that can aid you, can aid me. Everything you've done, every step you've taken, has been to help me. And the best part? You didn't even realize it."

"I'd never help you," I hissed, thrashing against my Atomic Cuffs. I sent my Chaos through the lock, as I'd done with them before in the Smiths' backyard, but they refused to break. I had a feeling Katherine had done something to them to superpower them, knowing I'd be able to free myself.

"Think about it, sweet-cheeks. Do you really think I'd have let you keep that dusty old book if I hadn't needed something from it? Do you really think I'd have let you near it, knowing that it was invented solely to kill me? I don't have a stupid bone in my body, Harley. I let you keep it for a reason. I do everything for a reason."

My eyes widened, as I realized she was right. Imogene had known about the Grimoire, which meant Katherine had known about it. And yet, she'd made no move to stop me. I knew the Grimoire was a sentient item that chose who it decided to let near it, but this was Katherine we were talking about—if she'd wanted to take it from me, in some way or another, she would've.

"Then why let me go through all that trouble with the Hidden Things spell?" I shot a nasty look at Davin. "Since *he* is here, I'm guessing you knew about that. I'm guessing you were in on the whole damn thing. So why let me get that far?"

She grinned. "Oh, I was so hoping you'd ask that question. It's always hard to segue into a stinging blow without a prompt, you know? Otherwise, it just sounds forced, like I've been rehearsing it. And I hate to sound rehearsed." She let the bracelet drop to the ground, since she didn't need to uphold the pretense of being remotely human anymore. "I'm going to use your body, once I ascend as a Child of Chaos. The Grimoire is going to give me that, but you needed to find the right spells first. Since you managed to uncover the secrets, I'm guessing you already have them. Even if you haven't quite found them yet, I'm going to have you read all those wonderful pages out loud to me, after I'm done ascending. Think of it like a bedtime story—the greatest one ever told."

"There's nothing in there for you," I muttered. "All of it is intended to kill you. If you have me read it out, I'll make sure I serve that purpose. So, you can be the one to think of it like a bedtime story. One that's going to put you to sleep forever."

She laughed. "Wrong again, Miss Righteous. I already know there's a spell I can use. One that will turn your body into precisely the vessel I need. Didn't you ever wonder why Odette was in that tragic state when you found her? I tore her mind apart to find what I needed. I shredded it to pieces, until she gave up the goods. The trick to torture is knowing your victim. Push the right buttons, and they all start babbling, sooner or later. Remington was my key. I know everybody's dirty little secrets, and even Librarians aren't infallible. They might have given up their past lives, but emotions die hard. Fortunately, I got her to squeal like a piggy before all of her marbles went missing. It's a fine line, and I tread it so very, very well."

Odette... I pictured her in the Paris Coven's infirmary, rocking back and forth on the windowsill, her eyes blank. Her mind had been traumatized, leaving her a shadow of her former self. And now I knew exactly why.

"Don't do this." I gritted my teeth and tried to fight against the Atomic Cuffs. It was a weak argument, I knew it was, but I needed to buy time to come up with some kind of a plan. Not that I had one. My own mind had all but given up, knowing I was moments away from being forced to wave the white flag.

"Oh, of course, let me throw away all these years of hard work. You're quite right, why would I want to continue with something I've been thinking about since I was a child? You've changed my mind, Harley. Thank you, from the bottom of my heart. Thank you for making me see the error of my ways. Please, allow me to untie you and let you walk free. And, while I'm at it, why don't I just let all these children go, too? Let's just forget about these silly rituals, shall we? And I'll let the cult fold, too, as a gesture of goodwill." She collapsed in a fit of hysterics. "Oh, and let me apologize for killing your parents. I shouldn't have done it. I really shouldn't have. I should have just swallowed all of their insults, and let them walk all over me, and channeled all of my energies into becoming a nun. Wouldn't I look gorgeous in a habit?" She winked at Davin.

"I think you would look gorgeous in just about anything... or nothing, for that matter." He grinned.

"Come on, Harley, you can do better than that." She smirked at me. "Why not beg? I'd like to see that, I really would. Let me see just how much you want these children to live. Plead, on your hands and knees, for their lives. It won't change anything, but it'll give me something to giggle about."

I glowered at her. "I wouldn't give you the satisfaction."

"Did you hear that, kiddos?" She glanced over at the cowering children. "She doesn't care enough to beg for your lives. She thinks you're disposable. How heartbreaking for you. I bet you all thought that now that the mighty Harley was here, you'd all be off the hook. Sorry to disappoint you."

"You are wondrous, my darling," Davin purred.

"And you can shut your trap, too!" I snapped. "You're a leech, clinging to that evil bitch because you think you're going to get something out of her. Let me be the first to tell you, the moment you piss her off, you'll be exploding into a spray of blood before you can even say, 'I'm sorry, *darling*.'" I roared the last word, hating his guts.

He laughed tightly, as though he wasn't quite sure if I was bluffing. "I like to stay on the side of the most powerful. And the most beautiful. Sadly, sweeting, that isn't you. And if that makes me a leech, then I am only too happy to suckle upon the supple flesh of my darling Eris."

"You make me sick!" I snarled.

"Put your head between your legs, then," Katherine retorted. "Even if it doesn't help with the nausea, you won't have to see what is coming next. Although, I'd hate for you to miss it. I've prepared quite a show. I might even throw in a few pyrotechnics, if I'm feeling particularly dramatic."

"I'll never read out those spells for you. You can scream until you're blue in the face. You can hurl all the hexes you want at me. I won't do it. Chaos will protect me." It was my last-ditch attempt at saving face, in the fragile hope that I might be right.

Her cold laughter immediately shattered that hope. After all, she knew everything. She probably had my reading out the Grimoire planned to the letter. If she'd known about this spell that she needed since before I'd seen Odette in Paris, then she'd been thinking about it for a long time. Far longer than I'd even known what the Grimoire had in it.

"You will read out the spells, Harley. Don't forget, I broke Odette's mind—like, I literally broke it. Yours will be child's play, and Chaos won't be able to do a single thing about it. Chaos rules, remember? No direct intervention. It can't move the goal posts now. It isn't allowed. Isn't that funny? It has all of this power, running through every magical in the world, and yet it can't stand in my way because of a rule *it* created. Talk about shooting yourself in the foot."

I sank back against the tree, trying to think of something to say, one searing comeback that would render her silent. Instead, I was speechless. She'd played her game so well, never slipping up, and we hadn't even known we were the pieces in play. We'd gone running off in so many directions, always reporting back to Imogene Whitehall, our avenging angel, only to find out that our angel had horns propping up her crooked halo. She'd played the long game, and now it was paying dividends, all of it coming together in exactly the way she'd wanted. I hated that more than anything—that we'd walked right through every hoop she'd set up without question.

"What, no witty repartee?" Katherine smiled. "Have I finally silenced the Great White Snark?"

I literally couldn't think of a single thing to say to her. What could I say? The Grimoire satchel was over by her, too far for me to reach, and we had no way of getting out of here with Jacob unconscious on the ground.

She's done it... she's won. I squeezed my eyes shut as a fierce, angry tear rolled down my cheek.

All of this had been for nothing. All of my time researching the Grimoire, all of the missions we'd endured to secure it, all of the effort and stress and strain, trying to come up with a way of stopping Katherine —it had all been for nothing. She'd been the puppet master this whole time, and we'd just been dancing on her strings. She'd won, and there was nothing else I could do or say to change that. And now, I'd have to watch as she stole the lives of these children, helpless to lift a finger to save them.

THIRTY-NINE

Harley

"Not you, too," Katherine muttered, as she turned back to the line of shaking children. "You could fill a swimming pool with all these tears. And they're completely pointless, by the way. Sniveling isn't going to make me change my mind. So why not be brave, instead? Why not lift those chins up and take it like troopers? After all, you're serving the most precious purpose that any magical can be gifted with."

The kids' desperate sobbing echoed back, making my heart break. I couldn't save them. Even if I didn't have my hands tied behind my back, one of Katherine's minions would have knocked me down again. Without a direct exit strategy, I couldn't do anything, and that hurt more than any pain I'd ever endured before. For the first time since I'd started this vengeance mission against Katherine, I felt like a total failure.

Meanwhile, Katherine strolled in front of the children, continuing her latest monologue of impending doom.

"It's high time you all realized I don't have a hoot to give about your feelings. I don't care if you suffer. I don't care if you're in pain. I dispensed with empathy a long time ago, and if you want to blame someone for that, you can blame your 'hero' over here." She jabbed a finger back at me, clearly wanting me to feel like this was my fault. "Well, her father, anyway. He taught me not to trust anyone. He taught me not to be weak. He taught me not to care. So, in a way, I've got a lot to thank him for, though I doubt you'll all be lining up to congratulate him. It's probably for the best that I skewered him. Right, Harley? Oh, what's that, still got nothing to say? Katie got your tongue?"

Don't let them see that you're defeated. I lifted my head as proudly as I could and looked at the children, trying to offer them some comfort. They just stared back in hopeless desperation, their eyes wide and panicked. They wanted me to get up and save them. They wanted me to do something. But I… I just couldn't. She'd already won.

"I'm not entirely heartless," Katherine continued. A gasp of hope went up from the children. "Oh, no, don't get it twisted, you're all still going to die, but I'm not going to drag it out for too long. This will all be over soon, and then you won't have to worry about anything, ever again. You can all die in the knowledge that you've given me the ability to ascend, resulting in a world far better than the one you'll be leaving. And your families, if you have them, will be well rewarded. As for the orphans and unwanted amongst you—you'll just have to be satisfied with the gift of giving me all-consuming power. Sorry, I don't make the rules… not yet, anyway."

The children howled, some of them crumpling to their knees, only to be dragged back up by the guarding cultists. A few begged for their lives, but the majority were too panic-stricken to do anything but cry and wail. Only Louella continued to hold her nerve, refusing to show fear.

Katherine came to a halt and raised her arms, standing right in the center of that circular stone slab as she urged the cultists to bring the children forward. Moving as if they'd practiced this, they set each child at equal intervals around the disc, making them look like the points on a clock, with Katherine in the middle. Once they were in position, she smiled and raised her arms. A bright bronze light swelled in her chest, pulsing as she started to speak.

"Filii chaos hora venit. Ego autem duodecim discipuli et venerunt ad praemium peto. In animabus suis: Ego offerre mea provocatione ad vos." Her words boomed through the ancient ruins as if she were talking through a loudspeaker.

The pulsating light in her chest grew brighter as she continued and took a step toward the first victim, who'd been placed at one o'clock on the disc. It took me a moment to realize, but the kids around the clock had fallen silent, their eyes closed. I frowned, trying to figure out what was happening. Their faces were blank, as if they weren't quite here anymore. In fact, they looked like they were sleeping, their bodies held up by the sheer force of Katherine's magic. *Maybe she has a sliver of a heart.* She wasn't keeping them awake or conscious while she performed the last ritual. They'd be oblivious to all of it. Though I wasn't quite sure what "it" was just yet. All I knew was that she'd told them they were going to die.

I didn't even see the knife until it was too late. The blade slashed through the air, and my heart lurched, fearing the worst. But the blade didn't make contact with the girl at all. Instead, Katherine had made a cut in the atmosphere itself. Weird, purple tendrils snaked out toward the girl. They reached her chest, and her body spasmed as Chaos abandoned her, particle by glinting particle, carrying the essence back to Katherine for her to absorb. The purple tendrils poured out, thicker and faster, crashing into Katherine's chest until the girl went limp and fell to the ground, disconnecting from the magic that had held her upright.

Is she alive? I leaned forward, desperate to see some sign of life. It was hard to tell from where I was sitting, but she still seemed to be breathing. A shallow movement of her chest and a faint flicker behind her closed eyes gave me hope. But would she ever wake up?

"You monster!" I yelled, but Katherine couldn't hear me over the roar of the magic.

I realized that she'd told the children they were all going to die, in order to scare them. Either that, or she'd been fully prepared to watch them die to succeed. There was every chance that she'd had no clue what would actually happen to them when she began the ritual. *You really are sick.*

All I could do was watch, helpless, as she made her way around the clock of children. After each repetition of the spell, she absorbed the Chaos from another child, until her whole body glowed with horrifying purple light, illuminating every vein, every capillary, every cell beneath her skin. Tears poured from my eyes, my heart shattering as the knife darted out, making its cuts in the air, and evaporated the magic of child after child, all of them dropping to the ground, unconscious, as they disconnected from Katherine's energy. I knew the clock was ticking down to the moment she reached Micah, Marjorie, and Louella. They'd been positioned at ten, eleven, and twelve, and I just knew Katherine had done that on purpose. She wanted me to suffer. She wanted me to feel her victory, in all its horrifying glory. *But at least there's a chance they're not dead.* I forced myself to focus on that as she kept going.

But they weren't the only ones I recognized. The two older girls, Sarah McCormick and Cassie Moore, who'd been so close to each other at the SDC, swayed with their eyes closed, completely expressionless, as though they were on a different plane of existence, numb to everything going on around them. At least they'd been spared the pain of this final act. I, on the other hand, couldn't do anything but watch and try to keep hold of the contents of my stomach. It was awful to watch their Chaos get wrenched away. With every absorption, Katherine got stronger, and soon, she'd be unstoppable.

Katherine swiped her blade in front of Sarah, the Supersonic girl, and absorbed her powers, just as she'd done with the children who'd gone before. I wanted to look away, but I couldn't. I felt I owed it to them, in some strange way. If Sarah hadn't been cuffed, she'd have been able to run from this. But we were all stuck, in our own way, just as Katherine had planned.

"Stop it!" I howled. "STOP IT!"

Cassie came next, just standing there with that same listless expression as the tendrils grasped for her Chaos and made their way back to Katherine. All of the Empath and Morph ability poured out of her, filling Katherine up.

Mina Travis and Emilio Vasquez were next in line. I couldn't recall what their abilities had been, or if we'd ever truly found out, but, if they were here, then it had to have been worthwhile for Katherine. I covered my eyes as she slashed her blade across the air, using the tendrils to lap up their Chaos. *And I can't stop her.* They were expendable to her, not worth sparing a moment for.

"You sick monster, you sick monster," I repeated. I wished I could've torn out my eyeballs so I didn't have to look at those swirling tendrils anymore. If there'd ever been a morsel of humanity in her, it was long gone. Nobody with any feeling whatsoever could do this. Nobody. That's where Chaos had gone wrong. They'd made the rituals so awful and so strenuous that they probably hadn't expected anyone to go through with them. And then Katherine had come along.

Passing through child after child, she reached nine o'clock on the circle. My throat was raw with sobbing, my eyes burning with tears, my heart in pieces. She was almost finished, and that meant she was one step closer to her end goal. A victory I couldn't stop. That hurt as much as watching the Chaos being removed.

"Is this worth it? Is it really worth it?" I roared. "You were a mother, Katherine! What the hell is wrong with you?"

Katherine shot me a look. "And look what I did to Finch," was all she said, as she swiped the blade and released more of the purple tendrils.

Micah was next, swaying gently as the trance held him. The tendrils hit him, and he fell to the ground, just as the rest of the children had done. I watched for that telltale rise and fall of his chest, finding a scrap of comfort in the sight of that steady movement. *They're alive... they're alive*. If they were still breathing, then it meant I might be able to fix the state she'd put them in.

"Heartbreaking, isn't it?" Katherine snickered, her eyes violet. "Two left. Best get on with it, eh?"

She smiled as she turned to Marjorie, the fledgling Clairvoyant who'd made the choice to go to LA, following Imogene as we'd all done. But it had been Katherine leading the show. It had never been Imogene. Her crocodile tears over the stolen kids had all been part of it.

With each passing second, the enormity of Katherine's operation became clearer. Every time we'd thought Imogene was helping us, it had been Katherine, moving another piece into place. She'd had the kids exactly where she wanted them. It hadn't mattered that we'd brought them to the SDC, thinking they were finally out of harm's way, because she'd always planned to put them exactly where she could see them. In a high-security facility, run by her, watched over by her, planned by her, until she could swipe them without detection.

"I'm sorry, Marjorie! I'm so, so sorry!" I wept, utterly destroyed, but she couldn't hear me.

"You should've kept her with you. I'd still have gotten her, in the end, but at least you could've pretended she was safe." Katherine chuckled as the knife lashed out, the tendrils pulsing, taking Marjorie's Chaos away forever. As the energy poured into Katherine, she moved to Louella. "And then there was one. I thought I'd save you for last, given all the hassle you've caused me. Though, I suppose it all worked out nicely in the end."

Louella smirked. "You should have killed me first."

Katherine paused in surprise. "Why aren't you in a trance?"

"It doesn't work on Telepaths, apparently. Lucky for me. And I've been listening, Katherine. You should hear what I've been hearing."

"You haven't heard anything. Stop stalling. It won't change your fate."

"Then why are you stopping?" Louella held her ground. "I can hear Chaos whispering all around the Garden of Hesperides. And it wants to make something clear, you evil cow. Chaos doesn't want you as its Child, just like the magical world didn't want you. Like your son didn't want you. Like Hiram Merlin didn't want you."

What are you doing? I leaned forward, not wanting to miss a word. Somehow, I still hoped she'd get out of this. Maybe, just maybe, she was smart enough to. Maybe she could stop the ritual at eleven, making Katherine fall at the final hurdle. If she couldn't, then it would be game over.

"Nobody wants you, Katherine," she pressed on. "Nobody wants you because your heart is black, and everything you are is pure evil. You're selfish and self-serving, and you're not going to get what you want, no matter how much you kick and scream. You could kill a thousand of us, and it wouldn't make the slightest bit of difference. Because the truth is, Katherine, you don't deserve Chaos, no matter how hard you try and push your way through. You'll see... maybe not now or tomorrow, but you'll see. Forcing Chaos through this Challenge will be the worst thing you've ever done, not to the world, but to yourself. I mean, you've said it yourself, all of your life... rules are made to be broken."

"Nice speech, chickadee, but it's not going to save you."

"It doesn't have to," Louella replied, her voice strong and firm.

Katherine rolled her eyes. "That's quite enough of you." The knife shot out and swiped at the air, unleashing the last bout of purple tendrils. A scream tore out of my throat. *She's awake! Oh God, she's awake!* As her Chaos began to disintegrate, flowing into Katherine, Louella turned to look at me, a pained smile on her lips. *I'm sorry. I'm so sorry.* Louella had been one of us, one of the Rag Team, and now she was out cold on the floor. And I couldn't see her breathing. Why couldn't I see her breathing? Had the trance protected the other children, somehow?

"Louella!" I shouted, as if it might rouse her.

But she lay still, her body limp, no hint of life stirring her. One of the brightest minds in the world, and Katherine had snuffed her out. No light would ever shine as bright as she had. And I didn't know what to do or say. I didn't have words powerful enough to show how sorry I was. I'd allowed myself to hope that everyone might be okay, after seeing the rest of the children breathing, but Louella… Louella was gone. I didn't need Tatyana to tell me that. I could feel it. An emptiness, floating across the landscape toward me, and she was at the numb epicenter.

Two of the cultists stalked toward me, dragging me off the ground and hauling me toward Katherine. They threw me down at her feet, so close to the Grimoire I could almost taste it. But it was in the bag, hidden from my grasp. I stared up as Katherine loomed over me, wondering if I was about to suffer the same fate as the twelve children. Instead, she slashed the blade across my cheek. Blood spilled out and trickled down my face. Sliding the knife back into her dress, she leaned down and swiped her fingers across the cut she'd made, until the crimson liquid dripped onto her palm.

"Two uses for the price of one. I love a bargain," she jeered, as she licked the blood away. As soon as it hit her tongue, she started the Latin chant again, her body disappearing inside a haze of blinding light. From within, I heard her shout, at the top of her lungs: "I challenge you, Gaia! Come forward and meet your fate!"

Gaia?

I'd always thought she'd choose Nyx when the time came, what with him being the weakest of the Children. But no, in true Katherine style, she'd gone for the big game. And I just hoped Gaia had the strength to pound her into dust, because if Katherine succeeded, then she'd be the mother of them all.

FORTY

Katherine

Oh, this felt good. So good. Better than anything I'd ever experienced in my entire life.

I had my arms wide open, waiting to welcome Gaia into our final showdown. It wasn't the simplest choice, but it would be the most satisfying. Gaia was the Mother of these Children—the ringleader, the boss, the oldest of them all. Go big or go home, right? And I didn't plan on leaving the Garden of Hesperides until I had what I'd come for.

"In lumine chaos ego ad te Gaia!" I called out my challenge again in Latin, just in case she tried to pretend she couldn't understand. I knew she was listening. Now, all I had to do was wait. The ritual hadn't specified whether she'd come immediately or take her sweet time, but I was a patient woman.

The energy from those delicious children pulsated in my veins. I was slightly disappointed at Chaos's cowardice—I'd been looking forward to watching these twelve die in front of my eyes, but I'd just worked myself up for nothing. And now I had eleven unconscious bodies to deal with, and one dead one. It had protected them in some way, putting them into a trance-like state to keep them from experiencing the hollow despair of having Chaos ripped away. *How weak—yeah, I'm talking to you, Chaos.* But if they woke up and started crying again, I couldn't make any promises that I wouldn't finish the job myself.

But at least I could enjoy their Chaos, feeling it swell inside me. Purple light shivered beneath my skin, making me look like a real-life blacklight, uncovering all the secrets of this place as I cast my glow about. I felt as though I could rip this whole otherworld apart with a flick of my wrist. I'd earned this power. Nobody was going to take that from me. In fact, it looked like the Garden of Hesperides was already quaking in its boots at my mere presence.

Good, you should be afraid. You should all be afraid.

The supernatural haven shuddered and shook, the creatures in the canopies howling for their lives, as birds took flight in a bid to escape me. Poor things. This was all as new to them as it was to me. But the truth was, there was nowhere far enough for them to fly, nowhere they wouldn't feel the singe of my fire. There was nowhere far enough for anyone to fly.

"Take them away!" I commanded, gesturing to the bodies on the ground. "But leave Merlin." The cultists did as they were told, dragging the unconscious children and Louella away to the sidelines. And not a moment too soon.

The stone circle beneath my feet splintered with a deafening *crack*, Harley wriggling about like a worm about to get skewered on the end of my hook. I would've laughed at how pathetic she looked if I wasn't watching the skies and trees surrounding me, waiting for Gaia to make her dramatic appearance. All Children of Chaos were the same—they loved the drama. That was why I was the perfect fit. And Gaia had been in the spotlight for much too long. Time for someone else to have a turn. *And here I am, ready and waiting. Whenever you feel brave enough, Gaia.*

Tendrils of Darkness slithered out from beneath my emerald skirts, making them billow like Marilyn friggin' Monroe standing over a grate. I smiled as the Darkness spread out, each vein connecting until a steady black fog swept across the landscape in front of me. In its wake, it left desolation and decay, everything in its path collapsing and withering at its deadly touch—leaves, grass, trees, Gaia's creatures, all of it. Only those belonging to *Homo sapiens* seemed able to withstand it. I still needed

Harley, and Jacob, and Davin, and the rest of my cultists. I didn't want them getting swallowed up by this fog, not with their potential still untapped.

With every fresh death of a blade of grass or curled-up leaf or branch bleached white and fragile, the life essence trickled back toward me through the earth, bolstering the extreme glow that shone through every pore of my being. My body was positively thrumming, as if I'd just swallowed an entire sun and lived to tell the tale. I was metamorphosing. I'd been trapped in my cocoon of ordinariness for so long, and now I was breaking out, more magnificent than ever. A rare creature, seen once in a lifetime.

This is it... the moment you've all been waiting for. I grinned as I reached my arms skyward, feeling the power growing exponentially inside me, consuming my flesh like wildfire. You would've thought it would hurt, but it felt like nirvana. As if this was always supposed to happen. As if this had always been my true state, and I was finally having it realized. Plus, I didn't plan to be a watery haze of energized goo. I had Harley to fix that. Other Children of Chaos might have been happy to drift about the place, only materializing when called or when they were in their otherworlds, but that wasn't enough for me. I wanted to be worshipped, and for that I needed a solid body.

I wasn't an ordinary magical, and I didn't plan on being an ordinary Child of Chaos, either. Ordinary was for those with limited imaginations, and mine... well, it stretched beyond all possible limits.

"Stop," Harley wheezed at my feet, the dark smoke filling her lungs and turning her eyes a suitably creepy shade of black.

"Why, because you're asking me to?" I shot back.

I wanted to smack her head into the stone circle, if only to knock some sense into her. Hadn't she just watched me kill her little pal and absorb the Chaos of the rest? Hadn't she just watched me drink in all of their sweet, sweet abilities? Hadn't she just watched me call upon Gaia? I guessed she had to make a show of defiance, but I was getting sick of her endless whining.

"Because you're a monster. Look at what you're doing," she rasped. "You're killing everything you touch. If you do this, the world will burn.

You won't make it better. You'll be ruling over a wasteland and a sea of skeletons."

I grinned. "Am I supposed to be scared?"

"You should be."

"I don't know the meaning of fear, Harley, but *you* should." My eyes hardened. "You should be very afraid, not only for yourself, but for your little chums back at home. I might need you still, which, believe me, is as much of an inconvenience to me as it is to you, but I don't need *them*. And I'm going to make you pay for all of your indiscretions. Did you think I'd let you waltz away into the sunset? Did you think I'd let your infiltration of my cult slide? Did you think I'd forget all of the irritation you've caused me?"

There were tears in her eyes as she forced a smile onto her face. A surprisingly dark one. "You mean like taking away your precious lieutenant? Haven't you been wondering where she is? She's supposed to be your most loyal follower, isn't she, but I don't see her anywhere. Do you?"

"I will find my lieutenant when I ascend," I replied. "I haven't had the time to go searching for her. I'm an incredibly busy woman. She's probably out searching for more children, as a way of proving she's not entirely useless. Still, she'll be so very disappointed when she finds out that I've gone on without her. She was eager to see the final ritual in action."

Naima was my loyal sidekick. Nothing on this earth would have stopped her from coming back to me. This was nothing but Harley attempting to taunt me, and it wouldn't work. I wasn't fond of many people, and Naima had pissed me off more than most, but she was a part of me. I would know if something had happened to her... wouldn't I?

"She isn't searching for anything, Katherine." Harley smirked. "It's pretty hard to look for things when you're dead."

I froze. "What did you say?"

"She's dead, Katherine. I killed her myself. If you *had* bothered to look for her, you'd know that."

"Impossible. She would never have allowed herself to die at your weak hands."

"She probably thought that, too, until I squeezed the life out of her." Harley held my gaze, unwavering.

"You won't get a rise out of me, Harley." I smiled back defiantly. "I don't believe you. I think you're trying to buy yourself some more precious time, but you're fresh out, sweet-cheeks."

Harley shook her head. "You don't have to believe me. It doesn't change the facts. I killed her. It was her or me, and I did what anyone would've done. I chose me."

"I would know."

"Well, apparently you don't. She's dead, Katherine. What, did you think you could reach this point without any casualties on your side? This is war, if you needed reminding. So, tell me, what are you going to do without your loyal muscle beside you? I bet you had this whole vision, didn't you? You as a goddess with Naima at your side, instilling fear just by snapping her jaws at anyone who tried to cross you. You threatened my people—what did you expect? Did you think we'd just roll over? You take from me; I take from you. You took Louella and Isadora, and so many others, so it only seems fair that I even the score a bit."

I stared at Harley as anger burned inside me. Despite her shortcomings, I'd cared about Naima in my own way, and being told that she was dead was starting a strange reaction in my veins that made me glow even brighter.

"Hurts, doesn't it?" Harley hissed.

"You really aren't the sharpest tool in the shed, are you? Do you think it wise to tell me this, after I've already completed the final ritual? Thanks to you, everyone you've ever cared about now has a massive target on their backs. Anyone who's ever come into your life—I'll crush them all, even if it's just the delivery guy who spoke to you once. *Anyone* who's ever been associated with you has gone right to the top of my list, where they'll meet the same fate as Louella and Isadora."

My voice carried a bitter edge. Naima had been part of my future vision, just as Harley had said, and she'd dashed that. I hated the destruction of a perfectly crafted aesthetic. A giant, half-tigress woman standing beside me would have made me all the more formidable, and now I'd have to do all of that fearmongering myself. I'd miss having someone I could trust entirely.

She faltered, as I knew she would. "You won't touch anyone I care about, or you won't get anything out of me."

I smirked. "I will, and, what's more, you know I will. You're out of options, dear."

Her eyes glittered with hilarious anger. "I bet it just boils you up inside that we managed to kill her, doesn't it? And she won't be the last, I promise you that. When I'm done, you won't have a single person left in this world who's devoted to you. And then what will you do? You might have all these dreams of becoming a great goddess, but it's lonely at the top, Katherine. You'll find that out when you have nobody left who gives a damn about you. You see, I've got my own list."

"Ooh, I wouldn't poke the bear if I were you." I was prone to acts of impulse, and I was about ten seconds away from smashing her skull wide open like a juicy watermelon. I would never have admitted it, but I realized I'd made a mistake. I should've stopped to find Naima, but I just hadn't had the time, in the end. The Challenge was more important than traipsing after errant cultists I could always find later. Only, there wouldn't be a later for Naima. I turned away from Harley, wondering where the heck Gaia was. That coward was taking her time.

"Nothing to say, Katherine?" Harley jeered.

"You should learn when to keep your mouth shut," I shot back. "Although, I've got to commend you. It seems you're more like me than you'd care to admit. Removing the hurdles that stand in your way, without being afraid to get your hands dirty—that's very me, even if you won't admit it. You could've been something tremendous, if you'd chosen the right side. I would have paved the way for you to reach your full potential, but now you're going to be nothing but a shell, destined to hold my energy for the rest of time. I hope *that* burns you up inside."

Her mouth set in a grim line. "You've still got a Child of Chaos to kill. I wouldn't be so cocky if I were you. You've had it easy so far, but Gaia is going to stop you."

I rolled my eyes. "You haven't been paying attention. That's very disappointing. Do you think I'd put myself through this if I didn't know I was going to win? I'm not a fool, Harley. Every risk I take is calculated, and failure is never an option. I haven't reached this point by blind luck. I know my enemy, and I always know how to defeat them."

"You're all talk, Katherine. You're frightened, I know you are."

I laughed. "Please. I've never felt more confident in my entire life."

I had to pause as energy surged through me, more powerful than ever. I was getting stronger by the second, the fabric of time and space opening before me, like doors I could walk through whenever I pleased. Bliss pounded through my veins. This was what it must feel like to be a Child of Chaos, to be able to transcend every facet of the universe, bending it to my will. *Chaos rules? Pfft, more like* my *rules.* And I was getting tired of waiting for this last challenge, before I could take my throne, once and for all.

"*In lumine chaos ego ad te Gaia. Venite ad me et detrimentum faciat animae tuae est,*" I called to Gaia again, changing it up so she couldn't avoid me any longer. It was part of the Challenge instructions, that if she didn't come, she automatically forfeited.

"Well, looks like you got what you asked for," Harley muttered, her gaze fixed on something behind me.

I turned as Gaia emerged from behind the crashing waterfall and drifted toward me. *What did I say about a flair for the dramatic?* Coming out of a waterfall was more conceited than anything I'd ever done. The sight of her threw me for a second, though. She had long red hair and bright green eyes, her face a mirror image of mine. She was even wearing an emerald dress, which annoyed me. Nobody liked showing up to a party in the same outfit as someone else. Only, hers seemed to be a delicate patchwork of leaves and flowers, woven together to look like fabric, ending in a train of gauzy petals that swept across the sea of dead grass. *How is she even keeping that together?* It wasn't practical, but I sure as heck wanted one when I took her place.

"You summoned me," Gaia said. It wasn't a question.

"Did I?" Sarcasm dripped from my words.

"I do not wish to do this, as I do not believe in violence. But you have left me with no alternative." Even her voice sounded like mine, only more distant, like it was coming from the crumbling trees around us.

"Lucky for you, I just *love* a bit of violence." I flashed her a defiant grin.

"Don't let her win, Gaia," Harley begged. "Don't let her win."

I threw back my head and laughed, feeling no hint of fear whatsoever. After all, who was more deserving than me?

FORTY-ONE

Harley

In the end, I knew it wasn't up to Gaia.

All she could do was fight and try to win, but I had no idea if these two were evenly matched. Katherine was glowing like a purple beacon, turning everything she touched to death, while Gaia was her usual, majestic self.

"You have Challenged me and I have answered, and so our battle must begin," Gaia said, dipping her chin to her chest and opening out her arms.

"Let the best Child of Chaos win," Katherine shot back, as she followed suit.

The two women erupted into blasts of blinding light. I squeezed my eyes shut to avoid burning my retinas. Only when the light had faded did I dare to look at what they'd become. Towering over the Garden of Hesperides were two gigantic, humanoid masses of pure energy, churning and fizzing as they faced off. Katherine had turned into a seething swarm of obsidian black peppered with purple sparks, while Gaia had turned into a mass of emerald green. It was a silly thing to notice, but I knew it would be burning Katherine up inside to see someone else take her favorite color.

Katherine made the first move. A tentacle of smoky black shot out and grasped one of the ancient spires of the ruins, hurling it right at Gaia. She moved effortlessly out of range, grasping for a chunk of rock from the waterfall and sending it careening into Katherine, who exploded outward, before gathering herself back together.

They'd become titans, fighting for supremacy. They grabbed for whatever they could find—mountains, clumps of forest, enormous pieces of ruins—and sent them smashing into one another. Sometimes, one of them would get out of the way in time, but sometimes it would barrel into them, sending parts of their teeming masses splintering off before they got drawn back in again. As terrifying as it was, it was freaking mind-blowing to watch.

"Don't let her win, Gaia!" I yelled, as I scrambled back toward Jacob, covering him from the falling debris that blasted everywhere. I wanted to protect Louella's body, and the still-living children, but the cultists had hauled them away to the far edge of the ruins. I'd already been hit by twigs and stones and shards of exploding rock, my body stinging with the impact, but it was nothing compared to the thundering blows these two supernatural beings were raining down on each other. I could feel each one ricocheting through the earth, causing it to crack.

"Are you trying to tickle me or fight me, Gaia?" Katherine taunted, her voice echoing weirdly from the center of her titan self.

"Pride comes before a fall, Katherine," Gaia replied, weirdly calm. Did she know something I didn't? Because, right now, they looked like they were on even footing.

Katherine uprooted another sharp spire and hurled it at Gaia's chest. Gaia tried to surge backward, but it struck her right where her heart might've been, though I didn't know the anatomy of Children of Chaos. Or humanoid masses, for that matter. Her emerald energy sputtered for a moment before she regathered herself, dragging the cascading waterfall into her enormous palms and sending the thrashing torrent right at Katherine's head.

Katherine swerved out of the way, flattening a section of trees in her hurry to dodge it, but the torrent followed her like a homing missile, making her leap through the air and right over Gaia's head. Gaia barely had the chance to lift her hands as the water thudded into her.

"Textbook error, Gaia," Katherine jeered, but Gaia wasn't out of the running just yet. Using Katherine's moment of gloating, Gaia raised her palms, bringing up a tangle of tree roots with the motion. They wrapped around Katherine like an egg, trapping her inside.

"YES!" I screamed, just as the egg erupted in a burst of flames. Katherine emerged from it like a phoenix, hauling a mountain out of the forest and bringing it down on Gaia's back. Her titan form crumpled for just a moment, but she got back to her feet, the edges of her emerald mass fizzing. Katherine was proving to be a relentless foe, unwilling to back down for even a moment, hammering Gaia with everything she had, matching her every move.

"Had enough, Gaia?" Katherine cackled.

"I will not allow you to usurp me." Gaia took to her feet and sprinted away through the forest, flattening it as she went. Katherine followed her in hot pursuit, running full-pelt, the two of them throwing boulders and entire trees at one another.

I had no idea how long this was going to go on for, or how it would end. I mean, how could someone kill a mass of energy? You had to see it to believe it, and even then I was having a hard time figuring out how it would come to a final conclusion. My money was firmly on Gaia. Katherine had the initial burst of energy, but Gaia would have the superior stamina.

Please let me be right.

The sky overhead darkened, storm clouds swelling as they rolled in. The titans were still throwing whatever they could find at one another, but it looked like things were about to step up a notch. A fork of lightning shot out of the stormy swell and exploded close to where gigantic Katherine stood. She staggered back, steadying herself, before she brought down her own fork of blinding lightning. It hit the canopy of the woodland, smoke rising up from the spot where it had hit.

As gale-force winds howled through the trees, whipping up around me, I caught sight of a figure disappearing into the nearby forest. *Davin?* I wondered if he was making a quick exit, just in case he found out he hadn't joined the winning side, after all. But that wasn't Katherine's style at all. Every cultist served a purpose for her, and Davin was no different. No, he was up to something. I just didn't know what.

What had once been a beautiful, verdant Garden of Eden had turned into something else entirely—a horrifying, nightmarish world, filled with storms and lightning and destruction at every turn.

I lifted my head to try and see what the titans were doing, but it was hard to get a good view of them. Gaia froze. Something had happened. I didn't know what, but it was enough to make her pause and glance down, as if there was something at her feet.

"NO!" I roared, though I was too far away for them to hear me.

Katherine seized her opportunity and brought a colossal lightning bolt down into Gaia's skull. It shivered through her emerald body, the particles of her being lighting up with a pulsating white jolt. A moment later, Katherine leapt at Gaia, her titanic hands closing around Gaia's throat as she knocked her to the ground. I felt the earth-shattering thud, Katherine wrestling to keep her grip. I could see them now, through the trees. Katherine had Gaia pinned, her hands squeezing tight, sending wave after wave of some unknown purple-tinged magic into Gaia's body. Gaia tried to fight back, but Katherine held fast.

"GAIA!" I screamed as loud as my lungs could manage. But it made no difference. Katherine was too focused to care about my screams. With one final blast of searing purple light, Gaia went limp, her emerald glow dimming until there was nothing left. I prayed with everything I had that this was just a trick, to make Katherine think she'd won, but the seconds passed and Gaia still didn't move.

It was over… It was over, and Katherine had won.

Silence settled over the Garden of Hesperides. The winds died down, and the storm clouds rolled back to reveal the serene azure sky. Not even the remaining leaves on the trees dared to rustle. I could barely breathe. How was I supposed to process this? How was I supposed to accept that Katherine had defeated Gaia, leaving her spot open for Katherine to take? It didn't seem possible. It couldn't be possible.

And yet, I knew it was done. This was Katherine's plan, and she hadn't made a single wrong step. She hadn't come into this fight thinking she'd lose, and, for some reason, Katherine always seemed to get whatever she wanted, through the sheer force of manifestation. My stomach churned, while anger seared my heart. Katherine had played us all, even Gaia. Everyone had expected Katherine to choose Nyx, or one of the weaker Children of Chaos, and I guessed Gaia had, too. Perhaps, if she'd been better prepared for this, there might've been a different outcome, but what was the use in thinking of what might've been? It wouldn't change what had happened, right here, right now.

And, very soon, Katherine was going to come for me. She'd told me she intended to use my body to hold the spilling energy that hers couldn't hold anymore. I didn't know how she planned to do that, but I understood now that she had everything orchestrated in her mind. She had a way. Otherwise, I wouldn't still be alive.

Oh my God...

All of my worst fears had come true. Katherine had completed the final ritual and the final Challenge, and Gaia's place amongst the Children of Chaos now belonged to her. We hadn't stopped her; we hadn't even come close. We'd never stood a chance.

I can't give up. I can't.

With panic rising up my throat and my whole body trembling, my eyes shot toward the Grimoire, still resting in its satchel beside the stone circle. Leaving Jacob where he was, I jumped up, my arms still behind my back, and raced toward it, skidding to a halt. Wriggling to get the right angle, I shuffled the loop of my arms down my butt and legs and stepped backward out of the loop so that I had my arms in front of me instead of trapped behind me. It was a feat of gymnastics, but, fortunately, I was flexible. For a moment, I tried to drive my Chaos into the locks again. But it didn't work this time either, not after whatever Katherine had done to make the Cuffs even harder to break. I wanted to scream the worst expletive I knew, but that would only bring Katherine's attention to me quicker.

Instead, I focused on the Grimoire. Even with the Atomic Cuffs clapped on my wrists, I could open the satchel and get the book out on the scorched ground. Desperate didn't even cover what I was feeling. I was already way past last-chance saloon, but maybe there was a last-ditch outhouse I didn't know about. Tugging the Grimoire closer, I fumbled inside the bag for the black lens and lifted it over the pages, frantic for a solution to this gargantuan mess. I supposed I'd hoped that, somehow, Chaos had accounted for this, too.

Come on, Chaos, get the spell to just jump out at me. Screw the rules. I had no idea if it was listening, but I prayed it was.

"Come on, come on, come on!" I muttered as I flicked through page after page, urging Chaos to show me the way. To be honest, my mind was so scrambled that nothing was making sense. Even through the lens, it might as well have been a jumble of squiggles and sigils, for all the good it was doing. And I knew I was almost out of time. "You wanted me for this, so freaking help me!"

My head whipped around as the silence shattered, a figure storming through the trees to my left. Katherine had returned to her regular-sized form, and she was dragging Gaia by the hair, the train of Gaia's beautiful gown trailing dead leaves and flowers as Katherine yanked her through the undergrowth without a hint of respect for the dead. It turned my stomach to see Katherine pulling her along, considering Gaia was an exact copy of Katherine. Macabre didn't cut it. It was almost as though Katherine had murdered the mere mortal she'd been, so that she could be reborn as Eris. This was her killing her last scrap of humanity.

Seeing Gaia, limp and unmoving, not fighting back, I knew for sure that it was over. She was definitely dead, and nothing could bring her back. She was already starting to disintegrate into tiny sparkles of bronze light, beginning at the train of her elegant gown. Before long, there'd be nothing left of her.

Nature itself rumbled around us, the Elements reacting violently to what had just happened. The storm clouds rolled in again, as though they'd changed their mind, and torrential rain poured down, as if they were crying for what they'd lost. The winds whipped up again, screaming now, wailing out their mourning cries. And beneath me, the earth trembled. The only Element missing was Fire, though it made itself known a few seconds later, as lightning cracked again, turning the nearby forests into a smoldering inferno. Nature didn't want Katherine here. The

Garden of Hesperides didn't want her here. This world, and all the other-worlds, didn't want Katherine reigning over them, and they were making themselves heard.

Katherine laughed triumphantly, turning her face up to the skies and letting the rain lash down. "I have completed the Challenge! I have defeated Gaia, and I claim her place! Chaos, I have done all you've asked. Now, give me my rightful position as your Child! You can no longer deny me!"

I gripped the Grimoire to my chest and watched helplessly as bronze light erupted from within Katherine in a devastating pulse that swept outward like the aftermath of a nuclear blast. It leveled everything, as far as my eyes could see—a hundred miles, at the very least. It was all I could do to throw myself to the ground, the Grimoire trapped under my chest, and hold onto the stone circle for dear life. I closed my eyes, blinded by the bronze light that rushed out of her, fearing what I'd see when I opened them again.

Seconds passed, and I felt a strange heat in front of me, as if I was standing too close to a furnace. The hairs on the back of my neck stood up, like I was about to bear the brunt of an electrical storm. I opened my eyes to find Katherine standing right in front of me, incandescent and ethereal. The glow coming out of her was mesmerizing and godlike, but her eyes were jet black. Smoke spilled down her cheeks like evil tears.

"Rise, the last of the Merlin dynasty." Her voice had changed beyond recognition. It was like thunder and gravel combined, bombarding my eardrums until I thought they'd cave in. "Witness the dawn of a new era. The birth of the Goddess of Chaos and Discord. The birth of… Eris."

It was like my voice had been ripped out of my throat. I couldn't find any words. All I could do was clutch the lens and the Grimoire close to my chest and pray for a freaking miracle, even though I knew, all too well, that it was too late for divine intervention, now that she was the divine one.

Katherine smiled. "Address me as Goddess from now on, you worthless mortal. You will obey me. You will not look away from your Goddess."

I couldn't have looked away, even if I'd wanted to. She was hypnotic.

The only thing preventing me from tipping over into total defeat was the knowledge that she still needed me. It wasn't exactly a lifeline, but it meant I had more time. *To do what?* That was the problem… I didn't know anymore.

"Come to me, my Children of Eris," she cried, lifting her arms. The air thrummed as though it was about to disintegrate, as portal after portal tore holes in time and space all across the ancient ruins—or what was left of them, anyway. I noticed Davin walking back across the flattened landscape, a smug look on his smug face. I didn't know what he'd done in those woods, but it had been enough to let Katherine win. "Join me, my Children. Join me, your Goddess of Chaos, and walk with me into the future. Walk into my brave new world and see yourselves rewarded!"

I watched her so-called Children step through the portals to join her, my heart sinking ever further as a few familiar faces approached. Vice President Caldwell—well, President Caldwell now. Officer Mallenberg from Purgatory, who'd watched over Finch after Kenneth Willow's attempt on his life. *Is that how Katherine did it? Is that how she got Kenneth in?* It was dawning on me, more and more, that Katherine literally had people everywhere.

Next came Stella and Channing, whom I'd met while they were on loan from the LA Coven to help us out with the missing children, followed by Clara Fairmont from the SDC, whom I'd thought Wade was crushing on when I'd first arrived at the coven. The LaSalles—the ex-Angels who'd come to the SDC for their retirement. Even the French nurse who'd taken care of Odette during her time in the infirmary. I realized she must've been the one who'd let Naima in to kill Odette. And then, Preceptor Sloane Bellmore stepped through, her eyes catching mine for a split second before she turned away again. So that was where she'd gone. She hadn't taken a sabbatical, or personal leave, or whatever the hell she'd called it. She'd joined Katherine instead.

Spineless coward!

Some of them were practically bristling with excitement, ready to take their place in Katherine's warped hell. Not all of them seemed as thrilled, though. Some, like Bellmore, looked terrified. *You should be, you idiots!*

I couldn't even begin to wrap my head around all of this. I was literally sitting front row at the end of the world, and there was nothing I could do but watch Katherine and her minions roll the credits.

FORTY-TWO

Katherine

You proud of me, Grandpa? His eyes would have burst out of his head to see what I'd done, if he were here now.

Well, his eyes were already pretty much melting out of his head after that idiot Necromancer's botched spell, but the sentiment remained.

All of his dreams, and all of my dreams, had come true. And it felt magnificent. I was omnipotent; I had all-consuming power at my fingertips and a horde of followers just begging for my next command. How many people could say they'd become a bona fide goddess, through sheer grit and determination? Forget sainthood, being deified was where it was at.

Look at them all—they're all here to worship me.

And I was drinking it in, every single second of my reward. I'd created this out of nothing, carving out an army for myself, and a position amongst the closest thing these magicals had to gods.

I could've soared forever on this wave of idolization, but there was one tiny problem. Something was wrong with my body. It couldn't contain all this power—I felt the wild energy pushing against my skin. The damn Chaos loophole that came with this position. Ultimate cosmic power, but no solid place to put it all. I wasn't about to fade into the background, like the rest of these godlike punks. I'd worked too friggin' hard to just drift into obsoletion, only remembered when someone wanted something, or when summoned by a mortal like Harley. *Ugh*. And my body wasn't going to be able to hold out for much longer. I could feel it disintegrating already.

"Worthless mortal." I turned to Harley, addressing her with her new name. "It's time for you to read. I'm in need of that bedtime story."

"You can float away for all I care. You asked for this, you deal with the consequences!" she shot back. *Still defying me, even now?* The girl had gall, I had to give her that. But I wasn't about to let her embarrass me in front of my shiny new legion of followers. Any hint of weakness, and they'd turn tail and run. All mortals were cowards, even the ones who'd chosen the winning side.

"Wrong answer." I grabbed her by the hair and dragged her across the ground, scraping her face across the stone circle. She cried out in pain, and the sound was music to my rapidly decaying ears.

Throwing her back to the ground, I lifted my palms and sent a pummeling wave of Electro and Cellular energy into her, careful not to push them too much in case I accidentally blew her up. She screamed as it hit her, the electric shock stabbing at every cell in her body, just the way I wanted. Torture was easy once you had the knack, and I'd had plenty of practice. With my newfound powers, this would be a walk in the park. I gave her ten seconds, max, until she started to read.

"It... won't... work," she roared.

"It will, Niece. Just give it time. I'm not done with you yet." I sent another surge of Chaos into her, combining reverse Empathy and Electro, sending all those feelings of desperation and despair into her body, letting her know that she had no choice but to obey. Tears sprang into her eyes, her face crumpling, but she made no move to open the book.

"NO!" She glared at me, clawing in breath after breath.

"Let's try that again, shall we?" I moved into Squelette territory—the magic of manipulating skeletons and bone—combining it with the Cellular energy. Adding pressure, I pushed her bones until they were almost at breaking point, while her cells swelled as far as they could go without exploding. I could sense each one straining. She had to be in agony by now—she had to break soon. I could see it on her face, and she was screaming so loud it was hard to hear myself think. Plus, she was causing a heck of a scene. All of my followers were staring at her and staring at me. They didn't know why I needed her, and I wasn't in the mood to answer any prying questions. But I couldn't have Harley making me look incompetent, either.

I released the combined abilities, giving her a moment to catch her breath. She opened her mouth, no doubt to throw some witty retort, but the words never came out. I hit her with another killer combo, her face contorting in a delicious mask of pure torture, a bestial howl rasping from the depths of her struggling lungs.

I'll show you, Harley Merlin. I'll show you what I'm capable of, since you don't seem to be learning.

I just wished I didn't have to keep her intact. Her head would've been enough to read out the Grimoire, but I needed the whole shebang, as funny as a genuine talking head would've been.

"Ready to read now, my little bookworm?" I released her again. It was an absolute joy to see her in such pain, and I could've gone on all day. Unfortunately, my human body had other ideas. I was sorry, beyond words, to have to say goodbye to this shapely physique that had served me so well all these years. But needs must be met, and I could always make a few cosmetic adjustments to Harley's plain-ass face. I hadn't lost my Shapeshifting ability, after all. It would be nothing more than a temporary departure from my beautiful self.

Harley, crying and heaving, stared me dead in the eyes. *Bold.* "I'm not… reading it! You want what's in there, you… read it your damned… self!" She smiled, her face twisting up as she collapsed in a fit of bizarre hysterics. "Oh wait, that's right… you can't! The great and powerful Katherine can't… read a simple book."

Anger and embarrassment spiked through my chest like a white-hot blade. It was mortifying to know that, even as a glorious Child of Chaos, even as Eris incarnate, I couldn't read the blasted thing myself. Harley knew that, and she knew everyone was listening. She was trying to put holes in the vision I'd created, by showing my one weakness in front of my cult. I knew what she was trying to do, and that pissed me off even more. She should've been on her knees by now, spilling those spells for all she was worth. Even Odette had been easier to break than this, and her mind had been like Fort Knox. Then again, she hadn't had all of Chaos on her side, scrambling to find ways to stop me. It wasn't letting up, even though I'd already completed its rituals.

Sore losers, huh?

"Why aren't you killing her?" I whirled around to find out who'd dared to speak. Nobody moved a muscle.

"Who said that?" I snarled.

A shaky hand went up as Sloane Bellmore stepped forward. She was trembling so hard I thought she might keel over. "I did, Eris. I don't understand, that's all... Why torture her if you can just end it now?"

"Oh, you don't understand? Do you think you know everything that's going on in my head? Would you like to come up here and try to usurp me?" I glowered at her. They didn't know what I'd learned from Odette, and they didn't know about the proviso in reaching these lofty heights. But that didn't mean they could ask. They were nothing. Nobodies.

She shook her head violently. "No, no, I was just wondering—"

I didn't let her finish. Swiping my hand, I sent a torrent of Squelette Chaos into her, gripping my fingers back into a fist. The splinter of her bones cut through the air, the perfect percussion to Harley's ongoing torture. Her scream was the sound of cymbals crashing as her execution reached its towering crescendo. I broke every single bone in her body, until she was nothing but a sagging heap on the ground. Gasps whispered through the rest of the gathered cult.

"Would anyone else care to question me?" I smiled sweetly, observing the quaking crowd. It was like the sniveling children all over again, but that's what I got for recruiting weak magicals. Despite being blessed with Chaos, at the end of the day they were nothing more than mortals. And I loathed mortals.

I stopped as I reached Davin. He was staring at me strangely, his sensual mouth set in a not-so-sexy grim line. I'd never been too good at reading the male species. Even if I brought forward a magical and poured Empathy into them, forcing them to tell me his emotions, I still wouldn't have been able to tell how he felt about me now. Still, he was here, and he didn't look like he was about to bolt. And he'd created the distraction I needed to take down Gaia, using his Necromancy to drag up a face she remembered. Some historical sidekick who'd been Gaia's human mouthpiece a long time ago. He'd really gone to town on that, so maybe he had the balls to stick around and see this through.

Stay... I sent the thought out to him, and hoped he heard. Greatness was embedded in my future now, the ink of my majesty already drying. Those who'd joined me would all witness it, if they had the strength. Those who'd opposed me would suffer and die, just as Bellmore had done. Not that I hadn't been dying for the opportunity to end her. I'd seen enough of her, as Imogene, to rank her as expendable. The same went for most of these folks, if they tried to cross me.

The world is mine now. Join me or burn with it.

There were no alternatives.

FORTY-THREE

Harley

My whole body was on fire, aching like I'd been put through a meat grinder twice. Every bone hurt, and every vein felt as though it was on the verge of collapse.

And my heart… I wasn't sure I had one anymore, not in the figurative sense, though the chunk of muscle was palpitating in my chest.

I'd seen so much horror and tragedy in the past who knew how long, and it'd broken me down into tiny shards, just as Katherine had promised. I was a shell, and I'd seen too much to ever be the same again. Maybe I was no different than the husks that I feared the children had become.

Now, I understood why soldiers who'd seen the front line had a haunted look in their eyes. I imagined my own eyes looked pretty similar, my mind plagued by those poor, defenseless children having their Chaos forcibly removed. Children I'd known and couldn't save from that fate. *And Louella...* I couldn't think about her without crying, which meant one thing: I wasn't hollow and heartless just yet.

I can't give up now.

It might've seemed hopeless, but I refused to give Katherine what she wanted. I still had some cards to play, and she'd given them to me, keeping me in the game. Without me, she'd have to drift off into the ether like the rest of the Children of Chaos, fated to retreat into her otherworld until she was summoned, all-seeing but unable to act directly. And who in their right mind would ever summon her? In order to roam free, she needed me. I was her loophole, and I sure as heck wasn't about to cooperate.

But I needed to come up with a way out of this mess, or I'd have no choice but to become Katherine's meat suit. A few more of those blasts of torture, and I wouldn't have the strength to disobey anymore.

"Now, where were we?" Katherine tapped her chin.

"I was telling you to stuff it up your—" I tumbled backward as a rush of air hit me square in the chest, knocking me to the ground.

At first, I thought Katherine had unleashed another bout of torture on me, but this was way too weak to be her doing. I sat bolt upright in time to see a portal gaping open behind Katherine, with magicals spilling out from the real world. Dozens of them, sprinting out, casting spells and curses left, right, and center, while Chaos abilities of all kinds sparked from their lifted palms.

My eyes darted to the cult members, but they were so stunned by this turn of events that they just stood there. Some of them fell, crumbling at the hands of Remington, O'Halloran, an army of security magicals, and Wade's parents—I remembered Felicity from our awkward encounter after the Paris Coven visit, and the guy beside her looked too much like Wade for it to be a coincidence. There were more besides them, but I couldn't put names to all their faces.

It looked like the big kahunas who hadn't succumbed to Katherine's influence had come out to play. And running behind them all, bringing up the chaotic rear, was the Rag Team, including Finch and Wade.

I wanted to join in, but I could barely lift my hands. Instead, I gripped the Grimoire and watched as the literal armies of good and evil clashed. Santana's Orishas were buzzing around like ferocious fireflies, dive-bombing the cult and taking over their bodies, decimating them from the inside out. Next to her, Tatyana was glowing almost as brightly as Katherine, a cluster of shimmering, transparent figures walking at her side. The spirits seemed to grow more solid as Tatyana pulsated, their spooky hands reaching out to grab at any cultist they passed. Their victims screamed as the spirits dragged them away from the living world, the way I'd been warned they could, when I was in the tunnels of Eris Island on All Hallows' Eve. It meant they were only good for one shot, but that was all that mattered, considering the number Tatyana had brought with her.

Dylan pounded through the throng of enemies—literally pounded through them, his fists flying as he brought his Herculean wrath down on everyone who stepped in his path. Behind him, Kadar had taken the reins of Raffe's body, his skin a vibrant red while black smoke trailed behind him, as he made a bloody mess of the cultists that swarmed to attack him.

"This is more like it!" the djinn roared, evidently delighted that he could go wild without any restraint whatsoever.

"You can say that again!" My mouth fell open. Levi, or rather, Zalaam, was hurtling right alongside Kadar, the two djinn taking down huge swathes of cultists at once. Those suckers just couldn't get out of the way fast enough, and Zalaam and Kadar weren't taking any prisoners.

Astrid was standing to the edge of the ruins, gripping Smartie, her fingers blurring as they swiped across the screen. Overhead, I heard a faint buzzing sound. A team of drones swept down over the cultists and dropped bombs that exploded in clusters of entrapment stones, pinning the cultists to the ground with shining green ropes. Garrett followed the drones, shouting out the spell that got the stones to work as he tore through the crowd with a sword in his hand. I had no idea where he'd gotten it from, but it looked ancient, the blade flickering with Fire as he slashed left and right. In fact, quite a few of the allied squad had weapons I'd never seen before—all of them looking like they'd come out of the pages of a dusty tome on ancient magical warfare. O'Halloran had a pair of shimmering daggers, while Remington had a pitch-black saber that seemed to suck light into the blade.

"Keep 'em coming, Astrid!" Garrett yelled back as he came to a skidding halt in front of Channing. "You?!"

Channing nodded slowly. "Guess you weren't expecting this, huh? Neither was I, to be honest, but I suppose we're fighting on opposite sides now."

Garrett scoffed. "Not gonna go easy on me, are you?"

"Afraid not," Channing replied, lifting his palms to send out a wave of Chaos.

Garrett lunged forward with his sword, the fiery blade cutting across Channing's arm. Twisting threads of silvery Chaos burst out of the wound, until they shrouded Channing in a glinting mist. He fell to the ground, unconscious. Stella screamed and tried to protect him, only to be swept to the side as Felicity Crowley came charging through, sending out powerful waves of Fire and Air and Telekinesis. Cormac Crowley was at her side, the two of them working in perfect synchronicity. I even saw her roll over his back to shove a blast of Fire in the face of the French nurse, which made my jaw drop. Talk about cool parents.

I spotted Finch in the fray, running full-pelt at Officer Mallenberg.

"Finch Shipton, you chose the wrong side, buddy," Mallenberg jeered. "I should've put you out of your misery when you were lying in a coma. Shame there were too many cameras."

"Instead of flapping your lips, why don't you put your head between your legs and kiss your ass goodbye!" Finch sent out a lasso of Telekinesis, wrapping it around Mallenberg's throat and tossing him as far as he could over the barren landscape. I lost sight of Finch a moment later as he darted back into the crowd, Shapeshifting into about a hundred other people until I couldn't spot him anymore. I tried to find Wade, too, expecting him to be close to his mom and dad, but he was nowhere to be seen.

My attention was drawn by the group of preceptors who were ploughing through the cultists like a combine harvester during high season: Rita Bonnello, Oswald Redmont, Lasher Ickes, and Marianne Gracelyn. Good old Dr. Wolfgang Krieger was sprinting right along with them, putting his Organa Chaos to less than healing means, sending fizzing blasts into the cultists that made them drop to the ground like sacks of potatoes. Somehow, Hiro Nomura was with them, too, his two katanas slicing through the enemies, a bloodcurdling shout bellowing from his chest.

"Shinsuke!" His war cry made several cultists freeze, and I couldn't blame them. It sounded like the howl of a madman.

Katherine pushed him to this. She pushed us all to this.

I glanced at her to try and gauge her reaction, but she was simply watching the whole debacle unfold with an amused smirk on her face. That couldn't be good. Still, the arrival of this army of good had bolstered that last flickering flame of hope in my chest, making it burn like a bonfire. Even if Katherine wasn't showing it, I knew she had to be shocked. There was no way she could've anticipated this.

She looked right back at me. "Don't think for a second that this changes anything." She winked. "Backups, sweet-cheeks, backups. I think it's high time I flexed these new muscles of mine, don't you? Shall we start with death rays? It's the only thing for a true badass to use, don't you think?"

"You're bluffing."

She laughed. "Oh, am I?" I stared in horror as she lifted her hands, a swirling vortex of pure white light forming in each of her palms. She took a breath, about to start firing off her death beams, when the waterfall spiraled away from its rockface and hit her in the chest, knocking her backward.

I glanced around frantically to try and see who'd done it. The earth shuddered underneath me as vines swept up, wrestling Katherine and the rest of her cultists to the ground. Air whipped up in volatile winds that were focused solely on the enemy. An entire group of cultists were twisted right into the center of a tornado that went zipping off across the barren wasteland of the Garden of Hesperides, taking them far away.

After slamming into Katherine and stopping her death rays, Water turned its attention to the cultists. Manifesting as a gigantic, weirdly human titan of Water, it stomped on the enemy, drowning them in its swirling legs, their bodies rising with no way to escape the watery body. Fire appeared next, standing beside Water in a similarly humanoid form, like the Human Torch, only massive. Screaming, the cultists went up in flames, some of them trying to run at the legs of Water, only to get caught in the current and dragged inside.

Gaia's children are intervening!

It didn't seem possible, but it was definitely happening. Even now, tornadoes were appearing all over the place as Air took its vengeance, grasping for the enemy and hurling them away. Now and again, one of our side got caught in the fray, but I supposed that was inevitable, no matter how devastating it felt. This was war, after all.

The image that the Chains of Truth had shown me burst into my head. The screams, the shouts, the crackle of Chaos, the groans of the wounded. It was all here, in this moment, playing out in real time. My heart beat faster—if this had come to pass, then did that mean the rest would? Had they been premonitions, after all? I tried to find the Rag Team in the midst of the battle, terrified for their lives, but it was like an impossible game of Where's Waldo.

My body was wrenched backward. I whirled around, half expecting to see Katherine leering down at me. Gaia's children had been giving her one hell of a beating, but she was stronger than all of them. The moment she wanted out, all she had to do was portal the two of us out of here, somewhere she could torture me some more. Instead, Wade and Finch were pulling me along, hauling me toward the spot where Jacob lay.

"What the—"

"No time to explain now, Sis," Finch replied. "Trust us... for once."

Wade nodded. "We didn't think Gaia's children would intervene. But now's our chance to get the upper hand again."

"British asshole, two o'clock," Finch muttered.

"Where?" Wade frowned.

Finch rolled his eyes. "Dude in the suit you wish you owned."

I turned to see Davin staring at us, but he didn't move. *What's he doing?*

Across the ruins, the first portal closed with a snap, only for another one to open right beside us. There was so much going on that it was hard to keep my focus on one thing. I tried to keep my eyes on Davin, but something else snagged my attention. Through the portal that had just opened, I could see a room of some kind, as though I was looking through an *Aperi Si Ostium* doorway instead of a portal. There, sitting on the ground, pale as a corpse, was Isadora.

My heart lurched, a gasp escaping my throat. Alton was crouched on his haunches behind Isadora with his hands on her shoulders, heaving breaths into his lungs, looking like he was as close to death's door as she was. Purple magic swirled around them both, Alton's eyes black as night, with two purple dots in the center, while black veins spiderwebbed across his skin. Realization hit me—he'd performed the same spell he'd done on my mom and dad, bringing Isadora back from the afterlife. And he was struggling to keep her here, by the looks of it.

"How is this happening?!" I asked.

"Not important now," Finch replied.

"We can tell you everything once you're out of here, away from Katherine," Wade added, as he bent down and scooped me up into his arms. Finch did the same thing to Jacob, struggling under his dead weight.

"Not quite so romantic, huh? I guess I'll let you be the hero, this time. Although, my sister is anything but a damsel in distress." Finch smirked as he hurried for the portal, jumping through with Jacob in his arms.

I looped my arms over Wade's head and around his neck as he followed Finch. We were almost at the portal threshold when I heard an ungodly scream tear across the Garden of Hesperides, so piercing and gut-wrenching that it made everyone stop for a moment. Katherine had spotted us. And that scream belonged to her. *What, don't you have a backup for this?* I wanted to laugh, but I didn't want to count my chickens before we were out of this place.

"GET THEM!" she bellowed. "DAVIN, GET THEM!"

Gaia's Children swarmed in on her, tornadoes of Air and Fire spinning around her, creating a circle of flames that blocked her from getting to us. Through the flickering haze, I saw vines shoot up, lashing at her wrists and ankles in an attempt to drag her down. She dispensed with them quickly, but the tornadoes were another matter. Not to mention the two huge titans of Water and Fire that were preparing to stomp on her if she tried to reach us. It was all she could do to keep them at bay, despite her fancy new role as a Child of Chaos. As it turned out, there were some things that even all the power in the world couldn't stop.

I glanced at Davin, who was still standing perfectly still at the edge of the ongoing mayhem. He took a deep breath before he started running toward us. I guessed it wasn't worth his life to disobey a direct order from the Queen Bee herself. As he broke into a sprint, I watched the Rag Team split off from the battle, emerging through the crowds and tearing across the open expanse toward the portal. Santana, Tatyana, Raffe,

Dylan, Astrid, and Garrett, followed by Levi, O'Halloran, Remington, the preceptors, and the Crowleys. Only Nomura stayed in the fight, with the rest of the allies. I got the feeling he didn't care if he survived or not.

Come on, come on, come on... I didn't want to know what would happen to my friends if they didn't make it in time.

Wade carried me through, but the portal stayed open, giving me a full view of Gaia's otherworld. Remington was leading the pack, brandishing his black saber, catching up to Davin before he could pursue us through the portal. He leapt onto Davin's back, yanking him down to the ground, where the two men wrestled in the dirt, and Davin tried to avoid the jet-black blade. Meanwhile, the others tore past them. Santana, Tatyana, Raffe, Levi, Dylan, Astrid, and Garrett jumped through with ease, joined by O'Halloran. The rest were so close.

Before they could reach the portal, it suddenly snapped shut, Alton collapsing in a heap on the floor. Remington, the preceptors, and Wade's parents hadn't made it in time.

I looked around in shock, unable to believe that I wasn't in the Garden of Hesperides anymore. I couldn't make sense of any of it. All I knew was, we were alive. Broken and battered, but alive.

FORTY-FOUR

Harley

I looked around at my new surroundings as I tried to stand on my own two feet, even though my knees were shaking and my body was more or less on its last legs. I'd expected to see some familiar part of the SDC, but this definitely wasn't the coven, not unless it had a cabin I didn't know about.

The group was gathered in a large lounge with comfortable sofas facing a fireplace and two bookshelves full of well-loved novels. Wind-chimes made of shells and sea-glass and tiny silver bells tinkled as they began to still after being swept wildly by the air from the portal. And, to the far side, colorful, gauzy drapes covered expansive windows that looked out onto the sandy shores of a glistening lake.

"Where are we?" I croaked, sinking down onto the arm of one of the sofas.

Santana smiled. "This is my family's cabin, deep in the heart of Mexico. We'll be safe here."

"Is anywhere safe now?"

"My family warded this place, mainly for privacy. The Catemacos are kind of a big deal in Mexico, so sometimes it's nice to get away from it all," she explained. "That's why they built this cabin, to keep it hidden from everyone and everything."

"Even from Katherine?" I couldn't believe that was possible, but she nodded.

"She won't find us here. Isadora made sure there was no trail for her to track. Maybe she'll catch up to us at some point, but for now, we're good. I promise." She walked over and put her arm around my shoulders, giving me a tight squeeze. I leaned into her, grateful for the support—mental *and* physical.

It was definitely peaceful here, with nothing but the sound of the small waves lapping the shore to break the strange silence. My head was still ringing with battle cries and sparking spells, making the quiet seem weird and somehow unnatural. It would take some getting used to.

I glanced at Wade, opening my mouth to thank him for getting me out. I froze as I saw him, the words dying on my lips. He was staring into the space where the portal had been, shaking. I could hear his sharp, shallow breathing and knew he was in pain. His parents were still trapped in the Garden of Hesperides. They hadn't made it.

"Is there a way back?" He whirled around, staring at the limp, unconscious bodies of Alton, Isadora, and Jacob. "There's got to be a way back, right? My parents are still out there. They came to help us. I need to get back. I need to make sure they're okay."

O'Halloran slipped his daggers into his belt and put his hand on Wade's shoulder. "I'm sorry, lad. We can't go back." He gave a heavy, defeated sigh. "The whole crew, everyone we brought with us—they're all stuck there, too. And I don't know that we'll ever see them again."

Katherine will kill them all. I didn't dare say it out loud. Wade was already struggling, and I wasn't going to be the one to kick him while he was down. But the stark fact remained. Once Katherine dealt with Gaia's Children, she'd move on to everyone who'd waged war against her army. And, with no way of escaping, it didn't seem likely that any of them would get out alive. Not Remington, not the preceptors, not Nomura, and not Wade's parents. And the children who were still there, alive but unconscious… If Katherine managed to regain control, they'd all be going from the frying pan into another raging fire.

"They knew… they all knew what they were getting themselves into,"

Finch said quietly, saying what I couldn't. "There were never any guarantees."

"Nevertheless, we will find a way to save them or avenge them. This was a dangerous leap of faith, and that deserves due diligence and respect," Levi chimed in, his voice thick with emotion.

His eyes weren't red anymore, which was comforting. The djinn didn't care much about losses or collateral damage, and we needed all the humanity we could get, to remind ourselves that the game wasn't over. As long as we had our humanity, we still had a chance. I was surprised to see it again in Levi. He hadn't shown emotion like this since President Price died. Sure, he was a coward, and we'd never see eye to eye on most things, but he'd joined the battle against Katherine, when he could have stayed put. That counted for something, as far as I was concerned.

My gaze shot away from Levi as Isadora's eyes flew open, a raspy breath escaping her lips. I ran to her, not caring about the pain that threatened to floor me. Skidding to my knees, I grasped her hands, even though my wrists were still bound, lifting her into a sitting position. Her lips were blue, her skin sunken, her eyes covered in a milky film. Somehow, she was still alive, even though Alton was on the floor behind her, comatose, barely hanging by a thread. Krieger was already seeing to him, in full doctor mode, trying everything to get him to wake up.

"Isadora? Isadora, can you hear me?" I asked urgently.

Her eyes blinked slowly as she gazed up at me. "There you are… my sweet niece. There you are."

I nodded. "I'm here, Isadora. Just hold on, okay?"

"I can't, Harley." She smiled sadly. "I'm tearing Alton up inside, just by staying here. If I stay, he'll die."

"Please don't go." I held her hands tighter, pressing them to my face.

"I was ready to die a long time ago. I should've died when Hiram did." A tear trickled down her cheek. "I held on for you, but you don't need me anymore. I'm sorry I won't be able to stick around to watch you kick Katherine's ass."

I choked out a laugh. "I love you, Isadora. I couldn't have done any of this without you. None of us could."

"I'm going to miss you all." She stared at the others as though she couldn't quite focus. "You're going to pull through this, Harley. You're going to do it. It was always your destiny. And I know you've got it in you. I love you, sweetheart. I love you, but I've got to go now. They're waiting." Her eyes turned toward an empty space in the air, a smile spreading across her lips.

"Please don't… please don't go."

"Wreck her, do you hear me? Wreck her. Do it for all of us who haven't made it. And… And tell Jacob that I said goodbye, when he wakes up." Isadora brushed her thumb across my cheek, only for her hand to fall limp a second later. The light sputtered out of her eyes, and she started to fall backward. Krieger lunged and grabbed her, laying her gently down on the floor as Death claimed her for the second, and final, time.

I sank down onto crossed legs and lowered her lids over her eyes. I'd already said my goodbyes to her body in the Crypt, but I still felt like I hadn't said enough—like there were a million more things I wanted, and needed, to say.

"I told him not to do this," Krieger murmured, his voice dragging me away from total collapse.

"Is he okay?" I stared at Alton's apparently lifeless body, fearing the worst. The Rag Team gathered around in an unsettling vigil over his unmoving figure.

Krieger shook his head. "I've been struggling to keep him steady since he came back from France. Davin left him for dead after a fight in the church, by all accounts. He hid from Davin and waited until he'd gone, and then proceeded to exhaust himself further by trying to get the stolen bodies and the ghoul bones back to the SDC through a chalk door. Presumably, he needed to gather the bones to awaken Isadora. I'm surprised he's still breathing, in all honesty. He was already far too weak, and then he went and did this. I was coming back from his office to collect some medication when I was apprehended by Katherine et al in the infirmary."

"I've got some gaps in what happened," I admitted. "I don't remember much after Zalaam knocked me out. Thanks for that, by the way." I shot a cold look at Levi, who had the decency to look sheepish.

"My apologies, Harley. I had no control over the djinn at that point, though I believe he was only acting in order to fulfill a deal he'd made with Katherine—a deal that would save Raffe and Kadar. I had no say in it."

I turned back to Krieger. "What happened, Krieger? Tell me all of it."

"Well, Alton had returned and called for me, after collapsing in his office. As I was tending to him, his phone went off. I answered it, and Wade was on the other end, calling from Montana. He explained that you'd run off, and he didn't know where you were, but he was worried you were in danger. He said he was going to try and track you down. In the meantime, I needed to fix Alton, so I went to the infirmary. Finch was already out cold, and so were you. It all happened too quickly for me to stop it. I was knocked out, just as the infirmary began to collapse around us. Next thing I know, I'm being woken up by O'Halloran and a team of security magicals, who'd come to investigate the disturbance after seeing something worrying on the CCTV. They got Finch, Levi, and me out. With Zalaam's help, Finch immediately went after Wade, using a chalk door to get him back from Montana. While he was doing that, I rallied the Rag Team to explain everything, and Santana called her parents to arrange our use of this cabin. We mobilized this entire operation from there, working as quickly as we could."

Wade nodded, his expression strained with worry. "Finch and I gathered everyone we could think of and had them call in as much trustworthy backup as possible—Remington, the preceptors, the security magicals, everyone. Remington suggested we raid the SDC's museum for ancient artifacts, which is where Garrett got the Avenging Angel, and where O'Halloran got those magical daggers."

"The Avenging Angel?" I raised my eyebrows.

"Big fiery sword," Finch replied. "And then djinn boy decided to give Levi back to us. Apparently, they came to a bit of a truce after knocking you out, Harley. Levi told us everything he'd learned from Zalaam about the deal he'd made with Katherine, to save Raffe in exchange for a favor. Knowing what would happen next, more or less, since you'd been nabbed along with your fancy book and stuff, we had no choice but to go full Rambo. Alton was the one who suggested his Necromancy voodoo, so we'd have a way in with Isadora's Portal Making. I mean, it worked, right? Chaos came through, *finally*. Better late than never."

I should've been crumbling, totally broken by everything that had happened and everyone we'd lost, but I wasn't. I didn't know if I'd seen so many horrible things that I'd somehow managed to numb myself completely, or if I'd simply gone past the point of feeling anything, but my insides were hollow, my brain perfectly alert and steady. I might as well have been catatonic, because I was way too calm and composed considering what had just gone on, and what was still happening in that war-torn otherworld.

"I already saw this coming. In a way, we all did," I said, my voice eerily matter-of-fact. "Fighting against every step of Katherine's mission was a reflex. It was the only thing any of us could do, really. But I knew she'd make it, no matter what we did. She tore the Chaos straight out of all those innocent children, right in front of my eyes, and it was like I was seeing a nightmare that I'd already had. Micah, Marjorie, Samson, Sarah, Cassie… Louella." I glanced at them all. "Louella didn't make it. The ritual couldn't hold her in the right trance that would've protected her, and Katherine killed her."

A gasp of pain rippled around the room.

"She's gone?" Krieger's eyes glistened with tears.

I nodded. "The other children were still alive after she'd finished, but I don't know what'll happen to them, with that battle raging." I lowered my gaze again. "There was never anything we could do. I think I finally understood that all our hard work had been pointless when Katherine revealed that she'd been Imogene all this time. Her web was so tightly wound that we'd never have been able to unravel it, even if we'd had years."

"Harley…" Finch took a step toward me, but I stepped back.

"No, hear me out." I took a breath. "She might have ascended, but it's not over yet. Katherine wants to be more than any Child of Chaos that has gone before. Children of Chaos are generally kept to their other-worlds, only intervening in the real world when they're called upon. Katherine needs a loophole that will allow her to walk *between* worlds, giving her omnipotence no matter where she is, power that isn't restrained by any rules. Otherwise, she'll be fighting against Chaos for the rest of her existence, in order to achieve what she wants to achieve. I'm the loophole."

Wade frowned. "What do you mean?"

"Katherine needs me to read out some spells in the Grimoire that will make me a suitable vessel to hold all of the energy she's acquired by ascending. She needs me in order to bridge that gap. Before you arrived, she was torturing me to try and get me to read the Grimoire pages to her." I paused. "I was so focused on using the Grimoire to prepare for stopping Katherine's ascension, rather than focusing on what might come after, and how to deal with that. But… I knew, deep down, that she'd make it that far. I'd be a liar if I said otherwise, even if I never fully admitted it to myself."

"Here. You look awkward as ass in those things." O'Halloran walked toward me and took out some keys, sliding them into the lock on my Atomic Cuffs to release them. They might've been supercharged by Katherine, but there was no magic quite like good, old-fashioned technology.

I rubbed my wrists. "Thank you." I glanced at him. "And you're okay? Not under Katherine's spell anymore?"

He smiled awkwardly. "I realized my water tasted weird, so I stopped drinking it. Katherine must've been putting something in it, because the effects wore off pretty quickly. My head's all clear again. I can talk about Echidna and Katherine without flailing about like a fish. Sorry for all the hassle before. Never take anything from strangers, right?"

"Right." He really did seem like himself. And there was no way he would've been out on the field with the others if he'd still been under Katherine's spell.

"You know this isn't your fault, right?" Finch eyed me.

I shrugged. "I keep trying to tell myself that."

Santana raised her hand. "I've got a question."

"What is it?" I replied.

"Why did you try and push us away?"

I'd been wondering when this would come up. After all, if they knew everything, then they knew what I'd done to Wade, and what I'd done in the church in France with only Alton to help.

"I made a promise to the Chains of Truth—that I was willing to sacrifice anything, even my friends, to defeat Katherine." I lowered my gaze. "I couldn't live with that, because you're all too kind and too loyal for your own good." I forced a smile. "The only way I could make sure nothing happened to you was by pushing you away and trying to do this on my own. Didn't really work out though, huh?" I thought of Louella again. I hadn't been able to save her. Even if I could have managed to get her through the portal, somehow, there was no way Alton would've been able to do anything for her. Not now.

"The Chains of what now?" Santana frowned.

I sighed. "They were keeping the doors to the New York Coven closed. We all had to answer questions to get inside. Mine involved all of you. I was so scared it was more than a promise—that it was, somehow, a premonition—that I made the decision to keep you all out of it, just in case."

"Is that why you left me?" Wade's voice broke my otherwise numb heart. On top of worrying about his parents, stuck in the otherworld with Queen Psycho, he had this revelation to deal with.

"I'll make it up to you, like I promised I would. But now isn't the time," I said. My head was starting to bang, my stomach churning with sudden nausea. *I pushed myself too hard again.*

"I understand, I really do," Wade replied, his tone edged with sadness. The uncertainty surrounding his parents was clearly never far from his mind. "We need to keep looking forward, in whatever way we can, and worry about the rest later."

I looked around at the Rag Team, who all nodded at Wade's words, wearing empathetic expressions. I was unbelievably relieved to have my friends around me again.

"How did Alton even resurrect Isadora? I thought her body had been tampered with." I glanced at the group for answers.

"Alton forced himself to do it," Finch replied. "He went all veiny and crazy, pushing all kinds of boundaries. Nothing was working, but then he cried out that you needed help, and the lock just kinda broke. No idea how, but Isadora's skin did this creepy rippling thing, as if something he'd done or said had broken Katherine's magic. And then, bingo, she was awake and portaling her heart out."

Raffe nodded. "He's got hidden depths, Alton does. He pushed himself beyond his limits to save us all."

"Well, most of us, anyway," Astrid murmured. I kept waiting for her to break down at the sight of her dad unconscious on the floor, but I guessed she and I were in the same boat. We were numb and hollow, missing some vital piece that made us feel anything.

"My parents are still there," Wade said quietly. "Remington and the others, too."

"And who knows what she'll do to them if she catches them." Dylan shook his head, getting a sharp jab in the ribs from Tatyana. "What? I was just saying what everyone's thinking."

"What have I told you about putting a filter on what you say?" Tatyana replied, but I could tell she agreed. It was written all over her face.

"Right now, those Elemental beings are dealing with Katherine, so maybe the others had time to get away." O'Halloran stepped in. "And they wouldn't have left the children if they spotted them."

"Yeah, what were those things?" Garrett asked, leaning on the hilt of his sword now that the Fire had gone out. He'd been staring at Astrid this whole time, no doubt wondering the same thing as I was.

I glanced at him. "They were Gaia's Children."

"And they're allowed to get involved like that?" Santana cut in. "I thought there was a whole rulebook that Chaos had to follow. Do those rules not apply in the otherworlds?"

I shrugged. "Your guess is as good as mine. But, right now, we have to just hope they're keeping Katherine on her toes. In the meantime, we need to think about what happens next. Katherine has ascended, and it won't be long before she gets out of that otherworld, since she's still technically got a body that can carry her. So, here's the big question—what the heck do we do next?"

Silence echoed back. *Yeah, I thought so.*

FORTY-FIVE

Katherine

How'd you like them apples?

The towering Water monster was nothing but a puddle of sopping wet earth, and the Fire titan was sputtering its last a short distance away, setting the tinder of the flattened forests alight. Black smoke billowed every which way, making it hard to get a fix on the little bastards who'd come pouring in to try and weaken my army.

They'd be back, no doubt. Elements weren't exactly destroyable. But they seemed to understand that their number had been called and their time was up. Even the winds had died down, and the Earth had given up trying to wrestle me to the ground with its spiky little vines.

I dusted myself off, on red alert for any pesky resurgences. *Don't you get that I'm the Mama now?* These irritating Elements were still fighting for Gaia, even though she was nothing but a pile of petals and curling leaves on the ground. I'd make Gaia's griping little kiddos bend to my will soon enough. Same as everyone else. Human, magical, Elemental—I'd have them all bowing and scraping by the time I was done.

At least I had the satisfaction of seeing a landscape littered with the bodies of my enemies. That took the edge off slightly. Most of the insurgents were dead, but not all. And I hated a half-assed job more than anything. I swept my hands through the air, clearing the black smoke to get a better view of what had once been the Garden of Hesperides. It looked like a wasteland now, but I wasn't too bothered. I didn't plan to spend much time here. It was nothing more than tearing down an ugly house to make room for something shinier.

Now, where have you gone, my pretties? My soldiers were picking themselves up and dusting off their shoulders. But there were too many of my enemies unaccounted for. How hard could it be to find them in a place that had nothing but flattened earth in a hundred-mile radius? Apparently, quite hard. And I knew they weren't smart enough to be hiding without help. Gaia's Children were trying to grind my gears again.

Frankly, it was infuriating. Chaos didn't like the outcome, so it'd decided to change things up a bit. What right did they have to get in the way? If they didn't want someone becoming a Child of Chaos, they should never have put the rituals out there in the first place.

Stop getting distracted.

I scoured the landscape. I should've been so much more by now. Sure, I'd ascended, but that didn't count for jack until I had Harley's supercharged body at my disposal. She was my loophole, my bridge, my gap between what a Child of Chaos used to mean and what I intended for it to mean. Until I had that, I was somewhat limited. Not a comfortable place to be in, to be honest. I wasn't used to limitations. And now, that constant, itching, festering boil of a Merlin had disappeared. And my son along with her.

Of course you were involved, you sad little cretin.

I should've known that leaving him to die in the SDC's infirmary wouldn't be the last I saw of him. He had a unique way of lingering like a bad smell and reappearing like that cockroach that simply wouldn't be squished. At least it was manifesting a change of heart in me. As Eris, I couldn't be weak in any way. And if that meant killing my own child, then so be it. I'd procrastinated over the issue for far too long. Next time I saw him, I wouldn't hesitate. He'd had his chances, and I wasn't feeling generous anymore.

You've only got yourself to blame, Finch.

The cult regrouped, all of them staring at me in awe. *Well, that's a start.* They were mesmerized by my godly aura, and who wouldn't be? I'd taken down titans of Water and Fire, and even managed to get the winds to stop. All on top of smashing a Child of Chaos to bits and leaving her in the dust. Who else could say that? At least this little inconvenience hadn't altered their view of my almighty power. I'd lost a few, yes, but they could always be replaced. Everyone but me was an expendable commodity, even if they didn't know it.

"Do not fear," I said, in my most majestic voice. "Others will join our ranks, and, together, we will watch them swell until our army covers the globe. The cult will continue to grow, and all of you, who have proven yourselves today, will be at the forefront."

"That was a remarkable feat, my divine Goddess." Davin approached and sank down onto one knee in front of me. *Nice touch.* "We have all seen your strength and fortitude in action, and we will not falter as we join you in your endeavors. We will fight at your side. We will see your new world come to fruition."

"I hope that you do." I smiled down at him. Everything wasn't quite as perfect as I wanted it to be, but I wasn't done yet. I could still get to that pinnacle of awesomeness. After all, I'd only been reborn an hour ago, and even newborns had some trials to endure before they reached steady footing. But I had this whole new life ahead of me, and I'd be damned if I was going to let Harley ruin that for me. I still had some tricks up my sleeve.

"As we look toward the bright horizon of our interwoven future, the plan must continue to unfold, as I have foreseen it." I ramped up the mystique, just to add some awe-inspiring flavor. They'd have no idea what I was going on about, but if it sounded intriguing, they'd follow me like sheep.

No one here knew what was in store, but when the time came, they'd have no choice but to understand and accept it.

Or die.

FORTY-SIX

Harley

Some minutes had passed, and nobody had answered my burning question.

Instead, we'd brought each other up to speed on any glaring gaps in collective events, though some things remained a mystery. Like how the Children of Gaia were able to react to their mother's death without Chaos getting involved.

As it turned out, Isadora had managed to track me to Gaia's world, which was how she knew where to portal everyone. I was pretty impressed by how quickly the Rag Team had mobilized once they'd realized what was about to happen. Despite that, they just kept going on about what a colossal failure this had all been, which I had no interest in whatsoever. A defeatist attitude wouldn't get us anywhere, and as far as I was concerned, we hadn't failed—we just had to rethink our offensive.

"We fought so hard for nothing," Raffe murmured.

An unexpected rush of anger hit me. "No, we didn't. You all need to realize that this was always going to happen, like I said. Moping isn't going to do a freaking thing, so pack it in, all of you," I snapped. "Louella was standing right in Katherine's face, telling her she would never win, even if she ascended, and she was seconds from death. Does that sound like failure to you? Because it doesn't to me. She'd be kicking all of your asses right now if she could hear you. Make her death count, make the loss of Chaos those children suffered count—don't wallow in what we could never control."

The Rag Team stared at me.

"What? Would you rather I was in a ball on the floor, sobbing about the injustice of it all? Well, you're not going to see that, so you can all stop waiting." I balled my hands into fists. "I'm tired of feeling sorry for myself, when it serves absolutely no purpose. Do regrets change past events? No, of course they don't. So we all need to stop it. If that seems cold, then it's your tough luck."

"Easy, tiger." Finch stepped toward me and put his hand on my arm. "People are just a little freaked out at the moment. Not everyone turned into a human bulldozer when we came back through the portal."

"Well, they should have." I held the collective gaze of the startled Rag Team. "Who are your tears for, huh? Because they're not for Louella, and they're not for Isadora. They're for yourselves, and if you say otherwise, you're not being honest. Louella and Isadora wanted us to keep fighting, not bury our heads in the sand and just hope this all blows over. I've got news for you; it's not going to."

"Harley, you really need to calm down. You're shouting." Wade took a tentative step toward me.

"I am calm. Calmer than I've ever freaking been."

"No, you're not. Look at the state of you." He held my shoulders. "You're shaking."

Sweat dripped down the back of my neck, my temples throbbing. "So what if I'm shaking? I almost had my bones broken and my cells blown apart, but you don't see me giving in or breaking down. You didn't see what I saw. If you had, you wouldn't be wasting a second on your own egos. I could be at breaking point, and I wouldn't stop. We've got too much to do, too many lives to avenge. You're alive, aren't you? So get over it, and let's get on with it, while our hearts are still beating and there's still breath in our lungs."

"Just breathe, Harley. You need to breathe. Ease up a little. You've been through a lot. We all have, but you more than anyone." He gripped me tighter, but I was losing it. That cool, calm exterior was morphing into something dark and ugly—a rage I couldn't control.

"How about *you* ease up?" I yelled, pushing away from him. Everything around me vibrated wildly, glass jugs teetering off shelves, the windchimes clanging so loud I wanted to tear each one out of the ceiling. The rainbow drapes flapped like plastic bags in a storm, and even the sofas juddered as my raw anger pounded through every particle in my proximity.

"Harley, cut it out!" Finch yelled.

My head was spinning now. "Something's wro—"

I gasped. Pain like nothing I'd ever experienced gripped my stomach, splintering out through my entire being like wildfire. A scream erupted out of me, and my arms flew wide. My muscles spasmed as something spilled out of my body. It felt syrupy and weird, oozing out of my pores like oil. Black smoke spiraled around me.

"She's Purging!" Santana shouted.

She leapt over the back of the sofa and sprinted for a cupboard, snatching a jar. I guessed, for a magical family, having a couple of spare Mason jars was as normal as a human family having good china for when guests came around. She skidded into position to catch the giant cloud of black smoke, while Wade ran forward with a handful of entrapment stones. I didn't know if they were the same ones I'd trapped him with, but the first flicker of guilt hit me as the Purge beast continued to pour from my veins.

The sudden headache... the nausea... It made sense now. All the warning signs had been there, I'd just ignored them, putting them down to fatigue and stress.

And I had no clue what was going to emerge from the smoke.

I sagged as the last of the Purge smoke evacuated my body, my legs almost buckling. I staggered back onto the edge of the sofa and gripped the fabric until my knuckles turned white, determined not to black out. Instead, I focused on the enormous cloud of black smoke that had filled the cabin lounge. It thrummed with an unsettling intensity. I could feel everyone's panic hitting me in wave after wave as they scrambled to get the thing under control. I had a horrible feeling it might stay that way, just a hazy mass, like the Purge beast that had come out of Alton in the French church.

"What is that thing?" Dylan gaped.

"I don't know, but it's powerful," Tatyana replied, her eyes transfixed. "*Very* powerful."

"And dangerous," Raffe added. "Can't you feel that?"

"It's unlike anything I've ever experienced." Krieger had stopped what he was doing to stare at it, as though it was sucking him in, somehow.

Levi was cowering in the corner of the lounge. "Trap it! For Pete's sake, trap it!"

"Anytime today, Wade!" Santana yelped, unscrewing the jar's lid.

His fist gripped the entrapment stones tight, his hand shaking as though he was trying with all his might to open out his fingers. But he couldn't.

"Wade, the stones!" Santana howled, although she seemed to be struggling too. Her arms were trembling, like she was doing everything within her power to keep the lid off the jar. Meanwhile, the mist swirled closer in front of Wade, strengthening the strange hypnotic power that it seemed to have over him. I could see him fighting it, but whatever this beast was, it had a firm grip, stopping him from scattering the stones across the ground.

"Obey me!" I shouted, with what little air I had left. Naima had obeyed Katherine, and Tobe had obeyed Selma. Maybe this thing wasn't anything like them, but even gargoyles and imps listened to the person who'd brought them into existence. The feathery snake that Santana had Purged still bristled excitedly whenever she got close to it, like it knew who she was and understood their bond. My Purge beast couldn't be much different. But it wasn't behaving like any Purge beast I'd ever seen.

The mist whipped around. Though it didn't exactly have eyes to show where it was looking, I just knew it was focusing on me. My body stiffened as it held me in its power, putting me in that same state of hypnosis. I couldn't fight it.

Wade broke out of his trance. Without hesitation, he tossed the stones at the black smoke. The red ropes shot out, crisscrossing so tightly that they formed a net to cover the mass. They thrummed, creating a forcefield to keep the creature in. Santana snapped out of her trance and lunged forward, sliding the Mason jar toward the beast. The black smoke trickled out, the forcefield controlling the steady pour. The wisps were sucked straight into the jar, and the charmed glass glowed. Within seconds, it was over—the Purge beast was inside the jar and Santana had dived for it, screwing the lid back on tight. The smoke creature slammed against the glass, twisting in a tiny vortex. But at least it wasn't getting out.

"What the heck was that?" Santana gasped, as she sat back against the sofa, wiping the sweat off her brow. "I couldn't friggin' move when it looked at me."

Wade shook his head. "Me neither."

"How do you know it was looking at you? That thing didn't even have eyes!" Finch stared at the jar.

"I can't explain it. I *felt* as though it was looking at me, and I froze." Wade glanced in the same direction, panting heavily.

"Is anyone else disappointed?" Finch grinned, clearly trying to lighten the mood. "I thought it'd be something cool, like Tobe. A big, smart, suave-as-heck monster, not a big blob of black mist. No offense, Sis."

"None taken." I sank back, totally spent, but feeling weirdly triumphant. *I survived my first Purge.*

"That was remarkable," Krieger murmured, mesmerized.

"Yeah, remarkably dangerous," Raffe shot back.

Krieger frowned in thought. "Perhaps. Perhaps not. All I know is, I've never seen anything like it before, and I have seen a great many Purge beasts in my time."

"Tobe would know more about this stuff," I said. "Speaking of which, where is he?"

"He had to deal with the Bestiary and separate it from the SDC when Katherine put that spell on the place," Krieger replied. "But you're right, he may know more about this. We should find him."

I was about to agree, when my body finally gave way. I collapsed, fighting to stay conscious. A shadow loomed over me, and I felt arms holding me tight, pulling me into a firm chest, filling my senses with a scent that was more familiar to me than any other in the world. *Wade...*

He held me close, sitting down on the floor and moving me into his lap, his hand smoothing back the sweat-soaked tendrils of my hair.

"You didn't know that was going to happen, did you?" he said softly.

I shook my head. "No idea."

"Well, I guess now we know why we were all getting a stern talking to." Finch was teasing me, but there was an edge of sadness in his voice. It made me feel even guiltier about all the things I'd said during that outburst.

"It's no wonder you didn't feel it coming," Santana chimed in. "You've had so much on your plate. And so many emotions. I'm just glad we were here to help catch that thing."

"But I didn't even do a spell," I murmured. "Can that happen?"

"Are you forgetting about the uber-complicated Hidden Things spell you did?" Raffe smiled, coming to stand in front of me.

"But why didn't I Purge right after?" I couldn't understand why it'd chosen now to manifest.

Tatyana joined him. "It doesn't always happen like that. Sometimes, it can be a strong reaction, or a lot of pain, or even a moment of pure joy. You've gone through the first two today. Combined with the residual effects of the Hidden Things spell, it's not surprising that it hit you like that."

"It came from anger?" I thought about Katherine and all the hate for her that burned inside me.

"Or grief," she replied. "You had to see some terrible things today. They were bound to take their toll, one way or another."

"Wait, does that mean that's an angry Purge beast?" Dylan frowned.

Santana lifted the jar. "Looks pretty peeved to me."

"The timing may be perfect," Krieger said. "A beast like that would be very useful in the ongoing fight against Katherine. It transcends Chaos, in a way. And if it is filled with the anger and grief that Harley has been feeling, due to Katherine's actions, then it may already have an innate desire for vengeance against her."

"A big old ball of pure hatred." Finch grinned. "Way to go, Sis. I knew you couldn't be all sunshine and rainbows."

I forced a smile. "When have I ever been sunshine and rainbows?"

"Good point." He chuckled, the sound comforting to my ears.

"We just have to hope it isn't powerful enough to break through the glass," Krieger warned.

"It could do that?" Levi squeaked from his hidey hole.

Krieger shrugged. "At this point, I have no idea what this creature is capable of. But we must be prepared for any eventualities."

"That's not the only thing we have that might be useful," I said, gaining strength from Wade's arms.

"What do you mean?" He gazed down into my eyes.

"We've got one last sliver of hope." I raked in a breath. "The Grimoire. I still have it."

"But I thought that was what Katherine wanted from you," Astrid replied.

I nodded. "It is, but it doesn't change the fact that she's terrified of it. There are things in here that can still be used against her. And I know it's got something to do with the last spell my dad put in here. I think we may have another sliver of hope, too."

"What is it?" Wade brushed his thumb across my cheek.

"Davin," I replied.

Finch's face instantly changed. "That British asswipe? Are you kidding? He's Katherine's lackey. You saw him. He came running after us the minute Katherine said 'jump' to him."

I shook my head. "Not immediately. He hesitated, and I don't know why. I'm not saying he's remotely trustworthy, but there's got to be a reason he just stood there. I can't explain it, but I think he let us get away."

"Pfft, he was probably just limbering up," Finch muttered. "Making sure he didn't pull one of his precious hamstrings."

"I'm not saying he's switched sides, but he's an opportunist. A dangerous one, for sure, but he wants to be on the winning team. If he hesitated, then maybe he's wondering if he picked the right side. That doubt might be useful. It might be the chink in Katherine's armor that we're looking for, especially considering Katherine goes all goo-goo eyed at the sight of him," I said.

Finch shook his head. "I've never seen Katherine go goo-goo eyed in my entire life."

"Then you haven't been paying attention when she's with Davin."

"Ugh, she always had the *worst* taste in dudes." Finch looked suddenly sheepish. "Our dad aside, of course."

"Well, for her, he was a bad choice," Santana interjected.

I glanced around the room at my friends, my chest gripping with regret. "I suppose I owe you all an apology, don't I?" I lowered my gaze again. "I'm sorry for trying to keep you all in the dark. It wasn't my decision to make, not really, but I made it with the best intentions."

"You don't owe us an apology, Harley," Tatyana replied. "We were miffed when we found out, sure, but you had your reasons and you explained them. We understand why you did what you did. I imagine every single one of us would've done the same thing in your position."

I groaned. "And now you're being nice about it."

She chuckled. "You heard something none of us did when you spoke with the Chains of Truth. We weren't there to reassure you it wouldn't happen. Fear and love make us all do crazy things. You made your decision because you were afraid we'd get hurt, or worse. It doesn't mean we weren't mad, but it makes things easier to understand."

"And we'll just forget about what you said during your pre-Purge outburst." Finch winked. "I mean, you were really taking us all to the cleaners."

"Although, you made some good points," Raffe interjected. "We shouldn't be wallowing. And we shouldn't be letting our emotions bog us down so we can't find the drive to carry on."

"Plus, we'd definitely be monsters if we bore a grudge, after everything you've been through today." Santana grinned at me. "Heck, you could've called every single one of us a *pendejo*, and we'd still have to forgive you after the things you've seen."

I smiled halfheartedly. "I'm still sorry."

"And we still forgive you," Garrett replied.

"Maybe things would've been different if I'd brought you all in on what I was doing." I sighed wearily.

"I doubt it," Astrid said. "Wade would certainly be dead if you'd taken him with you. So maybe your decision was the best one to make, given the circumstances."

Finch nodded. "You'd have been sad if any of us had been killed, but we'd be mopping you up right now if she'd done anything to Wade."

"You'd be mopping me up if she'd done anything to any of you," I insisted. "None of you are expendable. None of you."

"I still don't think it would've made a difference," Astrid continued, her voice oddly empty. "Katherine had played us as Imogene for much too long. She knew everything. We voluntarily told her everything. We didn't really stand a chance."

"Maybe you're right." I leaned into Wade's chest, just as he drew in a sharp breath, his whole body stiffening unexpectedly. My head whipped around as the rest of the Rag Team froze, a look of horror etched across their faces. I was about to ask what was wrong, when something slammed into my chest, pushing the air right out of my lungs.

Chaos thrummed inside me, in a sudden, almost panicked pulse. I felt it leave, ripping away like wax strips tugging at my skin. It hurt, it really hurt, and it took a moment for me to fully realize what had happened.

The magic was going out of us, one by one.

FORTY-SEVEN

Katherine

I stood in the smoking remains of the Garden of Hesperides and stared at my reflection in the mirror that I'd erected, right in the middle of the ravaged battlefield. Beauty amidst the wreckage, in an act of poetic glory.

I'd decided to take a moment for myself, to check the proverbial damage, while my cult members branched out to look for Harley, all of them disappearing through portals I'd made until there was nobody left. Well, nobody but Davin.

I'd instructed my cultists to scour the entire planet until they found my little niece. They knew the consequences of failure. I'd already proven my might by stripping them of their magic, although I'd given just enough back for them to complete this task. Their faces when I'd taken their Chaos had been a wondrous thing that would ease me to sleep at night, like a steaming mug of hot cocoa. The shock… the blissful, beautiful shock.

But I was currently the one getting a nasty shock as I looked over my reflection. My body was already beginning to suffer the effects of having so much power inside me. Children of Chaos weren't supposed to have solid forms, and that was making itself flagrantly understood. My smooth, diaphanous, painstakingly primped skin was starting to crack. A black, oily substance oozed through the cracks, as if I'd been overstuffed and it had nowhere else to go.

"This is ridiculous!" I snapped, smearing black ooze off my face and flinging it into the dirt. "Why shouldn't my body be able to withstand this? I'm a Shipton, born of the Shipton bloodline. My heritage is ancient. Why shouldn't I be able to contain it?"

Davin put his hand on the small of my back. "You look beautiful still, my darling. You are radiant. You are a goddess amongst women. And this is only a temporary measure, dearest heart. Soon enough, you will have Harley's body, and you will be as you were, in all your true glory. Eris incarnate."

I crossed my arms. "This is totally stupid."

"In Asian culture, objects are all the more revered when they have been cracked, and they are duly repaired with care and attention. You will be revered in the same manner, loved with even more ferocity because you have suffered for your position as the Goddess of Discord. And I will be the one to restore you, with all the care and attention I possess."

"And yet you continue to irk me by refusing to pledge yourself?" I narrowed my eyes at him, but he offered a charming smile in return.

"I will pledge myself to the Cult of Eris once you acquire Harley's body and take your true form as a goddess of all worlds."

I frowned in surprise. "Why wait until then? I've shown what I am capable of."

Davin sighed and cupped my face in his hands. "Because, my darling, you are yet to win this. If your body is vanquished before you retrieve Harley, then you will not become the Goddess of Discord, as you have envisioned yourself. In essence, you will become a haze of frustrated energy, forced to exist in an otherworld. The exact opposite of what you aspire to become."

It was sound logic, playing on my own fears, which were starting to creep in with every crack that appeared in my beauteous face. But I didn't like to hear it laid bare like that. It suggested a lack of faith, and I wasn't a fan of fence-sitters who couldn't pledge themselves. If it had been anyone but Davin, they'd have been six feet under by now.

So why am I letting him get away with it?

I was already frustrated as hell. Did I really need the added grievance of yet another man with commitment issues?

"It's that treacherous djinn, Abracadabra. I'd stake my money on it," I muttered, changing the subject. "He's doing something to hide Harley, I know he is. And those devious Catemacos, and whoever else is still rooting for that insidious little bitch. But it's not over yet. Oh no, I'm just getting started."

"I know you are, darling," Davin purred, stroking a tingling line up the curve of my spine. "It is why I'm still standing here, at your side. Once you have succeeded, you will have my allegiance eternally. Once you have her body, it will forge a bond between us that can never be broken. I can already feel those links slotting into place, binding us to one another. All you have to do is complete the task, and I will be your everlasting servant."

He was making it sound as though joining the cult was like joining me in a relationship. I hadn't jumped through hoops for a guy in nearly two decades, but I supposed this served me as much as it served him. I wasn't going to be a haze of frustrated energy, not after everything I'd put into reaching this goal. I didn't like the implication, though, that I had to prove myself to Davin.

Your head would be on a spike if you weren't so charming.

I knew I should just kill him and be done with it. I'd already made too many concessions for him by allowing him to keep his abilities after I had stripped everyone else of theirs—except those going after Harley. What did that make this? Stupidity? Temporary insanity? I didn't know, but I just couldn't resist him.

Feeling like crap about my cracked face, I needed a little TLC. And I knew just where to find it. Grasping the back of Davin's neck so hard he almost got whiplash, I pulled him into a deep kiss, letting him know that he was mine, whether he liked it or not.

The smirk instantly left his face, his eyes smoldering as he closed them, sinking deeper into our kiss. His hands moved to my neck, his thumb running down the line of my throat, making me shiver with anticipation. It was his display of possession, but mine was stronger, as I moved my lips against his with an almost violent ferocity. It was more like a fight than a kiss, which suited me just fine. I'd never been into gentle displays of affection, resulting in my fair share of terrified men running for the hills.

But Davin wasn't weak, and he wasn't like ordinary men. I would win this one, just as I was going to win against Harley. He was my toy now, to play with as I saw fit, whether he wanted to be or not. Soon enough, I'd have him begging to wear the seal of Eris on his skin.

It's not over yet. I'm not singing.

I had so much work to do, and so little time until my body caved in.

But I was going to get through this. I was going to win, and I was going to get every damn thing I'd ever dreamed of.

FORTY-EIGHT

Harley

"Raffe? Raffe, what's happening?" Santana reached out to him, the two of them clinging to each other as the magic drifted away.

"I don't know, I don't know," he replied frantically, clutching her tighter.

"My Chaos… it's gone." Tatyana patted herself down, practically tearing at her skin. "Why can't I feel it anymore? I can't hear the spirits. I can't see them."

Dylan held her wrists. "I don't know, Taty. Please, you have to stop. Stop or you're going to hurt yourself."

"How can I stop?" she screamed. "It's gone, Dylan!"

"I know, Taty. I know." He let her sink into his arms, holding her as he visibly struggled with his own realization. We had all lost our Chaos.

Garrett was staring blankly ahead, while Astrid looked around in confusion, not understanding what was happening. Levi was trembling in the corner, though that wasn't anything new, while O'Halloran was just looking down at his hands like they didn't belong to him. Finch had gone deathly silent, a look of pure hatred setting his eyes alight, and Krieger was still seeing to Alton, as though he hadn't even noticed anything had happened. I guessed this was his defense mechanism—keep working and you could pretend everything was okay.

I peered up at Wade, who was looking right back at me, terror and panic glinting in his eyes. My heart felt like it was about to break, my mind desperately reaching for any spark of Chaos that remained. I tried to delve deep inside myself, but nothing happened. It was like a huge wall had gone up, and I couldn't get through. My body felt physically drained, my veins crying out for something that used to be there.

"Wade?" I whispered, my eyes wide.

"I know. I feel it too," he replied hoarsely. He already had enough to deal with, without this. But he was trying to be strong—I could see it in the twist of his features, as he fought with his emotions.

"It's gone." I kept expecting it to keep hurting, but I just felt... empty.

He nodded. "I can't feel it anymore. I can't feel any of it." He lifted his hands and closed his eyes, but his Esprit's ten rings stayed dull, refusing to light up. I did the same with my Esprit, convinced there had to be a shred of something left, but the gems were just gems now, the Esprit just a useless piece of jewelry that served no purpose.

"I knew she'd do this," Finch muttered. "I knew it."

I was so shocked I couldn't even cry. I could hardly breathe. It was like being told a loved one had died, but the words hadn't quite sunk in yet. It was that terrible precipice on which everyone teetered, right before their lives changed forever. And I was teetering now, about to topple right over the edge.

A sharp gasp stole my attention away from the devastation that surged inside me. Jacob sat bolt upright, sucking in deep breaths, his eyes wide and confused as he looked around. I leapt out of Wade's arms and ran to him, putting my arm around him to keep him sitting up. He stared at me, his mouth opening and closing.

"Jacob?" I urged.

"I... I heard it all," he wheezed. "I... heard... everything."

"What do you mean?"

"I... heard everything. I was... conscious... inside here." He reached up a shaky hand and tapped the side of his head.

My heart lurched as I pieced together what he meant. He'd been awake, on the inside, this whole time. Had Katherine said something to him while she was masquerading as Imogene? What did he know? I was desperate to ask, but I didn't want to rush him. He'd been out cold for a long time, and it would take him a while to get everything back in working order.

"Tell me what you heard," I said. "Take it slow. In your own time."

"Katherine… I heard everything. She took… your Chaos," he rasped. "And I… know why."

"Why?"

"Taking Chaos was… always the first thing… on her to-do list." He dragged in another stilted breath. "She still needs you. She still… needs your body, but… it's still… viable without your Chaos. She'll give… it back when… she gets you to… read for her. There are powerful things… that exist, even without Chaos. Your bloodline… is one of them. But she will… get you to read the spells… when the time comes. She can't continue to exist, the way she wants… without you. Sooner or later, she will… find you, and she will take you. So she can fulfill her… wish of pouring her new self… into you."

I shook my head. "We're safe here, for now."

"No, we're not," Santana replied, tears streaking her face. "All of the Chaos is gone, which means my parents' charms won't work anymore. I don't know if there's anywhere safe now."

"There's more," Jacob murmured, getting stronger. "Katherine is going to reassign Chaos to those she… deems worthy—those in her cult. Soon enough, when she's… ready, she'll reveal magic to the humans across the globe, looking to… blend the two worlds of human and magical into… one."

I held my nerve. "As long as I'm away from her, we've still got a chance." I had no idea if that was true, but I had to put on a brave face.

My eyes drifted toward the Grimoire sitting on the floor by the sofa, and frustration boiled inside me. I had all these insane spells to use against Katherine, but no Chaos to actually perform them. Isadora was dead again, never to be resurrected. Alton was likely on the verge of death, already comatose, with Krieger unable to rouse him. The world was completely without magic, if only temporarily...

My gaze fixed on Raffe, a thought emerging. "Raffe?"

He turned. "What?"

"How's Kadar?"

He frowned and closed his eyes. "Still here."

"How about his djinn energy?"

"Still going strong, sweet-cheeks." Kadar's voice echoed back.

I looked to Levi. "Is Zalaam still with you?"

"I… I think so," he replied.

"I am here." Zalaam's voice boomed out a second later. "And my energy is untouched."

It looked as though the Levi men had managed to retain their natural Chaos, despite Katherine's attempts to drag everything away from the magicals. All that slipping hope reversed, filling me up with a bright, burning faith that it wasn't quite over yet. *It can't be over yet.* As long as there was still some magic in this world that didn't belong to Katherine, we still had a shot. A slim one, but a very real one.

If the djinn were still going strong, then that meant their connection to Erebus was undisturbed, separate from all the rest of this global mayhem. I didn't know if there were other beings like the djinn, who were connected to other Children of Chaos in the same way, but that didn't matter too much.

If I was going to get to Katherine, and stop her, then I needed the other Children of Chaos. Somehow, I would have to reach out to them and get them to intervene. Maybe they could give me some sort of mojo that would allow me to perform the Grimoire's hidden magic. I didn't know if that was even possible, but I had to try. If the djinn could contact Erebus, then that ticked one off the list.

"Your Purge beast is going wild," Krieger said, his eyes fixed on the jar.

"Do you think it can sense what just happened?" Wade replied.

I shrugged, getting closer to the jar so I could see the swirling creature better. *What if…* "If my Purge beast is still here, that means Katherine couldn't take its Chaos away. Which means she couldn't take it away from the other beasts, either. I mean, they're made from the stuff, right?"

Krieger nodded. "Right."

"Then we're not defeated yet," I said, with a smile. "We might not have magic anymore, but there are still beings in this world who have it by the bucketload. The djinn, Tobe, and even Leviathan could help us, if we're feeling particularly brave. And maybe this little beauty can help us, too, if there's a way of taming it."

The Rag Team gathered around the Mason jar.

"Is that possible?" Garrett asked.

I shrugged. "We've got no magic, but that doesn't mean we can't use magic against Katherine. We have to find a way—through the remaining Children of Chaos, through the monsters, through those weapons you nicked, and through every single supernatural thing on the fringes, out there in the world. We have to rise up in the only way we can."

"One little problem with that," Raffe said. "The Children of Chaos can't intervene. It's Chaos—"

I cut him off. "Please don't say 'Chaos rules,' or my head is going to explode."

"Okay, I won't say it," he replied warily. "But the fact remains."

I collapsed in hysterics, laughing like a madwoman.

"You okay there, Sis?" Finch gaped at me.

"The Challenge is over," I said, wiping tears from my eyes.

"And?" Raffe waited expectantly.

"The other Children of Chaos couldn't intervene in the Challenge, that's true. But the Challenge is over, it's complete. Now, there's nothing stopping the Children of Chaos from reacting or finding ways to punish Katherine."

Krieger shook his head. "But Children can't kill other Children."

"Who said anything about killing?" I smirked. "They don't need to kill her, not when I'm planning on having that particular pleasure. But nothing says they can't help magicals like us defeat Katherine. After all, Chaos channeled itself through my mom and dad to write the Grimoire spells. It left a couple of windows open where the doors were shut."

Finch chuckled. "Holy crap, I think you're on to something…"

I nodded slowly, rising to my feet.

Katherine had tried her hardest to crush me into smithereens, but I had news for her: I wasn't broken yet.

The next Harley Merlin book

Dear Reader,

Thank you for reading *Harley Merlin and the Challenge of Chaos*, and for accompanying her through this journey.

*Harley Merlin 9: **Harley Merlin and the Mortal Pact*** will be the resolution to Harley and Katherine's conflict, and it releases on **June 30th, 2019**.

Finch will be joining Harley back in the spotlight, and I'll be doing my best to make this showdown worth the wait…

Visit: **www.bellaforrest.net** for details.

Thank you, and see you there!

Love,

Bella x

P.S. Sign up to my VIP email list and you'll be the first to know when my next book releases: **www.morebellaforrest.com**

(Your email will be kept 100% private and you can unsubscribe at any time.)

P.P.S. Feel free to come say hi on **Twitter** @ashadeofvampire; **Facebook** www.facebook.

com/BellaForrestAuthor; or **Instagram** @ashadeofvampire

Read more by Bella Forrest

HARLEY MERLIN

Harley Merlin and the Secret Coven (Book 1)

Harley Merlin and the Mystery Twins (Book 2)

Harley Merlin and the Stolen Magicals (Book 3)

Harley Merlin and the First Ritual (Book 4)

Harley Merlin and the Broken Spell (Book 5)

Harley Merlin and the Cult of Eris (Book 6)

Harley Merlin and the Detector Fix (Book 7)

Harley Merlin and the Challenge of Chaos (Book 8)

Harley Merlin and the Mortal Pact (Book 9)

THE GENDER GAME

(Action-adventure/dystopian/romance. Completed series.)

The Gender Game (Book 1)

The Gender Secret (Book 2)

The Gender Lie (Book 3)

The Gender War (Book 4)

The Gender Fall (Book 5)

The Gender Plan (Book 6)

The Gender End (Book 7)

THE GIRL WHO DARED TO THINK

(Action-adventure/dystopian/romance. Completed series.)

The Girl Who Dared to Think (Book 1)

The Girl Who Dared to Stand (Book 2)

The Girl Who Dared to Descend (Book 3)

The Girl Who Dared to Rise (Book 4)

The Girl Who Dared to Lead (Book 5)

The Girl Who Dared to Endure (Book 6)

The Girl Who Dared to Fight (Book 7)

THE CHILD THIEF

(Action-adventure/dystopian/romance.)

The Child Thief (Book 1)

Deep Shadows (Book 2)

Thin Lines (Book 3)

Little Lies (Book 4)

Ghost Towns (Book 5)

Zero Hour (Book 6)

A LOVE THAT ENDURES

(New! Contemporary romance)

A Love that Endures

A Love that Endures 2

HOTBLOODS

(Supernatural adventure/romance. Completed series.)

Hotbloods (Book 1)

Coldbloods (Book 2)

Renegades (Book 3)

Venturers (Book 4)

Traitors (Book 5)

Allies (Book 6)

Invaders (Book 7)

Stargazers (Book 8)

A SHADE OF VAMPIRE SERIES

(Supernatural romance/adventure)

Series 1: Derek & Sofia's story

A Shade of Vampire (Book 1)

A Shade of Blood (Book 2)

A Castle of Sand (Book 3)

A Shadow of Light (Book 4)

A Blaze of Sun (Book 5)

A Gate of Night (Book 6)

A Break of Day (Book 7)

Series 2: Rose & Caleb's story

A Shade of Novak (Book 8)

A Bond of Blood (Book 9)

A Spell of Time (Book 10)

A Chase of Prey (Book 11)

A Shade of Doubt (Book 12)

A Turn of Tides (Book 13)

A Dawn of Strength (Book 14)

A Fall of Secrets (Book 15)

An End of Night (Book 16)

Series 3: The Shade continues with a new hero...

A Wind of Change (Book 17)

A Trail of Echoes (Book 18)

A Soldier of Shadows (Book 19)

A Hero of Realms (Book 20)

A Vial of Life (Book 21)

A Fork of Paths (Book 22)

A Flight of Souls (Book 23)

A Bridge of Stars (Book 24)

Series 4: A Clan of Novaks

A Clan of Novaks (Book 25)

A World of New (Book 26)

A Web of Lies (Book 27)

A Touch of Truth (Book 28)

An Hour of Need (Book 29)

A Game of Risk (Book 30)

A Twist of Fates (Book 31)

A Day of Glory (Book 32)

Series 5: A Dawn of Guardians

A Dawn of Guardians (Book 33)

A Sword of Chance (Book 34)

A Race of Trials (Book 35)

A King of Shadow (Book 36)

An Empire of Stones (Book 37)

A Power of Old (Book 38)

A Rip of Realms (Book 39)

A Throne of Fire (Book 40)

A Tide of War (Book 41)

Series 6: A Gift of Three

A Gift of Three (Book 42)

A House of Mysteries (Book 43)

A Tangle of Hearts (Book 44)

A Meet of Tribes (Book 45)

A Ride of Peril (Book 46)

A Passage of Threats (Book 47)

A Tip of Balance (Book 48)

A Shield of Glass (Book 49)

A Clash of Storms (Book 50)

Series 7: A Call of Vampires